'Scarily g[...]
'Sharp is part of a very small [...]
the talk and walks the walk. [...]
when she writes it, it feels more real than most non-fiction books.
Sharp deserves a genre all her own.' **Jon Jordan**, *CrimeSpree Magazine*

'Zoë Sharp is one of the sharpest, coolest, and most intriguing writers I know. She delivers dramatic, action-packed novels with characters we really care about.' **Harlan Coben**, bestselling author of TELL NO ONE

'Male and female crime fiction readers alike will find Sharp's writing style addictively readable.' **Paul Goat Allen**, *Chicago Tribune*

'Zoë Sharp is a master at writing thoughtful action thrillers,' **Meg Gardiner**, bestselling author of UNSUB

'This is hard-edged fiction at its best.' **Michele Leber**, *Booklist* **starred review** for FIFTH VICTIM

'I loved every word of this brilliant, mind-twisting thriller and even yelped out loud at one of the genius twists.' bestselling author **Elizabeth Haynes** on THE BLOOD WHISPERER

'Sharp is a writer of extraordinary skill.' **Maggie Mason**, *Deadly Pleasures Mystery Magazine*, **Rating A**

'Superb.' **Ken Bruen**, bestselling author of the Jack Taylor series, THE GUARDS, BLITZ

'Zoë Sharp has an apt last name. She delivers yet another sleek, sharp thriller.' **David Morrell**, bestselling author of FIRST BLOOD

'If you don't like Zoë Sharp there's something wrong with you. Go and live in a cave and get the hell out of my gene pool! There are few writers who go right to the top of my TBR pile—Zoë Sharp is one of them.' **Stuart MacBride**, bestselling author of the Logan McRae series

'Well, holy sh*tballs! What a book!...an intense, compelling and totally engrossing read.' **Noelle Holten**, *CrimeBookJunkie*, **5/5** on FOX HUNTER

ALSO BY ZOË SHARP

For more information on Zoë Sharp's writing,
see her website: www.ZoeSharp.com

DANCING ON
THE GRAVE

ZOË SHARP

First published in Great Britain 2018
by
ZACE

Registered UK Office:
143 Burneside Road, Kendal, Cumbria LA9 6EB

ISBN-13: 978-1-909344-40-2
ISBN-10: 1-909344-40-0

for Lee Child
a wonderful author and an even better friend

ABOUT THE AUTHOR

Zoë Sharp opted out of mainstream education at the age of twelve and wrote her first novel at fifteen. She created her award-winning crime thriller series featuring ex-Special Forces trainee turned bodyguard, Charlotte 'Charlie' Fox, after receiving death threats in the course of her work as a photojournalist. She has been making a living from her writing for thirty years, and since 2001 has written fifteen novels, including twelve in the Charlie Fox series, standalone crime thrillers and numerous short stories. Her work has been used in Danish school textbooks, inspired an original song and music video, and been optioned for TV and film. Find out more at **www.ZoeSharp.com**

f facebook.com/ZoeSharpAuthor

y twitter.com/authorzoesharp

PART I

1

It is a bad day to die...a perfect one to kill.

The sniper lies in cover towards the upper northeastern edge of the valley. His right eye is up close behind the ten-power scope attached to the receiver of the rifle. He is watching a massacre as it unfolds below him.

Between heartbeats, he tightens his forefinger round the trigger.

As he does so, the killer jerks back, a pink mist spraying from his torso. Lifeless limbs flail as he sprawls into the long grass. The crack of the report reaches the sniper's ears a fraction of a second later. He flinches. He checks the scope, knowing the target is down. Knowing the kill is good.

Knowing, too, that he did not fire the shot...

IT WAS Grace's habit to approach death the same way she approached life, with calm deliberation and an open mind. And while others might mistake that detachment for coldness, she reserved her compassion for more private moments.

She knew she would weep over the scene of carnage laid out before her, but it would be later, alone. Not now. Wailing at the graveside helped nobody, least of all the departed.

So she paused a little way back from the body and waited for the signs of death to speak to her, as she knew they would. First in half-caught whispers then louder, more stridently. Grace was patient, and three years as a Crime Scene Investigator had made her a good listener.

She stood easy, with the strap of the Canon digital camera over her shoulder, her head tilted to tune out the raised voices behind her. The farmer, arguing with the pair of uniforms who'd been first on scene. The bereaved, shouting for retribution.

And she stood motionless, casting a long shadow. It was still early enough for the sun to be climbing steeply and the dew sparked and shimmered on the spider webs in the grass at her feet. Ever since her childhood Grace had loved the ethereal light at this time of day.

Around her, the flies had already begun to feast. Blowflies—always the first to gather—drawn by the irresistible scent of blood, thick in the air. Grace hardly noticed. There were six corpses lying in the field. She'd studied each in turn but only one arrested her attention.

This one.

It was different from the others, not least in the manner of its death. The body lay stretched out on one side with the head thrown back, the teeth bared in defiance. Beneath one outflung limb Grace could see the blackened circle of the undoubtedly fatal gunshot wound to the chest, although at this stage she took nothing at face value.

"What a waste," she murmured.

"Come on, Grace," said a voice behind her. "It's only a dog."

She turned, found the younger of the two uniformed PCs at her elbow, Danny Robertshaw, cradling the farmer's confiscated shotgun. When she didn't respond he waved his free hand towards the other bodies. "And look at the number of lambs it savaged. Had it coming, if you ask me."

"Perhaps." Born in the country, Grace well knew the usual response towards any dog caught worrying livestock. Although, 'worrying' was putting it mildly. "But if it's so clear-cut Daniel, why did you need me?"

Robertshaw coloured, a ruddy flush that stained a neck still raw from the morning's hasty shave. He ducked closer, lowering his voice.

"Because of them two." His eyes shifted to the couple. "They were screaming blue murder when they rang it in." He shrugged unhappily. "Turns out they've got some clout."

"And since when has Cumbria Constabulary been operating a two-tier policing system?" Grace asked lightly. "One law for the locals and another for the incomers, is it?"

He wouldn't meet her gaze, suddenly fascinated by a hang-nail at the side of his thumb. "You know how it is, Grace. You, of all people."

Do I? She tried not to let that sting, instead asked, "You'll be sure to take a sample of the spare cartridges for comparison, won't you?"

"For what it's worth," the young policeman grunted. "But old Know-It-All Airey reckons the shotgun's not been fired for days."

Grace paused in the act of retrieving an evidence bag from her kit, eyebrow raised. He flushed again. "I've nothing against hobby bobbies as a rule," he said in a rush. "We need 'em when things are tight. It's just Airey who winds me up. Wrong temperament for the job."

As a civilian attached to the police, Grace stayed out of station politics as much as she was able, but the superior, swaggering attitude of volunteer Special Constable Jim Airey had reached her ears, even so. A bully, who abused his position to throw his weight around—and there was certainly plenty of that.

Nevertheless, his day job as a butcher's assistant hardened him to the sight of blood and bone. He hadn't flinched at today's scene, and she knew he was often sent to the nastier smashes on the motorway that snaked up the eastern border of the county, revelling in his own unshockable reputation.

Without comment, Grace nudged the shotgun upwards and, mindful where she put her face, sniffed the end of the barrels. Oil and metal and dust, overlaid with the faint ammonia smell of manure.

"Mm, in this instance I would agree with him." She bagged the gun. "But we should still follow procedure, don't you think? You'd better ask Mr Airey to make a perimeter sweep." Her voice was grave even as her lips twitched. "Cast his expert eye over the scene, as it were."

Robertshaw let his eyes roam the sizeable length of dry stone wall that bordered the field, at his colleague's generous girth as the man stood with feet arrogantly apart, between the owners of the dog and the field gate as though to prevent their escape.

The youngster grinned, suddenly not looking old enough to drive, never mind put on the uniform. He reminded her of the cheeky little boy with skinned knees he'd been back when she used to babysit him as a teenager.

"Right you are, Grace."

Grace unshouldered her camera, began quartering the view from the body. It was standard practice at any crime scene, allowing the victim's position to be precisely located long after the scene was cleared.

In this case, the view was of the squat lime-washed tower of All Saints Church peering through the trees to the south—the only visible part of Orton village itself. To the northeast, the road climbed towards the Scar, an expanse of windswept limestone pavement populated mainly by the hardy local sheep.

"Excuse me, but how much longer is this going to take?"

She turned, saw the couple who'd called in the death of their dog approaching. They were late middle-age, dressed in casually expensive clothes that to Grace's eye indicated a long and comfortable association with money.

It was the man who'd spoken. Tall, wiry, he had the whippy build of a long-distance runner, staring her down over a hawk-like nose. His voice was clipped with impatience and something that Grace recognised as unease.

"I'm going as fast as is prudent," she said pleasantly, and glanced at the returning Robertshaw. "I assume we have someone with authorised Firearms experience on their way out to this one, Daniel? You could ask the control room to divert an ARV if there are any in the area."

Several of the Cumbria force motorway patrol cars doubled as Armed Response Vehicles. Considering most of the Traffic boys seemed to think they were the next Lewis Hamilton in waiting, the chances were one could be on-scene without delay.

"Better than that." Robertshaw was smiling broadly. "They're sending down that new hotshot DC to show us how they train 'em in the big city."

"Surely it isn't necessary to keep us here all morning?" The woman nodded to the bagged shotgun the young PC still cradled under his arm, and slid her eyes meaningfully to the farmer, sitting on a mud-splattered quad bike only a few metres away. "We all know who killed poor Ben."

The farmer glared at that. He was a big thickset man, leaning with his elbows on the quad's fuel tank as he watched the scene play out. His reddened hands dangled loosely to reveal cracked knuckles misshapen by decades of hard work in all weather. Crouched sideways on the seat behind him, tongue lolling, was a wall-eyed Border collie.

"I didn't shoot 'im," the farmer said, gruff but without rancour. "Not that I wouldn't 'ave done, mind. Losing this many lambs at one go, it takes the profit right out of the year. 'Course I would 'ave shot 'im, if I'd got 'ere sooner. But somebody beat me to it, and tha's a fact."

The woman let out a pinched breath, her lips hardening into a narrow line. Grace recalled a teacher at her long-ago boarding school with a mouth like that.

"Regardless of *who* shot poor Ben"—the man forced a thin smile—"it's clear what happened here. I'm prepared to make full restitution."

Ah, you've *changed your tune.* Grace saw Robertshaw stiffen as though a bribe had been offered.

"We have a duty to investigate, sir," he said, aiming for stern but quailing under the couple's withering stare.

The woman had drawn breath to launch into some stinging tirade when they heard the sound of an engine approaching at speed. Grace caught a glimpse of something bright blue and sporty as it braked to a showy halt by the gateway.

"New bloke," Robertshaw muttered.

"*Well,*" the woman said. "Now we might actually get somewhere."

Grace turned away, glad of something to refocus their attention, then paused, mentally backtracking.

What hotshot new DC? She frowned after Robertshaw's departing figure, but her attention was already back on the body of the dog.

"Since it patently *wasn't* the farmer who shot you," she murmured, "let's hope this city boy is all he's cracked up to be…"

DETECTIVE CONSTABLE NICK WESTON was in a vile temper and drove accordingly.

His car usually responded to being pushed hard. The Subaru was his weakness, a sop to the last remnants of the boy racer in him. Much as he knew the WRX model wasn't helping him integrate into the hierarchy at his latest posting, he couldn't bring himself to part with it.

Might have to, soon, though.

For once, even thrashing down the motorway failed to lighten his black mood. He'd covered the eighteen miles of M6 from Penrith down to Tebay in a shade over eleven minutes, rarely dropping below a hundred. Good job none of the miserable lot from Traffic were patrolling that stretch or they'd have nicked him for it.

But maybe he was being taken seriously at last. The uniformed sergeant who'd found him skulking over paperwork in the CID office at the Hunter Lane station said the shout was a suspicious death out near Orton, a possible shooting, that the on-scene CSI was calling for an expert assist.

"Everybody else's out," she'd said, her flat tone making it clear he was her last resort, "but you used to be with the shoot 'em up boys, didn't you, detective constable?"

"Used to be."

She raised a cynical eyebrow at this reticence. "Well then, I thought it might be right up your street—you being a city lad."

She sniffed. "Saw enough gun crime down there in Manchester and London, didn't you?"

Nick attempted to shake off his misery as he got to his feet. "Right, I'm on my way." He'd tried what he hoped was a placatory smile. "And...thanks. Wendy, isn't it?"

That earned him another sniff. "I think 'sergeant' will do just fine."

Still, it was good to know that the two years Nick had spent with Armed Response had some ongoing benefit after all, even if he'd let his Firearms ticket lapse when he moved up out of uniform. Perhaps something might actually be salvaged from this disastrous career cul-de-sac.

Now, Nick almost missed the gateway to the field where this supposed shooting had taken place. He'd been accelerating up the long climb out of Orton village and had to brake hard when he spotted the marked-up Ford Focus sitting half-hidden behind some galumphing great pickup truck on the verge.

"What the hell are they playing at?" Nick muttered. Surely by now this unknown CSI should have arranged some marker for the investigation team?

When Nick joined the force, Scenes Of Crime Officers—he couldn't get used to calling them CSIs—came from the ranks. They had years of experience at the sharp end of policing. *Not like these bloody amateurs.* A quick day-release college course and they thought they were God's gift to forensic science.

He left the Subaru as far off the road as he could, paused at the unguarded gateway to note with irritation the presence of three obvious civilians in the middle of the field. The vicious headache that had plagued him all morning returned to pulse behind his right eye.

How incompetent are *these yokels?*

Scowling, he struck out across the grass. Within a dozen paces, the bottom three inches of his trousers were soaked through, which meant a dry cleaning bill on top of everything else. The realisation made him glower at the young uniform who approached, balancing a bagged-up shotgun under his arm.

"Who d'you think you are, sunshine—Wyatt Earp?" Nick demanded, just low enough not to carry to the people nearby. He nodded curtly to the gun without breaking stride. "That the possible murder weapon? Well, don't carry it around like some bloody trophy! Get it locked away before this becomes a multiple homicide."

"But…it already is."

"*What?*" Nick thought he caught something crafty in the other's voice, but a glance at his face revealed only blankness. "How many?"

"I think at the last count it was half a dozen," the young policeman said, stony. "Grace—er, CSI McColl—will be able to confirm the numbers."

He nodded towards a lone figure, camera in hand, who seemed to be wandering aimlessly at the far side of the field, with little thought to her responsibility for this organisational shambles.

McColl. Nick had heard the name, recalled occasional glimpses in the corridors of Hunter Lane of the tall superior redhead with her nose in the air. He was conspicuously excluded from the usual jungle telegraph but he'd heard about her, even so.

In certain circles, it seemed she was almost as unpopular as he was. And if her performance here was anything to go by, he could understand why.

He sighed, ran a frustrated hand through his hair and tried a sympathetic smile that was woodenly met.

"Look, I'm sorry I jumped down your throat. Looks like it's going to be a bad day for all of us. What's your name?"

"Danny—Danny Robertshaw."

"All right, Danny. Take a minute. Keep it together and get the job done, OK?"

The young policeman nodded, ducking his head and scurrying away.

Nick strode across the field, almost brushing aside the couple who stepped forwards—pompously, he felt—to intercept him.

"Well?" he snapped as soon as he was close enough to the CSI not to shout. "What's all this about?"

Her only response was a single raised eyebrow. She waited for Nick to reach her before she replied, which only annoyed him further.

"Good morning," she said pointedly. Her voice had a drawl that instantly put his back up. "Clearly they don't teach you any people-skills down there in sunny Manchester."

Nick's head came up, eyes glittering. "And clearly they don't teach *you* crime scene procedure up here in sunny Cumbria."

She put her head on one side as if considering whether to take offence or not. "You're very rude, Mr Weston," she said then, as if voicing a remote observation.

"And you're very sloppy, Ms McColl." He stuck his hands in his trouser pockets, looked about him. "Where's the rest of your team? Why isn't this whole area cordoned off? Where's your protective gear and your common approach path?" He fixed her with a glare that served him well in Interview. "You don't seem to be treating this as a proper investigation."

Nick heard the words coming out of his own mouth like they were being spoken by someone else, and gave an inward groan. *How to win friends and influence people.* Taking his anger out on her would only make his job worse.

Crime scene technicians like Grace McColl were the first response to any incident, and frequently led the initial stages of the investigation, giving it direction and focus. Antagonise them and you could find yourself sent off down a total blind alley, just for the hell of it. As if he hadn't already come up against enough resistance...

"Well," she said, finally matching her tone to his, icy, "if *you* are all they've sent me, it looks like nobody else is treating this as a *proper investigation* either, are they?"

He opened his mouth again—to apologise this time—but she had already looked away.

"Now," she said blandly, "if we've *quite* finished banging our egos together, would you care to take a look at the remains?"

Touché. He paused, frowning, still trying to feel his way into a reluctant apology, but then he caught the flicker in her face and realised his hesitation might be mistaken for a weak stomach.

"Lead the way."

She inclined her head, almost regal, and moved on ahead of him. She was only a few inches below his own six-foot-two which made her tall for a woman, and she moved like a race-horse, all smooth-gaited co-ordination and long muscles.

He felt the usual twinge of conscience that always nagged him when he had cause to admire another woman. He shrugged it aside and made an attempt at solidarity.

"Do we have an ID on the victim?"

The CSI glanced back over her shoulder, frowning again. The action caused a little dent to appear between her eyebrows.

"According to those two, his name was Ben." She indicated the couple he'd ignored with a cool slide of her eyes. Nick had initially thought they were pale brown, but now he realised they were hazel, flecked through with green and chestnut and gold.

"How old was he?"

She'd turned away but he saw one elegant shoulder lift briefly. "Difficult to say." Because he couldn't see her face, the pity in her voice seemed more apparent. "Only a youngster, though."

Oh, God, every copper's nightmare. Her casual attitude to the scene rose up again to anger Nick. "A child?"

She stepped smartly aside, so that he found himself staring at the stretched-out body of a black-and-tan German Shepherd.

"Of course not," she said. "He's a dog."

"A DOG?"

Uh-oh. Grace heard the deadly quiet in the fair-haired detective's voice and suddenly all his earlier comments made sense.

"Of course," she repeated blankly. "What were you expecting?" She shut her eyes a moment. *Stupid question.*

"What do you mean, what was I expecting?" he snapped. "A human being, not some...animal."

Grace stepped in closer. "If you'd an ounce of compassion left in you, detective, you'd keep your voice down." Her eyes flicked to the couple, watching their every move. "This may just be *some animal* to you but—to them—Ben was a member of the family."

She saw him take a breath and struggle to govern his temper. He wasn't as young as she'd first thought, she realised. Early thirties rather than late twenties, which made him old to still be a DC. *Unless he's incompetent, or insubordinate, or he's come late to the job.*

He was tall, wide across the shoulder, but it was his eyes that struck her most strongly. They were deep-set, watchful, and an amazing liquid pale blue with a darker edge round the iris, framed by lashes a woman would kill for.

He moved with barely suppressed aggression, as though something was constantly simmering beneath the surface. *Perhaps temper's kept him back?*

She could almost hear the low rumbling growl coming up from his throat. Just for a moment, the similarities between the man and the defiant snarl of the dead animal behind her were starkly defined.

"They didn't tell you, did they—when they sent you out here?"

He pressed his fingers over his right eye socket. "Yeah, well, something obviously got lost in translation."

Grace heard the defeat in his voice and preferred it, on the whole, when he'd been angry.

"I explained the situation quite clearly." She paused. "I take it this isn't the first time someone's dubious sense of humour has got the better of them?"

He stilled momentarily and his hand dropped away. "No, it isn't. They're going to laugh their socks off about this, aren't they?"

"Why?"

The question clearly surprised him. "Because they're just going to love the idea of me charging off like some damn Don Quixote to deal with a dragon that any fool could see was just a windmill." His mouth twisted and he started to turn away with a final sour parting shot. "I'm considered an outsider, Ms McColl —an offcomer—and this is the price I pay for it."

"Do you honestly think I have so little to occupy my time that I would have called for a second opinion if I didn't think it was necessary?"

He stopped at the sudden vehemence in her voice. "Some dog was killing sheep and the farmer rightly shot it. End of story. The boy wonder back there"—he jerked his head in the direction of Danny Robertshaw who was furtively hovering as close as he dared—"has the weapon used. What do you need me for?"

"Well, not for your sparkling wit and winning personality," she murmured, allowing a small smile to cross her lips to shift the emphasis from her momentary anger. "But since you *are* here, detective, perhaps you wouldn't mind casting your eye over the victim?"

For a moment she thought he would refuse. And she needed him to take this seriously. To take her seriously.

"Please," she said. "Humour me."

He shrugged, stepping round her to move closer to the body. Grace handed him a pair of blue nitrile gloves and at least received a curt thanks as he pulled them on.

"The entry wound's smaller than I would have expected for a shotgun," he observed after a few seconds, almost talking to himself. "He could have it fully choked to give him a tight spread pattern, I suppose, or been firing solid shot."

She shook her head. "He wasn't. I checked already."

The detective scowled, more in concentration now.

"Well, in that case, he must have rammed the barrel right up against the dog's chest and pulled the trigger, point blank."

"If the shot was point blank, as you say, there would be a stellate pattern—starring—round the entry wound as the skin itself was ripped by the force of the projectile passing through it."

She smoothed her gloved fingers delicately through the fine hair. "As you can see, there isn't any, nor is there any charring from burning gases leaving the end of the barrel, which means it must have been fired from several feet away at least."

For a moment he regarded the dog in silence and Grace caught a hint of pity in his eyes. *So, he's not quite as heartless as he'd like to make out.* She was surprised to be relieved by that fact.

"No tattooing around the wound and no spread of shot," he said at last. He looked up and something had quickened in his face now. "Not a shotgun—handgun or rifle, maybe. And no small-bore, if the size of the wound is anything to go by. Can't tell you more than that at this stage."

Grace smiled more fully. *And he's bright, too.* "Very good, Mr Weston. There's something else you ought to see." She shifted the camera round onto her back and leaned over the dog. "If you'd give me a hand to turn him over? I've already photographed his position pretty thoroughly and I don't believe we need to call a doctor to pronounce life extinct on this one."

To his credit, he barely hesitated before helping her roll the animal first onto its back and then its opposite side. The flies rose in an angry swarm at the disturbance. Weston was firm but respectful, she noted. Rigor mortis had yet to set in and the limbs felt floppy and not yet entirely cool to the touch. *Like he was sleeping.* Grace closed off the thought.

The blood had pooled and congealed under where the body had lain. The flies spiralled into a new frenzy at its exposure. They both stepped back until the insects settled. She heard him suck in a surprised breath.

"The blood gave it away," she said, neutral. "The shot was

clearly fatal—almost instantly, I would estimate—and when I saw how little had come from the entrance wound, I suspected there must be an exit wound as well."

"And you were right." His eyes narrowed. "Rifle, without a doubt. A handgun wouldn't pack enough punch to cause that kind of damage." And something in his voice suggested he'd seen this before, or something very like it.

"Hm." She nodded slowly, as though he'd offered confirmation rather than revelation. "So the next question I asked myself was why our unknown shooter watched Ben kill five times, but drew the line at six? After all, anyone out here with a rifle is likely to be a hunter. They would understand how serious worrying livestock is—the cost of it to the farmer."

He eyed her intently, raising one eyebrow. His nose had been broken more than once, she noticed. He had a physical self-assurance that said he could handle himself in the rough stuff and had proved it. "And?"

"The only answer I could come up with was that he didn't—watch, that is." Grace saw his quick frown. "Look, I'll show you."

She walked in a direct line towards the dry stone wall that bordered the field. At its closest point it was a little over three hundred yards from the body and around four feet high, but on the other side the ground sloped away steeply. When she turned back, she found the detective was frowning at her again and she realised belatedly that he'd been trying to keep the legs of that rather nice designer suit out of the long grass.

"Why here?" he asked shortly, rubbing at his right eyelid.

Grace eyed him silently then reached into the leg pocket of her cargo trousers and pulled out a plastic bubble pack.

"Here." She tossed the pack across. He made a grab and missed, had to go fishing in the grass. "Why don't you stop being such a martyr and take a couple of paracetamol for the stinking headache that's making you such an ogre? I won't work with you if you're just going to snarl at me." She met the narrowed stare of those remarkable eyes without flinching. "There's a bottle of water in my bag if you need it to swallow them." *Or, indeed, your pride.*

For a moment she thought he'd snap at her. His mouth opened to deliver some biting retort, then his brain caught up and he shut it again, letting his breath out on a long hiss. Something of his bad humour seemed to go with it.

"That obvious, huh?"

"Painfully so."

Hangover? she wondered. *Something else that would have held him back.*

He dry-swallowed the pills, sending her a rueful grin as he did so that made him seem far closer to twenty-something than thirty-something.

"So—if you'd be so kind," he said with a little bow that mocked himself as much as her, "why here precisely?"

"Topography." Grace smiled. "I can hazard a guess, from the position of the body, the direction from which the shot was fired. The way the land drops away, this is the first point our shooter would be able to see clearly what Ben was up to. Any further back and they might have heard the noise, but wouldn't have been able to tell exactly what was going on."

"What makes you so sure they weren't in the field already?"

"If that was the case, why let the dog kill so many before shooting him?" Grace said. "The nearest gate is fifty yards further down that way. If they'd come through it and then seen what was happening, surely they would have fired from there."

He shrugged. "They could have climbed over."

"Have you ever tried climbing over a hundred-year-old dry stone wall, Mr Weston? You're as likely to end up sitting on your backside amid a pile of rubble. They can be rather unstable unless there's a stile." She studied the wall with a critical eye. "This stretch hasn't enough throughs—those long stones that go right through to tie it together securely. I certainly wouldn't risk climbing it."

"And you're an expert on scaling wobbly walls are you, Ms McColl?"

"Not really," she said with just a hint of a smile. "I prefer climbing trees."

She turned and looked back across the field and saw it again as it was, as it must have been. The quick ghosted blur of fur and muscle and teeth. She brought her arms up as though holding an imaginary rifle, shutting one eye as if to sight along the barrel. "No, I think our shooter heard the commotion, reached the other side of the wall, saw the slaughter, and fired."

The finger pulls the trigger…and the bullet leaves the gun.

The mental image faded and she let her arms drop. She glanced back at the detective, not sure how he'd reacted to her flight of fancy, but his face showed concentration now rather than derision.

"So, you reckon it was a gut response. Then panic, possibly, when they realised the consequences."

Grace shrugged. "I don't know about panic. But, whoever the shooter was, they knew enough to police their brass." She leaned carefully over the top of the wall and indicated a flattened area amid the nettles on the other side. "You can see this area's been disturbed. I've checked it thoroughly and didn't find the casing."

He frowned again, ran a hand round the back of his neck. "Could have been something that doesn't automatically eject the casing," he said. "An old bolt-action .303 perhaps? Or the grass could've been trampled by that lot."

He nodded to the young bullocks occupying the neighbouring field. Large chestnut-coloured animals who had gathered about fifteen yards away to watch the interlopers, blowing out noisy breaths as they shuffled their feet and nudged each other like big stupid kids on a dare.

"Cattle don't nettle themselves," Grace said coolly. And when his silence betrayed his doubt, she pointed to a couple of torn leaves lying crumpled nearby. "And, even if they did, I've never come across one that tried to take the sting out of it with a dock leaf."

She watched the detective as he turned slowly away from the wall, eyes straying to the couple who owned the dog, now barely containing their impatience.

"A rifle of the calibre to have caused that kind of injury, it's the sort of weapon you'd use for hunting deer. A .270 or a .308 maybe."

"The season's over for hinds," Grace pointed out. "And this is hardly the right terrain to take down a big stag."

"So who would go to all that trouble over a dog, using a weapon that's bound to raise flags, when a shotgun would have done the job with no questions asked?"

"Ah well, I only deal with the *what*, *when* and *how*." Grace's lips twitched. "The *who* and the *why* are your department."

5

"Ah, inspector—at last," the thin blonde woman said pointedly. "I'm Angela Inglis—Mrs *Duncan* Inglis." She paused, clearly expecting the name to have resonance.

"Detective Constable Weston, ma'am," he said in a neutral tone, taking the limply proffered hand of a professional meeter and greeter.

"Detective *Constable*, did you say?" She regarded him blankly. "I must say, I rather expected someone a little more...senior. When my husband can tear himself away from European affairs of state, he plays golf with your Chief Constable," she went on, allowing herself a small smile. "Lovely man, and his wife's delightful. We've known them for years."

And, having whacked that ball firmly onto his side of the court, she eyed him with arrogant expectancy. *Your turn.*

Ah, that *Mrs Duncan Inglis*. The name finally clicked and Nick suppressed a groan as he mentally re-ran his arrival, trying to work out if he'd been rude enough to drop himself in it. The headache had returned with a vengeance and he forced his right eyelid not to droop under the weight of it. The last thing he needed was the wife of a local bigwig to accuse him of winking at her.

She was a handsome woman rather than outright attractive. With her glacial looks and immaculate dress, she could have been modelling for some kind of country pursuits catalogue. They both could. Nick nodded to the silent man alongside her.

"I take it you're not Mr Inglis, sir?"

It was the woman who answered, drawing herself stiffly upright. "Of course not," she snapped. "Giles is simply a friend."

"Ben is my dog, Mr Weston. Or rather, he *was*." He cleared his throat. "Bad business, this. Not much more than a pup. Bit boisterous, but no real harm in him."

Nick thought of the lambs with their throats taken out and wondered if the farmer would second that opinion.

"Your full name, sir?" Nick retrieved his notebook from an inside pocket, saw the man's eyes flicker. "Sorry about this. Just formalities, you understand."

"Ah, yes, I suppose so." The man sounded doubtful, as though Nick had just suggested something vaguely indecent. "Erm, yes, Giles Frederickson."

There was another hesitation before Frederickson reeled off his address, as though considering every piece of information before releasing it. He lived in Warcop village, he revealed, giving an address that consisted of a house name but no number or street, a haphazard system that was becoming all-too familiar to Nick. Cumbria didn't have the manpower to send him out teamed with a local officer, so he'd been told, and it made finding anywhere a nightmare.

"Pretty little place," Nick ventured, trying to put him at his ease. Warcop was about twelve miles from Orton, picturesque but bordered on its northern side by one of the main cross-Pennine routes. Nick had driven through the village once or twice when he'd been getting to know the area. Sunday drives with... He bit down on a scowl. "Must be a bit noisy, though."

"We're not *that* close to the A66."

"There's an army firing range nearby, isn't there, sir?"

"Ah, yes, I see." Frederickson's tone was offended, as though he'd been personally criticised. "Can't say it bothers me."

"Can you tell me what happened here this morning?" Nick asked, his raised eyebrow inviting either of them to pitch in.

Frederickson cleared his throat again. "Erm, I'd popped over to talk to Angela—Mrs Inglis—about the local agricultural show next Saturday. We're both on the organising committee."

Nick assiduously jotted this down. "And what time was this, sir?"

The pair glanced at each other.

"About seven-thirty, I would say," Angela Inglis offered. "Perhaps a little before."

Nick looked up. "Bit early that, isn't it, ma'am?"

"Of course not." A snap, which she belatedly tried to soften with a little laugh. "Both Giles and I are larks rather than owls, detective constable. You've no idea how much can be achieved while most people are still lounging in their beds."

Keeps emphasising the rank to put me in my place. And the rest.

"Really, ma'am?" He slipped doubt into his voice just to be awkward. His natural body clock had him up and out before six every morning, running the quiet streets around Kendal. "And where was Ben during this time?"

Again, a sideways look passed between them. "I'd, erm, left him in my car," Frederickson admitted. "Angela has a couple of Siamese cats and Ben has a tendency to…"

"Go after them?" Nick finished for him and there was a long pause before Frederickson gave a quiet, embarrassed nod. "So you left him locked in your car?"

"One could hardly say it was too warm for him at that hour." Frederickson flushed, two small coins of colour that highlighted his angular cheekbones. "I'd parked in the shade, watered him and cracked the windows. Unfortunately, seems I cracked them a bit too far, and he gave us the slip."

"Really, detective constable," Angela Inglis broke in, an edge to her voice now. "I wouldn't presume to tell you how to do your job, but don't you think your time might be better spent questioning that wretched farmer, rather than giving poor Giles the third degree?"

"Angela, my dear—"

"According to our crime scene technician, the farmer's shotgun hasn't been fired for days," Nick cut across Frederickson's half-hearted protest with a dangerous softness, "and it would also appear that the an—, er, *Ben*, was shot by someone using a rifle."

She closed her mouth again, her lips forming a tight line.

"Look, Weston, don't you think you're making a meal out of this?" Frederickson said quickly, ignoring the quiet gasp from the woman alongside him. "What I mean to say is, on reflection, I accept that Ben committed a serious offence and paid the price." He tried a small smile that didn't quite make it to his eyes. "I view this as a tragedy, believe me, but it would be a blatant waste of police time and public money to take this further."

"Oh, but surely—"

Frederickson held up his hand and Angela Inglis fell silent immediately.

"Please, Angela. Ben was *my* dog and you must let *me* decide how best to handle this."

For a moment they fenced silently before she let her gaze drop. *Interesting,* Nick thought, watching them. Maybe there was a bit more spine to the old boy than had been first apparent.

"Of course, Giles. Do forgive me for interfering, detective constable." Her composure was firmly back in place. "I'm understandably...upset by what happened."

"Of course," Nick echoed blandly. He glanced at his notes. "Nevertheless, I'm sure you understand that regardless of whether you feel this was rough justice of a kind, we *will* be making further enquiries about the firearm that might have been used."

Frederickson looked as though he would argue but then gave a resigned nod instead.

"If you're looking for someone with rifles, detective constable," Angela Inglis said suddenly, "then perhaps you should look to your own."

"Meaning, ma'am?"

"Jim Airey." Nick recognised the faintest tinge of triumph when she said the name, as though she'd been waiting for this opportunity and was determined to savour it now. "He's not a *real* policeman, of course, but if you people are prepared to hand out uniforms you must take responsibility for who puts them on. Jim Airey," she repeated, when Nick didn't immediately react. She glanced about, frowning. "He was here when you arrived. You must know him, surely?"

"I'm new in the area, ma'am." Nick wrote down the name, adding an underscore and a question mark. "Are you suggesting that Mr Airey might have shot Mr Frederickson's dog?"

"Of course not." Just when the pounding in Nick's head notched up a beat, she added, "but his daughter might."

"His *daughter*?"

"Edith. I gave her a little menial job last year after she left school. A few hours a week—cleaning and so forth. But I had to let her go at Christmas. A certain item went missing from the house." She coloured primly. "A rather valuable item. I spoke with her father and, naturally, agreed not to take action, but her position was clearly untenable. She was somewhat...resentful about it."

Nick noted the hesitation. "And you think she might have been involved in this incident, ma'am?"

Angela Inglis nodded. "She made some silly threats at the time—just an immature teenager throwing a tantrum, so I thought."

Nick's scepticism must have shown, because her face tightened. "Edith used to get rid of vermin in the garden—magpies and grey squirrels." Clearly sensing his distaste she added, "We're in a red squirrel conservation area, detective constable. That means keeping the non-native greys out—they're larger, more aggressive, and they carry disease. If any are spotted, there are local people one can call on to...take care of the matter."

"And a teenage girl was one of those people?"

It was Giles Frederickson's turn to nod. "She might only be a slip of a thing—all skin and bone, but she is a quite remarkable shot with a rifle."

They're lying to me, Nick thought as he walked away. *Not sure what about yet, but I know they are.*

He caught young Danny Robertshaw over by the gateway chatting with the farmer, who was still on his quad bike.

"Where's Airey?"

"Er, I think he's just nipped off." Robertshaw had the grace to look sheepish. "Said he'd got an errand to run. Had to pop home to sort something out."

His daughter, most likely.

"Yeah," Nick muttered, "I'll bet he did..."

6

S<small>PECIAL</small> C<small>ONSTABLE</small> J<small>IM</small> A<small>IREY</small> roared out of Orton village on the Tebay road. He was aware of a tight resentment spreading through his chest, but it could simply have been heartburn.

Damn you, Edith. Wait 'til I catch up with you, my girl...

The Aireys lived in a grim little brick terrace that backed onto the railway line in Tebay. Although only a few miles from Angela Inglis's grand residence in Orton, socially the two villages were separated by far more than just the motorway junction.

The Inglis residence. That was how she'd answered the phone that time—six months ago, just after New Year—when Airey had been forced to go and grovel on his daughter's behalf. Cap in hand, like some peasant. Mrs High-and-Mighty Inglis had just loved that. He still smarted at the memory.

Every time their paths had crossed since, she'd pointedly asked after Edith. "And what's that daughter of yours up to now, Mr Airey?" with a knowing smile on her face.

The trouble was he couldn't be certain that Edith hadn't done what she was accused of—stolen a pair of antique cufflinks while she'd been serving daft little bits of stuff off a silver tray at one of the Inglises' swanky parties.

Mrs Inglis had caught her upstairs where she'd no right to be —all the wait-staff had strict instructions to use the downstairs cloakrooms only, so she said. Privately, even Airey admitted that his daughter was shifty and evasive about what she'd been up to. Seventeen. It was a difficult age. Mind you, she'd always been a moody kid.

He'd had to do some fast talking so Mrs Inglis didn't press charges. What would happen to his Special status if his daughter was exposed as a thief? Mrs Inglis had seen through his sudden parental zeal and that made him resent the woman even more.

It irked him Edith was such a little liar. Airey would be the first to admit he could be inventive with the truth himself when the occasion demanded, but his daughter was in a class of her own. *World* of her own half the time, Edith, and a dream world at that.

Jim Airey didn't have much time for other people's dreams.

She shouldn't even have been able to get her hands on *that* rifle in the first place. When any of those loony lot—offcomers, mostly—started getting all upset about having seen the wrong colour squirrel and wanted Edith to do her thing, she had her own little .22 locked away, all tight and legal.

His *other* guns, the ones he didn't declare for his certificate every year, he kept somewhere else altogether and Edith certainly shouldn't have had a key for those. How had she done it?

He chucked the marked-up Ford Focus through the round-about and booted it up the hill, ignoring the screaming engine.

At the top of the incline was a sharp right-hand bend. Airey cut it, almost clipping a van coming the other way. The driver braked hard and flashed his headlights, police car or no. Normally, Airey would have gone after him for that. Not this time.

The side-street leading to the dour little row of cottages angled steeply off the main road and was a devil in the winter. He careered down it, reckless, slewing to an untidy stop without making any attempt to park.

His front door was locked but that was no sign. He fumbled with his key, shoving the door open so hard the inside handle bounced against the wall and gouged another lump out of the plaster. The wife would give him earache for it later.

"Edith!" he roared into the silent house. "Where are you?"

Nobody spoke, but he thought he heard the faintest muffled clatter from somewhere at the rear.

He charged down the narrow hall and straight through the back sitting room, boots heavy on the thinly carpeted floorboards. His daughter was in the kitchen, a gawky stick insect of a girl who'd entered the awkward stage early and appeared set never to leave, with rounded shoulders and mousy hair that she never bothered to brush since her mum stopped doing it for her. She was fussing with a tea towel and looking, to his eyes at least, guilty as sin.

He halted in the doorway, feeling the anger in the bunching of his shoulders under the confines of the uniform and the stab vest, the pounding of the blood in his ears. For a moment there was silence while Airey eyed his only child with dislike close to loathing.

The intensity of it surprised him. You were supposed to love your kids, that was normal. But Edith had been a sickly baby and a sulky child who flitted through the periphery of his life without generating much emotion one way or another.

There'd been a time a few years ago when he'd thought she might turn out interesting after all. A bit clingy, but the nearest he'd ever come to being hero-worshipped. Flattering, really.

But she'd hit puberty and burrowed in on herself. If truth be told, Airey had already begun to find her an irritation, her sudden absence a relief. By the time he'd realised that he missed her, whatever bond they'd shared was broken clean. His attempts to repair it were met with monosyllabic indifference. He hadn't tried hard.

"What the hell have you been up to, Edith?" He stabbed a warning finger, galled by the way she jerked back, as if he'd ever laid a hand on her. "And *don't*" —his voice knotted itself with rage—"don't you *dare* lie to me, my girl, or you'll be sorry."

For a moment she stood there looking gormless, a rabbit in the headlights. Then she shut her open mouth abruptly and swallowed, and an ugly red flush rolled up the sides of her neck.

"I haven't done nothing." Her voice was thin and whiny, but her eyes were everywhere. Airey had heard that tone, seen that look, a hundred times before. From teenage toerags off the council estates in Penrith, claiming outraged innocence one breath and calling for the duty brief like old lags the next.

Airey took a stride into the room, a big one, and Edith gave a theatrical gasp, retreating until her bony hips bumped up against the edge of the sink. Even then she cringed away, clutching the wash-worn cotton tea towel up in front of her chest like it was made of Kevlar.

"Do I *look* stupid to you, girl?" He rummaged in his inside pocket, dragged out the ejected shell casing he'd taken from the crime scene in the field, and thrust it close to her face. When he spoke again his voice was low and gritted. "Did you think I wouldn't recognise one of my own reloads?"

She swallowed again, gaping at him, but he saw first the bloom of realisation, then the fear. Quickly followed by a sly scrambling as her brain started to race. Her teachers always used to tell him his daughter was a bright girl. She just didn't bother to use it, that was the trouble.

Without giving her a chance to invent, Airey grabbed her arm and dragged her towards the cellar door. His thumb and index finger almost met around her scrawny bicep and, briefly, Airey doubted she was physically capable of taking the shot that killed the dog, never mind the skill involved.

Because *he* didn't have it, he acknowledged. The admission of his own inadequacy, even unvoiced, brought with it a fresh rage that made him more careless with her than he'd intended.

He ploughed over her feeble resistance, using sheer bulk to hustle her down the crumbling steps and into the cool mustiness below. He flung her away while he reached to his belt for the keys, scowling when he found none missing.

Edith stayed where she'd landed, half sprawled against a mildewed stack of deckchairs, snivelling.

In the far corner of the cellar, under the front step of the house, was what had once been the chute into the coal store. With a last contemptuous glance, Airey unlocked the door to it, pulling the grubby string to activate the naked bulb.

Inside, on racks, was Jim Airey's illicit gun collection. He expected to find one missing, but they were all in place and accounted for. Except something wasn't quite right about...

Ah, that's it!

The centrepiece of Airey's display was a piece of firearm history, a Kalashnikov AK-47 assault rifle that dated back to the early fifties. A classic—Russian-made, not some Chinese copy—with a solid wooden stock and handgrips, and distinctive curved magazine.

Airey had been a gun nut for years. Losing the first joint of his right forefinger in the sliding breech of an old air rifle when he was still a teenager had failed to dampen his enthusiasm. Even if it meant he was never quite as good a shot as he could've been, before the loss.

He'd taught Edith to shoot when she was barely big enough to get the butt into her shoulder. She'd always been fascinated by the AK but he'd never let her touch it.

Looks like she finally helped herself.

In her haste, Edith had put the rifle back with the strap twisted. For someone who'd happily let his wife pick up his dirty towels and discarded underwear, Jim Airey was meticulous when it came to his firearms.

He spun back to face her, triumphant, and waved the cartridge casing in front of her face again.

"Did you honestly think I wouldn't know my own?" he repeated, quietly furious now. Her reply was more racking sobs.

He turned the casing over in his hands, smoothing his thumb across its surface. Pure luck he'd been sent to walk the field boundary, that his foot scuffed against the spent brass as he'd trudged through the long grass. It had been worth scrabbling through that nettle patch after all.

Because if that snobby redhead had got hold of this casing, it would have tied the gun straight back to him. He knew the casing was marked just as uniquely by the firing pin and the ejector mechanism of each gun as the bullet was by its passage through the barrel.

Not only that, but Airey reloaded his own ammunition. So each casing bore the marks of the clamps and tools used to repack it with propellant and the fresh projectile. Wasn't easy, getting hold of bullets for a gun that had never been legal in this country, and he had all the kit for putting together his own, so why take the risk?

Only now it was another nail in his coffin.

He tried to work out if anyone at the station had ever *seen* any of his reloads, but he didn't think so. With the incriminating evidence in his hand, he was free and clear.

So that just left Edith, and the fact that she had wilfully taken one of his guns and used it to kill an animal connected to someone with *influence*. Someone who could make real trouble for them. For that alone, he was seething.

He tossed the cartridge casing into a plastic storage tray that was already half full with empty brass, hiding one among the many. His daughter was still crying noisily, but when he glanced at her sharply he found she was watching him from behind her lank hair.

"I should wash my hands of you for this," he growled. "How could you be so thick?"

"It was killing lambs," she muttered, hanging her head further so all he could see now was the prominent vertebra at the back of her neck. Her voice rose to a wail. "They should've been *grateful*."

"Grateful? Ha! Don't you know whose dog that was?" He let out his breath on a snort. "'Course you do. After all that trouble at Christmas, she wants your hide, you stupid girl, and I've half a mind to give it to her."

"You *wouldn't*." Her face jerked up then, a mess of tears and snot. Some women could cry with dignity but Edith wasn't one of them. *Who'd want to comfort that?*

Airey sighed. At the end of the day, she was still his flesh and blood. Took after her mother, of course, but still bore his name. And he was protective of *that*, if nothing else.

"They've got nothing. All right?" She took her time about nodding and he glared at her until she did. "Now, hand it over."

"What?"

"The key, Edith. Don't test my patience, girl."

Slowly, reluctantly, she dug down the front of her shirt and pulled out a thin silver chain. The copy key, when she placed it defiantly in his outstretched palm, was still warm to the touch. Airey stared at it, then jerked his head towards the cellar steps.

"Go on. And you better ask my permission before you set one foot on those stairs in future. Got it?"

She mumbled something that he took to be assent and flounced back up to the kitchen. As they reached the top, Airey's radio crackled into life. He recognised Danny Robertshaw, agitatedly asking his location. Just for a moment, he considered ignoring the call.

"I said I'd not be more than half an hour, Danny. Can't it

wait?" he demanded, tilting the microphone towards his mouth without taking his eyes off Edith.

"Er, not really," came the cautious reply. "Er, DC Weston needs you back here sharpish, mate."

"Well, make some excuse, can't you?" Airey snapped.

There was a pause, then an entirely different voice came on. "What kind of an excuse would that be?" it asked, the pleasant tone not quite masking the underlying threat. Airey's stomach sank. "I'd hate to have to report you to your inspector," the voice went on, still calm and reasonable, "for unauthorised use of a police vehicle."

Airey let go of the transmit button long enough to swear under his breath. *All right, don't get your knickers in a twist.* "Yeah, er, sorry about that. I'm on me way."

Weston knows, Airey thought, feeling the panic gorge on itself. He flicked a glance at Edith, just in case she was finding the slightest amusement in his discomfort. But she was just standing there, apparently oblivious, staring at the lino under her shuffling feet, her pointed little shoulders hunched and shivering.

He glared at her, even so. "We'll have words about this later, Edith," he warned darkly. "Understand?"

She gave an unwilling nod without raising her head. Airey eyed her for a moment longer before his impatience got the better of him and he turned for the door.

"There was somebody up there," she said, bringing him up short. "On Orton Scar. Lying hidden with a rifle, watching it all."

He wheeled back to find she'd finally got her chin off her chest far enough to look him in the eye, defiance in her face now.

"*Somebody lying,* eh? I'll bet. But I'd lay money there's no mystery man up on Orton Scar."

"There was!" Edith burst out, colour flooding her face now. "He had a long gun—a big rifle—with a sight on it, and a sort of big square block on the end, and it was on bipod legs. I saw him—"

"*That's. Enough.*"

His roar stopped Edith dead, looking hurt, of all things. As if he was going to believe *that* kind of fantasy.

"What did he look like, then, this bloke?" he demanded, and when she shrugged he rolled his eyes and jeered, "You'll have to do better than that, Edith, if you saw him so clear."

"Dunno," she muttered. "He was covered in all camouflage stuff. Grass and weeds."

"What—a ghillie suit?" Airey asked. He'd shown her pictures, years ago, of the methods used by Scottish ghillies to hunt game in the Highlands. They weaved in surrounding vegetation to blend so perfectly with the scenery that they could almost get close enough to touch their prey.

"Yes!" Edith latched on with suspicious eagerness. "He had a ghillie suit."

"Seen many ten-point stags roaming majestically across Orton Scar, have you?" Airey said derisively and he turned away again.

"He wasn't facing that way. He was pointed down the valley towards the village, and *her* house," Edith grumbled.

Airey regarded her a moment longer, aware that the more he delayed, the more trouble he was in.

But, if Edith *had* seen something, that might go in his favour. He could claim he was following a lead, a hunch. Trouble was, if it turned out to be just another of the girl's stories, he'd look twice the fool for repeating it. And what was there to shoot at in Orton? Nothing much to interest a serious poacher, that was for sure.

Damn the kid...

"You must think I'm all kinds of an idiot if I believe that fairytale," he growled, annoyed as much with himself for giving it credence, however briefly. The finger stabbed out another warning. "You just keep your mouth shut and say nothing, all right? You can manage *that*, at least." He regarded her with a final contemptuous glance before heading towards the door. "Never did have much to say worth listening to, anyway."

"But—"

"Give it a rest, Edith." Airey didn't look back, exasperation making his voice harsh. "Just for once show me some respect and remember what I've said, will you?" And he slammed out of the house.

It was only as he gunned the Focus back up the narrow street that he realised in his anger he'd never asked Edith just what she'd been up to. What on earth *had* she been doing—out there in the fields at that time in the morning with a loaded AK-47? Whatever her original plans, the dog had not figured in them.

And the fact that Jim Airey's palms felt suddenly clammy against the hard plastic of the steering wheel had little to do with the speed he was driving, nor the prospect of an ear-bashing from some jumped-up detective when he reached his destination.

7

I WANT TO DIE!

Edith Airey flung herself onto the single bed in her mean little bedroom at the back of the house and listened to the harsh note of the patrol car engine dying into the distance.

When she'd left home that morning it had all seemed so clear —what she had to do, how she planned to do it. Going to the house of that *cow* had seemed the perfect location to end it all. She imagined Angela Inglis hearing the shot and running out to find Edith's pale elegant corpse on her lawn. Oh, the self-recrimination, the wailing!

Taking the AK from her father's illegal collection was the perfect crowning act of defiance. He might still treat her like a kid, but that would've taught him to take her seriously!

But reality never matched the images in Edith's head. She'd been so caught up in planning her own demise that she hadn't given much thought to the act itself. It had been like one of those old black-and-white war films her mother watched in the afternoons—stealing the key, getting it copied and putting the original back, planning her route across the fields so she wouldn't be seen.

She was the tragic heroine, imagining herself in a long black Cossack coat and a fur hat, meeting her contact in a lonely wood or deserted church to accept a dangerous one-way mission.

Only, things hadn't quite worked out like she planned. They never did, she thought mournfully. When she'd heard the frightened cries of the lambs, seen the dog running amok, she'd just had time for a burst of relief that she wouldn't have to go through with it after all.

But even as she'd lined up the open sights—as some part of her brain had taken into account the direction of the dog's run, the way the breeze was stirring the grass, the slight elevation— another part had recognised Ben and known there'd be hell to pay.

So she'd run. Abandoned her careful plan and turned tail like a coward, hoping she'd be able to get home and put the gun back without anyone realising.

Should've known I wouldn't be that lucky.

The tears spilled hot down her pinched cheeks. They blurred the old film posters and the childish pattern of the wallpaper around the window on the far side of the room. She knew her father's outburst was just the beginning. She hadn't expected to be around to answer for anything.

Her parents, naturally, hadn't noticed anything was amiss. And the more they'd breezily ignored her towering wordless rage, the more uncommunicative Edith had become, punishing them in advance for their indifference. She'd made her plans in sullen silence up in her cramped bedroom.

It wasn't that they hated her—that, at least, would have been something to rail against. You can't push against something that doesn't push back.

They just don't care. Nobody cares about, stupid, ugly, fat Edith.

She had no idea how her father had discovered her escapade so fast. Just her luck that he'd been out playing at policeman, today of all days. The memory of his words brought on a fresh wave of mortification and she buried her face in the pillow until the worst of it passed.

She fingered the empty silver chain around her neck. He'd guard the key more jealously after this, she knew, but there'd be another way. She clenched her fists until the nails dug painfully into her palms. There *had* to be another way.

She sat up, scrubbing at her leaking eyes, determination chasing away the lassitude. If she couldn't use one of her father's illicit guns, there were plenty of others. Something bigger than her own little .22 Gaucher. Something guaranteed to do the job, instant. All kinds of people had firearms about the place in the country, if you just knew where to look…

Edith wondered where the unknown sniper on the hill had got *his* gun. Even though he'd disguised the weapon in strips of sacking and grass, she'd known right away she'd never seen anything like it. So, who was he? Some mysterious spy with a secret agenda of his own? For a moment she allowed herself the warm fantasy that her hated ex-employer was the object of the sniper's deadly skill.

If only…

It still galled her that her father had thrown the information in her face, like she didn't know what she'd seen. Like she was making it all up.

But she *had* seen it, just like she'd said. And if he was too stupid to listen, what did she care? It was his lookout, the sweaty old sod. Just another grievance. Another thing they'd be sorry about in the end.

If it was the last thing she did, Edith was determined to make sure of that.

8

HIGH ON ORTON SCAR, a man going by the name of Patrick Bard-well lay behind the scope of his rifle, motionless in the long grass.

He'd been there since before dawn, tabbing in until he was within sight of habitation and low-crawling into final position on his belly, moving a few inches at a time, towing the gun labori-ously alongside him in a canvas drag bag.

Then he'd waited, patient, for a moment that never came, and so witnessed without emotion the massacre as it unfolded in the fields below.

Bardwell had never completed formal education beyond the basics at fifteen but he'd spent a good deal of his professional life waiting for action, in one corner of the world or another. When not undergoing constant training, he'd passed his free hours immersed in books and learning.

So, he knew that massacre was the right word to describe what he'd seen: *indiscriminate slaughter, especially with cruelty.*

Bardwell calculated he was roughly a thousand metres from the scene and, because of the topography, approximately sixty metres above it. Far enough that he couldn't hear the cries of the lambs, despite the stillness of the morning air. What little breeze there was had come nominally out of the east, carrying any sounds off west of him. And for that, at least, he'd been grateful.

In ideal circumstances, Bardwell would have had a spotter with a laser range-finder to call the distances for him, but the circumstances weren't ideal. So, he'd based his computations on features of the landscape, carefully noted during recon, drip-filtered through a lifetime of experience like water through rock.

Before the girl had appeared, Bardwell had considered taking out the dog himself. A tricky shot, but not impossible, and it presented some technical challenges that interested him. He'd got as far as sliding his right index finger inside the guard to caress the curve of the trigger itself, knowing exactly how much pressure was required for it to break.

He had allowed for the elevation. The sights were calibrated and set to eight hundred metres, but the extra was well within the capabilities of both man and weapon. At this distance, it was simple mathematics to work out the hold-off without adjusting the scope, to neutralise the target without compromising his position. He might even still be able to remain on station and complete his original mission.

And then the girl had walked into view, passing so close that he still couldn't be sure she hadn't seen him. She'd glanced over a few times, but had seemed nervy anyway. And when he'd recognised the rifle slung over her shoulder, he'd understood why.

There was something horribly familiar about the sight of her, bone thin, almost childlike, carrying a Kalashnikov. It brought back all kinds of memories, none of them good.

He had faith that the all-engulfing ghillie suit would keep him hidden from all but the most sustained search. He'd made it himself with care and minute attention to detail, using a pair of khaki coveralls as a base and building on it, layer by layer with narrow strips of camouflage material, long enough to sweep the ground when he was lying prone.

He'd added the final weave of real vegetation only after he'd arrived at his location to keep it alive for as long as possible, given the same treatment to a floppy wide-brimmed bush hat with a veil of cam netting to cover his face and a short train at the back that melded with the rest of the suit. Bardwell knew that from anything above a few metres away he was well-nigh invisible. At one time his life had depended upon it.

So he'd done nothing to take the offensive as he'd watched the girl walk down the hill towards the village, carrying her gun slung on its webbing strap. She'd had to get much closer to the field, of course, before she'd seen what was going on there.

And when she did so, she swung the rifle up to her shoulder with a practised ease that surprised him. It had only taken her a moment to work out that the distance was too great and she'd begun to run, awkward and ungainly, into the dip of the neighbouring field, then up to meet the wall, swift as any advancing soldier.

Without a moment's hesitation, she'd levelled the rifle over the top of the old stones and bent her head to the sights.

Bardwell tracked the dog again, saw it pause, turn its head in the direction of the intruder. Blood coated its muzzle and dripped from its open jaws. Now it had the taste, would it change to human prey?

The corrected aiming point he'd selected on the crosshairs of the scope's reticle pattern lined up perfectly on the killer's chest.

But before he could fire she had beaten him to it. He jerked in conditioned response as the sound of the shot reached him. When he had eyes on the target again, it was to see the predator's dying throes, one foreleg just visible above the softly waving grasses.

By the time Bardwell shifted the scope focus back to the girl, her own legs had folded under her. She'd slid down with her back against the wall, hand pressed to her mouth. It was only then, through the magnification of the scope, he realised that he knew her.

He'd never have suspected such a meek little mouse would have such talent. One shot, one kill. It was the sniper's holy grail and she'd achieved it with a certain amount of luck, he acknowledged, but also with open sights and a careless facility that intrigued Bardwell as much as it somehow terrified him.

If the way she'd upped and fled was anything to go by, it had frightened her just as badly.

After she'd gone he'd remained to watch the couple appear. They'd played out the expected range of emotions, of course, from shock and outrage to an impotent kind of fear. The arrival of the farmer with his shotgun complicated things nicely. If it was taken at face value, then Bardwell reckoned his own purpose might be concealed a little longer.

He hadn't expected the police, not for something like this, but he'd noted their response time and their actions in every detail. The foot soldiers behaved as foot soldiers always did, methodical, uninspired, doing the job drummed into them by constant repetition. He allowed the minutest smile to twitch his lips as the right word came to him: *plodding*.

He'd been watching as one of the policemen discovered the ejected shell casing at the base of the wall where the girl had stood. To Bardwell's amazement, the man sleighted the casing into his tunic like nothing had happened.

And under his camouflage, Bardwell smiled to himself. *Looks like I'm not her only guardian angel*, he thought, although why the policeman should have done such a thing he'd no idea. But it intrigued him further still.

And the redhead, she was different from the others. She'd looked beyond the obvious and put it all together, quickly, precisely, even pinpointing with surprising accuracy where the shooter must have fired from. Bardwell watched her go through it for the benefit of the fair-haired man who'd come later. The one who'd arrived with temper visible in every line of him, but who'd soon become caught up in what the woman had found.

The woman and the girl. The girl and the woman. Whether they were aware of it or not, invisible threads now connected them— to each other and to him. Bardwell could feel them tugging at his mind, distracting him from a plan that, while simple, would need all his concentration and resolve to see it through. He couldn't afford to let a couple of mere women divert him.

But both would have to be somehow accounted for, he knew, before his work here was done.

9

NICK WESTON STIFLED a yawn as he started up the Subaru Impreza's engine, turning the climate control onto full heat in an attempt to dry out his trouser legs. To counterbalance the soporific effect he stabbed a finger on the electric window switch, dropping the tinted glass all the way.

By his reckoning, he was running on less than three hours' sleep and he was desperately tired. The paracetamol Grace had given him had yet to take the edge off his headache, which still seemed to be doing its best to kick him to death from the inside out. He rubbed a weary hand across his face but even the small movement of his skin over his bones hurt.

The dressing-down he'd given Airey on his sheepish return had done nothing to alleviate Nick's bad temper. The other man had been deliberately obtuse, weathering Nick's threats with a pretended incomprehension that was difficult to overturn. *Damn woodentops.* But Nick had seen the quick clench of the man's hands, the knowing smirk, and had to forcibly restrain himself from clouting the fat Special.

Instead, he'd told him flatly they had reason to believe his daughter, Edith, was involved in the shooting and they'd be investigating her closely. That had wiped the self-satisfied smile off his face.

A PC had been despatched to baby-sit the girl until Nick could question her, but Airey was demanding that a female CSI carry out the necessary examination. He knew there was only Grace and probably hoped he could claim cross-contamination later if he needed to.

Grace consulted her boss back at Hunter Lane and announced she could maintain the integrity of the evidence if she detoured home to shower and change on her way to Tebay. There was no triumph in her voice, but Airey deflated visibly just the same.

With his window down the sound of the big Nissan Navara pickup jarred loudly in Nick's ears as it pulled alongside the Subaru, nose to tail. He glanced sideways in irritation and found the CSI looking down at him. No surprises there—she'd been doing that all morning.

"If you'd care to follow me," she said through her own open window, "There's a lay-by at the top where you can turn round if you don't fancy risking the gateway."

He heard the implied criticism of his low-slung vehicle but hadn't the energy to argue. Instead, he nodded shortly and sped away up the hill, finding a large gravel area full of potholes with only an elderly Land Rover in occupation. Nick swung his car round and gunned it back down to fall in behind.

She set off right away, piloting the big pickup briskly through the twisting corners. This latest example of her competence irked rather than surprised him.

In Orton village, she turned off the main road onto a narrow lane bordered by thick hedges. After only a few hundred yards she pulled to the left through an open gateway and onto a gravel area in front of a pair of pretty stone cottages.

Nick slotted the Subaru in next to her and climbed out, looking about him. Whatever kind of a place he'd imagined Grace McColl living, this wasn't it.

She'd already jumped down from the pickup, shouldering her camera bag, and was waiting for him with a slightly quizzical expression on her face. He shook his head apologetically and moved to join her.

As she slid her key into the lock, Nick heard a frantic scrabbling on the other side of the door and, as soon as it was open a crack, a long snout thrust through the gap. Then a slender, mushroom-coloured hound burst out and threw itself at Grace's legs, whimpering.

Grace dumped the camera bag and went to her knees, wrapping her arms around the dog and burying her head against the side of its neck in a hard squeeze that was held a fraction too long to be just a normal greeting. Feeling an intruder, Nick looked away, over the low wall by the door to a brightly planted garden. *She's spent all morning picking over the remains of a dog without a flicker,* he thought slowly.

After a moment the dog tired and wriggled loose, retreating a few steps to watch its owner with unblinking amber eyes. It was only then that the animal seemed to notice Nick and something about it grew wary, the silky fur rising a little at the back of its neck.

"Don't take it personally, but I'm afraid Tallie doesn't like men very much." Grace rose, dusting off the legs of her trousers. She skimmed a brief hand over the top of the dog's head. It finally broke Nick's gaze and turned away, dismissive, to trot back inside the cottage.

"How convenient for you."

Grace glanced at him as she retrieved her bag. "For getting rid of unwanted admirers, you mean?" Her voice was gently mocking. "Yes, I suppose it is. But very few of them ever set foot inside my home, so she rarely needs to be so protective. Come through, Mr Weston." She toed off her boots in the tiny hallway.

Sideways on, he noticed for the first time the tiny crow's feet radiating outwards from the corners of her eyes. *Older than she looks. Late thirties, maybe?* Maybe that accounted for the quiet self-confidence.

He had to duck under the low door frame but, once inside, the layout of the cottage was not at all what he was expecting. The living room was open-plan to the exposed rafters revealing a galleried area that he assumed was a bedroom on the upper level. On the ground floor was a small office, and a kitchen at the back, divided from the living area by a breakfast counter.

"As long as you don't try to follow me up, Tallie should leave you intact," Grace said, pausing with one hand on the newel post.

Nick watched the dog amble across to lie down pointedly between him and the stairs, just in front of the French windows. She crossed her long forepaws elegantly and never took her eyes off him.

"What breed is she?"

"A Weimaraner," Grace said over her shoulder as she jogged up the staircase. "She has some convoluted kennel name I can never remember, and never quite lets you forget she comes from a long line of champions." And with that, she disappeared from view.

Alone, the dog and Nick eyed each other with open animosity. "I might have known you'd have a pedigree."

He stood for a moment, letting his gaze travel slowly over the interior of the room, recording every detail out of habit. The far wall held several paintings—bold, abstract originals, arranged with flair. Opposite, the triangle of wall space under the slope of the stairs housed a custom bookcase, shelves crammed at least two deep with well-thumbed paperback novels, lurid modern crime thrillers mixed in with the classics. He tilted his head to check out some of the titles and the floor lurched abruptly under his feet, making him stagger.

"There's a cool pack in the freezer," Grace's voice said from above his head. He glanced up and found her leaning on the balcony, looking down without expression. "If you wrap it in a cloth and put it on the back of your neck for ten minutes while I get changed, it will do wonders for that bad head."

He thought about claiming such a measure was unnecessary but the pain had become a throbbing stake through his eyeball.

"Thank you."

She smiled briefly at his capitulation and withdrew. A few moments later Nick heard the sound of running water in the shower. He tried not to allow his imagination to take charge, but the mental image of that long sleek body naked and slick with soap was unexpectedly vivid. He glanced at the stairs. The dog growled somewhere deep in her chest.

"Don't worry," Nick murmured, lips twisting in wry self-contempt, "Even if you didn't take my balls off, *she* certainly would."

Curiosity made him stick his nose into the study while the opportunity presented itself. A small desk filled the space below the window, home to a blank-screened MacBook, an anglepoise lamp, and a phone/fax with the message light flashing. Avoiding temptation, Nick turned his back on it.

Another bookcase lined the far wall floor to ceiling, filled mostly with textbooks and scientific journals, dotted with glossy tomes on the art of photography.

The remaining two walls were covered with the real thing—dramatic Lakeland landscapes, moody black-and-white cityscapes, a group of racehorses frozen at full stretch, and a stunning portrait of a well-kept man in early middle age with obvious Italian heritage and a widow's peak, captured staring straight into the lens with amused arrogance, a champagne flute in his hand. He was wearing black tie as though the picture had been taken at a formal wedding, with a sunlit stone balustrade visible behind him.

The subjects were diverse, but he recognised a single eye. Grace's own work, he guessed. It said something about her that she hid them away in here. He didn't claim to be an expert, but to him they certainly looked good enough for public display.

So, was she merely modest, he wondered? Or, deep down, just as insecure as everybody else?

Overhead, the shower cut off. Nick moved through to the kitchen area, taking in the lack of clutter on the immaculate work surfaces. It was a small kitchen, which might account for the unnatural order, unless...*ah!*

He'd opened the fridge door first, just to be nosy. All it contained was a bottle of rather good white wine with the cork untouched, a half-round of brie, some limp celery, and an open tin of dog food sealed by a plastic cap. The freezer was little better stocked.

So that's why it's so suspiciously tidy...she doesn't cook.

He grinned, pleased to have found a weakness, and quickly found the pack she'd described. As soon as he pressed the icy mass to the nape of his neck, the pressure inside his skull seemed to ease. *Damn women. Do they always have to be right about everything?*

Which brought him straight back to Lisa, the cause of his bad temper, bad behaviour, and bad head.

Oh, he couldn't blame his girlfriend for all of it, of course. When he'd first put in for the transfer to the wilds of the Lake District he'd been happy—even eager—to come here.

The arguments for the move had been sound enough, he

recognised bitterly. Lisa's retired parents still lived in the village north of Kendal where she'd grown up. They were itching to see more of their granddaughter, and the prospect of free childcare had added weight to Lisa's drip-drip campaign.

She could get back to her hairdressing, she told him, instead of being stuck in with the baby all day. Why should he be the only one with a career?

But Nick had loved undercover work with the Met. Loved it right to the point where it had nearly killed him. Still, he'd been prepared to give it up—if not for Lisa's sake then for little Sophie's.

Sophie was a delicate little slip of a thing, hair so blonde she could have been Swedish, eyes the colour of cornflowers. He'd known right from the first moment he laid eyes on her that she'd turn out to be a real heartbreaker.

Yesterday had been her fourth birthday.

Yesterday had also been the day Lisa told him it was all over. The day he could no longer pretend their separation was a temporary blip. As soon as he'd arrived at Lisa's parents' place in Staveley for Sophie's party, Lisa had started niggling away at him until he snapped, as she'd known he would. He wondered why he'd never seen it before, that the only reason she provoked him was so she could claim he was the one who started it.

Lisa liked a good row. She was a shouter and a stamper and a thrower of things. In their early days together Nick was shocked by her vehemence, even when he knew well her passionate nature. That was, after all, how Sophie had come along.

This row was different, though. *Premeditated* was the best way to describe it. And as soon as he'd taken the bait she'd sprung the trap.

She'd had enough, she told him. She wanted out. It wasn't working. He was too married to his job, too focused away from *her* needs, from Sophie's.

Too superfluous to requirements.

She hadn't actually said that last bit, of course. No need.

Nick hadn't responded well. Afterwards, he realised there probably wasn't a right response.

How long was she planning this?

He'd spent a restless and uncomfortable night alone in the flat they'd rented together in Kendal, staring at the ceiling, and went into work early to wrestle with paperwork. Normally he was organised, prided himself on it, but that morning the type all blurred into meaningless smears on the paper.

When the call had come, he couldn't have been more grateful for the sergeant's interruption.

10

WHEN GRACE PADDED DOWN ten minutes later, showered and changed, she found the detective sprawled on her sofa with his arms folded and his eyes closed. The cool pack was wedged between the back of his neck and the low cushion and his legs were outstretched, taking up an inordinate amount of floor space.

The dog, who'd been guarding this intruder with absolute attention, regarded her with reproachful eyes as she descended, bare feet silent on the treads.

In the shower, Grace had realised she hadn't done enough laundry lately to give her much choice of clothing. Eventually, she dug out another pair of cargo trousers, in slate grey silk this time, and a sleeveless T-shirt she'd bought at Glastonbury two years before. Not exactly the professional image she usually tried to convey. Still, she'd quickly learned not to wear expensive clothes for work. You never knew at the end of the day if you'd be putting them in the wash or in a bag marked 'bio-hazardous waste'.

Now, she paused on the bottom step, watching him. Even in repose, there was something coiled tight and seething.

"Seen enough?" he asked without opening his eyes. When he did finally lift those long pale eyelashes, she was struck again by the remarkable depth of colour to his eyes.

"I was going to ask you the same question."

He sat up, ran a hand through his hair and flashed her a quick grin, totally unrepentant. "Old habits."

"In that case, perhaps I should have asked for a warrant before I invited you in," Grace said. "Vampire rules do not apply, by the way—just because you've been across the threshold once doesn't mean you'll be allowed inside again."

He laughed, rising to hand her the now-tepid cool pack. "I'm sure your faithful hound will see to it that I'm kept at bay if need be."

She was aware of his gaze as she shoved the pack back into the freezer, collected her cameras, but gave no sign of it.

"You drive," he said when they were back outside on the gravel. He nodded to the Subaru. "I'll pick this up when we're done."

"It's only a few miles." Grace was reluctant to have him invade her personal space again.

"Exactly—turbo engines hate all this stop-start stuff."

"Mine has a turbo, too."

His smile was smug. "Turbo *diesel* doesn't count."

Grace shrugged and slotted the camera bag into the space behind the driver's seat, climbed in and started the engine.

"What is it about women and their four-by-fours?" Nick mused as they backed out into the lane. "Why on earth do you drive something like this damn great truck?"

"It does snow up here most winters, and I never know when I might be called to the middle of a field somewhere." Grace flicked her eyes momentarily away from the road, opted for truth because she knew he probably wouldn't believe it. "Besides, I grew bored of my Mercedes coupé."

He gave a snort and lapsed into silence.

A moment later, Grace's mobile began to ring in its holder on the dashboard.

"CSI McColl."

"Where the hell are you, McColl?" boomed a voice through the hands-free speaker. "I thought you were supposed to be on your way over to examine the Airey girl?"

Out of the corner of her eye, she saw the detective's head snap round and his eyes narrow. She smiled.

"Charming as ever, Richard," she said blithely to her boss.

"And you know full well that I had to clean up first, or whatever I got from her would be worthless."

"And *you* should know by now that gunshot residue fades within a couple of hours, my dear," Richard Sibson shot back. "Quite apart from the fact that she's probably scrubbing herself raw in the bath as we speak."

"There's a female PC with her until we get there," Grace said, placid, "and we're on our way now."

"'We'?"

"Myself and DC Weston." She slid Nick a sideways glance. "The station sent him out to help narrow down the type of weapon."

"Weston, Weston," Sibson muttered, as though sifting through his mental filing cabinet. "New chap? Hm, yes. Watch yourself there, my dear."

"He seems quite harmless." Her smile widened as the detective's face darkened. "Aren't you, Mr Weston?"

Just for a moment, something flickered in his eyes, then he said drily, "Thank you for that flattering assessment."

Sibson's only response to that was a grunt. "All right, McColl," he snapped, "but don't spend much more time on this one. If a major enquiry lands tomorrow I don't want to have to go cap in hand because we've wasted our budget on a dead dog. Remember we have human victims to deal with, hm?"

"The deer season's over, and yet someone is roaming the countryside with a large-bore rifle. If that's not something to be taken seriously, what is?" She was aware of her fingers tightening around the steering wheel, took a breath to level her voice. "This is no ordinary shooting, Richard. Let me prove that at least? Think of it as a training exercise."

"You were supposed to have finished your training when I took you on."

Battling for a lighter tone, she said, "Perhaps I just have an enquiring mind."

There was another grunt. "Hm, we'll see. But, just in case you're right, I've arranged for an old friend in charge of the veterinary medicine department at Lancaster Uni to carry out a post-mortem exam on the unlucky fido, first thing tomorrow. He's a good chap—Welshman, but you can't hold that against him. He should be able to confirm your initial findings."

"Thank you." Surprise turned her voice husky. "I—"

"Just get on with it!" She thought she detected laughter behind the irascible tone. "I shall expect chapter and verse when you get back." He cut the connection before she had a chance to react, and without saying goodbye.

Nick let a breath out. "Is he always so...abrupt?"

"Another one whose bark is infinitely worse than his bite."

He failed to look convinced.

Originally, she had been upset by Sibson's appallingly rude behaviour to all his staff in general and, it seemed, to her in particular. She learned inside her first week that by far the best way of dealing with his apparent displays of ill temper was to utterly ignore them, responding instead with a serene politeness that seemed to infuriate but actually engendered respect on both sides.

"He does seem to be taking this seriously if nothing else," Nick ventured.

Grace allowed herself a small smile that didn't quite reach her eyes. "Yes, he does. And that's what worries me."

11

WITH AN AIR OF TRAGIC DEFIANCE, Edith faced the uniformed woman sent to guard her. In front of them, laid out neatly on newspaper on the scarred Formica kitchen table, were the pieces of the stripped-down rifle she'd been cleaning when the knock on the door came.

In her mind now she was a heroine of the French Resistance, captured by the dastardly occupying forces just before her greatest piece of sabotage came to fruition. The Gestapo had been sent for and, if she could only hold out for long enough against whatever torture they devised, the charges would blow, the vital supply line would be disrupted, and the tide of the war would be turned.

She reflected, sombre, on the fact that her bravery would probably be commemorated for years afterwards, in black-and-white films and children's songs. Maybe even a national day of mourning to mark each anniversary of her execution by firing squad...

"How much longer are they going to be?" demanded her father from the kitchen doorway. He was in his shirtsleeves, rings of sweat staining the armpits and his fat belly straining the lower two buttons. He jerked his head in Edith's direction. "She should have been at work by now, and I've certainly got better things to do than wait around all day."

"Your guess is as good as mine, Jim," the stout woman PC sympathised. "How's your missus, by the way? Last time I bumped into her in Aldi she was having awful trouble with her feet."

"Still is," her father said gloomily. "And that new doctor's neither use nor ornament."

Below the level of the table Edith's hands gave a quick convulsive clutch. *Stop it! You're ruining it. You always ruin everything.*

She stared fixedly at the runs of spilt fat down the side of the old gas cooker and tried to blank out the policewoman's inane reply. She was still clinging to her fantasy that the woman opposite was a despotic jailer at SS headquarters, one who took delight in tormenting her helpless captives.

"So, Edith, how's school?" the PC asked cheerily. "Aren't you coming up for your exams soon?"

"I left," Edith said with disdain. "Last summer."

"Oh, and what are you doing with yourself now, then?"

"I work at a place called the Retreat," Edith said through her teeth, deliberately vague. "Down near Grayrigg. You'll not have heard of it."

"Well." The woman frowned. "That's nice for you, I suppose."

Her father made a harumphing noise. "She's a part-time cleaner in a glorified doss house," he put in nastily. "If she didn't wander round in a daze half the time, she might be doing better than mopping floors. But after—" he stopped himself just in time. "Well, jobs don't come easy for girls like our Edith."

"My nephew's just the same," the PC said. "Just lollops around the house all day waiting for his benefits, driving my sister mad and complaining he's bored."

"They don't listen." Jim Airey spiked Edith with a meaningful glare. "They don't *do as they're told.*"

She glared back at him. *Do you really think I'm that stupid?*

He'd arrived back a few minutes after the woman PC turned up, making out all innocent, like he hadn't already been home once. Edith would never forget the way his eyes bulged when he walked into the shabby little kitchen and saw her sitting there with the gun all spread out before her.

Just for a moment, the colour had dropped straight out of his face, before he'd looked again and he realised what she'd done. And, just for a moment, she'd seen the appreciative gleam replace the shock. Then he was glowering again. *Jealous because he didn't think of it.*

"Ooh, I know," the PC said. "I remember—"

But whatever dull reminiscence she'd been about to share was cut short by the sound of the front door and footsteps in the hallway.

"Hello!" the policewoman called. "We're in the kitchen."

As if, Edith thought sourly, *they wouldn't be able to find us otherwise in this rambling mansion...*

The man who walked in was not in uniform, but he would have been just right in the Nazi guise Edith's imagination had painted. Tall and, if not quite Aryan blond, he was at least fair-haired, with a forbidding expression and startlingly blue eyes. Their chilling intensity would have been the perfect foil for an iron cross at his throat, maybe an artificial hand in a black glove.

He stepped forwards and swept his gaze over the dismantled rifle before turning on the policewoman.

"What the hell is this?"

"You needn't take that tone with me," the PC said, stoutly pink. "Everything's exactly as it was when I got here." Her voice was a lot more tart than it had been when she was speaking to Edith's father, who blustered forwards.

"Just hold on a minute, Weston! You've no right to come in here and bully my daughter—"

"If you want to see bullying, Airey," the man said with icy contempt, "then keep on the way you're going, by all means."

Perhaps it was something about those eyes that made her father back off. Any other time Edith would have cheered to see him taken down a peg or two. Now she despised the ease with which the detective had him cowed.

"Oh, do stop it. Nobody's going to bully anyone," said a new voice from the doorway. Edith looked up and saw a tall glossy redhead. Older and quieter, she was casually dressed, but she had that kind of unconscious style some women achieved with no effort. The kind who could turn up anywhere in jeans and make everyone else feel *they* ought to be wearing them too. Edith was instantly jealous.

She had agonised over her meagre wardrobe before the PC arrived, eventually selecting a pair of dark green slacks and a short-sleeved jumper. She'd topped it off with a carefully knotted scarf at her throat for that added touch of relaxed sophistication. Now, she felt frumpy by comparison.

The woman put her bag down on the worn lino and smiled straight into Edith's eyes. "Hello Edith, I'm CSI Grace McColl. I don't know if you remember me but we met last year—I gave a talk at your school. Did you ever pursue your acting?"

Edith had a sudden flash of a careers day where an unguarded admission had led to brutal teasing. She flushed scarlet, ignoring her father's derisive snort.

"No," she mumbled. *What's wrong with wanting to be famous?*

But the memory tripped her concentration. She needed more time to prepare every answer, for Edith the Spy to steel her nerves. When Grace asked her if anyone had explained what this was all about, she just shrugged.

Grace smiled again as though that was a perfectly acceptable reply. "I'm going to carry out a standard Firearms Discharge Residue test, just to eliminate you from our enquiries." She glanced at the overcrowded table without expression. "We'll use the other room for this, I think."

In the back sitting room, she lifted a Jiffy bag out of her kit, ripped it open and spread a thin polythene sheet across the gateleg table, pulled on the disposable gloves provided. The gloves were one-size-fits-nobody. It all seemed a bit cheap and low-tech to Edith's eyes. Catching her disappointment, Grace pulled an apologetic face.

"So, is that your rifle in there, Edith?"

"What if it is?" her father jumped in, bristling.

Hasn't got the balls to take on the man, Edith decided in contempt. *But happy to prove what a hero he is by standing up to the woman instead.*

The redhead didn't seem in the least intimidated. She slid her eyes briefly towards him in gentle admonition, "I'm carrying out an FDR test, James. I need to know if—or when—your daughter last handled a firearm."

Only Grandma Airey had ever called him James, and then in an ominous tone of voice that must have had him quaking, back when he was in short trousers. Edith's remembered dislike for Grace abated a little.

"Yeah, it's mine," she said.

The CSI swabbed her own gloved hands first, dropped the

little piece of cotton into a sealed tube marked as Control, and reached for Edith's right hand, wiping it briskly, sealed the sample. She repeated the process with the other hand, her face, scraped underneath her nails, even combed through her hair. The swabs had a wet chemical coldness. Grace worked quickly, without hesitation, and Edith envied her dexterity on top of everything else.

"Where did you go out shooting this morning?"

He was asking the questions now, voice clipped and impatient. Edith felt the tension form a solid mass in her chest, expanding until it was an effort to breathe.

She shrugged again. "All over," she muttered, heard him sigh.

"All right, let's be more specific. Where were you between, say, six-thirty and eight o'clock this morning?"

Somebody must have seen me. Not that they'd remember fat little Edith, but if I lie now, and he already knows...

"Up on the Scar." She risked making eye contact and wishing she hadn't.

"Orton Scar?"

"Yes." *Now what?*

There was a pause. "And you were using *this* gun?"

She shifted uncomfortably on the hard wooden chair, making it creak, checked her father's stony face again, repeated, "Yes."

He let his gaze roam over the dismantled parts, pursed his lips slightly. "Nice piece," he said dispassionately. "Gaucher .22 —French, isn't it?"

After her father had locked away the AK-47 and stormed out, Edith had given her predicament some furious thought. If her father knew, others might also suspect her. Especially when it came out who owned the dog.

She'd gone to the *other* gun cupboard—the legitimate one built into the alcove by the fireplace in the back room, not the cellar—and brought out her own smaller-calibre rifle, the one she used for pest control. She'd been out with it the night before at dusk and had yet to pull through the barrel.

She'd watched enough TV cop shows to know she had to admit to firing something or they'd catch her in the lie. The Gaucher, already fired, fitted the bill. So she'd part-cleaned the weapon and left it spread on the table for them to find, pleased with herself for her speed of thought. *All in a day's work for Edith the Spy.*

"Who added the scope?" the detective asked now.

Her eyes jerked back to his face, slid across and dropped away. "I did."

She saw him glance across at her father as if for confirmation, but Jim Airey couldn't take credit for that one. He'd lost interest in her shooting abilities long before Edith had saved up her puny wages to buy the best telescopic sight she could afford.

She'd made the journey all the way down to Fawcett's old-fashioned shop in Lancaster, agonised over the choices, and eventually came away with a second-hand 4x20 scope cradled almost reverently in her arms. She'd hugged it close all the way home on the bus. Her little secret.

The policeman, Weston, reached towards the scope and an involuntary noise of protest escaped Edith's throat. He froze with his hand hovering over it, probing her with those mocking eyes.

For a moment he didn't speak, didn't move, just looked at her. She felt the heat steal up her cheeks.

"I got it all set up perfect," she said, in such a rush that she stumbled over the words, had to stop and untangle her tongue. "And I–I don't like nobody messing with it."

Almost to her surprise he gave the slightest of nods, as if he understood. But just when she thought he might be softening, he asked in a coolly accusing tone: "So, what are you shooting that you need a telescopic sight for, Edith?"

"She shoots rabbits for heaven's sake!" Her father was angry now, but it was the empty kind. Thunder not followed by lightning.

"Rabbits," the detective repeated flatly, rounding his focus onto her father.

"There's plenty round here who are partial to a bit of rabbit pie. And they're vermin. They breed like...rabbits." Jim Airey tried for a lighter note to cover his outburst, but his jovial came out as desperation. "Doing everyone a favour, aren't you, love?"

"Can anyone confirm where you were this morning, Edith?" Weston said. "Did you see anyone, speak to anyone, while you were out?"

"No." She lifted her head with what she hoped was quiet dignity. "I went out early 'cos I wanted to be alone."

"No friends who go with you, then? Boyfriend perhaps?"

The flush, which had begun to subside, raced back up her skin, scalding like steam from a boiling kettle. She bet it was that bugger Danny Robertshaw who'd opened his big mouth about her. Ever since she let him do what he wanted in the back seat of his car that one time, he'd been slagging her off to all and sundry. Edith let her head drop and mumbled a negative reply.

"Did you hear anything while you were up there?" Grace asked, gently. "Or see anything out of the ordinary, perhaps?"

Edith checked her father's face again. He'd tensed, the lines cutting deeper into his fleshy jowls.

What do I say now? They'll know, if I was where I say, that I would have heard the shot, so do I admit or deny it?'

"Well, Edith?" Weston prompted.

"I was thinking," she said, bold enough to be waspish, making a big show of concentrating on her recall. "Maybe I did hear something. A shot. But it sounded a bit, I dunno, weird, I s'pose."

"'Weird' how?"

Edith knew exactly what the gun had sounded like. Without ear defenders, it was going to take days to get rid of the faint ringing in her ears.

She shook her head and heaved a big sigh. "Not like a shot-gun. Bigger, somehow." She thought he'd worry at her on that but he switched tack again.

"You used to work for Mrs Angela Inglis, but she fired you. Why was that?"

"She never did—I walked out!" Edith protested scornfully, chin jerking upwards. "And I never did nothing, anyway. What would I want with a pair of stupid old cufflinks?"

"So it's best to say you don't get on," Weston said, and she got the feeling he was sneering at her again.

"She's a stuck-up old sow," Edith shot back, reckless, and didn't miss the twitch of Grace McColl's lips as she stripped off her gloves, that emboldened her still further. "And you can tell her I said so!"

"Hm, maybe I will."

Grace began to pack her kit away and, unaccountably, Edith felt disappointed by the anticlimax of it all.

"I thought you could tell, right away." She peered at the squashed swabs, rolled up inside the tubes. "Don't they go purple or something?"

"Blue," Grace said. "But quite a lot of things other than firearms residue will give you a false positive result—cosmetics, say, or tobacco. We prefer to test everything more thoroughly in the lab."

"Is that it?" her father demanded. "Are you done?"

"Just one more thing," Grace said. "I'd like to take a DNA sample from Edith." And when he began to bristle again, she added calmly, "Purely for elimination purposes. It won't be permanently stored."

Edith saw him hesitate, knew that refusing wouldn't look good.

"Oh, go on," he said, grudging, and then Edith had to submit to having the inside of her cheek scraped.

They all stood and watched the CSI work, uncomfortable, although she seemed totally oblivious to her audience. Weston never took his eyes off Edith, which made her fidget all the more, worrying at a hangnail on the side of her index finger with her teeth before she realised that her hands tasted of gun oil. She wiped her mouth on her wrist and let her hands drop.

"How many rabbits did you kill this morning, Edith?" Weston asked.

She shrugged again, forcing her shoulders to relax. "A few. I dunno."

"You don't know?"

She glared at him, struggling not to let her dislike spit out.

"I buried some of them."

"Why?" It was the first time he'd sounded genuinely puzzled. *Does he know nothing?*

"They were the myxi ones," she said, aiming to be difficult.

"Myxomatosis. It's a virus," Grace McColl put in, not looking up from packing away her bag. Her voice was neutral. "Farmers deliberately encouraged it in Britain in the 'fifties, I believe, to try and control the rabbit population. But it's particularly nasty—the poor things go blind and ultimately die of respiratory failure."

She smiled at Edith again. "Killing the sufferers might be considered an act of mercy."

Weston absorbed this information without comment. "What did you do with the rest?"

She heard the challenge in his voice and got to her feet without a word, moving to the back door. They followed her out, all four of them, overcrowding the cramped yard with its drooping washing line and the weeds poking through the cracked concrete. There was a tiny outhouse backed onto the kitchen, a thick layer of moss holding the slipping roof slates in place. Edith flung the door wide to reveal a grim little space full of spiders and dust.

But there, hanging from a row of hooks on the beam like convicted traitors, were four dead rabbits, their stiffened corpses swinging gently in the disturbed air from the open doorway.

12

"God, that was bizarre," Nick said as Grace steered the Navara back up the steep slope towards the main road. He let out a long breath and shuddered. "That kid gave me the creeps."

"She has problems, certainly," Grace said in a detached tone of voice, unsmiling. "I'm more interested in what lies behind them."

Nick twisted slightly in his seat so he could watch her. The T-shirt she wore was tight and stretchy, the lack of sleeves revealing long slim muscles in her upper arms as she drove. And the way the diagonal of the seatbelt emphasised the curve and separation of her breasts had his mind plummeting instantly off the job at hand.

When she reached the junction and leaned forwards slightly for a better view of traffic, he quickly averted his gaze.

"What kind of a name is *Edith* for a kid in this day and age, anyway? Difficult birth, d'you reckon?"

That at least raised a faint smile although she didn't speak right away. Nick let her thoughts order themselves at their own pace. He was a good enough interrogator to know when to push and when to let things glide, and silence had never worried him. Perhaps, if it had, he might have seen other things coming, he reflected.

Grace interrupted this sour contemplation. "She's unnaturally thin and her breath smelt of pear drops. If I had to guess,

I'd say bulimia rather than anorexia—her teeth are starting to go bad."

Then it was Nick's turn for stillness while he re-ran his encounter with the girl in his head, overlaid now with the framework of this new perspective. *It fits*, he thought, but… "What difference does that make—the state of her teeth?"

"Bulimics go through a cycle of bingeing and purging with excessive use of diuretics and laxatives," she said. "They also regularly induce vomiting. Stomach acid is highly corrosive to the enamel of the teeth."

"You're a mine of fun facts, aren't you?" Nick grimaced. "The roots of all those eating disorders are reckoned to be psychological, aren't they? You've met her before—any thoughts?"

Grace slowed at a crooked humpbacked bridge to let an oncoming elderly Land Rover over first, lifting her right hand briefly from the wheel to acknowledge the driver's nod of thanks.

"From what I recall, she seemed desperately unhappy when I met her at school. I would say she was being bullied. But any one of a number of things could have triggered it—a thoughtless remark by some boy when she was at a sensitive age, perhaps." Her voice was even, but he heard something else, little more than a shadow.

"I have to say I didn't like the way Airey hovered over the girl while we were questioning her," he said when Grace didn't continue. "It wasn't quite protectiveness. There was something else…"

"Fear?" She shrugged at Nick's sideways glance. "He certainly seemed very anxious what she might say to us, don't you think?"

"Hm, but about the death of Frederickson's dog, or about what he might be doing to his own daughter behind closed doors?"

"That's a bit of a leap. Have you considered it might simply be your scary interrogator demeanour thoroughly intimidated the pair of them?"

"Me?" He flashed a brief, boyish smile. "As it happens, I was thinking the same about you."

"Really? I think you'll find I haven't bitten anybody for *weeks* now."

He gave a bark of laughter that quickly faded. "All the same, there was something off about the way Airey interacted with his daughter, and I intend to find out what that was."

Paedophilia had always pushed the button of Nick's temper. Pushed it and held it down. The thought of a father having those kinds of desires for his own child made him bitterly sick as well as angry.

"Maybe we should bring her in, get her away from home and see if she'll open up," he said. "One of the DSs is the motherly type. I could ask her to have a word."

Grace lifted one shoulder by way of reply.

"What?" Her lacklustre response nettled him.

"I think you should be very careful with Edith," she said slowly, all evidence of humour gone. "As soon as we walked in there I got the feeling she was putting on a show for us, like a precocious child. She claims to have been out rabbiting all morning, yes? And according to her father, she was supposed to be at her cleaning job down near Kendal before lunch, and yet there she was all dressed up in those dreadful middle-aged clothes, like she was going to a play. Or maybe taking part in one..."

Her voice trailed off and Nick's eyes narrowed.

"She knew we were coming." His voice was hollow. "And she was ready for us." *Damn Airey!* He shut his eyes, picturing again the kitchen table with the gun spread out across its surface. "She wasn't just cleaning that rifle—it was on display for us, wasn't it?"

"Hm, that's my guess." Grace turned into the lane that led up to her cottage. "And those rabbits were in full rigor. It takes eight hours to develop in humans. I'd have to check, but I'd say it's unlikely they were killed this morning."

"But, what does she gain by any of it? I mean, we've only hearsay linking her to all this, and you know as well as I do that if Lady Muck wasn't involved, we probably wouldn't have bothered taking it this far. It's as if Edith *wants* us to look at her more closely."

"She's seventeen and once expressed an ambition 'to be famous'." Grace slid him a sideways smile. "Who says there's any logic to her thought patterns?"

Nick grunted. "So, we have a disturbed hormonal teenager

with a grudge against her former employer and a penchant for firearms."

It was Grace's turn to raise an eyebrow. "Shooting rabbits and squirrels is hardly the sign of a psychopath."

He shook his head. "When I was interviewing Frederickson, he mentioned she was a remarkable shot. Then she didn't want me to touch the scope in case I knocked it out of alignment. *That* tells me just how serious she is about it." He ran a frustrated hand through his hair. "Sounds like a recipe for disaster to me."

"For Edith," Grace murmured, "yes, it probably is."

PART II

13

GRACE STOOD, Canon poised, on the tiny flagged patio outside the French windows. A few metres away, dangling by one back foot from the peanut feeder on the cherry tree, was one of the red squirrels Angela Inglis was so keen to protect.

The cottage was an outbuilding conversion that barely allowed for the frivolity of garden space. Grace had utilised every inch and now, with the early dew still misting every leaf, was the time she loved best.

My own work, Grace thought. Not just the design, but the actual digging, the planting. All of it. Her eye absorbed its every nuance and she smiled faintly as she carefully lifted the camera. The squirrel, alerted by the slightest movement, catapulted back into the branches and darted away.

"Bad luck." Behind her, Max Carri's voice contained the same lazy amusement it always had, back when they were still married and Grace's photography was a hobby he indulged. "The amount of food you put out, I'm amazed you're not beating them off with a stick. There'll be other days."

"Perhaps." Grace flipped the lens cap into place. She slid the Canon back inside the open bag on the wrought iron garden table and closed the lid. At one time Max's refusal to take seriously anything she did had infuriated her but she'd learned to be impervious.

Max took a sip of his coffee and smiled over the rim of the plain white bone china mug, the action crinkling the skin around the corners of his eyes. It was the only noticeable sign, she thought, studying him with a dispassionate eye, that her ex was just a couple of years away from fifty.

He'd always taken great pains over his appearance, but she'd never considered him outright vain. Sprawled in one of the uncomfortable chairs that went with the table, he managed to look relaxed and totally at home.

And she didn't want him to be.

The cottage was *her* home, not his. He hadn't been able to impose his choices, his tastes—his *will*, even—on any of it. Simply having him here felt like an imposition.

She allowed nothing of that irritation to show on her calm features, although she carefully remained standing because she knew he expected her to join him, acquiescent, and sit.

"You're looking well," she said politely.

He shrugged. "Business is good," he said, which was about as much as he'd ever deigned to tell her about the intricacies of worldwide property development.

In his beautifully tailored black suit, he looked smooth and slick and successful. The suit, like the startlingly white shirt underneath it, was made-to-measure rather than off-the-peg, and everything about him reeked quietly of money.

Grace knew, without undue conceit, that she had played her part in helping Max acquire that gloss. Her family came from money they no longer possessed. Max's origins were diametrically opposite. He'd fought his way up from nothing and was justifiably proud of the achievement. Her biggest achievement, as she saw it, was stopping him from becoming too smug.

Besides, it wasn't Max's money that had attracted her in the first place, but his sense of grounded stability. Her own father had never seemed to be there. Max, as it turned out, was there too much.

Grace was never much interested in her husband's finances while they were married, and even less so when the relationship was being legally dissolved. Her solicitor had almost wept when she'd told him she had no wish to lay claim to half of her husband's fortune as recompense for twelve years of matrimony.

After Max's initial anger and surprise, theirs had been an amicable split. Civilised. He prided himself on his urbanity and secretly it pleased him, she knew, that three years on they didn't snipe and bicker at each other like so many of their friends whose marriages had come unstuck.

And that brought her back to the reason for his unexpected early morning visit.

"I can't go to Florence with you in a fortnight, Max." She managed to sound suitably regretful. "It all sounds lovely, but my work—"

He gave a slight flick of annoyance with one hand. "You know you wouldn't have to work if you'd let me make proper provision for you." He leaned forwards a little and lowered his voice conspiratorially. "That legal man you hired was a fool."

"He was only following my instructions. I don't want more than I have." *Except, perhaps, my privacy.* "And, besides, I enjoy my job."

He sat back in disbelief. "Poking around at crime scenes, photographing rotting corpses? How the devil can that be classed as enjoyable?"

"I make a difference," Grace said quietly. "I find it...satisfying."

Most of the time. And I have amends to make, still.

"There were other things you could have involved yourself in —schools, charities." He waved vaguely. "You didn't have to take up something so *gruesome*, darling, just so you can feel useful."

Grace paused, surprised at the vehemence, the plaintive note that she should prefer the company of the dead. *How can I explain it, why I need to do this, when I never entirely confided in you at the time?*

Max glanced away, put his cup down very precisely.

"In a few weeks it's our anniversary—or would have been," he said with dignity, eyes fixed beyond the hedge at the bottom of the garden, on some distant point away across the fields. "Fifteen years. I thought you might like to mark the occasion."

"We're not married any more, Max," she reminded him gently. "It's a kind and generous offer, but I'm sorry. I can't go."

"Can't or won't?" While his tone was light, Grace caught the sulky thread beneath it.

"Can't, Max." She smiled to soften the blow. "My life is very different now."

He shrugged, scowling at the bulky camera bag.

"Ironic, isn't it? When you first told me you were interested in photography, I assumed you were thinking of modelling," he said, wry. "I wasn't sure whether to be delighted or appalled."

Grace lifted an eyebrow. "And now?"

"Oh, appalled, definitely." He broke into a full-blown smile that showed off his white teeth against the natural tan of his skin. He rose, buttoned his jacket, shot a cuff to glance at his watch.

"What time is your flight?" Grace asked to cover the relief that he was leaving.

"I'm using up some of my hours on the jet. They'll wait," he said in a tone that suggested they better had. "I'm only away a few days. I've promised to be back for some local show next Saturday." He grimaced. "I was browbeaten into being their main sponsor by a fearsome woman who's the wife of our local MEP."

"Not Angela Inglis?" A picture of a furious icy blonde in a field of dead lambs sprang into Grace's mind. "I can't imagine you letting her bully you into anything."

Max turned. "You know her?"

"We've met only once. I don't think we really hit it off."

"Her husband is someone it's unwise to annoy," Max said. "Worth a day spent at some local shindig, anyway. Otherwise, I might be tempted to extend my trip and give it a miss."

"And where is it you're jetting off to this time?"

"Oh, somewhere I can hardly pronounce in Kazakhstan."

She paused, frowning. "Is it likely to be dangerous?"

"Worried about me, darling?" He smiled at her again, a little patronising this time. The old Max. "Don't be. I'm taking every precaution. And they're so desperate for Western investment I very much doubt my hosts will let anything happen to me. They're the kind of people who take their security very seriously."

"Ah," she said, grave. "I do hope you're not getting mixed up in anything I should be taking a professional interest in."

She'd meant it as a joke, but something in his face hardened. "I've always played fair, Grace—hard, but fair. In business and always with you."

Grace saw him to his car. Watched silently while he reversed the big Mercedes out of the driveway and listened to the opulent note of its exhaust fade away down the lane.

Her thoughts turned unbidden to the detective, Nick Weston. He had something of the same intensity about him and, knowing she found the characteristic attractive, Grace made a mental note to be wary in his company. Perhaps inviting him into her home had been a mistake, she admitted.

Grace knew that she was the subject of some speculation around the station and had gone to some pains to keep her private life just that—private. If he chose to use the knowledge he'd gained to imply any kind of intimacy, it would be round the place faster than any schoolyard rumour.

But it was difficult to discount his compassion—his attitude towards the girl, Edith, for instance. He'd been unmistakably angry at what might have been done to her. An anger which transcended any feelings of foolishness that he'd been taken in, however briefly, by her act with the stripped-down rifle.

Interesting.

The awkward loneliness of the girl spoke to Grace in ways she found difficult to ignore. But as to Edith being capable—physically or psychologically—of carrying through such an act was another matter. Nick had called her a recipe for disaster and he was probably right.

Edith's Gaucher rifle had been taken away for comparison, of course, but Grace already knew its .22 calibre could not have inflicted the injuries she'd documented.

So, what did?

Collecting her camera bag and the empty coffee cups, she moved inside, latching the French windows behind her. Tallie, lying with her back against the bottom step, raised her head briefly and huffed out a breath.

Grace moved through to the small study and booted up her MacBook, inserted a thumb-drive to make another pass through the crime scene pictures she'd downloaded the night before. She did so with an impartial gaze, disconnecting her emotional response from the scenes of slaughter.

Just as she was about to close the program down, something caught her eye. It was in the distant background to one of the overall shots she'd taken from the position of the body. Little more than a smudge of pale colour in the upper left-hand corner, near the top of Orton Scar.

Grace zoomed in as far as the resolution allowed. The shape solidified into a definite mass. There were no houses, so it could only have been a vehicle. Something square and blocky, like a delivery van.

She recalled a rough lay-by at the top of the hill affording a clear view out over the valley. It had been early morning, but perhaps this unknown driver saw or heard something?

Perhaps I'll suggest to Nick that he follows it up, she thought. A faint smile hovered on her lips. *Carefully.*

14

NICK RAN. When the insomnia gripped him, exercise was the only thing that soothed his mind. The only drug he was willing to take.

It was 5:45 a.m. but the sun had been up nearly an hour. For as long as he could remember, Nick had run at this time of day. Something about the quiet of the early morning always helped him to achieve some measure of peace as his feet found a rhythm all their own through the deserted streets.

It hadn't taken him long after moving to Kendal to work out a series of testing routes. There was plenty of hill work. Every road out of the grey stone town involved a steep climb. The only drawback used to be tearing himself away from Lisa's warm body.

Not any more.

He could still remember the day, weeks ago, when he'd got home to find Lisa gone, and Sophie gone with her. Lisa had taken her clothes and most of Sophie's favourite toys. It had been all he could do not to weep. He increased his pace, feeling the muscles start to block and burn, glad of the pain.

They'd had a pretty combative relationship but he'd always thought they were well suited, underneath the sparks. It was certainly never dull. He still couldn't work out where it had all gone wrong.

At least having a case of sorts to work on would keep him from wallowing. Otherwise, before you knew it, he'd have the old photo album out, and the Jack Daniel's, and he'd seen too many friends take *that* long slide to oblivion.

No, better to sweat it out. What better way to outrun his demons?

This morning he'd chosen the most punishing circuit. He was on the home stretch, alongside the River Kent, past the weir and, on the far side of the river, the old Provincial Insurance building that had been converted into upscale apartments. There were two swans in the water, a dead tree, a flutter of ducks.

Nick crossed over the narrow footbridge, ran the length of the car park on New Road and dropped back onto the path again before he checked his watch and finally slackened his pace as he reached the nearby flats. The wind was sharper here, funnelled by the concrete, bottled in. His sweatshirt was stained dark and the early chill bit right through.

The case was not as interesting, he acknowledged, as the CSI who was working it. There was something about Grace that triggered responses he'd thought were dormant. He was aware of momentary reflex guilt, shrugged it away.

The path widened out. Up ahead was another footbridge across the river to Aynam Road where home was a flat in what was once an old organ works. Not much industry left in the town now—not with the insurance giant and the shoe factory gone.

As he approached the bridge, Nick glanced over and saw a man on the other side, near the entrance to his own building. A brief glimpse of a smallish, slimmish figure in a dark suit, not an obvious threat. But something about him pricked Nick's senses, and he hadn't survived five years of undercover assignments by ignoring his instincts.

He allowed his fatigue to show while he considered his options. There was a time when he'd never gone anywhere without a weapon, even out running. *Especially out running.* It took a moment to remember he didn't lead that kind of life any more.

Nick jogged up onto the bridge, slowing as he neared the midway point and finally recognised the man. Matthew Mercer. There'd been a time when Mercer had known Nick's habits well enough to realise where he was likely to be at this hour, if his car was in its designated bay and there was no answer to the bell.

Nick stopped altogether then, leaning forwards with his hands braced on the guard-rails at either side of the bridge.

"Mercer," he said, not loud, but loud enough. "What are you doing here?"

Mercer crossed the deserted road without haste, climbed the steps onto the bridge, and started out towards him. Nick was surprised. From what he remembered of him, Mercer wasn't the type to meet you halfway on anything. He waited until he was a few yards away.

"What do you want?"

Mercer stopped, stuffed his hands into the pockets of his suit. "Oh, Nick," he said with that wide open smile of his. "Is that any way to greet an old mate?"

"No," Nick agreed flatly. "Call me fussy, but I don't count people who've tried to have me killed as mates. Sorry." He showed his teeth without humour, added, "Sir."

If anything, Mercer's smile broadened. "Operational snafu. That's the way it goes sometimes with undercover. You of all people should know that."

"You lot covered your own backsides and left mine swinging in the wind," Nick said. "I don't think it qualifies."

Mercer shrugged, dismissive. "Well, you're looking fit, anyway. No lasting effects. Still getting those headaches?"

Nick ignored him, turning sideways to rest on his forearms and stared down into the water eddying around a half-submerged rock. He tried to work out if the momentary satisfaction he'd gain from chucking Mercer into the river would be compensation for a ruined career.

Way things are going, will it make much of a difference?

"I can't believe you've come all the way up from London just to enquire after my health. So, what nasty little business does Special Branch have in a backwater like this?"

"Don't flatter yourself," Mercer said cheerfully. "I'm on my way up to deal with some 'nasty little business' in Glasgow, so this is just a detour. And you're behind the times. It's the CTC now—Counter Terrorism Command. Should have joined us while the offer was on the table, Nick. We have all the best toys to play with."

"Yeah, but I'm fussy who I work with, too."

Mercer laughed. "And this coming from a guy who used to mix with the scum of the earth…"

"Exactly."

The laughter dried but Mercer continued to regard him with a lingering smile. Irritated that he recognised the bravado for what it was, Nick straightened, moved to step past.

"So, you're reduced to investigating dead dogs." Mercer's voice was conversational but enough to halt him. "Is that all you're up to these days?"

Nick opened his mouth in instant denial, was afraid he might not pull that one off convincingly. *How the truth hurts.*

"Come to gloat? What do you want, Mercer?" he asked again, wearily. "Last chance." He gestured down at his damp clothes. "I'm dirty and I want my breakfast, and unless you have something to say, I feel the need to wash away the stink."

The sideways insult didn't go unregistered, he noted, but it was interesting that Mercer didn't rise to it.

"Yesterday morning you were called out to a Firearms incident involving the wife of a Member of the European Parliament. Angela Inglis."

"Bit outside your remit, isn't it?"

Mercer lifted a careless shoulder. "Anything that concerns the politicos falls into our lap, as it were."

Nick shook his head. "A dog was killing sheep. That's considered a crime in these parts. Someone shot it," he said flatly. "And if you want to know more, might I respectfully suggest, *sir*, that you put in an official request for a copy of my report."

Mercer let him take a couple of strides.

"Your inspector's name is Pollock, isn't it?" he said casually. "Is he an early riser, do you know? Because otherwise, I'm just about to get him out of bed to tell him one of his junior officers is refusing to co-operate with the CTC."

Nick glanced over his shoulder and found Mercer a picture of innocence, holding up his mobile phone.

Nick let his breath out on a long sigh and delivered a clipped précis of events that gave the bare bones of what had happened without adding anything of Grace's conclusions.

Nevertheless, Mercer said, "Sharp, this CSI, isn't she?"

"Very," Nick snapped. "So, are you going to tell me what your interest *really* is in all this? I don't believe you go haring off round the country every time some politician's wife clicks her fingers. What's so special about this one?"

"We do random checks every now and again. I promised Angela I'd make sure it was being taken seriously."

Angela. Something about the way he said the name plucked at Nick's nerves. Familiarity and connection. More than just professional. More than just a random check. *A slip.*

"I take every case seriously."

"Of course you do." Mercer smiled. "Best man for the job."

An elderly woman in a tweed cape appeared from the direction of the flats pulling what appeared to be a small fluffy rat on a lead. She didn't notice the two men until she'd actually stepped onto the bridge, and then she grew wary, tugging the rat tightly against her ankles as they passed. Mercer turned and gave her another of his wide smiles. She gripped the lead even tighter and bolted.

Good judge of character, Nick thought sourly.

"The dog belonged to Inglis, not Frederickson, didn't it?" he said abruptly, after the woman had gone. "No way would you be going to all this trouble otherwise."

Mercer said nothing. Nick glanced at his carefully noncommittal face and nodded slowly.

"Why pretend it was his unless she was trying to side-step responsibility? Hardly going to cause a career-breaking scandal for her old man that, is it?"

The sarcasm got a response, not much more than a twitch, but something. Mercer was too aware of his disadvantage in height to step in close, get right in Nick's face, but his stare was a cool threat all by itself.

"Duncan Inglis is a big wheel. Plenty of people a lot further up the food chain than you or I, take a very close interest in anything that might affect him or his family." He paused, let his gaze flick across Nick's sweat-stained figure with the faintest sneer. "If you want to salvage what's left of your career, detective constable, you might like to bear that in mind."

He walked away quickly, leaving Nick standing in the middle of the bridge. On standby, an official-looking Volvo appeared out of the car park behind Nick's building and pulled up as Mercer reached the kerb. He gave Nick a jaunty wave before climbing into the passenger seat. The car had tinted glass and Nick couldn't see the driver, but he memorised the registration as they pulled away. Quite why, he wasn't sure; just a reflex.

In the flat, he jotted the number down in his notebook, along with the gist of the conversation. Another habit gleaned from years of undercover work.

By the time he'd finished, the writing covered several pages and his hand had begun to stiffen. He rubbed it absently.

They'd broken all the fingers of his right hand, that last time. When he'd been compromised. Such a sanitised word for the mother of all cock-ups. The enquiry had never quite pinned down blame, but the way Mercer's Special Branch boys had scrabbled to distance themselves said more than enough.

Whoever was responsible, the result was that Nick's cover was well and truly blown. The gang he had successfully infiltrated did not take kindly to the discovery of a traitor in their midst. All smiles and slaps on the shoulder, they'd lured him to a meet in a disused warehouse, remote enough that nobody would hear his screams.

As well as his fingers, they'd broken three ribs, his nose for the second time, caused serious internal bleeding, fractured his skull. They'd been rushed, or they would have done more. He'd spent a fortnight either unconscious or so far out of it on the drugs the doctors had pumped into him as to make no difference.

For Lisa, it was the final straw. She'd gone crazy, had every right to. Difficult to repeat his glib assurances that the risks were minimal, calculated. Not with a pair of armed officers guarding the door to his hospital room. She'd caught him at a weak moment, mumbling promises he hadn't the heart or stomach to go back on afterwards.

Now, sitting in his empty kitchen, listening to the ache in his bones, it seemed to Nick, in a leap of twisted logic, that the man from CTC had cost him everything he held dear.

15

EDITH SLEPT BADLY and woke restless, filled with dread. And just for a moment, as the thin trickle of daylight slunk between the bedroom curtains, she imagined that she could wish it all away and start again. Yesterday. The last seventeen years.

She clamped her eyes tight shut, but the more she clutched at the tattered remnants of her fantasy the more it disintegrated and the wretched cold facts crashed over her.

She hadn't been able to clear her mind of the way the dog slumped as the round hit it, the jitters of its dying body. Sleep had been a long time coming and fitful when it had. And it did no good to remind herself of the brutal savagery of the attack on the lambs. Knowing she'd done the right thing did not make it easier to bear.

Edith had been shooting rabbits, rats, and squirrels unlucky enough to have the wrong colour coat, since she was barely into her teens. She'd never realised that something *bigger* would cause her to lie awake sweating at the awful memory of what she'd done.

Oh, last night she'd summoned up a sullen bravado to face her father's spluttering rage and her mother's weary disappointment. But up here, alone in the dark, that brittle façade had cracked and splintered.

On the far wall surrounding the window, the posters of her silver screen idols stared down at her, mocking. Edith had longed to join them, had aped their sultry pouts and sophisticated poses. Until a few weeks ago she'd believed she finally had a chance of actually becoming one of those beautiful, elegant, *desirable* women.

She'd foolishly believed the attentions of the local boys proved she was finally turning from an ugly duckling into a swan. Because they wanted her all right; in field gateways and bus shelters, in the backseat of cars, they'd expressed their lust.

Including Danny Robertshaw, who'd been her secret crush at school. The older boy who'd been so surrounded by his groupies he'd never given her a second look. Until a local band was gigging in one of the pubs in the market square in Kendal. He'd bought her a Red Bull and vodka, even though she was under age, and she'd gone down on him in one of the ginnels leading down towards the river. Hadn't known until after, as he was zipping up his jeans, that he'd just been seeing if the rumours about her were true.

Edith had never realised that by giving any of them what they wanted, she was taking it away from herself.

Stupid, ugly little Edith. Didn't she prove yesterday that she can't do anything right?

Edith screwed her eyes shut again, gripped the edge of the lumpy quilt until her hands pulsed. But still, the sneering voices wouldn't abate until, with a low moan, she twisted to face the wall. If that bloody dog hadn't done what it did, maybe she would have been saved all this now. It would all be over. But deep down she couldn't escape the craven sense of relief that she hadn't had to do it, after all.

"Edith! You are out of bed aren't you, lovey?" Her mother's voice, reedy and anxious, floated up the stairs. "You haven't forgotten Mr Hogg needs you to go in today, have you? Your breakfast's nearly ready."

Slowly, Edith rolled over onto her back and stared up at the sagging woodchip on the ceiling. *So, she's going pretend it never happened. No change there, then.*

Her mother's biggest reaction to the events of the day before came when she discovered Edith had broken one of her precious china ballerinas from the mantelpiece in the front parlour. It was the room saved for best and never used except when the vicar came round.

Her mother had bought the ballerinas, a matched pair, out of one of her magazines—the boring ones with the knitting patterns. Sent off the money week by week and twittered with anticipation waiting for the first of them to arrive. Edith had always hated those figurines, with their flawless white skin and their swanlike poise. Twin models of perfection that taunted her every clumsy attempt at grace.

Her mother cried a little over the broken pieces, mutely shaking her head when Edith's father had offered to see what he could salvage with superglue and a dab of putty. Instead, she'd swept up the shards, wrapped them lovingly in newspaper and laid them to rest in the dustbin. What, in the heat of the moment, had seemed to Edith like an act of final defiance, suddenly took on the tawdry hue of small-minded pettiness. She found herself awash with renewed self-loathing.

Her mother called again from downstairs, sharper now, a long-refined trigger for Edith to drag herself listlessly out of bed and into her clothes. As she descended the creaky staircase she could hear her mother bustling around in the kitchen, clattering pans. The smell of fried bacon hit Edith's stomach like a fist. She pushed open the back sitting-room door to see a dripping plate waiting for her on the gateleg table by the window.

"Don't look like that, lovey, you need a decent meal before you do all that cleaning," her mother said from the kitchen door- way. She eyed her daughter critically. "Honestly, Edith, you'd blow away in a strong wind." She disappeared again, carrying on the one-sided conversation over her shoulder as she went. "I'm rushing myself this morning. One of the girls is off sick and I've said I'll cover."

Edith knew better than to argue. She slouched into a chair and made a show of cutting up what was on her plate. Her mother sat down opposite, letting out a sigh as she got off her feet. She was forty-two and moved ten years older. A heavy woman whose once passable looks and figure had buckled under the weight of hard work and worry and too many nights of cheap ready meals in front of the telly.

She was already wearing the tabard for her shift in the canteen at the truck stop down by the motorway junction. Despite spending all day doling out greasy food, she attacked her fried breakfast with gusto, her eyes fixed on a magazine laid

open on the table in front of her, shovelling it in. Edith's movements faltered.

Maybe I'm adopted.

Her mother sensed her lack of enthusiasm and glanced up.
Edith put a small forkful in her mouth, chewed mechanically,
then put her knife down and reached for her milk.

Her mother had never questioned why Edith always drank
milk at mealtimes, and she dismissed it as a harmless quirk that
her daughter insisted on a mug, not a glass. The opaque liquid in
its equally opaque container was the perfect place to spit
unwanted food. Edith made herself leave half of what was on
her plate, and poured half of what she *appeared* to eat down the
drain afterwards.

When she'd hastily disposed of the leftovers and dumped her
dirty crockery in the sink, she gathered her cagoule and open-
face helmet, and made for the back door. The little Honda step-
through scooter was parked under a tarpaulin by the back gate,
with a chain wrapped through the rear wheel, even though all
the local kids knew better than to try and steal anything from Jim
Airey's family. Not because he was talented as a detective, but
because he was mean. He'd indiscriminately make all their lives
a misery by way of retribution.

"Edith."

Edith hadn't heard her mother follow her out and jerked in
surprise to see her, still in her slippers, standing by the gate.

"Look, I know your dad went on at you a bit yesterday, but
it's for your own good, lovey," her mother said haltingly. "What
you did…well, I know you *thought* you were doing the right
thing, but other folk won't see it that way if they find out it was
you. And Mrs Inglis is already against you after…well, after last
Christmas. People like us can't afford to make enemies out of
people like her. She's *important.*"

And we're not. I'm not. Edith didn't say it, just stared at her
with a thousand cutting words pouring from her brain to her lips
and dying there unspoken.

"I know."

Someone had let their dog lift a leg against the back wheel of
the scooter. *Deliberate, most like.* Edith unlocked the chain doing
her best not to touch it, half expecting that her mother would
retreat back inside the house. To her surprise, when she straight-

ened, the woman was still watching her from the safety of the step, hands clutched as though trying to work up the courage to say more. Their eyes met with total incomprehension for each other.

"You've got to find yourself a *purpose*, lovey," her mother said then, all in a rush. "You don't know how lucky you are, living out in the countryside, not like some of them inner-city tower blocks with junkies on every landing and the lifts never working. But you're throwing it all away if you don't *make* something of yourself." She stopped, took a breath. "You've got a good brain in there—all your teachers said so—but if you don't use it you'll never get anywhere."

She paused, as if hoping to see some instant effect from this badly-delivered little speech. When there was none, she floundered on. "You're never going to be famous, Edith, and you can wish for it all you want but it isn't going to happen. Things like that don't happen for people like us, lovey. You might as well wish for the moon."

She broke off, bit her lip as the fire went out of her. "Did you think I wanted to be scrubbing tables all my life? Always thought it was temporary. Until something better came along. Well, here I am, Edith, still scrubbing tables and mopping floors at my age. And that's all I see in store for you, unless you pull your socks up and *do* something."

For a long, disconnected moment, mother and daughter stood facing each other across a gulf too wide to ever be bridged.

Edith swallowed. "I gotta go," she said, forestalling whatever response her mother might have made to that by jamming on her helmet and hitting the starter. The two-stroke engine smoked into life with a ringing clatter. But when Edith glanced back there was something sad in her mother's eyes, in the hunch of her shoulders. *She knows...*

By the time the scooter had struggled up the steep hill to the main road, Edith could barely see for tears.

Throwing it all away... You'll never get anywhere... All I see in store for you... You're never going to be famous... It isn't going to happen... Not for people like us...

Not for people like us...

The litany hammered round and round in her head to the

rhythm of the tyres on the road and the beat of the motor, until she wanted to scream out loud.

She bent low over the handlebars and the scooter swooped down the next hill, gathering the momentum she needed to get her up the long climb on the other side. Only the buzz of precarious speed seemed finally to drive her mother's words out of her head.

"I'll show them," she muttered under her breath. "I'll show them what I can do and *then* they'll be sorry. They'll *all* be sorry."

16

WHEN HE WALKED into the CID office at Hunter Lane the first thing Nick saw was the dog sitting on his desk. A big cheap fluffy stuffed toy with misshapen limbs and a constipated expression. The sort of thing dragged around travelling funfairs by embarrassed teenage boyfriends, chosen purely for size, not quality, to kid them they'd won a worthwhile prize for their money. *Somebody,* he thought, *must have been delighted to palm off this one.*

He picked up the deformed animal by its front legs and wondered briefly if he could find a home for it. Sophie loved animals, but this would probably give her nightmares.

No, if nobody owns up, it's straight down the charity shop for you, sunshine.

The dog stared back at him, glassy-eyed, with a distinct squint. It was wearing a makeshift collar, from which hung an inscribed cardboard medal. 'For DC Weston,' the scrawled lettering read. 'For "dogged" devotion to duty.'

As he read it, he heard laughter squirt out behind him. He turned, the dog still in his hands, to find a bunch of them clustered on the far side of the office, waiting for his reaction. So far, he realised, he hadn't shown them one. And he was damned if he was going to.

"Hey, Nick, I heard you're getting rid of that flashy Jap car of yours, eh?" It was one of the younger DCs, Yardley, grinning inanely.

For a moment Nick failed to make the connection and they laughed all the harder.

"Heard you're going to buy a Rover instead, eh, mate. Rover —geddit? Woof, woof!"

Yardley's wit was greeted with renewed howls. He was the kid of the bunch, fresh-faced and gullible. No doubt he'd been the butt of everyone's jokes before they found this new target.

Nick bit back his instinctive sarcastic response. Taken individually, they weren't so bad but together as a pack they were vicious and likely to be driven to a frenzy by the first hint of blood in the water. He'd seen it every Friday night chucking-out time when he'd first started on the beat.

Oh, there was never anything overt, of course, nothing that couldn't be shrugged off as a bit of a laugh if he'd called them on it, but Nick had no illusions he was part of the team.

His only course of action was to show them nothing and hope they got bored, found a new victim, or that they finally accepted him, but he wasn't holding his breath.

He could see it taking years.

Nick realised he'd been onto a loser before he ever walked through the door at Hunter Lane. Coming from any city force was always going to cause friction in a rural area like Cumbria. And you couldn't get much bigger city than the Met. That wouldn't have been so bad had he not also inadvertently stepped straight into a plainclothes' vacancy widely expected to go to someone moving out of uniform on the local patch.

When his transfer had come through, Nick's old inspector had told him he was lucky not to have to reapply for plainclothes. Now he wished he had. A spell back in uniform, proving his worth, settling in, might have made all the difference.

Ah well, no help for that now.

. So he forced the semblance of a smile. "Very witty, boys. I suppose you all thought I was barking up the wrong tree, huh?"

There was a grudging wave of laughter at that, both with and against him. Nick noted the tone of it for future reference. Yardley looked vaguely disappointed as everyone drifted back to their desks.

"Got you good style with that one, didn't she?" somebody else said and, just for a moment, Nick thought he meant Grace.

The idea that the tall CSI was in on the joke after all froze the amusement off his features, making the other officer pause, eyebrow climbing. Nick saw the reaction and locked down his anger.

He meant the sergeant who relayed the original message, you fool, he berated himself.

"She did," he agreed, hastily rueful. "She did indeed."

He booted up his computer terminal, shrugged out of his jacket, got coffee. And then he started running searches.

He quickly discovered that Duncan Inglis, MEP, was enjoying what might be termed a quietly distinguished career, which meant he was never destined for a glory post, but probably in line for a knighthood and a cushy pension in the not-too-distant future. When Nick found the man's name listed on various subcommittees concerned with anti-terrorism measures and NATO, he understood the CTC's exaggerated interest.

Perhaps they had a hand in keeping Inglis's family out of the limelight. About Mrs Angela Inglis, Nick could find very little beyond her name listed on the committees of various worthy causes. When a Google Images search brought up a news shot of the Inglises with the Chief Constable and his wife at a charity event earlier in the year, he stifled a groan.

Maybe that was what had prompted Mercer's unscheduled visit? Perhaps experience had taught him that responding smartly to anything that affected the couple was the least troublesome way of dealing with it. Maybe that was why her name had produced such ripples from the CTC man. *There's history there.*

He reached out to exit his current screen but another thumbnail picture caught his eye. Taken at the same ball, it showed Angela Inglis smiling haughtily for the camera, alongside a tall man he recognised.

"Well, well," Nick murmured, with that familiar burning sensation in the pit of his stomach when something significant leapt up and punched him.

He knew they were dealing with a large-calibre weapon of a type not common outside the police, certain elements of the criminal fraternity, and the armed services. And now Nick knew just where the man who'd claimed ownership of Ben fitted into that picture.

Mrs Duncan Inglis with Major Giles Frederickson, the caption read. He dug around further and sat back in his chair with something resembling a snort.

No wonder Frederickson had been sniffy at Nick's comment on the noise from the firing range at Warcop Training Ground.

He ran the place.

Nick waited until the office was empty before he ran his final search. This time he used the internal police network to check out Special Constable Jim Airey. Nick knew he was unpopular enough without adding to his sins by getting caught nosing into another copper's affairs.

Disappointingly, there were no reports of injuries of the 'walked into a door' type on file for Airey's wife, nor did their daughter seem to have been especially clumsy as a child.

The one blip on Jim Airey's otherwise undistinguished service record was a drugs raid where he'd apparently been a little too enthusiastic during the course of an arrest, thrown a man to the ground hard enough to break his shoulder.

Of course, everyone else involved closed ranks, and swore that Airey and the suspect merely tripped and fell. It sounded just unlikely enough to be true. Besides, Nick had seen Airey's bulk first hand, and he certainly wouldn't fancy that kind of weight coming down on top of him.

Can't chase after some young scally for more than twenty yards, Nick thought, cutting, *but would kill one if he fell on him from a tree.*

The only other interesting note in the file went back a few years. Airey was a real gun enthusiast. Before Michael Robert Ryan's infamous killing spree at Hungerford in 1987 that led to their ban, he'd held licences for a number of semiautomatic rifles, which he'd dutifully handed in as required. He'd given up his handgun collection after the Dunblane tragedy nine years later, and was now listed as owning a couple of shotguns, and small calibre single-shot rifles, for pest control.

So, she gets it from her old man.

Nick sat back in his chair and swivelled a little, considering. If this was his previous posting, he would have simply asked around, got the juicy stuff on Airey that wasn't on any official record, but here they'd tell him nothing.

He sighed. No choice but to put in a formal request for a search warrant. There'd be hell to pay, but it was hardly likely to make him more unpopular than he was already, was it?

Perhaps Grace knows something? Or maybe she could talk to the girl?

The thought that he might have a legitimate reason for seeking Grace out, somewhere away from flapping ears and prying eyes, brought a genuine smile to Nick's face for the first time that morning.

17

GRACE RELAXED into the stock of the rifle and delicately squeezed the trigger. The gun jarred in her hands. She wore ear defenders, but the report was already reduced to little more than a phut by the Parker Hale sound moderator fitted to the end of the muzzle.

She worked the bolt to eject the casing and stepped back, glad of the framework into which the rifle was secured. It meant she didn't have to aim to produce consistent results, and the recoil was negligible. Grace was still only too aware that the gun's sole purpose was deadly, couldn't shake the feeling it was just waiting to lull her into carelessness.

She checked again that the rifle was clear and empty before removing her ear and eye protection and venturing out past the firing point, camera in hand.

Grace had set up a clay-filled box barely halfway down the seventy-five-metre indoor range at the Carleton Hall police HQ, and had been firing a variety of ammunition into it through Edith's Gaucher, meticulously documenting the results.

Officially, this investigation was on the back burner and Richard Sibson would not have been pleased to learn she was still devoting time to it. Unofficially, Grace had made use of a gap in the range's busy schedule and was on her own time. She wasn't sure why, except that something nagged at her about the whole business. She'd ignored such doubts in the past, and was still haunted by the consequences.

She measured the depth of the latest indentation into the clay, photographed it with a scale, and straightened slowly, thoughtful.

Definitely not enough.

When she turned back, it was to find Nick Weston watching her from the firing point, leaning against the side partition, arms folded.

He jerked his head towards the rifle. "Edith's?"

Grace paused a moment. "Good morning," she said. "Yes, it is."

"Sorry." He nodded to the rifle again. "What are you doing? I thought we'd already established this couldn't have been it."

Unwilling to confess her unsanctioned curiosity, Grace walked back, aware of his scrutiny, and ducked under the firing point. "I like to be thorough. I've also sent Edith's gunshot residue test, her DNA, and a sample of the ammunition we collected off to the lab." The cost of which, she was hoping to slip past her boss unnoticed.

"So, if this wasn't it, what was?"

Grace glanced up briefly. "You're asking me to guess," she said, smiling. She expected him to return the smile, but a flicker of annoyance crossed his features.

"Could it be military?"

She raised her eyebrow. "It could be any number of different weapons, military or civilian. I can't say for certain—"

He held up a hand. "OK, but just run with me on this. It *could* be military, yeah?"

"Determined, aren't you?" She gave a cautious shrug. "Yes, I suppose it could. Why?"

He began to pace. Grace watched the nervous energy and idly wondered if he threw himself into everything he did with the same total commitment.

"Because Giles Frederickson just happens to be an army major, in charge of Warcop camp. He transferred from active service twelve months ago."

She frowned. "Well, as I assume you're not suggesting he shot his own dog, where does that lead us?"

"Perhaps someone on camp thought they were in line for the promotion and then matey-boy gets parachuted in over their heads." His smile was bitter. "It's won *me* no friends, that's for sure."

He's taking this too personally.

"If that's enough reason," she said coolly, "perhaps you should be thankful you don't own a dog."

That stopped him, jerked his head back. Then he shook himself out of it, relaxed his shoulders a little.

"Speaking of ownership, I've reason to believe Ben actually belonged to Angela Inglis."

Grace considered. "That…makes no sense. It was bound to come out, so lying was foolish, and they didn't strike me as fools. Have you confronted them about it?"

"Not yet. I only received this information earlier today." His face twitched, almost a grimace, and he checked his watch. "I'm about to go over to Warcop and see what the good major has to say for himself."

At that moment the door to the range opened and the Firearms inspector stuck his head through.

"You all done, Grace?"

"Yes, thanks. I'll pack up my stuff and be out of your way in five minutes."

He nodded, cast a curious eye over Nick and left without comment.

"Anything I can do?" Nick asked.

"If you wouldn't mind retrieving the clay box?" Grace waited until he'd returned before she unclamped the rifle and laid it carefully on its side with the muzzle pointing down range.

"You're uncomfortable around them, aren't you?" he said, watching her.

Grace gave him a composed stare. "Anyone who's seen what they can do ought to be, don't you think? I don't feel that 'comfortable' is a state one should aspire to around firearms."

"I would've thought someone like you would have been brought up with them," he said, voice cynical. "Huntin', shootin' and fishin' and all that."

"Tell me, do you feel your tendency to leap to the wrong conclusions has held you back as a detective, Mr Weston?"

He had the grace to offer a rueful smile in apology.

Max enjoyed shooting, had tried to persuade Grace to join him on the grouse moor where so much valuable networking could be done alongside the sport. She had always declined. It was ironic that she had handled more firearms since her divorce than she ever had previously.

She unzipped the bag she'd used to transport the rifle and he stepped forwards, picking up the gun. As soon as it was in his hands a slightly wistful look settled over him.

"Nice balance. I'm not surprised she didn't want anyone else touching it."

He wound the strap around his left forearm as he lifted the weapon to his shoulder, almost fluid, aiming for a point at the bottom of the range. His right index finger crooked inside the trigger guard then hesitated.

Now there *is someone,* thought Grace, *who is very comfortable indeed around firearms.*

But whatever entranced him faded as quickly as it came. Silently, she held the bag open and he slotted the rifle inside quickly.

"You were a shooter," she guessed, closing the zip. "If you miss it, why did you stop?"

"Did two years with the Firearms boys in Manchester, before I transferred to the Met." He shoved his hands into his pockets, as if to remove them from temptation. "Let's just say I don't quite have the touch for it like I used to."

She would have questioned that, but the range door opened and the Firearms inspector reappeared, leading a practice group. Grace slung the rifle bag onto her shoulder, picked up her cameras. Nick grabbed her clipboard and the clay box. She didn't miss the stares directed at him as they went out.

They walked together, neither speaking until she'd unlocked her Navara and stowed the evidence inside.

"I assume you didn't track me down just to check my methodology," she said briskly. "Was there something you wanted?"

His hands were in his pockets again, like a schoolboy trying to proclaim innocence or nonchalance, she couldn't quite decide which.

"I need to know if there are any rumours circulating about Jim Airey, and I don't feel I can ask around."

"What kind of rumours?"

"Whether he's a drinker, gets out of hand at home. Any kind."

Grace's frown exposed her doubt. "And you think I'm in a position to ask questions like that?"

He shrugged. "Better than me."

She was silent for a moment, then shook her head slowly. "I'm sorry," she said. "I've tried very hard not to get mixed up in the politics of this place and I'm not about to start now."

As he took a breath to speak she cut him off. "*But*, I've said I'll try to have another word with Edith, see if I can get her on her own. If she tells me anything relevant, I'll let you know. Good enough?"

Nick gave her a tired smile. "Honestly? It's more than I expected."

And as he walked away Grace wasn't sure whether to be ashamed or insulted by that parting shot.

18

AN HOUR LATER, Nick found himself standing on another range, outdoor this time, watching a dozen camouflage-clad figures decimate their wood and paper enemy.

They were firing the standard British Army assault rifle, the SA80, from the prone position. The air was harsh with the rip and clatter of semiautomatic weapons, the smell of burned powder. Nick jammed his fingers in his ears and tried not to remember his own skills in that direction. Back before his broken hands had healed without the delicacy of touch he'd once enjoyed.

He'd been delivered up to the range by a taciturn female corporal who introduced herself as the CO's aide. She waited until the burst was over, then pointed out a man at the far end of the squad, just in case Nick missed the insignia, and left him to it. As the khaki Land Rover Defender disappeared back down the hill towards the main camp, he hoped Frederickson was going to be amenable or he was in for a long walk.

A short bulldog of a man, with spit-shined combat boots and a weather-beaten face like a local sheep farmer, intercepted him, bristling. He was barely placated by the sight of Nick's warrant card.

Giles Frederickson got to his feet, meanwhile, took his time about pinching out his ear defenders, giving Nick a thorough stare. Seeing him now, in uniform, made Nick wonder how he could have missed the man's military bearing. He'd rarely seen someone look so at home in fatigues.

"Well, sar'nt-major?" Frederickson said, not taking his eyes off Nick.

"Nice grouping, sir." The bulldog man turned to glare at the soldiers who were eyeing Nick with undisguised curiosity. "All right, you lot! Show's over," he bellowed. "Here, *you*, private. Make yourself useful and go paste up the holes in the major's target. And make sure you take plenty of paper squares, laddie, because you can bank on it there'll be plenty to cover."

The rest scattered, wary of a worse assignment.

Frederickson straightened his battledress tunic. "So, what can I do for you, Mr Weston?"

Interesting, thought Nick. Angela Inglis had tried to intimidate him by emphasising his rank. Frederickson's approach was not to give him the courtesy of a rank at all.

"Just a follow-up to yesterday's incident, sir," he said blandly, reaching for his notebook. "Sometimes we find things occur to people when they've slept on it." He paused inquiringly, contained his disappointment when Frederickson did not leap straight into a confession.

Instead, the major slid his gaze across the hovering warrant officer. "If you wouldn't mind ensuring my rifle gets back to the armoury safely, sarn't-major?"

"Yessir." The other man eyed Nick as though in favour of capital punishment for impertinence. He snapped briefly to attention and spun on his heel.

Frederickson watched him leave before he remarked, "Taking all this rather seriously, aren't you, Mr Weston?"

"Would you rather we shrugged our shoulders and said, 'ah well, he got what was coming to him'?" Nick asked. "Besides, after the whole Derrick Bird thing a few years back we take *all* incidents involving firearms very seriously, as I'm sure you'll appreciate."

"Naturally." Frederickson had the grace to look chastened. He didn't need the reference explaining further, even if it was before his time. It was before Nick's time too, come to that, but it had made the national news for days when a Cumbrian taxi driver had gone on an armed rampage, killing twelve people and injuring another eleven.

The major began to move, forcing Nick into step alongside. They walked in silence until Frederickson halted by another ubiquitous Land Rover Defender, leaned on the front wing and stared into the distance as if fascinated by the swathes of yellow gorse.

"Got up this morning and was halfway down the stairs to let Ben out before it hit me he wasn't there," he said, reflective. "I'll miss him."

"You hadn't had the dog long, though, had you, sir?"

Frederickson flicked him a wary glance, straightened and jerked his head.

"Hop in. I'll run you back down to camp."

Nick just had time to scramble into the rudimentary seat before the major fired up the engine and threw the Defender into a wide circular turn, as if hoping to distract him by reckless driving alone.

"Not long," he said then. "He wasn't much more than a pup, after all."

"Can I offer you some advice, major? When you leave the army don't turn to crime—you're a lousy liar."

Frederickson's head turned sharply in his direction, just as the Defender went airborne over a particularly nasty yump. Nick grabbed at the dashboard to brace himself. "You might have a future as a getaway driver, though."

When that gained him no response, Nick sighed.

"Look, we already know the dog belonged to Mrs Inglis, and if you think you're protecting her by claiming—"

"Ben *used* to belong to Angela," Frederickson said quickly. He paused, added with dignity. "She gave him to me some months ago. I wasn't lying yesterday, Mr Weston, when I told you that Ben was my dog, *my* responsibility. He was."

Nick digested this in momentary silence. "When, exactly, did she give you the dog?"

"Shortly after Christmas." He gave a brief rusty smile. "As I mentioned to you yesterday, Angela has two Siamese and Ben was an inveterate cat-chaser. Her husband's choice, but completely unsuitable, in my opinion. Wanted her to have something of a guard dog while he was away." He flicked his eyes sideways again, as if to see how Nick was taking all this. "I offered to take Ben off her hands. Felt sorry for the poor beggar, if you must know." He let out a quick breath, more of a snort, as he braked hard for the junction with the main A66 that divided the ranges from the rest of the camp. "Not much of a reprieve, as it turned out."

Nick took advantage of the momentary calm to make a note before the Defender lurched forwards again, heading for a gap in traffic.

"And you didn't think to mention any of this yesterday?"

"Frankly, I didn't see what relevance it had." They were alongside the football field now, which doubled as a helo landing site, its faded orange windsock billowing in the lazy wind. The major bent his head to peer at a group of cadets who were building what seemed to be a showjumping wall on the touchline.

"Military training exercise?" Nick asked drily.

"Hardly." Frederickson gave another of those austere smiles. "My lads are providing the main arena crew for the agricultural show next Saturday. I believe I did mention *that* yesterday."

He slowed to a crawl as they turned in towards the main gate, where two armed guards waved them to a halt and checked their ID. Nick had been through the same procedure on his arrival and he was pretty sure they must recognise their own CO by now.

"Bit jumpy, aren't they?"

"Standard operating procedure, Mr Weston," Frederickson said severely. "No point in doing a sloppy job."

After another couple of turns, he braked alongside Nick's Subaru, in front of the main office building. They went in, past the same corporal, who barely glanced up from her keyboard.

"See if you can rustle up some coffee, would you, Parrish?" Frederickson said over his shoulder as he strode through.

The major's office was hardly the plush command centre Nick had expected. The furniture wouldn't have looked out of place back at the station; an old desk, a line of grey filing cabinets that leaned slightly away from the wall as though the floor tilted towards the centre, and a pair of upright visitors' chairs that were not designed to be welcoming.

The only personal touch Nick saw was a line of framed photographs on the wall behind the major's chair, showing the man himself in various foreign locations going back probably twenty years. In all of them he was surrounded by sun- or wind-burned men in uniform, brandishing a selection of impressively fearsome weaponry.

Nick expected Frederickson to sit, but he moved to the window instead, gazing out with his back to the room.

"So, you can't think of any reason why someone might want to shoot your dog, sir?"

The major's back stiffened in irritation.

"Apart from the obvious—that he'd been running amok in a field of sheep, you mean? No."

"What about Mrs Inglis, sir?" Nick persisted. "Has she mentioned anything to you? Do you know if anyone would want to hurt her? Send a warning, a threat, perhaps?"

Frederickson turned then, his face mildly insulted. "Apart from the Airey girl? No." For the first time, there was snap to his voice. "Why don't you ask her yourself, Mr Weston?"

"I intend to, sir. Thank you for your time." He got to his feet, folded the notebook away into his inside pocket, nodding to the photographs. "You've done some travelling."

"A fair bit."

"That first one—Falklands, isn't it?"

"Yes." Frederickson followed his gaze, surprised. "It was taken just after Goose Green."

"And that next one...Iraq, at a guess?"

That tiny smile again. "Close. Liberation of Kuwait City. I served in both Gulf wars, Mr Weston. South Atlantic, Afghanistan, the Balkans, Northern Ireland. All the favourite holiday destinations."

"Quite a career." Nick met the major's eyes. "So, what did you do to end up in a backwater like this?"

Frederickson stiffened, colour threading through the veins of his gaunt cheeks. "Perhaps it was simply time this old warhorse was finally put out to grass." He paused, treated Nick to another assessing stare. "Why, what did *you* do?"

19

IAN HOGG HEARD the familiar rapid rattle of the Land Rover coming over the cattle grid at the bottom of the yard. He looked out of the farmhouse kitchen window just in time to see the ancient station wagon pull up on the far side of the concrete. Patrick Bardwell climbed down stiffly from the cab.

Hogg let his eyes track the other man as he unlocked the converted byre. Beside the door, a splash of red geraniums and violet aubretia now tumbled from the galvanised steel trough where the cattle had once stopped for water.

Bardwell's slightly shambling gait made Hogg frown. *Now there's a man who knows pain in greater quantities than he's a right to.*

Hogg was no stranger to pain himself. After his parents were killed in a car accident, he'd left the farm in his younger brother's care and answered calls from God and country to be ordained as an army chaplain. Until his last tour in the Balkans, when he'd been in the wrong place at the wrong time and seen two men he'd counted as friends blown to fragments before his eyes.

One moment they'd all been laughing and joking at the doorway to an abandoned house. The next, the world split apart in an outrageous crump of heat and light and sound. The explosion blew Hogg ten yards off his feet, partially stripped him, knocked him flat and sat on his chest to keep him down.

It was only when he tried to rise he realised the damage to his leg. They'd told him he'd been lucky not to lose it. When the pain kept him awake night after night he wondered if that were so.

But of the two soldiers, almost nothing remained. *Two more sealed coffins coming home weighted with memories and sand.*

Then, while he was in rehab, his brother drowned—a freak accident. The unfair shock of it, on top of everything else, made him put aside both vows and commission. He returned to Cumbria and became the country landowner he'd sworn never to be.

His brother had already converted most of the outbuildings into holiday lets after his livestock fell to the last outbreak of foot-and-mouth disease. Offering the accommodation to lost souls rather than tourists seemed a small transition, but one that dovetailed into circumstance and soothed Hogg's conscience. Visitors had returned to the Lakes only slowly, making business fitful anyway.

Patrick Bardwell had written to him six weeks previously. A short brittle note explaining that he'd been given Hogg's name by someone he'd served with in Bosnia. That he found himself suddenly adrift and in need of a place of refuge. Hogg had read as much into the spaces between the painfully scripted words as the words themselves. He offered welcome without reserve.

Bardwell travelled up to the tiny railway station at Oxenholme just outside Kendal—the only one locally on the London to Glasgow mainline. Hogg drove to meet him in the old Land Rover and found Bardwell waiting outside with his kit bag and his Bergen. A big unkempt man, long-haired and full-bearded, he was surrounded by a milling crowd and yet totally isolated. Hogg glimpsed someone at odds with whatever remained of his humanity, and perhaps in danger of losing his grip on it altogether.

He'd greeted Bardwell with calm restraint, made comfortably idle talk during the drive back up to the Retreat, filling the silences when he judged it prudent, letting them linger when he sensed the other man needed time to take it all in.

Bardwell had been subdued, thoughtful. A man who gave each question due weight and consideration. One who hadn't been allowed to speak his mind often enough to waste the opportunity with inconsequential chatter when it presented itself. But his few words revealed the residue of a quick mind and a quiet wit. Hogg found that he liked him.

Now, he sighed and glanced at the wall clock. He had a doctor's appointment in Kendal but there was just time to tell Patrick about Edith.

Sometimes that girl's more trouble than she's worth. Even as the thought formed, Hogg felt guilt follow.

Edith wasn't the kind of robust country wench he would have employed at the Retreat if he'd had much of a choice. The truth was, however, that finding staff willing to work this far out of town, and for what he could offer, was no easy task. He'd been obliged to take what he could get.

When they deigned to turn up, that is.

Trouble at home. That was the reason Jim Airey had given for Edith's unexpected absence yesterday. She'd be down first thing and do what was needed, without pay, he'd added in an ominous tone that made Hogg wary of inquiring further. He wouldn't get any kind of explanation out of the girl once she arrived, that much he knew. And she was already late—again.

He unhooked his cane from the edge of the sink, scooped his pipe and tobacco into a pocket, and moved across the worn stone flags to fumble into his wellington boots by the back door. The routine action immediately woke the elderly Jack Russell terrier from her basket by the Aga. She jumped up, staggering in half-sleep until she got her legs under her. Hogg waited patiently, holding the door open.

The terrier circled his heels as he limped slowly across the yard. Bardwell must have seen him coming. He stepped out of the doorway and waited without emotion as Hogg made his careful progress across the uneven ground, as though he'd remained a long time at the convenience of others.

Wanting to break that cycle, Hogg increased his pace, bumped his foot against the terrier as she crossed before him, slipped and almost fell. The cane went clattering onto the cobbles and Hogg flinched instinctively from the pain he knew would follow.

He never saw Bardwell move. One moment the man was yards away, the next he'd caught Hogg under the armpits, hauling him up before his ruined knee touched the ground.

Hogg had a moment to recognise the strength required for

that effortless rescue. Then he was swung round and set down perched on the rear bumper of the Land Rover, his cane propped next to him against the tow hitch before he'd even got his breath.

When his mind finally caught up with the averted disaster, Hogg blinked a few times, found Bardwell crouched a few feet away, comforting the dog. The terrier was lying on her side, showing her belly in abject submission as he smoothed her rough coat.

After a second, Bardwell glanced up and briefly met his gaze.

"Thank you, Patrick." Hogg was breathless and quietly shaken. "I thought I'd had it there. Stupid thing to do. Should have known my running days are over."

Bardwell shrugged, almost defensive. "Easy done," he said, and turned his attention back to the dog.

For a moment neither of them spoke. Hogg waited until his breathing had regulated before he picked up the cane and got awkwardly to his feet, still lightheaded. *Relief, probably.*

He tried a couple of unsteady steps, and leaned gratefully against the stonework by the front door of the byre, reaching into his pocket for his pipe. The terrier twitched out from under Bardwell's hands and rolled to her feet, rubbing apologetically round Hogg's legs. Bardwell rose, arms hanging loosely and face blank above the full beard.

Watching him now, Hogg could hardly credit the man's speed. He shook his head a little as he leaned down to fuss the terrier.

"So, how's the old girl behaving herself?" He strove for the mundane as he nodded to the Land Rover. "Everything all right?"

"She's a sturdy old barge," Bardwell responded, matching his tone. He leaned his hip against the front wing where bare aluminium showed through the flaking paint, and folded his arms. "Was thinking I might do a bit of patching up on her, though, if that's all right?"

"Patching up?" Hogg's frown was one of concern rather than disapproval. "I didn't think she needed anything. Got through her MOT a couple of months ago without a murmur."

Bardwell shrugged. "There's a couple of bits of chassis rail looking a tad scabby. This age, they can break their backs easy if you let 'em rot too far."

Hogg tapped out his pipe into the corner of the galvanised trough outside the cowshed door, lifting the trailing foliage to reach the steel. As he did so, he spotted a thin black cord reaching over the edge of the trough and disappearing into the soft earth. Puzzled, he wrapped it around his fingers, preparing to tug it free.

"Don't." The anxious note in Bardwell's voice had Hogg looking up, surprised. "Spare key." One corner of Bardwell's mouth lifted fractionally. "Always lose 'em. Better than leaving it under the mat."

"Yes...I suppose it is." Still troubled, Hogg let go of the cord and straightened, jamming the empty pipe back into his mouth. He hadn't sensed the agitation in Bardwell before, but he knew there had to be plenty. It was there in all of them. *Time and space*, he thought. *That's all he needs.*

"Tell you what, why don't you leave it with me?" He nodded to the Land Rover again. "I'll drop her into the garage next time I'm through and they can sort her out. If they missed something important, they should be the ones to fix it, don't you think?"

"S'no trouble," Bardwell said, quickly enough to have Hogg rubbing reflectively at his chin. "Only, I noticed you've got an old MIG-welding set-up in the barn there. I used to be a bit of a dab hand with that kind of stuff. Thought I could get back into it again."

He must have seen Hogg's uncertainty because he added with a bashful candour, "I thought, if it's only a bit of chassis, it wouldn't matter too much if it was workmanlike rather than pretty, like. Just 'til I get my eye in again."

The doubt cleared. "Of course," Hogg pushed himself away from the wall, found his balance again, smiling. "Help yourself —and let me know how you get on. I've a wheelbarrow that lets more through than it holds, if you need a bigger challenge."

Bardwell ducked his head and Hogg began to move away, clicking his fingers to the terrier.

"Well, that's a good sign, isn't it?" he murmured when they were out of earshot. The terrier looked up at him with adoration, hanging on his every word. "Our Patrick is taking an interest, thinking of the future."

It was only as he bumped down the potholed driveway

twenty minutes later, he realised he had forgotten to warn Bardwell of Edith's late arrival.

He braked, glanced back, but the farm buildings were already out of sight. Hogg contemplated turning round, but hesitated. Bardwell was an intensely private man. Today's exchange was far more than he usually ventured. Hogg had no wish to overcrowd him.

If Bardwell didn't want to be disturbed, well, the man was more than capable of telling Edith to come back to change his bed linen and clean another time. He checked the dashboard clock. He was already cutting it fine. Perhaps, this time, he would let Edith make her own excuses.

20

BARDWELL STOOD a little way back from the byre window and watched Ian Hogg's old Peugeot disappear down the driveway. Its progress was marked by kicked-up clouds of dried earth. Bardwell had served in plenty of places where such dust was a vital early warning system. He could read its swirling signature as clearly as a written word.

Another few minutes, he thought. *Let him get too far for it to be worth turning back.*

He stood without impatience, hands relaxed at his sides, face slack. Anyone watching at that moment might have thought him touched or maybe even simple, but he knew there was no-one watching. While some part of his mind held station, the remainder drifted in silent contemplation.

His sight turned inward. Although the image of the distant Lakeland hills was still imprinted on his retinas, it was overlaid by the stark ranges of another landscape altogether. Sheep transmuted into shaggy mountain goats, and the distant rumble of freight on the railway line filtered into the choppy thunder of rotary-wing air support.

Bardwell had killed his first man at nineteen in such terrain, had long since lost count of the others. But for the uniform, they'd have branded him a psychopath. But to his comrades, snipers like Bardwell were magicians, capable of visiting death on a distant enemy who thought to slaughter without fear of retribution. He'd earned the undying respect of the men he'd fought alongside. A bond written in fear and blood.

For years he'd performed the impossible without a murmur. The hierarchy had exploited his temperament and abilities as if he were merely an extension of the gun. Perhaps that was why they'd betrayed him so easily when he'd begun to question. There was no place in the field for equipment considered obsolete, but they'd trained him for this and nothing else. Who were they to say when it was over?

He shook himself, glanced at the clock on the oven and realised fifteen minutes had gone past without registering. He went through to the cramped bedroom, knelt as if in prayer and slid the rifle out from under the bed, wrapped in the ghillie suit.

He carried the gun outside and laid it across the rear seat. Carrying it openly like this had been a calculated risk, and he'd been anxious for the opportunity to minimise his exposure. Its current disguise wouldn't survive the most cursory inspection. If he'd been stopped yesterday, he would have been unable to explain it away.

It was what it was.

He paused, almost sniffing the air, then bent and carefully rearranged the trailing aubretia Hogg had disturbed while clearing out his pipe. Bardwell's fingers smoothed the edges of the thin cord, blending it a little further into the corner fold of metal.

He'd said it held a key, and that was half true. There were few locks could not be opened with the .357 revolver that was attached, safe in a waterproof oiled bag, to the other end of the cord. He had buried the ex-French police Manurhin revolver there, fully loaded, the night he'd arrived at the Retreat. *Insurance.*

He preferred a semiautomatic but, kept dry, the revolver could be relied upon to fire almost without question, no matter how long it remained hidden. He wondered if the former priest would ever know how close he'd come—or how Bardwell might have been forced to respond.

He drove the Land Rover straight up the yard and into the old stone barn next to the farmhouse without wasting any more time. It was cool inside—the thick sandstone walls as effective at keeping out the summer heat as they were the bitter Cumbrian winters—and musty from the stack of mouldering hay at one end.

Two fluorescent tubes strung from the rafters provided the barn's only artificial light. Bardwell pulled his hair back into a loose ponytail and lifted an inspection lamp off a rickety shelf, clipping one end of the cable to the battery. Squatting down to peer underneath the chassis, his movements were suddenly economical and sure.

There was nothing structurally wrong with the Land Rover. The mainstay of the British Army since their introduction, they'd seen service in every corner of the world. They could take the hammer, were respected for it.

But as soon as Hogg had arrived at Oxenholme to collect him, Bardwell had remembered the circular aperture in one of the Land Rover's main crossmembers for the power takeoff. It was almost tailor-made to hold the barrel of the rifle, snug and out of sight. All it needed was a quick-release bracket fabricating for the stock and he would have his perfect method of carriage and concealment.

He lifted the gun out, careful of its bulk, carried his burden across to the old scarred workbench along the back wall and set it down, almost reverently, like a child. The rifle was a Barrett M82A1 Light Fifty—one of the last made in 'ninety-two—and still as devastatingly effective as the day it left its Tennessee birthplace.

To Bardwell, the long gun's purposeful shape and sheer brutal power was a thing of beauty. He'd fallen for it the first time he'd handled one, nearly twenty years before. Fallen harder and faster than he ever had for any flesh-and-blood woman.

An inch over five feet from butt to muzzle-brake and weighing over twenty-five pounds, the gun was a hefty beast. They made some attempts to reduce the overall dimensions on later models, without sacrificing the monumental range and power. But Bardwell was a purist at heart, preferred the original. Besides, he was a muscular six-foot-three—the size and weight of the weapon didn't bother him.

He'd taken his time tracking down this rifle, revisiting old haunts, stretching the goodwill of old comrades and contacts to its limit and not caring.

There hadn't been as much time for testing as he would have

liked. Hard to find somewhere suitable. Familiarity with the breed was one thing, but each gun was subtly individual. At the kind of distances where the Barrett reigned supreme, even the curvature of the earth played a part in the fall of each shot.

Bardwell knew that when it mattered, he would have no margin for error. He should have had none yesterday. And, if circumstances had been different, he would have found out if he measured up to the task he'd set himself.

The first part of it, at least.

21

"ANYBODY HOME?" Edith tried for nonchalance as she pushed open the back door of the farmhouse, but sounded timid even to her own ears. She'd been surprised, even a little aggrieved, when there'd been no answer to her knock. *Knows I'm coming, don't he?*

OK, so she was late. *Very* late. Not her fault that her mother must have used the scooter and not refilled the tank. They were economical, but they didn't run on thin air. *Always down to Edith to do the dirty jobs.*

She stepped through the mudroom into the kitchen itself, calling out again. The only response was from the old terrier, in her basket by the Aga. She lifted her head, gazed through filmy eyes, then curled up again, dismissive.

Nobody's here, the girl thought mournfully. *Nobody cares about fat, stupid, ugly Edith.*

Her knees suddenly slack, Edith subsided into one of the wooden chairs by the kitchen table and stared at her shoes. Her tears, which had blown themselves out on the ride down to Grayrigg, bubbled up afresh. She tried to swallow them back into her aching throat, but little gulping whimpers escaped from her as she wrapped her arms around her skinny frame and rocked, crying, for what seemed a long time.

She couldn't have said why she was so devastated. It wasn't that she even *liked* Mr Hogg. OK, so he never shouted like her father, but he got this *disappointed* air about him. Took it personally when she let him down.

Some of her old teachers had tried that trick and it hadn't worked any better when she was still at school. "Oh, Edith, if only you'd apply yourself a *little* harder." But what had they to offer if she did? A bone-numbing job in telesales, or the check-out of the local supermarket? And then, at that last careers' day, some so-called friend had blabbed about Edith's secret dreams of fame and fortune. She'd hoped for encouragement. What she'd got was scorn.

How dare they laugh?

Edith never mentioned it again, but her resentment began to fester. She'd made her plans, quietly and without fuss, to exit this miserable existence. So when they mentioned her name in future, it would be in awed, hushed voices. And laughter would be the last thing on their minds.

Edith's bawling subsided into sobs, which grew more difficult to sustain. She'd been hoping that Mr Hogg would walk in and find her weeping tragically, at which point he'd coax the whole story out of her, all sympathetic.

Edith comforted herself with a brief vision of her employer on the phone to her parents, berating them for how badly they'd treated their daughter, how they'd come so close to losing her.

Naturally, they'd rush down there, all full of regrets, to cosset and pamper her, to tell her she was their best girl. Like they used to back when she was almost too young to recall if it was memory or craving. Back when she had yet to dissatisfy them in so many ways.

Eventually, it dawned on Edith that if the terrier was still in her basket, Mr Hogg had likely gone further than a walk around the yard, even with him being a cripple. He could be out all morning. All day.

Edith felt her last chance for salvation slipping away from her.

She slouched out of the chair, only then catching sight of the note addressed to her in Mr Hogg's looping hand. Hope flared again. In the time it took her to snatch it up, her imagination painted a heartrending plea not to do it. Perhaps some poetry, even a proposal.

The reality was a brusque instruction to clean the byre and give the old dairy a thorough going over before it was fit to let again. It finished: 'We really must talk about your time-keeping, Edith!'

You'll never get anywhere... All I see in store for you... You're never going to be famous...

Edith's face crumpled. She threw the ball of paper across the kitchen, causing the terrier to raise her head again briefly to see if it was worth the chase. It wasn't.

The sight of the old dog, gazing up at her with those trusting eyes, made what she'd done yesterday even worse.

If only that farmer paid more attention to his flock...

Edith straightened. Her father might have put the AK beyond her reach, but he wasn't the only one with a gun around here.

Still swallowing her tears, she hurried through the hallway to Mr Hogg's study. She knocked before she went in, just in case. The room was empty.

Propped behind the door was a twelve-bore Baikal, just where she remembered. The shotgun was old, speckled with rust. She'd never seen Mr Hogg pick it up, never mind fire it. Just for a moment, she worried that it wouldn't do the job.

Soon find that out, won't I?

The top shelf of the bookcase yielded a dusty box of cartridges. Decisive now, Edith opened it up and took just one, right from the centre, slipping it into her pocket. She put the box back, went through the kitchen pausing only to take a bottle of cooking sherry from the pantry.

Out in the brightly sunlit yard, she hesitated for the first time. *Where?* She looked around. Her eye lighted on the side door to the old barn next to the farmhouse.

22

HEAD CSI RICHARD SIBSON was engrossed in a report on the latest advances in DNA profiling, making occasional comments into a small memo recorder. He did not initially hear the annoying buzz of his office telephone. Eventually, with a sigh, he snatched the receiver to his ear.

"Yes!"

"And a good morning to you, too." Grace's slightly husky voice was placid.

Because she couldn't see his face, Sibson allowed himself a broad smile at the sound of her. He sat back in his swivel chair and rocked a little. "Ah, McColl—at last! Well, if you're going to gallivant off round the country for half the morning, you can't expect civility from me."

"Don't exaggerate," she admonished gently. "And I'd hardly call attending a post-mortem exam 'gallivanting', would you? My, what an interesting private life you must lead."

"Don't be cheeky, my dear. I'm both your elder and your better. So, what did that old Welsh charlatan have to say?"

"Well," she said cheerfully, "Professor Evans claims that you faked your degree and couldn't tell your—"

"About the dog, McColl, thank you *very* much!"

"Ah, well, on that subject he was less inclined to joke."

Sibson lost his languid pose. "Tell me," he said curtly. "Did Evans have any theories on the weapon?"

"Oh yes. In some ways, I wish he hadn't."

She gave her report in the concise, almost emotionless style Sibson had come to value. Laying out the facts without emphasis or bias, so he could absorb them in his own way. And she never seemed to miss anything. That photographer's eye. Unobserved, he smiled again. *She's a natural.*

Sibson knew when he took Grace on, still fresh from her studies and jaded from her marriage, there were some who questioned his judgement. Cumbria had received any number of applicants for the post of CSI and he could have had his pick. But something about Grace had stood out, even then.

And he wasn't just talking about her looks, although he'd had more than the odd sideways comment about his ulterior motives. Five years earlier, after a protracted struggle, Sibson had lost his wife to cancer. Some had thought he intended to seek consolation in the arms of his latest protégée, but in truth, he'd no designs on Grace. Even if he *had* entertained such an idea, she'd certainly given him no encouragement.

But he'd been surprised, he had to admit, that she'd been with that brash new chap yesterday. Grace was normally very wary of letting colleagues invade her personal space. She had an ability to keep herself slightly removed that Sibson secretly rather admired.

So his eyebrows climbed as she brought her verbal report to a close and asked, "Would you mind passing on the information to DC Weston?"

"Weston? My dear McColl, I'll be taking this straight to Inspector Pollock. Why deal with the oily rag, so to speak, when you have the engine driver to hand?"

"Because he was there," she said simply. Sibson heard the shrug in her voice. "I thought he deserved to know that yesterday wasn't all some wild goose chase."

"I'll make sure he's told," Sibson promised. "And no, Grace, if Evans' opinion is to be trusted—and much as it grieves me to say it, I rather think it is—then the last thing I'd call this business was a wild goose chase, hm?"

He put the phone down without waiting for her reply and stood up sharply enough to send the swivel chair skittering backwards. It hit a stack of textbooks, knocking them into a sprawl.

Sibson glanced at it with annoyance, then strode out of the office anyway. The books could wait. His report to Inspector Pollock on Grace McColl's findings, he considered, could not.

23

NICK RAISED his hand to knock on Detective Inspector Pollock's office door, pausing to take a deep breath before his knuckles made contact.

The Post-It note saying the inspector wanted to see him urgently had been stuck prominently to his computer monitor, but whoever put it there knew full-well he was out of the building. Pure chance that he'd called in to Hunter Lane on his way back from Warcop camp. *Another petty stab in the back.*

"Come!" barked a voice on the other side and he pushed open the door. "Ah, Nick, I was wondering where you'd got to, lad."

Nick hesitated. "Sorry, sir," he said, tone colourless.

Pollock caught it, though. There wasn't much got by him. His face twitched and he gave a reluctant nod. Nick knew the decision not to make excuses was the right one. His inspector would not take kindly to the implied criticism, even if he didn't like being kept in the dark about unrest in his team.

Wants to know, Nick thought sourly, *just doesn't want me to tell him.*

Pollock waved him into one of the chairs facing the desk, which looked no more inviting than those in Frederickson's domain. Out of habit, Nick swung the chair round so the door was no longer directly behind him. He knew Pollock didn't miss that, either.

The inspector leaned forwards, folding his hands on the

scrupulously tidy desktop and fixing him with a hard stare from under wildly sprouting eyebrows.

He was a big man who'd been a county-standard rugby player in his youth. A prop forward rather than some light-weight little winger. Now, two decades on, his wife was fighting a rearguard action against his weight, much to his disgust and her despair. Nick noted the half-drunk coffee by his elbow, the empty plate dotted with biscuit crumbs.

Photographs of Pollock's past sporting achievements hung around the walls, showing him aggressive and fearless on the field. He'd managed to preserve his ears and nose intact, although he'd sacrificed his teeth to the glory of the game. The front four of his upper set gleamed artificially white and straight. He showed them now, like war trophies.

"You were called out to a bit of a Firearms incident yesterday morning." His tone made it a question.

"Yes, sir." Nick kept his voice cautious, but there must have been some underlying harmonic.

"The lads have been giving you a ragging about it, have they?"

Nick forced a thin smile. "You could say that, sir."

"Well, I'm sure you've worked out by now that if you can't take a joke, you're in the wrong job."

Nick put his teeth together very precisely. "Yes, sir."

Pollock nodded again. "All right then," he said, sitting back. "I've read your initial report, but—"

Another knock at the door brought Pollock upright, glower-ing. "Come!" he bellowed, and in walked Richard Sibson, barely waiting for the invitation.

To Nick's mind, the balding CSI resembled a gangling spider, all sharp points and angles, his movements carefully precise, almost fussy.

"Ah, just the man." Sibson caught sight of Nick with satisfac-tion. "Morning, Brian."

Pollock gave a grunt. "Can it wait?"

"Probably," Sibson tucked his long limbs into the empty chair. "But I've just got the post-mortem exam results from Grace McColl and what I have to say concerns DC Weston anyway. I thought we could have one of those joint briefings the Time and Motion people are so fond of."

"Hang on—what post-mortem exam?"

Sibson sighed audibly. "On the dog, of course."

Pollock threw up his hands. "Hell's teeth," he muttered. "We have to account for every penny, and you're autopsying farm animals." He slumped in his seat again, which creaked ominously underneath him. "You set too much store by that girl."

"No more than she deserves." Sibson treated the inspector to a stern glance. "Besides, a dog hardly classifies as livestock. And I believe the correct term is a necropsy when it relates to an animal. Oh, relax, Brian," he added as the inspector's colour began to rise, "I called in a favour with an old friend. We're not being charged for his services."

Pollock grunted again. "Sorry to rain on your parade, both of you, but orders have come down from on high that we're to shelve this one."

There was a moment's silence. Not quite shock, but certainly disappointment. Nick recovered first.

"Might I ask why, sir?"

Pollock shot him a brooding look. "It's been suggested to me that 'pursuing the matter would not be the best use of our resources', unquote," he said acidly. "We're to put this one down to a lawful shooting, and leave it at that."

"Even though we know the farmer's shotgun was never fired?" Nick persisted. "And the rifle Grace took away from the girl was incapable of inflicting the fatal wound?"

Pollock glanced at Sibson.

"The veterinary pathologist confirmed the weapon used must have been at least a .303 or a 7.62mm," Sibson said mildly. "As we're well outside the season for deer, is the Chief Constable really quite happy for someone to be wandering around the countryside with something of large and illegal calibre, taking pot-shots at whatever takes their fancy?"

"No, he's not. We've been there before and look what happened then." Pollock gave a gusty sigh. "I understand Mrs Inglis has already been in touch with our beloved leader." His quick grimace was his only comment on people who tried to interfere with police business. "But he told her he'd every confidence in the abilities of his officers." His eyes narrowed. "No, this has come from further up the line." He spoke with a grim finality, but Nick shook his head.

"Sir, I've just been over to Warcop Training Ground. Giles Frederickson's the major in charge up there. He was being cagey about it, but the camp seems on alert for something. If this is some disgruntled squaddie on the loose, it could get out of hand very quickly. And if it comes out that we had prior warning and did nothing—"

"All right, lad," Pollock cut in heavily, raising a meaty hand. "You've made your point." He sighed, scowled at his desktop for a moment then looked up at the two men. "To be honest, I don't like it any more than you do, but I know which side my bread's buttered, and at the moment it's the side that lands square on me, face down, from a great height."

Nick heard the twist of contempt and knew in an instant who was behind this sudden order to bury the investigation. *Mercer.* Nobody else inspired such disdain.

"Not like you to buckle, Brian." Sibson's tone was bland.

"I've been in this job long enough to know when to pick my battles," Pollock replied placidly. He swung his attention back to Nick. "Something on your mind, lad?"

Nick glanced up, made another split-second decision, shook his head. "No, sir."

"Hm." Pollock put both hands on the desk as if preparing to rise. "Right, then, if there's nothing else?"

Nick got to his feet. Sibson followed suit, uncoiling out of his seat.

Pollock let them almost make it to the door before he said, "Oh, if you've nothing else on your plate at the moment, Nick, I've got a job for you."

Nick turned back. On his way out Sibson flashed him a half-smile of what might even have been sympathy.

Pollock picked up a bulging folder from the neat in-tray on one corner of the desk. "Quad bikes—been disappearing all over the county," he said, thrusting it into Nick's hand. "Word's come down it's an organised gang. Cast your eye over that lot, will you? See what you make of it. Could do with a result on this one."

"Yes, sir."

"Don't look so crestfallen, lad. They can't all be gunfights."

"No, sir."

Pollock paused, then reached into one of the desk drawers to pull out a piece of paper. Nick recognised his own request for a search warrant for Jim Airey's place of residence with a certain sense of foreboding.

"Nosing around your fellow officers—even Specials like Airey—will not help you fit in with that lot." He jerked his head towards the door as if to indicate everyone on the other side of it.

"No sir," Nick repeated.

The inspector nodded. "We'll say no more about it, then." He leaned over to feed the sheet through his office shredder, sat back and fixed Nick with a piercing gaze. "Just remember, lad, I picked you for this job. They told me it wouldn't be a popular decision in some quarters, but I read your record and thought you'd tough it out. Thought you were the best man for the job. Still do."

When Nick didn't immediately respond Pollock rose, impatient. "All right," he said gruffly, waving him away. "Get on with it—and don't prove me wrong, eh?"

"No sir," Nick said again and went out, closing the door with a quiet, controlled click behind him.

24

OVER THE YEARS, Patrick Bardwell had learned to trust his own survival instinct implicitly. Now, as he was juggling with Vise-Grips to tack the last part of the makeshift bracket in place to the Land Rover chassis, it tapped him on the shoulder and whispered in his ear.

You are not alone.

Casually, he slid out from underneath the vehicle and laid aside his welding mask. Carefully, he propped the rest of the rig so any residual heat didn't set fire to the straw-strewn floor of the barn, and climbed stiffly to his feet, placing both fists into the small of his back as though to stretch it out.

True, his spine was feeling the pinch from the awkward position, but it also gave him a good excuse to twist slowly in both directions.

Over to his right, on what remained of the haystack, he caught a tiny glimmer of movement that might have been someone ducking down. *Not a professional, then.*

One of the first things they'd taught him was never to move quickly unless sure he'd been compromised. The most astounding levels of exposure could be countered by the simple act of stillness.

Bardwell shuffled over towards the workbench, which brought him closer to the stack, while his brain ran possibilities with a glacial smoothness behind a blank expression. There was a door in the far back corner where his unknown watcher must have squeezed through into the barn and climbed onto the haystack.

But how did they know to look? And how much have they seen?

The Barrett squatted on its bipod legs, taking up almost the entire length of the bench. Bardwell had thrown a sheet over it, more to keep dust and dirt at bay than for disguise. But he'd uncovered the gun several times, to take measurements and to check the fit of the bracket. *If they'd been watching then…*

He clattered around at the bench for a few moments while he considered the risks, hands distractedly moving over the tools he'd laid out as though searching for some misplaced item.

There's still a chance they've seen nothing…

Then, from the other side of the hay came a sound, too loud to pretend he hadn't heard. A scrambling noise with a smear of panic to it.

They've seen it all right.

Abandoning his shambling gait, Bardwell threw himself at the wall of hay, hands grasping the thin twine binding each crumbling bale to launch himself up and onto it. He rolled down onto the other side amid a billow of choking dust, landing right on top of a scrawny teenage boy. The boy reared back, tripped over his own feet and went down shrieking.

Bardwell's only thought was to silence him. He piled in, using aggression and body mass to drive the boy down into the hay, clamping one hand over his mouth to cut the screams, grabbing for his throat with the other.

And suddenly he was plucked from the cool lushness of an English summer and plunged back into the harsh desert of northern Iraq. Back to when he and his spotter were compromised by a young Iraqi boy herding his goats through the wadi where they'd made their hide. They had already seen the dust haze thrown up by the rapid approach of the mobile Scud launcher they were tasked to disable, when the boy had begun to shout.

That time Bardwell had used a knife. He was a long-distance killer by training and temperament and it hadn't been as quick, nor as silent, as he'd been misled to believe. The boy had taken his time about dying, ugly, and Bardwell was forced to leave him drowning in his own blood to go back to his gun.

It was one of the rare occasions when he had missed the precise point he'd chosen on the target with his first cold shot.

This time, even the distance of a knife was denied to him. He gripped tighter round the boy's throat, feeling the skinny muscles start to tear. Already, his frantic struggles had weakened, the thrashing limbs beginning to flop.

And then, just as suddenly, the boy's flowing bedou coat shimmered into a gaudily-patterned shirt with an open collar, and the bleeding, dying Arab boy became a pale, terrified English girl. Not just any girl, but one who was known to him.

Bardwell let go as if stung. He flung himself away and jerked his hands up as if just to look at her hurt his eyes. The girl sat half up instantly and scuttered backwards on her elbows and bony rump, whimpering with fright. Her heels scrabbled for grip in the soft loose hay.

She'd barely gone two metres when he heard her hand connect with something solid. She grabbed and swung it towards him. Bardwell let his hands drop and found himself looking straight down the gaping barrel of a shotgun.

Just for a second, neither of them moved. The only sound was the insistent bleating of lambs in the nearby fields and the rasp of the girl's breath through her half-crushed windpipe. The sight of the gun pulled up into her shoulder tripped his memory, back to the field, and the dog.

So, she did see me after all.

He watched her hands tighten and knew he was as close to being killed here as he'd ever been in any godforsaken corner of the world.

And, in some strange way, he felt relief. If he died here—now, today—then the choice would be taken from him. There would be no more duty, no bonds of blood. It would all be over.

He sat on the edge of the bales and met the girl's eyes without flinching. Moving at all was a calculated risk. She could have pulled the trigger just out of fright and no-one would have blamed her for it.

But she didn't.

"Well, what're you waiting for?" he asked with gruff belligerence. "Didn't dither about with that dog yesterday, did you?"

Her mouth dropped open. "How do you know that?" she demanded hoarsely and he cursed under his breath as he heard the surprise in her voice, saw the wheels turning and the crafty glint in her eye. "It was you, wasn't it—with that big rifle?"

Coldly, Bardwell realised his mistake. Whatever she'd been doing up here, it wasn't to spy on him. He noticed the bottle of cheap sherry lying on its side with the dregs leaking into the hay, the flush to her skin that wasn't purely down to adrenaline.

The shotgun was heavy. The weight of it dragged at her narrow shoulders. Out of habit, Bardwell recognised it as Ian Hogg's old Baikal. He'd spent time in the farmhouse study, occasionally invited to engage in awkward conversation with the Retreat's owner. He'd always got the impression the gun was a relic of an earlier generation—that Hogg didn't really approve. It even crossed his mind it might not be loaded now.

Could still finish what I started…

"Aye, it was me."

But her angry response what not what he expected. "Then why didn't *you* shoot it?" she wailed. "You ruined *everything!*"

Bardwell kept one eye on her whitened trigger finger. "Ruined what?"

She paused, took a shaky breath and drew herself up. "I was going to kill myself," she announced with a dignity that was somehow pathetic.

Bardwell had dealt with a lot of things in his life, from fellow squaddies with their legs blown off to hordes of yelling fanatics waving spears. His reaction was to switch off emotion like a light, leaving only a cold logic behind.

"Not easy with a long gun," he said after a moment. "Don't go for a gut shot—you'll die screaming. Seen it often enough. Mouth's best. Instant, more or less. Take your shoes and socks off and work the trigger with your big toe."

He saw her shoulders begin to shiver, and for a moment he thought she might shoot him by accident if not by design. He braced. At that distance, in a confined space, there wasn't much else to be done.

Then, with something close to a moan, the girl sent the shotgun spinning away onto the bales and glared at him, eyes bright with the fever of unshed tears.

"See? *Everyone* wishes I was dead!" she cried, and bolted, slithering down the far side of the stack away from him.

Behind her, Bardwell sat bewildered, staring at the discarded shotgun and the empty bottle.

25

SQUEEZED into the narrow space alongside a block-built work-shop in Staveley, a few miles the other side of Kendal, Grace McColl hunched awkwardly over the single footprint she had just enclosed and cast. She nudged a gloved finger at the dental plaster to see if it had hardened enough to be lifted. As with anything watched over, it wasn't ready.

She sighed. Whoever had trodden in this patch of soft earth down the side of the building had not given any thought for the CSI who would follow their night of crime. The print was in a difficult position to get to, never mind photograph with the required measurement scale in place.

The workshop was on a small industrial estate in the middle of the village. Grace remembered Staveley when the main road up to Windermere and Ambleside had run straight through the centre of the village, jinking round the grey slate buildings at every turn. The residents had campaigned for a bypass and had got their wish. Grace wondered how many small businesses like this had suffered as a result.

She had spent the greater part of the morning at the sprawling university at Lancaster, observing the post-mortem examination that Professor Evans had performed on the remains of Ben. He'd turned out to be a neat, dapper little man with precise movements and a flirtatious manner.

She hadn't expected a full-scale investigation to follow, not on her say-so, but was surprised to be retasked so quickly.

Almost an admonishment. She'd debated on making a fuss but decided against. It would give her an excuse to pay another call on the girl, Edith. If only to tell her things were not being taken any further.

Grace leaned sideways onto the sagging pallet that partially blocked her access, wiped the back of her gloved hand across her forehead where the elasticated edge of her Tyvek suit rubbed irritatingly at her skin.

It was cool alongside the workshop, out of direct sun, which was why the loose soil sluiced down near the drain had not dried out, and now held a clear impression of what Grace thought might prove to be a Nike trainer. She had learned over the last couple of years to recognise the sole-patterns of most popular makes. As Max's wife, she'd once been able to identify all the major haute couture houses just by the cut of the cloth.

If her ex-husband could see her now, she mused drily, he would throw up his hands in total incomprehension.

She heard footsteps on the gravel behind her and was about to call a warning when they stepped dutifully onto the metal treadplates she'd put down to preserve the approach to the scene.

"So, you're in the doghouse, too, are you?" asked a familiar voice with its slightly flattened Mancunian vowels. "No pun intended."

"Mr Weston." Grace allowed a smile to form. She rose, twisting in the confined space. "I was just on my way back from Lancaster when Richard diverted me. I took it as a logical reassignment rather than some form of reprimand."

He'd been hoping for commiseration, she saw, and when his only answer was a scowl she allowed her amusement to slide through. "My word, you *do* have a chip on your shoulder, don't you?"

The detective had stopped several metres away, hands thrust into his trouser pockets. *Making sure he doesn't touch anything,* she realised. For a few moments, they stood there in silence.

"So," he said at last, a little grudging, "what have we got?" and without waiting for an answer he jerked his head towards the polythene sheeting flapping gently at a broken window near the front of the building. "I assume that's our point of entry."

Grace paused. "Eventually, yes."

"Eventually?"

"I believe they—there were at least two of them—first tried to force that little window right near the back." She turned to point. "The frame's going along the lower edge and there were tool marks where they tried to jemmy it with a flat-bladed instrument of some kind, a chisel or a screwdriver, most likely."

She glanced back, found him frowning. "Not the most obvious place," he said, almost to himself. "They'd have to know it was there."

She nodded. "The owner can't be certain no-one's tried that one before, of course, but the marks look pretty fresh. I've cast them for comparison."

Nick gave a grunt. "How much did he lose?"

"Two quads and a small trailer. From what I can gather, it's very much like the other break-ins—they just take a couple. Not too greedy."

"I'd say they're just limited by the size of getaway vehicle." Nick pulled out his notebook and jotted something down. "They must have been here recently, scoped the place out." He started to turn away. "I'll see if the owner remembers anything."

"You might also like to see if he has a dog," Grace said, halting him. At his raised eyebrow, she added, "I recovered some animal hair from the frame of the broken window. Just a few strands, but they could have come from the clothing or gloves our thieves were wearing." She shrugged. "It might be a break— I understand the other scenes so far were clean. It could help place a suspect here."

"*If* we find a suspect." Nick muttered, giving her a weary smile. "Thanks, Grace."

He folded his notebook back into an inside pocket but seemed reluctant to move away.

"Your boss mentioned the PM on the dog showed it *was* a military rifle?"

"Of that calibre, certainly." His stubborn determination not to let go of this one surprised her. "Why?"

"I knew Frederickson was hiding something," he said, fixing her with a fierce stare as if willing her to take him seriously.

Grace leaned down to prod the plaster cast again. *Needs another minute.*

"I would have thought it was perfectly obvious what those

two were hiding," she said over her shoulder. She stood again and found him staring.

"And when, exactly, were you going to let me in on *that* little secret?"

Grace met his scrutiny without flinching. "I haven't been a CSI very long, but the first thing I learned was to offer facts not opinions. If I'd uncovered any solid forensic evidence, you would have been the first to know," she said crisply. "As I've mentioned before, I don't like to guess."

She let him ponder that one while she tried the plaster again. For the next few minutes, she ignored the man behind her, concentrating on delicately removing the cast and documenting her methods. When she turned back she found his expression shrouded.

"So, without *hard evidence*, what makes you think there's something going on between them?"

She picked up her kit and stepped carefully onto the nearest treadplate, expecting him to move aside and let her pass. When he didn't, she leaned against the rough wall of the neighbouring building to wait him out.

"The way they stood so close together but were so careful not to touch." She shrugged. "If he was at ease enough to visit her at that hour of the morning, she should have been perfectly happy to put a consolatory arm around his shoulders, in the circumstances. Instead, they were desperate to emphasise the distance between them. Guilty consciences, wouldn't you say?"

He digested the information for a moment, eyes focused inwards. "Damn," he said at last. "Why didn't *I* spot that one?"

She could have told him that she'd spent years relieving the boredom of stuffy social gatherings with Max by playing spot the infidelity. *People give so much away when they're trying their hardest not to.* She smiled and said lightly, "Well, it's hardly surprising so many affairs go unnoticed."

"Is that what happened—your ex had a fling?"

Grace gazed at him levelly until he coloured, dropped his eyes.

"No. And I certainly would have noticed." For some reason, she felt an unfamiliar need to expand. "I simply found I preferred being alone."

He nodded, but she'd seen the way his shoulders slumped.

He looked tired, she realised. More than that, a bone-deep weariness.

"Do you ever...miss being married?"

"Of course," she said honestly. "But not often. Mostly, I'm... happy in my own company." And suddenly she thought of the forlorn figure of the girl, Edith, sitting defiant over the partially dismantled gun on her parents' tatty kitchen table. "Some people are just born lonely."

26

FIFTEEN MINUTES LATER, Nick caught up with the tall CSI as she was loading the last of her equipment into the crime scene van. She had already peeled off her nitrile gloves, and now she pushed back the hood of her unzipped suit, to rake her fingers vigorously through that mass of rich red hair.

"All done?" he asked as he walked towards her across the cracked concrete.

"I think so." She pushed the suit down to her knees and sat in the van's side doorway to wrestle it over her boots. Underneath, she was wearing faded jeans and a pale blue shirt with the sleeves rolled halfway back along her forearms to reveal what looked like a battered gent's watch.

What's she trying to prove? Nick wondered. The answer was immediate. *Everything.*

He leaned against the open sliding door, watching her. He was as old-fashioned as the next man when it came to female attire. He liked women to look like women; pretty clothes and makeup—just as long as he didn't have to hang around while they chose it.

"You were quite right, by the way. The owner says he only had the faulty catch on that window fixed last week. His insurance agent kicked up a fuss because the policy was coming up for renewal."

Grace stopped, thoughtful. "Good job he got round to it, or his claim might have been thrown out."

"Hm." Nick glanced up, squinted at the starkness of the sun and fished in his pocket for dark glasses. "So our thieves haven't been here since last week, or they'd have realised it was a waste of time."

"Or they knew the catch had been fixed and still reckoned it was their best option." Grace smiled. "Sorry. Just playing devil's advocate."

Nick found himself returning the smile. "And he doesn't have a dog, either. Allergic to them, apparently. Says all his regulars know to keep theirs outside."

"Well then." Grace pulled the last of the suit free and bundled it into a waste bag. "That's something, at least." She stood. "I'm sorry it's not more."

"Don't be. You've dug up more than anyone else has managed. You never know, we might actually be able to crack this one."

As he spoke he realised that something of his old eagerness for the job had returned. He'd come down here still troubled by the same bout of sullen irritation he'd been struggling to shake. But now he felt what might even have been optimism. *She might be a bit aloof, but there's no doubt she knows her stuff.*

It still annoyed him that he'd missed the signs of the affair between Frederickson and Angela Inglis, but he shrugged it aside. If Pollock didn't think it was worth taking seriously, who was he to argue?

Nick stepped back to allow Grace to slam the side door shut, van keys ready in her hand.

"I don't suppose," he said as she moved for the driver's side, "that you'd let me buy you lunch?"

She looked down that long aristocratic nose at him, nodded to the van. "It would be unprofessional to leave evidence unattended."

Nick jerked his head towards a café on the other side of the estate, obviously catering as much to walkers and passers-by as the nearby businesses. There were half a dozen chrome tables and chairs clustered outside, from which their vehicles would be clearly visible. "You wouldn't have to."

"Hm, it's very kind of you, but I don't think so," she replied in that slightly remote voice of hers. The disappointment flooded him, but when he looked closely there was a faint smile tugging the corner of her mouth. "I'm quite capable of buying my *own* lunch," she added. "You're more than welcome to join me."

"Right." He tried not to sound relieved. "I'll grab us a table, shall I?" And he walked away quickly, just in case she was tempted to change her mind.

27

A LOUD KNOCKING jerked Patrick Bardwell out of a fitful doze. His hand reached automatically for a weapon that wasn't there and he blinked into full wakefulness with a shuddering gasp like a man revived from drowning.

The noise stopped and the world righted itself, steadied. He was back in the cramped sitting room of the cottage, embraced in a faded wingback chair where he'd settled, waiting for them to come for him.

He'd been certain they *would* come. How could they not? The girl had seen him out there on the fell. She knew enough of guns to realise something of what he was about. And even if her word was doubted, the finger marks around her throat would shout their own story.

For a moment he strained, listening. Had there really been knocking, or was his imagination playing tricks on him again? He rubbed wearily at his beard and his hands came away damp and cold, like a fish. He could smell the fear in his own sweat, a sharp, bitter tang. A long time since he'd been afraid like this.

He'd taken off his watch, put it away so they wouldn't strip him of it when they took him, and now he'd lost his grip on time. The sun was too high for the dawn raid he knew they favoured, when they would hope to drag him disorientated from his bed.

Well, not him.

It'd taken a time to shake out of his daze after the girl fled.

He'd finally climbed down and gathered up the tools, putting them away like an automaton, some sub-level of his mind monitoring his movements without registering them.

He drove the Land Rover outside and carried the rifle back into the byre. A good soldier takes care of his equipment first and foremost. That had been drilled into him during basic training and proved in combat in the years since. So he drew the curtains and field-stripped the Barrett, his hands moving in a smooth and precise ritual.

The gun stood now on the low table in the living room, bipod legs spread and aligned exactly with the corners like a kit inspection, the hefty ten-round magazine laid alongside. Then he'd leaned back in his chair, hands quietly on the arms, and waited for them to come.

The knock sounded again and Bardwell's imagination exploded into a vividly coloured snapshot of black-clad thugs from SCO19, gathered round the cottage doorway with machine pistols at the ready. In his mind's eye, another pair ran in to swing a steel enforcer towards the hinges and—

Another knock and, as his alertness increased, he recognised timidity in the polite tapping.

The picture jump-cut to a solitary country bobby hovering uncertainly on his doorstep, a bit embarrassed perhaps at having to follow up the wild fantasies of a disturbed teenage girl.

Bardwell got to his feet, staggered, his limbs protesting the sudden activity.

"Just a minute," he called, gruff. "Give me a minute."

There was no response and, for all his earlier fatalism, now the moment was here his first instinct was to run.

He grabbed the Barrett and the magazine and carried both through to the tiny bedroom. The space was almost entirely taken up by the double bed in the centre, a legacy from the farm's holiday let days.

Bardwell knelt down and slid the rifle under the bed, draped in a blanket. He ducked back into the living room only to sweep the oil-impregnated cleaning cloth off the table and drop it into the coal bucket.

In the kitchen, he took a moment to calm himself before he finally opened the door. Outside was a visitor he definitely hadn't expected.

Edith.

He'd caught her just as she was looking back over her shoulder, nervous, like she knew coming here was a bad idea. At the sound of the door opening, she snapped back to face him, mouth rounding into a silent O. Her neck seemed too long and thin to support her head, with its shapeless cap of badly-cut hair. In that startled, ungainly pose, Bardwell was reminded, not of a young fawn but, less flatteringly, a giraffe.

For an endless, disconnected moment, they stared at each other.

The girl recovered first. His presence less of a surprise to her, however much she might have lost her nerve.

"Well then," she said at last, boldly, with a kind of jerky flick that might have been intended as a cavalier toss of her head but instead made it seem she'd gone into spasm. "Aren't you going to ask me in?"

Wordlessly, Bardwell stood aside. And just before he closed the door behind her, he made one quick survey of the deserted farmyard. If this went the way he feared, the fewer witnesses the better.

28

Outside the café in Staveley, Nick walked back to the table, careful not to spill the brimming glasses of lemonade he was balancing. Grace was gazing into middle distance, he saw, notebook open on the table, tapping absently at the page with her pen. She closed it with an apologetic smile as he approached.

"Sorry. Difficult to get your mind off the job sometimes."

"Hey, I'm the last person you need to explain that to." He managed to put both glasses down without slopping their contents and took the chair opposite.

The café was a glorified sandwich shop, with a small outside seating area cordoned off by narrow planters filled with geraniums, colourful enough to catch the eye of passing trade on the main street a short distance away.

Nick expected her to order a salad but when he nodded towards the menu, still folded on the table, her smile became conspiratorial.

"I don't need to see that. Not when I've been tantalised by the smell of bacon butties since I got here."

Nick shook his head and went back inside to order, wondering just how often this woman was going to surprise him.

When he returned, Grace was looking round, taking it all in, professional. Something told Nick she would be able to describe the place in great detail, long after she'd walked away from it.

"I rarely eat outside these days. Not since the smoking ban—

it's usually like an ashtray." She flicked her eyes over his hands. "Of course, I'm taking it for granted that you're not a smoker."

"Reformed," he said, reaching for his glass. "Nearly five years."

Grace smiled faintly and raised her own glass in a silent toast. "Nearly?" she queried.

He grinned, caught out. "Four years, six months and, oh, about fourteen days." *Can still remember the day I quit. The day Lisa told me she was pregnant with Sophie…*

"Was it hard—giving up, I mean?"

He shrugged. "I knew I needed to stop, so I did. Looking back, I only ever did it as a social thing. Stupid really, but I grew up in pubs at a time when everybody smoked. If you wanted to fit in, you did, too."

"You grew up in a pub?"

He smiled at the doubtful note, took a swig of his drink. "My dad ran a series of dives for one brewery after another. By the time I was twelve, I could bottle up a bar single-handed." *Often had to, when the old man had a death-grip on his bed in the morning.*

"What about your mother?"

Nick forced himself not to tense. "She left," he said shortly. "I was about seven, just a snotty-nosed kid. Can't say I blame her, though. My dad liked to play the field."

Grace nodded but didn't go through the usual sympathetic motions and Nick was grateful. Instead, she said, "It's quite a journey from running a pub to your current occupation," with enough interest in her voice to make it a question.

He sat back, as if considering. "Maybe I decided that if I had to break up fights every Saturday night, I might as well do it with CS spray and a warrant card, and get paid for the privilege."

It was glib. He saw from her face that she was disappointed by it, and added, "My first undercover job was getting myself hired to run the bars in a very dodgy nightclub, so the experience stood me in good stead."

She was leaning forwards slightly, putting all of herself into the attention she gave to him. Nick tried not to be flattered; it was just a technique. Grace would have made a good interrogator. People would talk just to watch her listen. The men, anyway.

"Was it successful?" she asked now. "Your first undercover assignment."

Nick gave a wry smile. "Even as we were being raided, the boss was telling me to keep my mouth shut and he'd see me right, so I think it's safe to say my cover was pretty solid." *Best not to remember the time when it wasn't.* He reached for his glass again and said, only half-joking, "So, what's a nice girl like you doing in a job like this?"

For a moment Grace frowned into her mineral water, then said candidly, "I was already involved in photography—strictly amateur, you understand—when a solicitor friend asked if I'd take some pictures of a building where a robbery had taken place."

"Like today, you mean?"

She gave an elegant shrug. "An office building, rather than a workshop, and I'm afraid the idea of the exercise was to prove the prosecution's witness couldn't possibly have seen what he was claiming, from the position he was supposed to have been in at the time."

"And were *you* successful?"

"That depends on your point of view." She sat back and crossed those long denim-clad legs. "We proved our argument, if that's what you mean. My friend's client got off and afterwards Richard Sibson approached me and told me—rather cheerfully, I thought—that I'd ruined his case. Then he gave me a card and said if I was ever interested in working for the side of the angels, he could use someone with my eye—his words."

"So you took him up on his offer."

"Not right away, no. After Max and I separated I enrolled at college over in the northeast. By the time my divorce came through I was qualified enough to accept."

There was something in her voice and Nick glanced at her, but her expression gave nothing away. Treading carefully, he asked, "Didn't your ex want you to take the job?"

She pulled a face that held amusement more than irritation. "He didn't want me to take *any* job. He was making enough to support both of us, so why did I need to work?"

Her matter-of-fact tone rankled him. As if all working husbands were faced with the same dilemma. "I assume, after the settlement, you still don't need to."

Grace picked up her glass again and gave him a cool stare over the rim. "And I would have thought in your job you'd have learned by now to assume nothing."

He grinned at her, raising his glass to acknowledge the point. "Speaking of which, do you want to let me have your *assumptions* about this robbery? D'you reckon they really didn't know about that window?"

They chatted over Grace's initial conclusions until other customers arrived. Then their food came out, two huge hot bacon sandwiches, and they gave themselves over to the business of eating in companionable silence.

She ate with delicate determination, Nick noticed, not picking through her food or worrying about the calories. *Perhaps she's just naturally slim?* He remembered the meagre contents of her fridge. *Or perhaps she just doesn't eat much at home.* And his thoughts turned to inviting her to share another meal with him. A quiet dinner, maybe, when they didn't have work on their minds...

When their plates were empty, she asked quietly, "You're still worried about the girl, Edith, aren't you? What are you going to do?"

Nick glanced across, found her frowning.

"I'm not sure." Like her, he kept his voice low, careful of the nearby tables. "I was hoping to get someone from the...office to speak to her, but that's going to be tricky. Her father will know I've been told to lay off, for a start."

"Mm. I could drop in on my way home—nothing official, of course—if you think that might help?"

Would it? "I think so." He flashed her a rueful smile and added frankly, "At least if word gets back to her father, he's not going to arrange for his mates to take *you* down a dark alley."

"How gallant," she said in that lightly husky voice that was a hair's breadth from laughing at him. And then her eyes shifted to a point just over his right shoulder and went blank.

Before Nick could turn, a voice behind him said, "Not interrupting anything, am I?"

"Lisa!" Even as he said her name, Nick knew there was guilty surprise on his face. *Damn!* He stood up sharply. "Listen, I—"

"Spare me," Lisa snapped. "I can see you're busy." Her eyes raked Grace up and down. "Bit old for you, isn't she?"

He groaned inwardly, but Grace didn't react to the barb.

"That entirely depends," she said calmly, "on what it is you think he's been doing with me?"

Nick saw Lisa gather herself. He grabbed her arm, aware of the staring eyes surrounding them. "Let's talk about this later, yeah?"

Lisa yanked her arm free. "What's to talk about?"

Nick recognised that simmering look. He took a deep breath.

"Look, all I'm doing is having lunch with a colleague," he said, aware his voice was weary with defeat. "We've been dealing with a break-in. So, say what you came to say without embarrassing yourself, hey?" And, even though he knew it wouldn't help matters: "You're the one who lives round here now, love, not me."

Her pretty face flushed, from anger or shame he wasn't sure which. She flicked her eyes to the rapt faces at the nearby tables, most of whom hastily shifted their gaze.

Mind you, Lisa was the type to turn heads anywhere. Small and blonde and petite, with an impossibly tiny waist and a heart-shaped face, she and Nick had met when someone had tried to rob the hairdressers where she was working in Manchester. Still in uniform then, he'd been first on scene, to find this diminutive figure furiously threatening to castrate the cornered would-be thief with a pair of heated curling tongs.

He couldn't claim he wasn't forewarned about her temper.

Today she was wearing a flowered summer dress that made her look impossibly dainty compared to Grace, but somehow not nearly so attractive…

"I recognised your car," she said then, stiff-necked. "I wanted to tell you I'll be popping round to the flat at the weekend, to pick up some of Sophie's toys."

Sophie's toys. That sliced, right enough. Nick turned away so she wouldn't see it. "Yeah, sure. If I'm not working I'll give you a hand."

"There's no need," she said, quickly enough to make him wince. "Our Karl's said he'll run me down to Kendal in the van so we can fetch her Wendy house."

Karl was Lisa's morose, lumbering brother. He and Nick had never got on at the best of times. Nick couldn't imagine things improving now there was no need for a pretended amnesty between them.

He resisted the urge to shove his hands into his pockets like a naughty schoolboy and asked awkwardly, "I...how are you? How's Sophie? Is she—?"

"She's with my mum. We're both fine." Lisa sniffed. "And so are you, by the looks of things."

She cast a last venomous look in Grace's direction, who bore it with polite disinterest, and flounced away.

The silence following Lisa's departure was deafening. Nick sat down again slowly, unable to meet Grace's steady gaze. For a moment, neither of them spoke.

"I'll make it easy for you," Grace said. "Lisa is your girl-friend, I take it, and Sophie is—"

"—our daughter," Nick finished for her. He tried to raise a smile that failed miserably. "She's four. Lisa took her when she walked out on me a couple of weeks ago."

"I see."

He saw her mentally put together the timings and his own temper threatened to make a reappearance. "Look, I'd rather you didn't mention this at work. You know how bad the station is for gossip."

"Yes, I do." There was a faint snap in her voice. Nick realised, somewhat belatedly, that she was probably the last person who'd spread rumours.

"I'm sorry, Grace, that was—"

"Tactless? Offensive? Yes," she said, more lightly now, "it was. But don't worry. Your secret's safe with me." She got to her feet, suddenly seeming very tall and self-assured. She gathered her bag and slipped a folded banknote onto the table, under her glass. "That should take care of my half of lunch. I'll let you know as soon as I have any results back."

But as she moved past him, she paused with her hand on his shoulder and looked straight down into his eyes. "You didn't see Lisa's face when she first saw the two of us," she murmured. "She was angry, certainly, but there was more to it than that." Those hazel eyes flicked over his face, as if searching for duplic-ity. "If *she* walked out on *you*, as you say, I think she might be having second thoughts. So, don't blow your chances, will you? If only for your daughter's sake."

She gave his shoulder a single pat and, with a dazzling smile to the waitress, she left.

Nick slumped back into his seat. Was Lisa really having doubts about leaving him?

The thought of getting little Sophie back made him ecstatic, but as for Lisa herself...? Why didn't the prospect of resuming *that* part of the relationship fill him with the same kind of joy?

Out of the corner of his eye, he watched Grace walk across the car park to the van. And he was honest enough with himself to admit that all he felt was disappointment that he wouldn't be getting to know the red-haired CSI outside of work.

He leaned his elbows on the table and stared into what remained of his drink to mutter under his breath: "Damn."

29

"*Damn!*"

Grace waited until she was behind the wheel before she vented her disappointment in a single quiet expletive, but quickly dismissed the plaintive thought. There was an edge to Nick's mind that she enjoyed and the occasional dinner would have been...pleasant. But she wasn't looking to share her life with anyone.

It had been one of the hardest things to explain to Max. It wasn't just that she no longer wished to be married to *him*, but that she no longer wished to be married at all. He'd even asked for first refusal should she ever change her mind, like they were discussing a painting, or a house. Perhaps that was another reason why she had divorced him.

As she pulled out onto the main road heading towards Kendal, she found herself uninsulted by Lisa's snide comments on her age. Grace was entirely at ease with having turned forty. She suspected the other woman was having a crisis about the big three-oh.

She'd discovered Nick was thirty-two—eight years her junior. An interesting little coincidence, given that Max was eight years her senior.

She'd first met Max at some arts event with her mother at the Theatre By The Lake in Keswick. He hadn't had the means to indulge his passion for art back then, but after a few minutes in his company, she instinctively knew he would achieve whatever goals he set himself. Grace had just emerged from a wishy-washy relationship that she'd mistaken for true love, and to find someone so incisive and unashamedly ambitious was a breath of clear air.

Max had tried to sweep her off her feet—the Italian in him— only to find her remarkably grounded. It had taken him three months to coax her into bed, and another six before she accepted his proposal.

Their interests were similar, they rarely argued, and everyone had assumed they had the perfect marriage. Looking back, Grace realised her own compliance had been partly to blame. Perhaps if she had pushed against him a little harder at the beginning, created a bigger space for herself, she wouldn't have found herself so utterly stifled at the end.

She thought back to Max's invitation to Florence. *Fifteen years,* she thought with just a twinge of regret. She still enjoyed his company, but they were not on their way towards retaking their vows, and a weekend in Italy was likely to have him making plans in that direction.

It was a shame Nick was unavailable. She could have done with a distraction. But a man with those kinds of attachments was definitely out of bounds. She was disappointed that she'd picked up an interested vibe from him. One or other of them should have known better.

It worried her that she'd found him so easy to talk to. *Maybe I just need a friend, someone I can talk to?*

Still, she shouldn't have told him about the robbery case that had started her career, however much she'd left out. He might mention it around the station, or ask Richard Sibson. Someone might tell him the rest of the story...

To say Grace wasn't proud of how it ended was putting it mildly. A month after his acquittal, the robber decided empty domestic property might prove a softer target. Only, the house he'd chosen turned out not to be empty after all. An elderly aunt of the holidaying owners was staying there. Disturbed, the burglar beat her senseless and tied her to a chair. He made his escape, leaving the old lady still bound, terrified and humiliated. Some hours later, she suffered a massive stroke, from which she would never recover.

Painstaking forensic investigation had tied the criminal to the crime, layer on layer, irrefutable.

It was Max who'd pointed out the newspaper story. Grace was never sure why. Perhaps he'd hoped to discourage her from dabbling, send her scurrying back to the safety of hearth and home. Instead, it was what finally drove her away.

Now, her hands tightened on the steering wheel, trying to force the memories out of her mind. She tried to concentrate on the girl, Edith. If she was allowed to slip through the cracks, who knows what disaster might be waiting to happen there?

Grace frowned over how best to approach her as she dropped down the hill into Kendal. She navigated the one-way system through the town centre, crossing over the River Kent and climbing the twisting road towards Grayrigg and Tebay.

It was just as she neared Grayrigg that she caught sight of a sign set back into the ivy surrounding what might have been a farm entrance. The Retreat.

Something jogged her memory. She checked the mirror and hit the brakes before backing up a few yards on the deserted road to turn into the driveway.

Edith works here, she remembered. *No harm in calling in, is there?*

30

BARDWELL RECOGNISED the tall redhead as soon as she climbed out of her vehicle in the middle of the farmyard. When he'd heard her approach, he was towelling himself dry from the shower, needing to clean up. Now, his hands faltered.

So, the girl sold me out anyway. It was all for nothing.

He'd certainly expected her to. What rational person wouldn't go straight to the police after seeing a man stalking with a gun? After being half strangled by him?

Even as the thought formed, the logical side of his brain dismissed it. Edith was far from rational, and if she'd called anyone for help before knocking so boldly on his door, it would not have been this woman. Even from his distant observation, Bardwell knew the redhead was some kind of technician, not a detective.

No, it would have been the heavy mob.

Still watching her, he dumped the towel and shrugged into a fresh shirt, the slide of well-washed cotton soothing against his skin.

The redhead turned a slow circle in the middle of the empty yard, taking in everything with a minute attention that disturbed him. She seemed to stare longest at the byre. He told himself it was the only one showing signs of occupation, not some darker reason. He'd brought the Land Rover out of the barn and left it outside his door, everything normal. Bardwell opened the kitchen door.

"Help you?" he called across the yard, keeping it neutral, neither unfriendly nor encouraging her to linger.

She was frowning as if something bothered her, and swivelled at the sound of his voice, advanced a few steps.

"Hello," she said, calm and easy, not intimidated by the size of him. "I'm looking for Edith Airey. I understand she works here. Is she about?"

Bardwell shrugged. "Dunno." He jerked his head towards the farmhouse. "If she's not up there, she'll have gone home by now, likely as not."

She gave him a nod and a brief smile. "Thanks," she said. "I'll give it a try."

Bardwell retreated inside while she made her fruitless journey. Motionless, he was still watching when she returned to her vehicle minutes later. She looked around again, nosy, before driving slowly out of the yard.

As she disappeared from view, he took a deep breath. Somehow, disaster had been averted. The gun was secure, the threat neutralised. Now, all he had to do was concentrate on the job at hand.

So why couldn't he clear that image of the woman with the fox-red hair? The first time he'd seen her was through the scope of his rifle. It forged an intimate connection that would not be broken, whether she was aware of it or not.

Their paths would cross again. The patterns swirled and solidified inside Bardwell's head. *I'll make sure of that.*

PART III

31

NICK STOOD by the bedroom window of the flat he'd shared with Lisa, arms folded, hands clenched, glaring down into the car park. It was his first Saturday off in weeks and this wasn't how he'd envisaged spending it—watching Lisa's lumbering brother, Karl, struggling to load Sophie's brightly coloured Wendy house into the back of a borrowed box Luton van.

It would have been easier to dismantle the awkward structure; it came apart in a few minutes if you knew how. But Nick's offer to help had been roughly rejected.

Lisa was supervising, getting in the way, and Karl's two boys —thugs in the making—were running riot across the flowerbeds. What else was new? They'd always regarded him, his profession, with a fearless insolence. Definite trouble there for the future.

Now, Karl came stamping up into the flat, Lisa following him in.

"That everything?" Karl's triumph only slightly tempered by the sweat of his exertions. Nick was thankful for that, if nothing else.

Nick had preferred being on an upper storey, and not just for security. There were nicer views, and it was better not to have neighbours overhead. Even though Sophie was no longer in her pushchair Lisa had still complained about the climb.

Well, she doesn't have to worry about that anymore, does she?

"I think that's it for the moment." Lisa wouldn't meet Nick's eyes. She gestured vaguely around the flat; the gaps on the bookshelf, the half-empty CD rack, the space where the microwave used to stand. "We'll sort out the rest some other time, Nick, yeah?"

"Yeah, sure." He shoved his hands into the pockets of his jeans and found he couldn't meet her eyes, either. "Whatever."

"Need to be off, Leese," Karl said, brisk, picking up the grubby sweatshirt he'd discarded earlier across the back of the cream linen sofa. "Promised the boss I'd have the van back before twelve." He pulled out his cigarettes, stuck one in his mouth but knew better than to light up in front of Nick.

"Yeah, OK, I'll be down in a minute."

Karl frowned, as if not wanting to leave them alone together. Nick gave him his best Moss Side cop stare.

"I'll be in the van," Karl mumbled.

They listened to his heavy feet on the stairs. It was a wonder the old building had survived. Nick could hear him yelling for the boys as he reached the outer door on the ground floor. Lisa still hadn't spoken.

Eventually, she sighed and pushed her hair back, then folded her arms, defensive, across her chest.

"Look, Nick, we need to get some things sorted out."

"Sorted how?" *You left. That sorted it.*

Another sigh, like she was being reasonable and he was being deliberately difficult. "About Sophie."

"Visiting rights, you mean?"

Her eyes slid away again. "No, child support."

Nick felt his chest tighten, something boil behind his eyes.

"Yeah," he said, a metallic taste in his mouth. "Yeah, right."

"You know you can see Sophie whenever you want." She tried a little smile, reaching. "'Course you can. She's your daughter, too, isn't she?"

Nick's gaze swept across the flat, stripped bare of a child's presence. "Is she?" he said, bitter, without thinking.

Lisa's face dropped through disbelief straight into anger like a stolen car off a quarry edge. Her hand snaked out, cracked hard across his cheek. A flashbulb went off somewhere close to his left eye as his head snapped back, riding the worse of it.

"You *bastard!*" she hissed, and slammed the door on her way out, hard enough to rattle the glass in the kitchen cabinets.

Well, I guess I deserved that, didn't I?

Nick slowly put a hand to his face. It was going to leave a bruise; they'd love that at work. *Better ice it.*

But as he turned away he caught sight of a smear on the back of the sofa, where Karl's sweatshirt had been.

That grubby little…

But when he looked closer, Nick realised it wasn't a stain. Face forgotten, he fetched a zip-lock sandwich bag from the kitchen and a pair of tweezers from the First Aid kit above the bathroom sink. Very carefully, he gathered a sample and sealed the bag, holding it up to the light and shaking the contents gently.

Unless he was very much mistaken, he'd just picked up dog hairs. Grace had found dog hairs at the crime scene in Staveley. It was lurking at the back of his mind. And much as he knew it was a very long shot, a part of him would cheer long and loud if, by some freak of chance, they turned out to be a match.

The rational half of his brain took over and his stomach sank. Because, if they did, the kind of problems *that* was going to cause, both personal and professional, didn't bear thinking about.

"So," he said aloud into the empty flat, "what else can go wrong today?"

32

FOURTEEN MILES NORTHEAST OF KENDAL, on a flat, rough-mown field that ran alongside the River Eden above Tebay, the agricultural show was moving into full swing. Giles Frederickson cast a critical eye over his cadets as they scrambled across the main arena, setting out obstacles for the dog agility classes. *Not a bad performance,* he decided, *but they could have done with another week's practice.*

In his time Frederickson had been involved in all manner of events from the Royal Tournament to the Winter Olympics. He tended to measure all other public displays by those standards and was rarely entirely satisfied. *Still, not bad.*

He recognised that the cadets were not responsible for his general ill temper. Even after he'd learned that the police were not going to pursue the shooting, he'd still told Angela it was time to end the affair. Besides, after today they wouldn't have a legitimate reason to liaise quite so regularly and openly. Not without her dim-witted husband beginning to suspect.

The major still derived a certain satisfaction from the fact that Angela had given her husband's gift—the dog—to her lover. And the poor cuckold had actually been grateful to him for having Ben taken off their hands. *If only he knew.*

He'd find Angela hard to forget. Under that icy exterior, she'd proved to be a woman of passion and stamina. *Thank God for Viagra,* he thought. He had no illusions that he was her first infidelity, nor any more than a fleeting diversion, but he liked to think she hadn't been ready to let him go just yet. He'd learned things in the Far East that Western women seemed to find surprising in bed, and Angela had been no exception.

She'd assumed, scornfully, that coming under police scrutiny had made him turn tail, and he hadn't disillusioned her. True, he'd been concerned about DC Weston. Frederickson could recognise a born hunter when he came across one. If he hadn't been told to let it lie, who knows what the detective might have uncovered?

"Ah, Giles, *there* you are. I was beginning to think you were avoiding me," Angela Inglis's voice stroked a nerve down the major's spine.

He turned. She looked perfect, as always, poised and cool despite the muggy summer heat, in a pale green dress that might have been raw silk, deceptively simple and ending demurely at the knee.

"Have you met Max Carri?" she asked, before he could speak. "Max is one of our wonderful sponsors."

The public address system blared into life at that moment, calling all junior Working Hunter competitors to make their way to the collecting ring, and judges in the floral arrangement category to the handicrafts marquee.

The interruption gave Frederickson a chance to study the man whose arm his former mistress grasped with such a light yet proprietary touch. Sweet-talking sponsors had been very much Angela's bag, so he'd heard about Carri but hadn't met him during the run-up to the show. He wasn't pleased by what he saw.

In contrast to the tweeds and florals so beloved of the natives, the man wore a Panama hat and a cream linen suit with the careless flair of someone who spent a good deal of time and money on his wardrobe. In Frederickson's instantly formed opinion, he was altogether too sleek, too smug, too...predatory.

Frederickson didn't like the purr of satisfaction in Angela's voice, either. Nor the fact that the two of them looked well matched.

Replaced me so easily, have you?

Carri, meanwhile, returned the scrutiny with only a twitch at the corner of his mouth giving away some inner amusement. Frederickson squared his shoulders inside his dress uniform and held out a leather-gloved hand. Carri shook it without any attempt at bone-crushing heroics.

"I must say, Angela's been singing your praises," Carri said.

Frederickson had been half-expecting an Italian accent to go with the colouring and the name, but the voice was classlessly English. *Elocution lessons,* he thought nastily.

"She's too kind." Frederickson's voice was bland.

"You've certainly got your boys well drilled." Carri nodded to the swarm of cadets. He gave a rueful smile. "If only my people could work with such coordination, I'd be a rich man."

"Oh, Max." Angela gave a breathy laugh. "You *are* a rich man."

He gave a self-deprecating shrug. "Comfortable, certainly. Enough to keep the wolf from the door and for indulgences such as this." He smiled at her and Frederickson felt his hands tighten. "But what's paying for a few trophies and a token of prize money without all your hard work to make the whole thing happen?"

Angela fluttered at the praise. Then, duty done, and possibly objective achieved, she began to turn away, stopping only to favour Frederickson with a final, gracious smile. "You'll join us in the refreshments marquee for lunch, Giles, of course?"

So I can watch you fawn over him some more? "No, I don't think so." He offered a slight smile to take the sting out of the refusal, nodding to the cadets. "Have to keep an eye on my chaps if everything's to run to schedule. The timings are pretty tight. Thank you, anyway."

To her credit, she managed to conjure disappointment. "We'll need you on the main stage for the prize-giving," she said firmly. "Three o'clock sharp. No excuses."

"No, ma'am. I'll be there."

33

"Richard, can I run something by you?"

Thirty miles away, at his desk in the Hunter Lane station, Richard Sibson looked up to find Grace in the office doorway.

He eyed the papers in her hand. "Does it involve looking at pictures of naked women who are not actually dead?"

Grace smiled. "Now I understand why you're working on a Saturday morning. You really ought to get out more."

He grunted, holding out a peremptory hand for the sheet. "Oh, let's have it, McColl."

"You remember I did an FDR test on Edith Airey?" she began.

Sibson pushed his chair back and let out what might be mistaken for an annoyed breath. "You're not still on that, are you? Did you not get the message from on high that we were to take no further action?"

"Of course. And I paid absolute attention to it," she said, unperturbed. "But I'd already sent the residue I collected from Edith off to the lab, together with a sample of the .22 ammunition we retrieved from her parents' house. Don't give me that look—you know as well as I do that it's standard procedure."

"Yes, yes, all right. And?"

"They don't entirely match." She finally relinquished the printout. "There was no doubt Edith had been shooting that morning, as she claimed, but the residue I recovered from her hands and hair had additional indicators to those present in the bullets she gave us."

Sibson frowned, intrigued in spite of himself. "Different batch perhaps?" he suggested.

"The box was half used." Grace hesitated fractionally. "I wondered if it might have been a different gun."

Sibson shrugged and handed the papers back. "Water under the bridge now." He started to turn back to his desk, paused and glanced back at her. "Weren't you going to have a quiet word, anyway? You and Weston thought there might be some funny stuff going on at home, I believe?"

"Mm. I called in at her work a few days ago, on my way back from the Staveley break-in, but she'd already gone, apparently. I've tried her at home a couple of times since, but no joy. I'll try again this afternoon, perhaps. Might stand more chance at the weekend."

"Speaking of the Staveley job, I've another just come in." Sibson searched his desk for the paperwork. "Ambleside this time, which should be a pleasant little run out for you. Looks like the same MO—repair shop, four quads taken this time, sometime during the night. Our little gang of bike thieves is getting more ambitious."

Grace took the sheet he offered and managed, he noted, to suppress her dismay at the prospect of having to fight her way through the weekend tourist traffic. "All right, I'm on my way," she murmured, scanning the page as she turned for the door. "And this could just mean they're using a larger van."

Sibson watched her leave, not shifting his gaze as she walked down the corridor until she reached the staircase and disappeared from sight.

ROAD SAFETY! I'll give 'em road safety!

Jim Airey sweated inside his stab vest and helmet as he manned the Cumbria Constabulary display at the back of the main arena. Black was not the colour to be wearing in this heat and there was no shade, unless he lurked behind the raised stage affair where they were going to present the prizes.

Airey resented being asked to cover events like the agricultural show. Waste of his time and expertise when, in his opinion, he could be out catching real criminals. That was his kind of work.

Danny Robertshaw came ambling towards him across the cropped grass, sucking an ice cream with a flake in it. It had melted down the sides of the cornet and dribbled across his hand. He held it awkwardly so it didn't drip onto his uniform, stopping every few yards to lick his fingers, and only succeeding in spreading the ice cream around his mouth like a five-year-old.

Airey rolled his eyes. *Least it's not chocolate.*

"All right?" Robertshaw called as he approached. "Anything exciting been happening?"

"What do *you* think?" Airey eyed the gooey mess sulkily. "And where's mine?"

A LITTLE OVER A MILE AWAY, eye hovering behind the Unertl sight, Patrick Bardwell tracked the young policeman's progress until he disappeared from view.

He lay behind the long gun in a hollowed-out hide that veed into the hillside above Bowderdale. A latticework of spindly branches holding up a roof made from turf cut from beneath him. In front was a partial curtain of nettles. From above, even close to, he blended into the terrain almost perfectly. Just a narrow pocket, like he'd opened up a piece of the earth and slipped inside, safe as the womb. Did it all before the sun came up. They'd have to be almost on top of him before they realised he was there.

Not that anyone was looking.

With the benefit of the hide, Bardwell had abandoned his ghillie suit. Good job, the way he was sweating. Instead, he wore nondescript hiking clothes, same as a thousand others out on the Lakeland fells on a Saturday in June when the weather hung slumberous and heavy.

Three water canteens were stacked by his right hand; two full and one sacrificed onto the hard-packed ground just in front of the muzzle to damp the telltale dust from the flare. The canteen had a wide mouth, too, just in case the need arose. Not that Bard-well expected he'd have to use it. Wouldn't be there long enough. But if so, a full bladder was a distraction he could do without.

He had the familiar feeling of slipping outside his skin, acutely aware of the atmosphere around him, of each lazy breath of wind that ruffled the grass between his position and the killing ground beyond. Everything else narrowed down, filtered out like distant background chatter as other senses came to prominence. It always happened, the outside world softening down until the only thing he could see clearly was the target, and even the beat of his own heart matched the trance-like pace he'd set. They'd tried to explain it to him as a form of self-protection, so he could make each kill without the reality of it troubling his conscience.

He'd nodded, impatient to be done with them, but in truth, he'd never had any trouble in that regard.

Even so, he recognised that this one was different. This was not the result of orders passed down, of tactical objectives decided further up the chain, of risks evaluated by some nerdy little analyst crouched safe in a bunker, miles from the fight.

This was *his* choice. He was here because he wanted to be. Because he'd promised. Because it needed to be done. And the only unexpected factor, the only thing that might possibly have compromised him, he'd dealt with.

"Well?" he demanded, gruff. "What can you see?"

Cramped alongside him, Edith Airey lifted her eyes away from the spotter's scope, blinked a few times as her sight adjusted to the dim closeness. She was wearing old jeans and the camouflage jacket she used for hunting rabbits, a pair of ear defenders bunched awkwardly on top of her head.

In the confined space he could almost smell her excitement.

"Everything." Her voice was filled with a fierce wonder. "I can see everything."

36

"WHAT CAN YOU SEE?" he asked again.

Edith twisted the focusing ring on the scope, the way he'd shown her, and the picture snapped into bright, hard, clean definition. Across the centre of the reticle was a graduated scale, marked in mil dots for calculating the range.

"Wow." She glanced past the scope, as if to satisfy herself that they really *were* all that distance from the field where the agricultural show was taking place. Without the ten-power magnification, the tents and banners and milling crowds of people and animals were reduced to tiny toy-town figures. She ducked back behind the lens. "I can count the hairs up their noses with this."

She'd been hoping for some kind of reaction from the man lying beside her, but Bardwell didn't laugh, didn't even smile, like he should have. *Weren't they partners now?*

She flitted her eyes sideways again, watching him, absorbing his total concentration. Even his voice was different, as though he'd shut down everything that didn't relate directly to the operation of the gun, facial muscles included.

———

WHEN SHE'D STEPPED into the byre that day to deliver her ultimatum, Edith hadn't known quite what to expect. It wasn't until later that she realised he could have just finished what he'd started in the barn, buried her body way out somewhere remote.

Then what would she be; just another teenage runaway? Her parents certainly wouldn't have kicked up much of a fuss, that's for sure.

But as soon as she'd crossed the threshold, she'd sensed the grief in him, the fear. And for the first time, she was aware of her own power. He was frightened of her. Of what she might do. She held his fate in her hands.

As soon as that realisation hit, Edith knew what she wanted from him. She'd only caught a glimpse of the long gun, that day out on Orton Scar, but it wasn't something she'd forget in a hurry. Not the weapon or the day.

She'd thought the AK was a monster compared to her puny Gaucher, but this was another world altogether and suddenly she wanted—craved—to be part of it.

"Show it to me," she'd commanded, regal, like a queen, and silently he'd done her bidding, shambling, defeated by the weight of expectation. That she'd turn him in for what he'd done already. For what he was so clearly about to do.

When she'd seen the Barrett in all its glory for the first time, when he'd fetched it and laid it out for her, the awe hit Edith so hard she could barely breathe. She'd stood there, in the tiny living room of the cottage where she'd cleaned for him every week, unnoticed and unthanked, and felt the balance of her whole life begin to turn.

"I want to be there," she said. "When you shoot. That's what you're about, isn't it?"

He'd shaken his head, sunk in on himself even more.

"Why?" Edith hated the whine in her own voice. "Why can't I be there?"

He lifted his head, stared at her with dead eyes. "Not your fight. No turning back from this, and you got a life ahead."

Edith had felt the tears come again. Who'd have thought she'd so much crying in her? "What life?" she wailed. "If you hadn't stopped me, I'd be done with it by now."

That scored a bullseye, she could tell. No idle threat from a hysterical girl. A reality he'd seen with his own eyes. Ruthless, she used it.

"If you turn me away now, I promise you I'll be dead by tomorrow. As dead as if you'd kept your hands round my throat and kept on squeezing." It sounded dramatic inside her head.

Too dramatic when it came out. She sank onto the sofa, perched there on the stone-hard cushions. "Please?" she said again, meekly. "I can help you. Let me help you."

He'd turned without a word, without a flicker, and walked out of the living room, back towards the bedroom where he'd had the rifle tucked away. Edith put her face in her hands, filled with a bleak terror that she'd have to go through with it now.

She waited, wiped her nose across the back of her hand, sniffed a little. Then heard his returning footsteps and couldn't bring herself to look up until he dumped something heavy in a cylindrical nylon bag into her startled lap.

"Sniper needs a spotter. I'll show you how to use that in the morning. Not got much time."

In surprise, in gratitude, Edith jumped up, flung her arms around his neck to hug him like a favourite uncle. Just for a moment, he recoiled and she flinched. Wasn't Mr Hogg always telling her how careful she had to be around his 'guests'? How *damaged* they were.

But then he trembled slightly, gathered her up and she felt the soft scratch of his beard against her hair, the heave of his chest. And Edith saw the moment of his weakness, that he wanted her.

"Oh, *Patrick*," she breathed, and kissed him.

It was a frantic kiss, on her part at least, filled with desperation. For a few long seconds, his mouth felt lax under hers, then began to move. And once it had, it was like she'd broken something free inside him. One big hand splayed across the small of her back, hauling her against him, leaving Edith in no doubt of his desire for her.

This is how it's supposed to be, she realised, exultant, as he swung her up, shoved her back until the wall bumped the breath out of her body, moulding it to fit his. Not the immature boys she'd fumbled with until now. *A real man!*

She grappled with his trousers, whimpering, urging him towards the bedroom before he came to his senses. The prospect of doing it—completely naked in a real bed—was a rarity that only heightened Edith's surge of lust.

Sex had always been a journey rather than a destination, searching for something it was never going to give her. And then she'd learned, only a week ago, what they were calling her behind her back.

Danny Robertshaw, who'd dazzled her with the uniform but proved no more adept than the teenage boys she'd been with before him. Maybe she shouldn't have made that plain, but he'd no right to go branding her the village bike.

The final straw...

She hadn't expected Patrick's body to impress her. He was old, after all, but when he shrugged out of his shirt she discovered a torso slabbed in well-defined muscle and no hint of a soft belly. In fact, everything about him was hard.

There was a driven intensity to him. Once he'd thrown back the covers he hardly even kissed her, turning her, his breath shaky against the back of her neck. No words other than a murmured, "I need you."

After that, she didn't care how rough he was. It all happened fast. As he forced a heavy hand between her legs, Edith fluttered a protest, stiffening in shocked pleasure at the accuracy of his manipulation, back arching in reflex. It was all the invitation he needed. He grasped her hips with callused hands and drove in deep.

Afterwards, he wept in quiet sorrow while Edith, no longer his inferior, cradled him close.

She'd thought she heard a vehicle arriving when she was in his shower, was suddenly mortified that Mr Hogg might catch them, but Patrick told her it was nobody.

And as she was leaving he'd put a hand under her chin, tipped her face up to kiss her, hard, on the mouth.

"Mess me about, Edith," he said, soft yet cold, face blank, "and I'll keep your promise for you. All right?"

She'd ridden the little scooter home in a daze, almost ran off the road twice. And that night, after her parents were snoring in their beds, she'd gluttoned out, eaten everything in the secret stash under the loose boards in her bedroom. Eaten it until she thought her stomach would burst, then brought it all back, heaving silently in the shadowed darkness, knelt shivering on the bathroom lino, clinging to the bowl.

At the end of it, she'd felt only a kind of peace, cleansed by the ritual. In control. Not just of her own life, but the fate of someone else's, too. All kinds of possibilities bloomed so hard, so fast, she could hear nothing for the roaring of them unfolding through her mind.

————

"FIND A REFERENCE," Bardwell said now in that hoarse voice. "Give me a range."

Chastened, Edith panned across the show field, hastily selecting and dismissing objects. In the competitors' parking area were row after row of big fancy four-wheel drives with horse trailers behind, drawn up like a battle fleet. Any number to choose from.

"Range Rover—that do you?"

Bardwell barely seemed to move. "Too far. Find me something closer to the target."

Edith slid the scope back, across a flash of coloured ponies, summer hats, balloons and candy floss, to the openness of the main arena where the cadets scurried to rearrange poles and wings and bits of brushwood to some grand plan. She moved on, caught something and moved back.

There!

"What about that big showjump—the red wall? Right in the centre. It's got to be six foot at the ends. That do you?"

Bardwell shifted slightly. "That'll do," he murmured. "Nearly time."

37

"COME ON, LADS!" Frederickson's voice boomed out of the speakers dotted around the main arena. "Twelve minutes precisely to the start of the next class. Look sharp!"

Inside the commentary post, Frederickson put down the PA microphone and wiped his dripping forehead. Outside the dusty glass, the cadets did their best to rally, adding a final row of hollow wooden blocks to bring the red showjumping wall up to height. First thing this morning they'd been racing across the grass like young pups. Now they could barely manage a jog.

Ice creams all round after this, cold drinks and a rest in the shade. Got to have the carrot as well as the stick.

Not that it was any cooler inside the commentary post. A grand title for little more than a thin plywood sweatbox on wheels. Even with the door propped back and the front windows wide open, it was suffocating inside.

The elderly retired colonel who'd been landed with the commentary for the entire event had been only too happy to relinquish his position to a lesser rank while they rearranged the course. Frederickson had last seen him heading for the beer tent with the dogged determination of a man on a forced march through the desert.

He studied the course plan with a frown of annoyance. Left to him, the layout would have been much simpler, much easier to change between the horse and pony classes and the dog agility display. As it was, they'd wasted valuable time recon-

structing part of the course halfway through the day. It felt...
untidy. *Typical civilian operation.*

"Still hard at it, I see, Major Frederickson."

He glanced across, found Max Carri halfway up the short
flight of steps leading to the box. The man had one hand in his
pocket so it pulled his jacket back with studied jauntiness, classic
Wayfarer sunglasses covering his eyes under the brim of his hat.

"Yes," Frederickson said with an icy smile. He felt the floor
rock a little as Carri moved to stand alongside him, and was
absurdly pleased to note the other man was the shorter by an
inch or two, even with the hat. He'd intended to be politely but
firmly dismissive and when it became clear this tactic had failed,
he stifled a sigh and looked up again.

Carri removed his sunglasses, hooked them into his handkerchief pocket. He had dark eyes with very long lashes, which he
kept fixed on the frantic work of the cadets out in the arena,
fanning himself with the Panama.

"Angela Inglis is a remarkable woman," he said at last,
without inflection.

"Yes," Frederickson said, in kind, "she is."

"I find her company...stimulating. But I wanted to reassure
you that I have no designs on her."

Frederickson stiffened. "Mrs Inglis is happily married," he
said, aware of his own pomposity.

"So? I was also very happily married—right up until my
divorce." Carri looked at him directly, amused now. "There's
something in her voice when she talks about you. You might
want to mention that to her, just in case her husband is more
perceptive than you give him credit."

"You'll excuse me for speaking plainly, I trust?" Frederickson
said, frosty, "but I hardly think it's any of your business."

"Oh, of course not."

Carri inclined his head and slipped the Panama back on. His
eyes shifted beyond the glass and Frederickson turned to see
Angela approaching.

"I thought I might find the two of you conspiring together."
She arched one brow.

"I was just admiring the major's technique," Carri said
smoothly as he came down the steps. He nodded to the cadets,

now converging wearily on the commentary post. "Looks like his crew are all finished. They've done a marvellous job."

"Oh, I couldn't agree more," Angela said with a little sideways glance. "In which case, Giles, you've no excuse not to join us in the refreshment tent, after all, have you?"

As Frederickson climbed down himself, he flicked his eyes over Carri again, but the man had retreated behind his sunglasses. Their dark green lenses gave nothing away.

It was stupid to be jealous, Frederickson knew, but he couldn't help it. Perhaps that was why he found himself saying, "Naturally," as Angela stepped forwards to take the arm Carri courteously offered.

He'd surprised them. Frederickson hid a dark satisfaction as he turned away, issuing brief instructions for the cadets to get themselves something to eat and drink. They scattered with renewed enthusiasm.

Then, with a wave of his arm, he indicated the arena, dominated by the red showjumping wall in the centre. The refreshment tent was directly opposite the commentary post on the other side.

"Shall we take a shortcut?"

"THAT'S OUR TARGET!"

Edith wanted to be cool and deadly. Instead, her voice came out like a Yorkshire terrier high on caffeine.

"Where?" Calm and slow.

"Middle of the arena. Group of three. There. *There!* Near the red wall thing."

"Clock face, boy, remember?" His voice was a low growl, still unhurried, his movements delicate.

"Oh, yeah, um, ten o'clock?"

"Asking or telling?"

"Ten o'clock! I'm telling you, aren't I? Ten o'clock."

"Got it. Range?"

The mil dots on the reticle of the spotter's scope were at a pre-set distance, Edith knew. If you knew the size of the object you were observing, it was an easy calculation to work out the range and vice versa.

But, now, she fumbled through the mental arithmetic, terrified of getting it wrong. She'd been good at maths at school— another useless talent. Until now.

"Eighteen hundred and thirty," she said, breathless, and glowed when Bardwell didn't even question it.

"Air temp?"

She read off the gauge from the probe that sat sheltered outside.

"Ears up," he said.

BARDWELL HAD no need of the amateur information provided by the warm body to his left. Boy, girl, they left only a hazy impression, like a graphics rendering. Outline only, nebulous and indistinct.

Through the rifle's own scope, he could work out the range from the size of a standing man without anyone's help. Done it often enough, and these were easier than most. They weren't prepared for the possibility of a sniper. Dug in, fortified, running between their sandbagged enclosures bent over and jinking like chased hares.

The targets he observed now walked slow and unhurried, stopping for minutes at a time, standing, chatting, as if taunting him with the brazenness of their own exposure.

As for the atmospheric conditions, he knew with ingrained instinct what effect the current temperature and the humidity would have on the shot. He'd absorbed the landscape between hide and target and read the intervening crosswind with narrowed eyes, taking in every ruffle of the grass, every shiver of the trees. He waited for the rhythm of nature to make itself clear, to find the lull before each breath. Art, as much as science.

Just before, he closed his eyes, let out a long exhale, opened them again. His dominant right eye was still settled close up behind the scope. The sight picture hadn't changed. His position was perfect.

And then, between heartbeats, Bardwell's right forefinger

tightened on the trigger.

Most shooters, he knew, were totally ignorant of what happened between the moment the finger squeezed the trigger, and the bullet left the gun. He was not. An almost-subliminal chain reaction went through his head every single time.

The leap of the hammer, the firing pin striking the primer cap with effortless precision. Its delicate mix of chemicals igniting, flaming through to the main charge. The instantaneous explosion.

Obturation. The superheated gases expanding at an exponential rate within the confines of the cartridge case; the casing itself deforming to create an airtight seal against the wall of the firing chamber and loosening its grip on the bullet.

The projectile launching into the constriction of the barrel; swaging to fit as it forces through the tapered aperture; moulding to the internal contours, engaging with the rifling to gain maximum acceleration from the erupting gases backed up behind it. The round branding itself with the distinctive lands and grooves along its length that tie it uniquely to the weapon from which it's fired.

In this case, the barrel of the rifle has twelve grooves with a right-hand twist. The rotation generated is a finely balanced compromise between the round's velocity, stability, and ultimate penetrative power.

And the round itself is no ordinary bullet. The outer copper-nickel jacket is precision-milled on a CNC lathe. The inner core is lead, with a hollow cavity in the nose, helping to shift its centre of gravity rearwards.

The ultra-precise profile produces very low drag, flattening the round's trajectory, reducing its lateral drift in crosswind, and causing it to decelerate less rapidly in flight, so that it arrives at its point of impact with its maximum kinetic energy intact.

By the time the half-inch diameter projectile spits from the end of the Barrett's muzzle, it is travelling at a shade under two thousand miles an hour—almost tri-sonic. Born amid a rage of conflagration and on its way. Dazzlingly lethal, superbly streamlined, it will arrive at its target, more than a mile distant, in a sliver under two seconds, towing its soundwave a fraction behind.

The recoil as the trigger broke slammed the butt back into Bardwell's shoulder. A kick like a World Cup Final striker presented with an open goal. Bardwell momentarily lost the sight picture.

By the time he reacquired it, there was nothing left to see.

MAX CARRI never knew what hit him.

One moment he was crossing the main arena with Angela Inglis on his arm, glancing back to smile blandly at Major Frederickson. The next he was on the ground, blinded, dazed, choking.

He thrashed feebly, a beetle on its back, not understanding why he couldn't rise or how he'd fallen. He couldn't see, couldn't open his eyes. One arm was pinned and there was something heavy across his legs. Distantly, muffled, he thought he heard screaming. His brain reeled, thought processes slurring.

A bomb? Never a far away assumption now, after the Twin Towers, Madrid, the London Underground. *Am I dead? Is that why there's no pain?*

"OHMIGOD," Edith muttered, over and over, in a small scared whisper.

"Status?" Bardwell demanded, still tight and controlled. Through her ear defenders, she could hear no hate or triumph in his voice. It was flat and level.

How can he do that? How can he bring about such destruction and it mean nothing to him? She stole a sideways glance at the gun, still now after its violent spasm and the far-reaching pandemonium.

"Is the target down?"

Edith jerked out of it, fumbled with the scope.

"Down?" she repeated, tongue suddenly thick in her mouth, a spreading fire in her belly that she recognised as exultation. "Oh yeah, the target's down all right. The target is blown away."

Bardwell nodded without satisfaction. "Then we're done here."

"GET UP, MAN! UP, *UP!*"

Carri responded to the command without assimilating the words. His struggles increased, almost frantic, until a hand grasped his elbow, wrenched him upward, then a shoulder ducked under his arm and forced him into a flat run across the rough ground, matching him stride for stride.

Still blinded, Carri's feet tripped and twisted. He went down as far as his knees, jolting away what little breath he had left. His rescuer dragged him on by sheer will, calmly furious. Then other hands grasped his arm, his shoulder, swung him round and shoved him down onto the ground again.

More voices, high with stress, panic. Through the ground beneath him, Carri felt the thunder of horses' feet somewhere nearby, plunging to escape an unexpected danger that plugged straight into their primal instinct. An instinct that told them to run like hell.

They weren't the only ones. Carri heard sobbing and was abruptly thankful, as well as terrified, that he couldn't see.

A hand scooped under the back of his neck, tilted his head. "Eyes tight shut, sir," the voice said, shaky. "Let's get the worst of this off you."

Carri flinched as liquid was poured onto his face. It was tepid, fizzing like acid on his skin. For a moment he panicked afresh before his sense of smell kicked in. Cola, he realised, sticky and cloying. Any port in a storm.

A stiff cloth scraped clumsily at his face, dragging at his eyelids, and at last he could open his eyes. As he did so, the cola ran in, biting and clinging, and that finally brought him round. He fought his way up to sitting, tipped his head forwards, tried to rub his eyes. Someone grabbed his hand to prevent him.

"Here, use this." Balled-up cloth was thrust into his reach and Carri blotted his face until the discomfort passed. He lifted his head timidly, blinking, discovered he could see colours. *Thank God!* Shapes solidified into a red cloth, scuffed brown earth, and the dark uniform of a young policeman who was bending over him, white faced, perhaps a tinge of green.

Behind him, another copper was crouched low, eyes darting, shouting into his radio, scared and excited both at the same time. They were in the shadow of the stage, a dozen of them, strangers, shivering like vampires hiding from sunlight.

"Where are you injured?" the young copper asked.

Carri opened his mouth, shut it again. "I'm fine," he said. *Ridiculous. I've just been blown up. How the hell can I be fine?*

The policeman's face said he thought the same, but didn't say it out loud.

Carri turned over the red cloth in his hands, searching for a dry patch. Underneath, it was pale blue. He froze. Then he stretched out his hands and found they matched the cloth. Red, as if dipped in paint, past his wrists and right the way up his arms. A deep, rich, glossy, glistening red.

Blood red.

The smell of the slaughterhouse hit Carri like a punch in the stomach. He reeled sideways, heaving. The young policeman lurched backwards, nearly overbalanced out of shelter. The other policeman lunged with creditable speed for a fat man, grabbed his colleague's stab vest and yanked him back again.

The younger copper landed hard on his rump, eyes wide, gasping.

"Wh–who—?" Carri began, dizzy, the dread curling through him, but the policemen's attention was elsewhere.

Major Frederickson came sliding round the edge of the stage at a dead run, feet first, bundling a pair of petrified cadets in front of him. He stuffed the boys down and crabbed over to the two policemen, eyes everywhere.

"That's the last of them," he said, taut with fury. A dark stain was splashed up the front of his dress uniform, a crusted smear across his cheekbone, soaked in along his shoulders.

He's the one who got me up, Carri thought with grudging admiration. He looked at the others. "But where's—?"

Frederickson shot him a narrowed glance, and all at once he knew.

My God. Angela...

"Didn't you see?" Frederickson demanded.

"See what?" Carri found himself floundering, fear turning to anger. "Listen, chum, I didn't see a damn thing. What *happened* out there?"

"At a guess?" Frederickson said. "Sniper. Somewhere further up the valley towards the high ground, I imagine. Best part of a mile, from the delay."

He leaned sideways to take a cautious look across the deserted arena. Beyond him, Carri could see the scattered debris left behind by a stampeding crowd—bags, food, even clothing, hats, the occasional walking stick as the lame miraculously found themselves able to run. Shivering little groups of humanity were huddled behind any solid object they could find, horses left to run loose.

"Cavalry's on its way, so let's all sit tight until they get here, yeah?" The fat policeman let go of his radio and edged in closer. "They're sending out the chopper."

"I'd tell them to keep it back, if I were you." Frederickson pulled off his gloves, used them to scrub his face. His peaked cap was gone and he looked older, his skin grey in the shaded light.

"Sir, I think you can leave this to the experts—"

"In a situation like this I *am* an expert!" the major snapped. "Use your head, man. Mrs Inglis was shot by someone with a high-powered rifle. A *very* high-powered rifle. She damn near disintegrated before my eyes."

His gaze flicked over Carri. *And into mine,* Carri thought and nearly heaved afresh. Frederickson seemed to see the weakness, despise it, turned back to the policeman.

"What do you think something with that kind of penetrative power is going to do to a civilian aircraft?"

The fat policeman's face turned ashen. He lifted his radio again.

PART IV

43

"How did you know?" Nick asked.

Giles Frederickson didn't reply at once. He was leaning against one of the police Armed Response Vehicles, arms folded, wearing a borrowed Tyvek suit.

The forensic people had taken his ruined uniform, bagged and labelled, and Frederickson looked uneasy because of it. No doubt the major had stripped enough captured enemy soldiers, Nick considered cynically, to be aware of the psychological effect.

Mind you, Frederickson had fared better than Max Carri. *Poor sod.* Inside the back of one of the ambulances over to Nick's right, he could still see the man Frederickson had dragged dripping from the killing ground. They'd taken everything, including his dignity, leaving him wrapped in a yellow hospital blanket and his misery. Nick saw Grace's tall figure hurrying up the back steps to go to him. Not quite how Nick had imagined her ex, but he admitted he probably wasn't seeing the successful entrepreneur at his best.

He returned his attention to the major, waiting. Frederickson's eyes were on the ragged debris scattered around the red showjumping wall in the middle of the arena.

Something had hit the wall after the shot, collapsing the centre. Nick didn't want to think what that 'something' might have been. The wall looked formidable but was constructed of lightweight hollow blocks, larger sections at the bottom, leading to individual bricks at the top to fine-tune the height. A test of horse and rider's boldness and skill but easy to knock down, for safety and to incur penalty points.

Angela Inglis scored four faults, then.

Eventually, Frederickson peeled his gaze away from the scene of devastation, met Nick's eyes.

"How did I know what?" His voice held that slightly dazed note common to victims of serious, sudden, violent crime. Once the adrenaline fades and the reality seeps in. But of all the people on that field, Frederickson was possibly the only one who'd been under this kind of fire before, and Nick noted his reaction with interest.

"The type of weapon?" he nudged. "How did you know?"

Frederickson's face ticced. "My entire military career has not been spent organising dog and pony shows, Mr Weston. Let's just say I've had enough direct experience with large-calibre sniper's rifles to identify one when it's used on a target within a few feet of me."

The streak of blood high across his cheekbone gave the major the look of a warrior, stained from the fight. His eyes shifted back to the arena, to what was left of the wall.

"You're sure this wasn't a rocket-propelled grenade perhaps?" Nick persisted, eyeing the damage.

"The effective range of that type of weapon is around five hundred and fifty yards," Frederickson said, offhand. "They have a relatively slow muzzle velocity—less than a thousand feet per second. Half the speed of an average rifle bullet." His eyes flicked over Nick again, hooded now. "I would have seen it."

No idle boast, Nick realised. He nodded, scrawled a note. The body armour they'd issued chafed as he moved and his shirt was already glued to his back and chest underneath it. Nobody was complaining.

Nick had been moping round Morrison's supermarket on the outskirts of Kendal when the call came through. It had been almost a relief to abandon his trolley in the cereals aisle. And he'd thought Lisa's visit was going to be the low point of the day.

He'd arrived to chaos, hundreds of people log-jamming the entrance to the field as the uniforms tried to move them to a holding area where at least names and contact details could be taken. The crowd was frightened, panicky. There'd been a couple of punch-ups. Nothing like a crisis to bring out the best and the worst in people. Traffic was still backed up and the Firearms lads were keeping the CSI teams away until they could confirm the area was secure. Personnel had been dragged in from all over the county for this one.

"Like to hazard a guess what they *were* using, major?"

Frederickson made a fractional movement of his shoulder, hardly enough to qualify as a shrug. "There are plenty of weapons with that kind of capability." He jerked his head towards the arena. "McMillan, Stoner, Barrett—they all make twelve-point-seven millimetre anti-matériel sniping rifles. One of those would be my best guess. The Gepard M3 is fourteen-point-five." He gave Nick a small tight smile. "That will punch a hole through an inch of armour plate at six hundred and fifty yards, so you can imagine what it will do to a fragile human body, even much further out." His eyes drifted, grew colder. "Well, you can see that one for yourself."

Nick understood his bitterness. "Care to estimate a likely range?"

"We heard the shot a good four or five seconds after A—" Frederickson stopped, swallowed. "After Mrs Inglis went down. About twenty-two hundred yards, maximum." He cleared his throat, gave another micro-shrug. "We had recorded kills in Afghanistan at that kind of distance."

"'We'?" Nick queried and received a flinty look.

"Don't ask, Mr Weston. You don't begin to have the clearance. Just take my word for it that you need to set up roadblocks at least two miles away, if you haven't done so already."

"I'm sure my superiors have come to the same conclusion, sir." He looked round at the blankly distant hills. "Although I suspect our man was long gone before we got here, if he's any sense."

The major snorted. "You think *sense* had any part to play?"

"Does this feel like a random shooting to you?" Nick asked quietly. "Even Derrick Bird, before he started taking potshots at passers-by, took out specific targets first. And I think our man here had a specific target in mind. Question is, did he hit it?"

Frederickson took an instinctive breath to snap at him, let it go, and something of his resolve went along with it. "It might help if you told me exactly what it is you want to know, Mr Weston," he said, more tired than angry. "Spit it out, man, for God's sake."

Nick pointedly shut his notebook. "Was he aiming for you?"

Frederickson's mouth flattened into a thin line. "Hard to tell. At that kind of range, a fraction of error in the calibration of the sight, calculating the windage, any number of factors, and you'd miss an elephant." He made a brief, dismissive gesture. "Who knows how much time he's spent zeroing? Or even how much experience he's had?"

Something about this last comment jarred on Nick's cop senses. He'd listened to any number of lies over the years, told with everything from absolute conviction to utter desperation. *False*, he knew instantly. Not even a conscious thought process, just a reflex response.

"Anyone who goes to the trouble of obtaining a gun like that has to be pretty sure of their ability to use it." He waited a beat, then said softly, "Who is he, major?"

Frederickson's gaze wouldn't lock. "How would I know?"

"First your dog, now your mistress." Nick saw the jerk of surprise. He stepped in closer, certainty burning brightly now. "He must really have it in for you. Someone you served with, maybe? Or against?"

The question lay where it had fallen. For a long time, the major didn't speak. Nick knew if he'd been way off the mark, the man's first response would have been denial, ridicule. But it wasn't.

"Neither." Frederickson straightened. He spoke without looking at Nick, staring off into the distance. "I suspect he may be someone who served under me."

"Who?"

Frederickson glanced at him then. "You were entirely correct when you asked what I'd done to end up here," he said with a grim smile. "I'm here as a penance. A man of my experience would not be shunted away into some little rural backwater at this point in his career otherwise."

Quietly, Nick said, "What happened?"

"I made a mistake," Frederickson said flatly. "A bad one. My last tour in Afghanistan. Kandahar region. I was in charge of coordinating a small group, snipers. The best we had. Too good, as it turned out."

"*Too* good?"

"We were given bad intel, which resulted in what's euphemistically termed a friendly fire incident." His shoulders squared a little, gaunt face rigid. "It was my operation, I was in charge, so I carried the can."

Nick heard the pain in his voice. More than that; a deep abiding sorrow.

"Who is it you think is after you?" he asked. "Some friend of the men who were killed?"

"No," Frederickson said. "Pete Tawney. The man who killed them."

Nick frowned. "But surely—?"

Frederickson gave a twisted smile. "Tawney questioned the order to fire. His spotter radioed repeated requests for target confirmation. At the time I had no reason to doubt, so I gave it. Somewhat forcefully, I'm afraid." He reached up to swat at a fly that was hovering around his face, drawn by the dried blood. "Afterwards, when the whole damn mess came out, he... punched me out, swore vengeance. Landed himself in the glasshouse at Colchester for his trouble. Military prison."

"I'm aware of the facility," Nick said drily. "When did Tawney get out?"

"Six months ago. The shrinks were claiming post-traumatic stress, of course, and he was supposed to report in regularly, but a week after his release he disappeared, dropped off the radar." He saw the question forming on Nick's face. "I had an email from an old friend down there, telling me I should watch my back."

"And this Tawney was capable of using one of the rifles you mentioned?"

"He had a liking for the Barrett Light Fifty, and he was one of the best we had. I've come across a lot of snipers in my time, Mr Weston, but Tawney differed from many of them in one important regard." Frederickson glanced back out across the arena again where the carrion birds had begun to gather. "He had no problem killing women."

44

SLOUCHED at the other side of the ARV, Jim Airey momentarily closed his eyes.

He hadn't meant to eavesdrop, but if you were in the right place and people started talking about something important, well, it was stupid not to listen, right?

A Barrett. Airey had never seen one for real. The IRA was supposed to have used a Light Fifty to take out Brit squaddies in Northern Ireland, shooting from way across the border in the South. Brought down a helicopter, too, so the rumours went. And he'd seen the videos on the Internet, supposedly of Yank snipers taking out Taliban guerrillas. The pieces just *flew*.

Airey swallowed. He hadn't been watching the arena at the moment Angela Inglis was hit, but he'd been in time to see what was left of her land, hard enough to bring down that wall. Didn't think he'd ever forget it.

A rifle. A big rifle...

What was it Edith said, that day he confronted her about the AK? Claimed she'd seen someone dressed in camouflage, out on Orton Scar above the Inglis place with a long gun, big enough to be bipod-mounted, with a sight on it, and a muzzle brake.

Thought she was lying as usual. But what if she wasn't...

Airey wiped a sly hand across his jaw. What if *he* was the one to provide the break in this high-profile murder inquiry?

He heard something, almost a growl, looked up sharply to find DC Weston glowering at him.

"What are you after, lurking about?"

"Nowt," Flustered, Airey's eyes slid over Major Frederickson's departing back. "I—"

But Weston caught the guilty gesture. "Just try and act like a real copper for once, Airey. I'm sure your mate, Robertshaw could do with a hand on traffic duty. It's chaos down there."

"Yessir."

Jumped-up little… If I hand them a premier-league lead they won't have me directing traffic, he thought, surly, *that's for sure.*

He trudged across the grass towards the snarl of cars and horse trailers desperate to escape the field. Well, if Weston wasn't interested, there'd be plenty more who were.

After all, Duncan Inglis was an important man. And the death of an MEP's wife in such spectacular and public fashion was going to be front page news all over. Journos always flashed the cash.

Comforted by that lucrative thought, Airey rapped on the window of a big Shogun 4x4 with a private plate, whose driver had just sounded his horn impatiently.

"All right, sonny," Airey demanded, cheerfully belligerent. "What's your game?"

45

"LOOK AT HIM, FAT OLD FART," Edith muttered under her breath. In the circle of the spotter's scope, her father loomed large as life and twice as ugly. "Parking cars. About all he's good for."

She was tucked in alongside Bardwell in the back of the Land Rover. The space between the wheel arches was narrow and, of the two, he was the one who needed comfort, position, so Edith was curled awkwardly around him. She was on her side, half-twisted so she could use the scope, with the ridged metal floor painful beneath her ribs.

By necessity in the confined bed, her pelvis was wedged against Bardwell's hip, her sternum pressing into his elbow. The enforced intimacy brought a flustered warmth to her cheeks, a quiver to her breath.

As soon as Bardwell had fired his first shot, they'd collapsed the hide and withdrawn, back to where the Land Rover was parked, hidden from the show field. It had only taken a moment to clip the gun into its hiding place underneath, Edith keeping watch. Then they pulled out sedately onto the road heading for Raisbeck.

It was only a short drive to the north. The ground sloped up towards Raisbeck Wood, with High Pike behind. Bardwell backed the Land Rover onto a grass verge at an angle, swinging open the rear door to obscure the outline of the Barrett, its bipod feet resting securely on top of the dry stone wall.

Now, he lifted his head a fraction from the gun, enough to meet her eyes. His were grey, nondescript, and he never seemed to blink.

"Want me to take him out?"

For a moment Edith's breath stopped. "You're not serious?" she gasped, her heart restarting with a jerk. "I mean, you'd really do that? For me?"

He twitched one shoulder, dropped his eye back to the sight.

Edith lay silent for a moment. Did she really want to be rid of her father? She'd wished it occasionally, but suddenly she was faced with it as a real prospect.

An image jumped into her head of the Colosseum in Rome. They'd done it in history at school, and everybody had seen the movies. She imagined herself sitting high above the bloodshed with the emperor, in the finest silks, waving a languid arm towards the carnage acted out for her entertainment below.

Her father's plump figure inserted itself into the fantasy, standing fearfully in the bloodied sand, still in his police uniform. A half-naked gladiator, agleam with the blood of his victories, stood over him with sword raised. The warrior lifted his eyes to meet hers, enraptured, asking.

Edith saw herself, a pale slender beauty surrounded by slaves, holding out a fist with her thumb concealed, teasing. Slowly, she rotated her arm so the thumb pointed upwards, which did not indicate mercy, the teacher had explained, but was an affirmation of the kill. The crowd swelled and shrieked, the sword flashed. And the last thing Edith saw was her father's disbelieving gaze...

"No," she said, unable to suppress a shiver. *What good is it if he doesn't know whose hand's behind it?* "Not yet."

"Who then?"

"You mean...I get to choose this time?" Edith squirmed, then froze, but he never gave any indication he'd felt her move against him, never mind been affected. She remembered his passion that day at the byre. *Wanted me then, didn't he?*

"You've already done who I wanted."

"So? Pick another." And there was something intense about him now. "Clock's ticking."

She felt her throat tighten at his disappointment, pressed her eye to the spotting scope again, scanning desperately. And then, amid the sea of white-clad figures, one leapt out at her. *There!*

"Got it."

"Sure?"

"Yes," Edith said, emphatic. "Final answer."

46

"*Finally*, we have access to the scene." Richard Sibson raised his voice slightly to be heard by the whole team. Grace, and half a dozen other CSIs they'd dragged in from all areas. *Not enough,* Sibson thought, looking round at them. *But it'll have to do.*

Sibson had worked with all of them. Steve Scott and Paul McKendrick up from Kendal; Ken Allcott and Tyson Frost from Workington; Chris Blenkinship and Tony Marsh down from Carlisle. CSIs brought in from across Cumbria in a mad rush, only to sit around and wait for hours for the chance to do their job. Frost and McKendrick might still be a bit green, but otherwise good experienced people. Even so, they'd never had to deal with anything quite like this.

"We have a large area to cover," Sibson went on. "And this is only the first crime scene we have to process today. With any luck, they'll find the position of our shooter. That will become our secondary scene." He glanced across. "Grace, I'd like to keep you in reserve for that."

"She's no use," Chris Blenkinship said bluntly. Sibson saw Grace's head turn, but she merely raised an eyebrow. "No good looking at me like that, pet," Blenkinship went on, shaking his head at her. "You know you've already had close contact with one of the witnesses here. Couldn't wait to get his clothes off, could you?"

Of course—Max. Sibson suppressed a sigh. *I should have*

realised. She wouldn't have been human if she'd stayed away from her ex-husband after something like this.

Grace favoured her boss with a slightly wan smile. "Sorry," she said, whether for the mistake or the fact that it was Blenkinship who pointed it out, he wasn't sure. "Chris is quite right, of course. Anything I got from the second scene might be deemed contaminated."

"If I can't trust you to follow procedure, I've been wasting my time training you."

"I'll take the second scene, then, shall I?' Blenkinship said. After Sibson himself, Blenkinship had the most time in with Cumbria police. A tall Geordie who attempted to disguise early baldness with a military-style buzz-cut, Blenkinship had tried out in his youth for Sunderland FC and still traded on his near-miss with fame.

He knew that Sibson had been toying with retirement and was positioning himself as natural successor. Sibson had little time for politics, mildly despising those who had the inclination and the talent to play that particular game. He respected Blenkinship's abilities, but couldn't bring himself to actually like the man.

"All right." Sibson ladled out a cool stare. "In that case, McColl can handle photo and video. We'll start with the victim." He didn't miss the little sideways look Blenkinship exchanged with Ken Allcott, caught the meaning well enough.

"McColl is by far my best photographer," he said flatly. "Would *you* like to explain to the chief constable why we failed to allocate our best personnel to the tasks to which they're most suited?" Blenkinship dropped the smirk.

"Right," Sibson said. "Tape the arena into zones, as usual. Take a zone each, work an organised grid search pattern. We need to be fast and thorough. Anyone finds anything out of the ordinary, they mark it and call McColl. I trust nobody *else* has any objections?" He allowed a hint of sarcasm to creep in, business as usual.

"What about the wall?"

It wasn't just the question that had Sibson swinging back, but the fact it was Grace who'd asked it.

"What?"

"The wall." She ignored the covert amusement around her.

"According to the witnesses, Mrs Inglis was passing in front of it when she was killed and it was knocked down in the process."

"Yes, yes, we'll clearly need to remove some of the fallen segments in order to retrieve all of the remains," Sibson said impatiently. "Any damage will be documented in due course."

"But we can't ignore the possibility, given the victim's position, that the round also passed through the wall itself. Don't you think it's important to find out?" She paused. "According to the information Major Frederickson provided, the sniper could have been more than a mile away. That's an awful lot of ground to cover. Surely, anything we can do to narrow down the area for the search teams ought to be a priority, don't you think?"

Sibson absorbed the implications, lips thinning.

Blenkinship, misreading his reaction, gave a snort. "We need to get this scene processed as quickly as possible," he told her. "I can't believe you want to waste time playing with building blocks."

"And *I* can't believe we didn't think of that earlier." Sibson nodded curtly to Grace, allowed his eyes to take up the smile his mouth ruthlessly suppressed. "Good thinking, McColl."

Blenkinship flushed. "Sir, with all respect, we need everyone on the ground. We can't just—"

"*Your* work won't start until we find that second scene," Sibson cut in. "Until then, I want you rebuilding that wall. If the bullet did indeed pass through, it may give us the elevation as well as an indicator of direction." And just before Blenkinship threw a sulk, he added, "Important task, Chris. Needs someone of your seniority."

Unimpressed, Blenkinship put his hands up, as if to ward off further flattery. "Fine. I'll get on it."

"Good," Sibson said. "Anybody makes a find, McColl will photograph it before it's bagged and tagged. Clear?" Everyone nodded. "Right, suit up and let's get this crime scene sorted before the wretched crows make off with any *more* of our poor unfortunate victim, shall we?"

47

GRACE, pulling on her Tyvek suit, glanced across the arena to where Chris Blenkinship was now discussing the exact dimensions of the showjumping wall with Major Frederickson. It made sense to consult him, since he'd been in charge of building it in the first place, but Grace was uneasy about the army man's involvement. He was too close, too...*connected.*

"You should be careful of him, my dear."

She turned, to find Richard Sibson at her shoulder. "Careful of whom?"

Sibson sighed. "Chris Blenkinship. He's after my job and I should imagine it won't be too very long before he gets it." He gave her a severe look over his glasses as he stretched his fingers inside the nitrile gloves. "You'd be wise not to make an enemy out of him."

"Well, Christopher is not someone I particularly want for a friend," Grace said easily, tucking her hair beneath the hood of her suit. "And I don't see you being wheeled round the park in your bath chair just yet, do you?"

"Nevertheless, my dear, just remember that you were my choice," Sibson warned. "Almost certainly, you won't be his."

His words lingered as the CSIs walked out over the arena. Grace had never tried to get close to the people she worked with. She didn't go for after-hours drinks, outings, shopping trips. After years of a social diary booked up months in advance, the freedom of being able to do her own thing on her own time was still a luxury she savoured.

"Make sure you get close-ups of the separation of the remains will you, Grace?" Sibson said, putting markers down in the grass by pieces of bloody cloth that might once have been pale green silk. "This spread pattern may well help identify the weapon."

He rocked back on his heels slightly while she laid down a scale and leaned over the area to take her shots, bracketing the exposure.

Grace straightened. "I thought Major Frederickson said it was —what was it? A Barrett Light Fifty?"

"And *I* thought I'd taught you never to try and make the evidence fit someone else's theories," Sibson returned sharply. "Besides, the major's working on nothing more than supposition. He believes this man Tawney *may* be after him but, as you'd be the first to testify, whatever did this is nothing like what killed the dog."

Grace frowned. "You told me never to trust in coincidence, either."

He sighed. "Do you have to remember *everything* I said, McColl?"

"Now Richard," she murmured, "you know I hang on your every word."

Sibson's only reply was a grunt. He bent to examine another piece of what had so recently been human, waving away the flies. "Whatever else, it was quick. She wouldn't have felt a thing, poor woman."

Grace wondered if Max would ever forget what he'd seen. She'd been horrified at her first sight of him huddled in the back of the ambulance, streaked with blood and bone. In all the years of their marriage, she'd never seen him so bewildered, so *vulnerable*.

He would never know how hard it had been for her, to treat him with the detachment required of her job, to bag and label his clothing, sticking strictly to procedure, keeping the chain of evidence intact, when all she'd wanted to do was offer the comfort he so badly needed.

Because of the strong sunlight, she attached a flashgun to the Canon to eliminate the contrast of shadows and snapped more pictures, then stood to quarter the scene from their position.

As she did so, a faint flash of colour caught her eye. She raised the camera to her eye, operated the zoom lens, just to be sure, and completely missed her boss's next comment. At her lack of response, he glanced up.

"What it is?" he asked quickly, irritation fading.

"Hm? Oh, I thought I saw something. A vehicle, perhaps," she said, pointing.

He followed her direction with narrowed eyes. "Well spotted."

Grace pressed the shutter and checked the image. "I'll fetch a tripod from the van." She put down her bag. "The less shake, the bigger I can go with the enlargements."

"And get someone onto it," Sibson added over his shoulder as she walked away. "If it's some farmer out doing whatever it is farmers do with their livestock, we may have another potential witness to add to the hordes."

Grace nodded, glanced around and spotted Danny Robertshaw near one of the incident vans.

"Daniel!" she called, loud enough to attract his attention.

He turned, started towards her. Grace passed through the crowd barriers that marked the edge of the arena and stepped into the sunshine. As she did so, she pushed back the hood of her suit, letting her hair fall loosely about her shoulders.

48

"THERE! LOOK—THEY'VE SEEN US!" Edith's outrage barely scratched the smooth surface of Bardwell's thought processes.

He felt nothing. Not for the depersonalised targets he viewed through the magnification of the scope, nor the body lying next to him. Her occasional wriggling was a minor irritation. Nothing more.

He had already assessed the possibility of discovery as soon as one of the figures pointed an arm vaguely in their direction. Shooting from the vehicle was a calculated risk. At this stage, all the search efforts would be concentrated in a direction that took them further away from Bardwell's present position. He hadn't expected them to try and pinpoint the hide from the angle of the shot through the wall. *Clever.*

But this next target would cause chaos by its very random nature. They would waste time looking for reason where there wasn't any.

Forcing the girl to make the choice had another bonus, too. *She* may have come to *him*, but could not have appreciated the reality of what he was about. He'd been surprised by her excitement after the first clean kill—disturbed by it, even—but Bardwell had come across a lot of people for whom death became more than just a job. It hovered around the borders of religion. Edith had the tinge of the fanatic about her. Better to ignite that flame and then control the burn.

So he'd made her choose, knowing that complicity would

bind her to him in a way no verbal promise would ever do. As soon as he took down *her* target, obeyed *her* command, she was tied to him by blood to the end.

And, by then, it would scarcely matter.

He'd never intended to take the girl to bed, but one look at her face when she'd hugged him at the cottage, and he knew instantly it wouldn't take much to turn her loyal as a dog. Less troublesome in the long-term than hiding her corpse.

Besides, it had been a while and there was something about that scrawny body, even if he could hardly bring himself to kiss her. But she'd been pathetically unskilled and eager, and didn't know enough to question his regret.

"Shoot!" Edith demanded now, her voice cracking. "You *tryin'* to get us caught? They're taking pictures. Do it now, for—"

"Enough," he growled, and barely registered that she turned in on herself, except at last that she was quiet and still. The wind had died, the trees barely stirring, and the distance wasn't quite so great, a little over a thousand metres. He selected his target, not asking her to call the range, not needing her to, slipping beneath the surface rhythms to feel when the moment was right. Delicately, precisely, Bardwell squeezed the trigger.

And at the very moment he did so, he caught a flash of movement and knew in that split second it had all gone wrong.

49

Sibson had twisted on his haunches to watch Grace speaking to the young constable. He was looking directly at the pair of them when the sniper's bullet hit.

Grace had pushed her hood back and was combing a hand unconsciously through her hair and Sibson wondered if she had any idea of the way Robertshaw was gazing at it.

Yes, lad, she has that effect, doesn't she?

Grace had just pointed to something and the young copper refocused with a sudden jerk, nodding profusely, a flush staining his neck. She smiled, dazzling, touched his shoulder as she moved on. Robertshaw stayed rooted for a moment longer, staring after her, then seemed to shake himself and turned away abruptly.

And as he did so, Robertshaw's right arm above the elbow exploded, as if he'd been holding a live grenade, an obscene pink mist spraying outwards. Sibson just had time to register the bizarre shock of the dispersal before the noise of the shot struck them all.

He had been a CSI for a long time. Had seen the aftermath of explosion, fire, suicide, tragic accident and murderous rage. Nothing prepared him for the grotesque experience of seeing a man go down from a single large-calibre round, breaking the sound barrier more than twice over, and hearing the whine and the crack and the rolling thunder that followed a terrifying two seconds later.

He remembered Major Frederickson's estimate of the time delay. Four or five seconds. *My God,* Sibson thought. *He's moved closer.*

Everyone had dived, woefully slow, the report alone knocking them flat. The public was largely evacuated by now, even with Jim Airey on traffic duty, but there were enough people left to panic. Sibson heard screaming, a cacophony of over-revved diesel engines as drivers instinctively put their foot down, animal trailer behind or no. The crash and grind of at least two vehicles trying to take the same route to safety, graunching against each other.

Sibson, on his belly, twisted round searching for Grace. He caught a flash of red hair, down on the ground about twenty feet from where the young policeman must have fallen. Sibson's view of Robertshaw's body was hidden by the wreckage of the showjumps between them and, in some ways, he was thankful for it.

"Grace! Are you all right?"

"I'm...yes, I'm OK, but Daniel's terribly injured." Her voice was clear, just a touch of an underlying tremor. "He needs help."

Sibson opened his mouth to shout a warning, but another voice cut across him in a familiar bellow.

"You keep your damn head down, McColl!" DI Brian Pollock yelled. Sibson looked across, found the thickset inspector had managed to wedge himself under the front bull bars of a 4x4 at the edge of the arena.

Pollock met Sibson's gaze across the bloodied grass, and the CSI read anguish despite the fierce tone. "You just stay where you are," Pollock warned. "Until we have this area secured, you will not move, do you hear me?"

"Grace," Sibson said gently, sensing her gather for the fight. "There's nothing you can do for him."

For a moment there was silence, then Grace's voice came again, icy in its composure. "Of course there's something I can do. He's bleeding out right in front of me. I can—"

"Darling, please, just listen to them!" Another voice—Max Carri. Next to the ambulance and still wrapped in his blanket, with DC Weston struggling to hold him back from going out to his ex-wife.

"No, you listen." Sibson heard the towering anger in her voice. It sent a cold streak of fear straight down his spine, because people were bravest when they were angry. And the last thing he wanted right now from Grace was the kind of stupid selfless bravery that gained dead soldiers posthumous medals and a twenty-one gun salute across their graveside.

"I'm going to help him," she said, ripe with it now. "And if I'm shot, you can say 'I told you so', but if I lie here and a young officer dies because I was too much of a coward to try to save him, I damn well deserve shooting. And, frankly, so do the rest of you."

Sibson saw Pollock shut his eyes. "Dammit all, Grace. Stay down." There was no mistaking the pain in his voice. "That's a direct order."

"You overstep your authority, detective inspector. I'm a civilian." There was a defiant edge to her now. "You can't give me direct orders."

"Richard, can't you control your own people?" Pollock roared.

"Hard to argue with someone determined to do the right thing," Sibson replied, even though his heart was a stone in his throat.

"Grace!" Carri called again, outraged, stricken. "Darling, for God's sake, you don't have to do this. *Please.*"

Sibson saw her head move, searching until she located him. "I'm sorry, Max," she said without a hint of regret. "But of course I do."

Sibson saw her bunch herself, preparing to rise. Outside the arena, Carri dropped his blanket to reveal a pair of designer boxers, and leapt into the back of the ambulance. Moments later, he reappeared with an armful of dressings and bandages. He did not look as ridiculous as a man in his position should have done, Sibson realised. Maybe it was the sheer courage that lent him some degree of respect. That and the fact he was still crusted with the blood of the sniper's previous victim.

"Weston—restrain that civilian," Pollock barked. "Arrest him if you have to."

Weston stepped in front of Carri when he would have started forwards. Sibson was too far away to hear what passed between

them, but he was at the right angle to see Weston take the dressings Carri held, stuffing them into pockets, clutching the rest
tight to his chest. Then, ignoring the howl of wrath from Pollock,
Weston turned and ran, doubled low, out into the field of fire.

50

It was Nick's turn to sit on the ambulance steps with a blanket draped around his shoulders. His forearms resting on his knees, hands dangling. They were still bloodied to the wrists. The shirt would have to go in the bin, if it wasn't required as some kind of evidence. Of what, he wasn't sure.

An hour had passed since his heart-pounding dash across the field to Grace's aid. He doubted he'd ever forget skidding to a halt alongside her and staring down at Robertshaw's mutilated body.

Robertshaw's right arm was...gone. Not broken or damaged, but simply not there anymore. All that remained amid the tatters of his tunic was a stump of whitened bone protruding from his shoulder, a few sinewy threads. The grass under him was a rich dark red as the blood gushed and pooled too fast even for the famished ground to drink.

Grace was already bending over him, Sibson by her side, working feverishly to stem the flow, coated like butchers. Robertshaw, mercifully, was unconscious, had remained so throughout.

Nick thrust the dressings into her hands. His mind shut down the reality of what he was seeing, doing, but his stomach revolted nevertheless.

"Breathe through your mouth," Grace said over her shoulder. "You're no use to him if you're going to throw up."

She had been rigidly angry, Nick realised, a raging stillness that utterly enveloped her. *Better than being scared.*

Because he'd been scared, he admitted privately. That deep down, bone-crushing, soul-numbing kind of fear. The kind that shrieked inside his skull all the while he'd been exposed. Once, he wouldn't have felt anything close to it. But now? Now he knew the price for failure. They said the body didn't remember pain, just the emotions associated with it.

And those, he'd found, were harder to forget.

They'd done what they could, Grace yelling furiously for a doctor until at last one of the paramedics overcame his fear, got behind the wheel and bounced an ambulance across the rough ground.

And all the time they'd been waiting for the buzzing zip of the next shot and the echoing boom that followed.

It never came.

They loaded Robertshaw onto a stretcher, pale and hardly breathing. The air ambulance had put down on the truck stop at the motorway junction at Tebay, a couple of miles away. They weren't being allowed closer; not for someone whose odds of survival looked so poor.

Grace gave Nick's shoulder a fast squeeze and went with Robertshaw, leaving Nick behind to face the music.

He knew he'd disobeyed an order and that was never going to play well with the man who'd given it, but he hadn't expected such uneasiness from the others. Sibson had muttered a quick, "Well done," and hurried back to supervise his tainted scene.

Nick shrugged. It wasn't like he'd lose friends over this. *Didn't have any to begin with.*

Max Carri, now in a Tyvek suit rather than his blanket, gave Nick a brief but heartfelt thanks. They'd arranged for one of the uniforms to drive him home in his own car, a big black Mercedes with a private plate. "I won't forget," he said.

But Pollock was not impressed with hotheads and made this position abundantly clear, getting right in Nick's face while he did so. Whatever the inspector had eaten the night before had been heavily spiced with garlic, which did little for the delicate state of Nick's stomach when he leaned in close. Vomiting on a superior officer, Nick reckoned, would not win him any brownie points.

When Pollock's invective wound down, Nick was left to sit alone and wonder. Why did the sniper shoot and grievously wound Robertshaw, but not complete the kill? If it was indeed this man, Tawney, out for revenge on Major Frederickson, why go for a policeman at all? What purpose did *that* serve?

And if that was all part of the plan then why, when he'd then been presented with *three* wide-open, almost static targets, hadn't he finished the job?

51

"YOU MISSED!" Edith's voice was shrill, close to tears. "How could you miss?"

She slouched in the passenger seat, fidgeting and chewing at her already bitten-down fingernails as Bardwell bumped the Land Rover carefully out onto the main road.

"He moved." Bardwell gave a shrug, little more than a twitch. "It happens."

"Well, why didn't you have another go?"

"One shot, Edith." He allowed disappointment to show in his voice. "Any more than that, they get a fix on you. Told you that, didn't I?"

"Yeah," she muttered. "But if he survives they'll make him out to be some kind of hero—"

"Don't push it." Softly now. "We're not going back."

She didn't reply to that, settling into a sulky silence. Bardwell's thoughts turned back to the failed shot. It didn't happen often and he always went over it in his mind, worked out why. Satisfying himself outside forces had been at work.

In this case, the man had chosen the exact moment of Bardwell's shot to turn unexpectedly. Bardwell had been centred on the largest area of his body mass, crosshairs settled on the man's chest. He'd gauged the range, the conditions, with the finest accuracy his experience could supply.

But the man had moved.

And regardless of what he'd told the girl, Bardwell knew he

would not have taken a second shot even if his cover had been perfect, his concealment impenetrable. It was if, by setting that rule, he yielded responsibility to some higher power. Lap of the gods. The man Bardwell selected chose that very moment to twist on his heel. Might even be enough to save his life. Who was he to argue with the hand of fate? He'd never had anything personal invested in his targets. Until now at any rate.

The Inglis woman had been his primary interest and he'd taken her out, clean, surgical. Even threaded the round past the man whose arm she was holding, and not a scratch on him. Have to dump that cream suit, though.

But the second target had been Edith's choice—could have been picked at random for all he knew. But at least he'd been in uniform, and that classed him almost as a combatant. Enough to salve Bardwell's conscience, more or less.

A flash caught his eye. A police car, lights and sirens blazing, appeared in his mirrors, closing fast. Bardwell lifted off, drifted towards the shoulder. Edith jerked upright, twisting in her seat, mouth dropping open.

"What do we do?"

"Nothing," Bardwell grunted. He flicked on the left-hand indicator. "You keep your trap shut, you hear me? Just remember —he was yours, that last one."

He started to brake, watching all the time as the pursuing vehicle leapt towards them. A big Volvo, maybe, from the shape of the front end.

No, wait—it was a Toyota four-wheel drive. A Land Cruiser full of armed Iraqi secret police, looking for the man who'd just taken out a general at eight hundred and fifty metres. The man had been one of Saddam's relatives. No surprise there—most of them were—but retribution tended to have a knock-on effect all the way down the line. Bardwell had already seen them slaughter a family in sheer temper, for nothing more than protesting the roadside search. Beat the father to death with the butts of their rifles, in front of his screaming wife and children. Killed the others just to shut them up.

He'd sweated inside his stolen robes as he inched the ancient van towards the roadblock, praying that the fake papers his contact supplied would pass. He'd been in the desert long enough to burn his skin dark, he knew the manners and the customs, but he couldn't escape the knowledge that his eyes might give him away. Not just the colour, but there was something in them he couldn't seem to hide. Not from men who knew what to look for. Who were just the same as he was, underneath.

The police car swerved out around the Land Rover, now barely crawling, and roared past, lurching as the suspension loaded.

Bardwell was almost stationary now and the patrol left them behind at an accelerated rate, disappearing into the distance on the straight stretch of road like a fast jet.

"Are you all right?" The voice seemed to come from a long way away, and he reacted to the anxiety more than the question. He looked up, shook himself, found his hands clenched tight round the top rim of the hard steering wheel. The sweat stung his eyes and he wiped them with hands too damp to make a difference.

Something nudged his arm. He glanced down, found Edith holding out a crumpled handkerchief with the hesitancy of someone expecting rejection. After a moment, Bardwell took it and mopped his face, not quite sure what to do with it after.

"'S'all right—keep it." She looked unaccountably pleased, trying for nonchalant. "I got another."

"I'll wash it. Let you have it back," he said, not understanding why that disappointed her.

She fell silent. The only sound was the frantic keening of the siren, growing gradually fainter in the distance, and the grumble of the Land Rover's engine ticking over.

"They won't find out, will they?" she asked then, in a small voice. "They won't catch us?"

Bardwell turned, found her staring fixedly at her hands, clasped in her lap. Her head was bent, showing the prominent vertebra at the top of her spine.

"How would they do that?"

She shrugged, awkward. "I dunno—all that forensic stuff you see on the telly. They can tell loads, can't they?"

Bardwell paused at the hopeful note. *Hopeful we'll get away with it? Or be stopped? Hard to tell.*

"From what?" he said. "A few photos? Be a miracle if they find the hide. We policed the brass. They'll never dig out the rounds. How're they going to catch us? What with?"

She shrugged again, an uncoordinated spasm.

He took the Land Rover out of gear and turned a little in his seat to face her. "Long as you don't blab to anyone, they've no chance." He saw something stammer in her face. "What?" He leaned forwards, sharp enough to have her head rearing up in shock, guilt even. "What have you said?"

"I haven't!" she protested, face flaming. "I haven't told anyone. I wouldn't!"

"You better not," Bardwell said, unsure if she was lying. Girls worked on different rules, sly and shifty.

He unclipped his seatbelt and edged towards her, hand sliding round the back of her rigid neck, locked his eyes with hers all the way in. Right up 'til hers fluttered closed as he kissed her, hard. Held it long enough to feel her fire up beneath his mouth.

"Just mind what I said, Edith," he warned, pulling back. "We're in this together. You and me."

He released her and her chin lifted. "Yes. We are, aren't we?" and now there was something else in her voice that Bardwell had no trouble recognising. Heard it often enough, from soldiers on all sides of every conflict he'd ever been involved in.

Pride.

PART V

52

THE MARKER LOOKED LIKE A GRAVESTONE. Grace stood at the exact spot where Danny Robertshaw had fallen, staring down at the dark stains still visible in the grass. Even without other indicators, the furious buzzing of the flies would have drawn her to the spot.

Why? she asked the unknown gunman. *What did you hope to achieve?*

She shook her head, recognising the fatigue that crept along her bones like winter frost. It was five a.m. after a clear night. The sun was already climbing towards the promise of another oppressive, airless day, but Grace felt she'd never be warm through again.

Robertshaw had remained unconscious during the short wild ride from the show field to the air ambulance. She'd wanted to go with him but they hadn't let her. She'd watched the helicopter lift off and swoop north towards Carlisle General. Afterwards, drained, Grace had briefly gone home. She'd stayed long enough to shower, change, feed the dog; then she'd gone straight back to the field.

The whole place was being treated as a crime scene, finally cleared of the public and swarming with official personnel. She signed the log at the gateway from the road. The young constable on duty asked about Robertshaw straight away.

"Me and him went through training together. I never thought...well, you don't, do you?"

Grace touched a hand briefly to his arm and walked on.

Chris Blenkinship had taken responsibility for the second victim, abandoning his work on the red wall. Grace felt a mild annoyance that it was being allowed to fall by the wayside but what right did she have to dictate what was done after she left the scene?

Young Ty Frost had taken over photographic duties, and Sibson was buried in his work, barely acknowledging her return. Feeling lost, Grace turned her attention to reconstructing the wall. She worked alone, documenting her progress, ignoring outside distractions, using that single-minded act to push everything else away from her, and hold on.

As the light faded, they brought in floodlamps, bathing the whole area in harsh light. In a rural area with little by way of streetlighting, their glow was visible from miles around.

Later, somebody left her a thermos but she couldn't have said who. She barely registered them, couldn't let herself be drawn into pointless speculation about Robertshaw's chances. She didn't see the hurt stares, the muttering. It wouldn't have made a difference if she had.

Just as the first streaks of dawn reached across the fields to soften the artificial brightness of the work lamps, she put the last wooden shard in place. As she lifted her camera to record this final piece, Grace noted automatically that she could close down the aperture another stop. Daylight was on its way.

Only then did she notice the flask for the first time. She unscrewed the cap and sniffed the contents. Coffee—milky and sweet. Not to her taste but she poured it out anyway. *Tepid*, she realised at the first sip.

And now the task was over, she felt yesterday's events drag at her shoulders. Stiffly, she sat cross-legged on the edge of the treadplates, cupping the foul coffee in both hands and staring through the hole she'd rebuilt in the jumping wall.

On the other side, it was relatively small—not much more than the diameter of a golf ball. A neat round insertion point that belied the damage the bullet had already done before it reached there.

But this side was another story. The exit hole in the hollow structure was huge by comparison, raw, jagged, surrounded by a starburst of shards and splinters as the flimsy plywood had simply been blown apart.

Grace hadn't had the time to collect every tiny piece of the jigsaw and painstakingly ease it into place, but she'd done the majority. Enough to work out the angle of penetration, to take a bearing that might track the path of the shot back to its point of origin. One of the accident investigators had promised to bring down a theodolite first thing, so they could accurately measure both the horizontal and vertical angles to get a precise bearing. *Too far for canes and string.* And once they had...

"Here, you look like you could use this."

"Mr Weston." She didn't turn round. "Could use what?"

She felt the metal plate vibrate slightly underneath her as he stepped closer, finally glanced up when he was right alongside. He had changed his clothes, she noted, wearing a wax cotton jacket against the dewed chill.

He lifted something wrapped in foil out of his jacket pocket, warm to the touch when he dropped it into her hands. The smell alone made her salivate.

"Bacon sandwich. Get it down you while there's still some heat left in it."

Just for a second the thought of it revolted her; then her stomach took over, the craving for food overriding any finer sensibilities.

She flicked him an upward glance. "Thank you, Mr Weston."

"Frederickson insists on calling me *Mister* Weston, just to keep me in my place. You do it to keep me at a distance. Why is that, I wonder?"

"There's supposed to be distance." She peeled off her gloves to unwrap her gift. Inside she found toasted bread, mayonnaise, sliced tomato, and lettuce, as well as the bacon. She bit deep, couldn't remember anything quite so welcome or tasting so good.

He didn't interrupt her while she ate, just strolled away, keeping to the treadplates, eyeing the rebuilt wall. He must have been watching her, too, because he timed his return just as she was wiping her hands at the finish.

He crouched to eye level, searched her face. "You're exhausted, Grace. You've done your job. Why not go home, get some sleep?"

She took her time to chew and swallow the last mouthful. "Like you have, you mean?"

"I grabbed an hour in the car," he said, dismissive. "I have a kid, remember? I can do without sleep."

"Whereas I am an old lady who can't, you mean?"

He almost smiled, a fleeting glimmer, jerked his head towards the wall. "Was it worth it?"

"If it helps us find him? The evidence to convict him? Yes." Grace rose, braced her hands behind her and stretched out her back, feeling the muscles quiver and twang. She missed her yoga.

"You think you can do that from a bullet hole in a few bits of wood?"

"It's actually two holes—one in, one out. With enough of a gap in between to measure an angle. If lining them up means we get a fix on the hide and find it before it deteriorates, or before the scene's contaminated by animals, or it rains—even another dewfall won't help—then yes, it will have been worth it."

She stooped to cap the lens, slip the camera into its padded bag. When she straightened again, she found him watching her steadily.

"What now?" he asked, and just for a second, any number of possible answers flitted through Grace's mind.

"Back to the office," she said firmly, swinging the bag onto her shoulder, resting her hand on it. "I need to download this little lot, pull up some satellite images and see what I can put together before the search teams really get under way again. What about you?"

He shrugged, beat her to the field kit. Grace debated on arguing that she could carry her own gear, decided she was too tired to argue. Let him be gallant if he felt the need.

"Me, too—back to the office, I mean. Pollock's had me looking into threats against Duncan Inglis or his wife. He's still not best pleased with me," he added, rueful, wiping a hand round the back of his neck. "You've no idea how many crackpots send them crazy letters every week. I've spent most of the night chained to my desk, knocking on cyber doors. No doubt I'll soon be out knocking on real ones."

They walked back along the treadplates towards the cluster of vehicles by the edge of the arena. The width meant they went single-file, didn't speak again until they reached the crime scene van.

"I assume someone's been trying to track down this man Tawney the major mentioned?" Grace asked, opening the sliding side door and depositing her bag inside. "Any trace of him?"

"Once he'd done his time, he just dropped off the map." Nick shook his head. "The man's a ghost."

"Hardly surprising," Grace commented, and when he glanced at her she said simply, "Well, wasn't that what the military trained him to do—how to disappear in hostile territory?"

Nick let out a long breath. "Yeah. Unfortunately, it was."

53

PATRICK BARDWELL CAME SURGING out of the depths of tortured sleep, on fire, drowning and deafened by silent screams.

For a long suspended moment, he grasped at the tatters of reality. His chest heaved, yet he managed to release no more than quiet whimpers. He was at once the frightened child and the monster that terrified him.

With a gigantic effort, he wrenched free of the nightmare and struck for the surface, gulping in lungfuls of hot desiccated air that he could have sworn tasted of burnt powder and aviation fuel. He ducked his head, waiting for the next assault on his senses. It never came.

Then the world righted itself, steadied, cooled, and he was back in the cramped sitting room of the byre at the Retreat, sprawled awkwardly on the rigid sofa like he'd been thrown there.

He sat up slowly. His hair had come loose, unruly, and he gathered it back, tightening the leather bootlace he used to secure it. Still couldn't get used to the length, around his shoulders like a girl.

The beard, too, was a small annoyance, wiry, itchy, threaded with more grey than he remembered, but too useful to dispense with. He'd had them before, of course. They didn't hand out razors to men in captivity.

And suddenly the walls of the sitting room started to pulse, woodchip wallpaper peeling away to reveal stained concrete beneath, scarred and stinking with desperation. He stumbled to his feet, lurched blindly through the kitchen, almost panicking when his fingers couldn't immediately release the lock on the door.

Then he was out into the stark clarity of early morning. It took him half a dozen lungfuls to clear the stench of confinement from his senses and he clung to the side of the Land Rover for support, gasping. And still he expected that any moment he would hear the outraged shouts of the guards behind him, would suffer their swift and violent retribution.

He straightened, embarrassed and shivering, but there were no witnesses to his foolish display. With a last deep breath, he forced himself inside, to close the door and turn the key.

Back in the sitting room, the Barrett stood on the newspaper-covered coffee table, stripped and cleaned and reassembled with a loving attention to detail.

He'd seen to the rifle last night. For Bardwell, it was all part of the liturgy. No point in having a weapon unless it was ready to fire. Just dead weight. Normally this process soothed him, cleansed him.

Not this time.

Maybe it was because, this time, he couldn't offload his guilt onto some faceless Rupert further up the chain of command. But he knew better than that. This was death by his design, a plan born of loyalty, sealed in blood, where a man's word, once given, was unbreakable. The money meant nothing, a means to an end.

No, it wasn't *that* kill that troubled him, but the other. The second shot that was neither hit nor miss. He'd always prided himself on the skill of what he did, precise like a surgeon.

Yesterday, he'd been a butcher.

Should have finished him.

Of course, the man might still die. Oh, she'd gone to him quick enough, that red-haired woman, with a bravery that caused Bardwell to wonder and admire, but few survived the shock of such an injury.

How the girl reacted might be a concern. Seeing the target go down was one thing. Over and done. But hearing the lad had survived could turn her mind away from it, a delayed death sparking guilt and denial. The last thing Bardwell could afford right now was for Edith to come over all noble.

That was why he'd brought her back here, straight after, bundled her into the bedroom and taken his time over her. And if he hadn't handled her as gently as he might have, she'd been right there with him, all the way.

He shrugged, fatalistic. If Edith failed him, he'd deal with her when the time came. Trying to pre-empt things would only push a possibility into a certainty, distract him from his task. He would accomplish it no matter what.

It was merely the first part that was over. Now he needed to concentrate on remaining at large long enough for the rest of it. And for that, he was going to have to do something about the Land Rover.

54

NICK PUT the phone down and rubbed a weary hand across his face, feeling the burr of stubble against his palm. His mouth tasted of old coffee and his eyes were burning. Since he'd got back from the field he'd been staring at his computer screen for four hours straight—and, before that, for most of the night as well. *The disadvantage of modern technology. It never sleeps, so neither do we.*

He always kept spare clothes in his car, so hadn't been home since yesterday. Nothing heroic about that—the whole office had the slightly sour tang of unchanged shirts and overwhelmed deodorant. An electric fan stood on one of the filing cabinets, wafting the stale air in languid sweeps. It wasn't helping much.

Nick glanced round and saw red-rimmed eyes and sagging shoulders, dogged determination in the face of exhaustion. *We're none of us doing any good here,* he considered, and knew they'd lynch him if he voiced the thought.

A few minutes ago, Jim Airey had stuck his head round the CID office door, nervy, looking for DI Pollock. Airey was in his civvies, clearly having eaten, showered and slept. The grumble of resentment that rippled outwards after he'd gone convinced Nick not to speak out.

He clenched his jaw, ignoring the ache in his back, his hand, and bent grimly over his keyboard, noted others doing the same.

Since his return, he'd been checking local firearms licence applications, old and recent, though heaven knows no-one had ever held a licence for the kind of weapon used out there. *Waste of time.* But it was procedure; someone had to do it.

Still, that didn't mean he couldn't extend the search a little to anyone who'd held collections before the gun ban, anyone who'd apparently handed everything over in dutiful fashion. Perhaps a little *too* dutiful.

Someone else had been given the job of checking into Pete Tawney and Nick had eavesdropped on progress. That was the promising lead, he could feel it. The military connection screamed at him. All the rest was going through the motions but he didn't have the standing to say so. It would make them dig their heels in, and right now he was more interested in catching this lunatic, however they achieved it.

Nick had been shot at twice when he'd been a Firearms officer in Manchester. Once with a combination of small arms and a sawn-off shotgun during a botched bank raid, and the second time by a drugs gang with an Uzi. Point and spray. Both times he'd seen the weapon before the shooting started. Only moments before, but enough to mentally brace for action.

He remembered the way Robertshaw had gone down, totally without warning. Wondered if he'd ever forget it. And Grace, defying orders, going out to him. An act of courage that terrified everybody who saw it. He'd fully expected her to disappear in a mist of blood and bone at any moment. Somehow, being out there with her had seemed preferable to watching from a cowardly distance.

And this morning, when he'd seen her sitting there amid such furious activity, dog-tired, vulnerable. It made her bravery all the more remarkable, set his stomach tensing. He sat up straighter, tried to roll the creases out of his shoulders. It didn't work.

The phone lines had been jammed since the early hours, and already the press were circling. No surprises there—an MEP's wife, shot dead in front of hundreds of witnesses. It had the glamorous smack of assassination. They were clustering around Cumbria HQ at Carleton Hall out near the motorway. At least that kept them away from the smaller station at Hunter Lane where Pollock was coordinating the official enquiry, cracking the whip over his team to get some kind of result before the whole thing was taken away from him. Not that they needed chasing.

Everyone was working themselves into the ground over this one.

"All right, lads, listen up!"

There were three female officers working plainclothes but Pollock's introduction never varied. Nick twisted in his chair.

The inspector stood in the doorway, tie hastily shoved up into the vee of a still-unbuttoned collar. He looked dishevelled and angry. There was a trace of humiliation, too, like a bear woken from hibernation and then made to dance.

The man next to Pollock had to be the cause of the inspector's ire. Small by comparison, slim, neat, in a dark three-button pinstripe suit and a tie that hinted at an old school. He stood half a pace behind the inspector, faux respectful, hands clasped in front of him and a newspaper folded under his arm. Nick almost groaned aloud.

"This is Detective Superintendent Mercer, from the Counter Terrorism Command," Pollock said flatly, eyes travelling over his weary troops as if to gauge how much more of a beating they could stand, then delivering another anyway. "He'll be taking charge of this investigation until further notice."

There wasn't a murmur so much as a collective drawing of breath. A couple of them sat back, slumped, as if their efforts had been for nothing. Mercer's gaze moved over them with clinical detachment, head tilted as though listening to instructions only he could hear. Nick recognised it was more than just fatigue that made him bridle.

Silence fell under this slow scrutiny. The only sound was the squeak of the oscillating fan as it ran through its tireless arc.

"Sir!" Young Yardley—it would be—slapped his hands on the arms of his chair like he was going to bounce up and make something of it. "With all due respect, sir, if we're looking for this bloke Pete Tawney, what's it got to do with CTC?"

"My department is concerned with the possible political ramifications," Mercer said with that deceptive smile below a cold gaze. "At this stage, it's not clear who was responsible for this incident—I understand Mr Tawney is just one line of enquiry, yes? Until we have confirmation, I'm afraid I've been asked to…oversee things, as it were. Particularly after this."

He seemed to look directly at Nick as he spoke, who felt a sudden sinking in the pit of his stomach, almost a premonition of

disaster as Mercer stepped forwards to flick the newspaper carelessly onto the nearest desktop.

People leaned in automatically. It was one of the red-top
tabloids, with a banner headline and a slightly fuzzy colour
photograph. The picture was of three people kneeling over
someone lying flat on the ground. He didn't need to get any
closer to recognise it, even without the headline: 'THERE BUT
FOR GRACE'

"A fine low-key job you're doing," Mercer said, mocking, and
didn't miss the venomous glances slipped in Nick's direction.
"So, would anybody care to fill me in?"

With plenty of glances at Pollock, people offered up halting
information, such as it was. Nobody had seen or heard any whispers. They'd had no joy tracking down their one possible
suspect, and forensic evidence still being gathered. There was
nothing to go on.

"And you've been here all night for that?" Mercer said
without inflection when the last of them petered out.

Nick sensed the trap and sat very still but there were a few
self-conscious nods. Pride, from those who'd put in the time.

Mercer nodded, too, as if agreeing with some internal
comment.

"Go home," he said.

"What?" Yardley again. "But, sir—"

Mercer's icy stare slapped him down. "Anyone who's been
here more than twelve hours, go home. Get some sleep. Get a
shower and some food that doesn't come deep-fried. Get a
change of clothes. I don't want to see you back here inside six
hours at the earliest. You're no use to this investigation running
on fumes and we can't afford mistakes. If you haven't found
something useful by now, you certainly won't find it in the state
you're in."

For a moment, there was no reaction. Mercer watched them
calmly, waiting.

Then someone reached for the power button on their
computer monitor, and that broke the dam. A dozen chairs went
back, jackets were shrugged into, keys and phones shoved into
pockets. They tried to look offended, reluctant, mostly couldn't
manage it. They filed out, trying not to meet their inspector's
eye.

Nick risked a glance at Pollock and saw a simmering resentment directed towards the CTC man. Not for trespassing on the inspector's turf, he realised, but for sending his people home when it was something Pollock should have done himself. For that alone, Mercer had just earned himself the inspector's intense dislike.

Nick stood, grabbed his jacket and prepared to follow the rest, but as he reached them, Pollock fixed him with a growling stare.

"Not you, Weston," he said, lip curling. "Mr Mercer's put in a special request for your services."

"Didn't expect to see you again so soon, Nick." Mercer's smile was broad as it was insincere as he thrust out his hand.

Nick would rather have offered his hand to a Great White shark, but short of outright mutiny, ignoring the gesture would have been childish. He was thankful that most of his colleagues had already gone, but there were enough left to tar and feather him for this, he noted bitterly. He kept it as perfunctory as he could manage, the tapping of gloves before the opening bell.

Mercer turned to the depleted team. "OK, everyone. I don't have to tell you that we need to catch whoever is responsible for this, and we need to do it fast before it becomes any more of a media circus than it already is. I would suggest we concentrate our efforts on who has the capability to make this kind of a hit, at this kind of distance. I think you'll find it's a pretty exclusive club." Mercer waited until he'd received grudging nods in submission.

"Duncan Inglis is flying back from Brussels this afternoon and however unlikely it may seem, we can't ignore the possibility he might be a secondary target, so he'll be under full protection," he went on. "As I know the man, I'll brief him. I can tell you now he'll want answers. We'll be issuing a press statement this afternoon regardless." His eyes flicked to the inspector. "I'm happy to let Mr Pollock here be the spokesman. Let's give him something worthwhile to say, yes?"

Nick didn't miss the way his inspector's hands gave a convulsive clench.

"Shall the three of us carry on this conversation in your office, Brian?" Mercer continued.

"Of course," Pollock said, toneless. "Follow me."

They didn't speak again until the inspector's door was firmly closed behind them. Nick fully expected Mercer to make a jump for the executive chair behind the desk, but it seemed he felt he'd stamped his authority enough. Instead, the CTC man went to the open window, hands clasped behind him and stared out at the limited view.

Nick mentally measured the distance. *Two strides, lock both wrists, heave.* He glanced at Pollock's stony face and wondered if his inspector would back him up on suicide.

"Well, Brian, this is a bloody mess, isn't it?" Mercer said at last, any hint of softness gone. "No concrete evidence, no clear leads, and it seems like every bobby in the north of England's done their bit to muddy the waters. Not to mention running to the papers with their happy snaps."

Pollock glanced sharply at Nick, unhappy to have a witness to this dressing-down, but Mercer smiled again. "Oh, don't worry about Nick. He and I are old mates, aren't we?"

Nick's eyes went to his boss. "I once had the misfortune to be involved in an operation with the superintendent, if that's what he means."

Something flickered in Pollock's face. "We have followed procedure. I ensured the safety of my personnel, preserved the evidence, and have my lads following up every lead we can find. We have the name of a possible suspect and we're making every attempt to trace him, but other than that we have no real motive for anyone to want Mrs Inglis dead. What more did you expect?"

Mercer studied him for a long moment and Nick caught a glimpse of something very dark in him, then his face cleared. "I didn't expect you to do more than you've done. So, no offence."

The emphasis was subtle, the insult sly. "Of course, statistically, a lone sniper is far more likely to have selected a target at random," he went on. "We'll keep Mr Inglis well under wraps, just in case, but I'll be concentrating on finding this guy, rather than trying to work out why he did it. Surely strangers stand out in this type of community? I thought that was part of the charm of living out here in the sticks?"

"We've already put out appeals," Pollock said, "and we're canvassing local farmers—see if anyone's noticed anything suspicious lately." He jerked his head towards Nick. "Weston's been going through firearms licences, checking if anything pops up there."

"Waste of time," Mercer dismissed, and the fact that he'd echoed Nick's earlier sentiment did nothing to appease Nick's own dislike of the man. "Put a couple of PCs on the number crunching, if you must. I want Nick as my liaison while I'm here. Tap into his local knowledge."

"He's not a glorified tour guide," Pollock said. "I can't spare anyone." *Even him*, Nick heard.

"Oh, I think you're being a little harsh on DC Weston's excellent abilities," Mercer said. "What do you say, Nick?"

Nick wisely kept his mouth shut.

"I'm well aware what Weston's capable of," Pollock gritted out, "but—"

Mercer held up a hand to cut him off, blinking momentarily as if calming himself.

"You misunderstand me. It wasn't a request. Nick was the officer who investigated the shooting of a dog that was recently given away by Mrs Inglis, less than a week ago. An incident which nobody here felt was worth pursuing—except him. Isn't that right, Nick?"

Nick cursed silently as Pollock glared at him afresh.

"It remains to be seen if those two incidents are connected," Mercer went on smoothly, "but until then, he's with me. All right, detective inspector?"

Pollock said nothing for what seemed like a long time, then turned away as if sick of the sight of both of them. "Do what you like with him. He's all yours."

BY THE TIME Grace had been at her own desk for several hours, the need for a decent cup of tea became tinged by obsession. She popped out to the Spar nearby for Earl Grey, was gone less than ten minutes. But the first thing she saw when she walked back into reception at Hunter Lane was the forlorn figure of Edith Airey sitting under the crime prevention posters.

The girl was wearing a dreary cardigan, the wool thickened from machine washing. It hung unflatteringly on her thin frame, bagged at the front pockets. She'd teamed it with an ugly skirt over scuffed old-fashioned shoes with a single strap and buckle.

Who dresses her? She looks more seven than seventeen...

Grace paused, holding the door, until someone cleared their throat behind her and she stood aside with an apologetic smile. Edith was staring into the middle distance, locked in her own little world, but she looked up with a flicker of annoyance as Grace took the chair alongside her, as if she'd been interrupted from something important.

"Hello, Edith. I don't know if you remember me, but we met—"

"I know," Edith mumbled, looking away quickly, colour blotching her cheeks. "I'm not simple."

"I didn't think for a moment that you were." Grace waited a beat. "Actually, I've been looking for you."

Edith flushed unbecomingly. "Why's that?"

"To see how you were."

Edith raised a bony shoulder. "I'm all right," she said, lapsed back into silence.

"You got your rifle back all right, did you?"

"Yeah." Edith gave her a withering look. "Needed re-zeroing."

"Are you on your own?" Grace looked round. "Or are you waiting for someone?"

Another shrug. She sat hunkered down into herself, not making eye contact when people came in.

"Would you like a drink, perhaps?" Grace went on, as if she'd started up a chatty conversation, mentally pushing aside the mountain of data waiting on her desk to be correlated. "It's a bit warm for coffee, although there's a little place in the middle of town that does nice latte. Or would you prefer a Coke or an ice cream?"

For a moment the girl frowned as if trying to decide, then she shook her head with another uncertain little flick of her eyes.

"Mm, I suppose you're right. We *are* a little busy to be taking time out." She pulled a casually rueful face. "You've heard about what happened yesterday at the show, I imagine?"

Her eyes were on Edith's bowed head as she spoke, and she saw the tiny shiver that ran through the girl, quickly stifled. *Ah. Something she's interested in. A chance for a connection…*

"Actually, I wondered if you had any light to shed on the subject?" Grace asked then, apparently engrossed in refastening the strap of her watch.

"What?" Edith's head jerked up, meeting Grace's eye more fully now, and there was fear where it had no right or reason to be. "Why would I?"

Grace watched the swirl of emotions the girl wasn't sophisticated enough to hide. "Well, you're quite a shot with a rifle yourself, aren't you?" She ignored the bitter taste at the back of her throat, kept her tone pleasant. "I thought you could offer an expert opinion about this man, whoever he is."

For a moment she saw the war going on inside Edith's head. Surprise swamping the caution, conceit swamping that. The girl straightened, playing with the matted corner of the cardigan, brow furrowed as though deep in thought. "You think it's a bloke?"

Grace let her eyebrows rise. "Well…we try never to make

assumptions without evidence, but...yes, I suppose we do. Why?"

"There was this Russian woman during the Second World War, see—Lyudmila Pavlichenko." She stumbled a little over the pronunciation. "She was Ukrainian, actually. By the end of the war, she'd had three hundred and nine confirmed kills." No mistaking the awe in her voice.

Grace forced an admiring look onto her face. "You're very well informed."

Edith scowled, still retaining a child's sensitivity to any sign of being patronised. "Saw a documentary about her and I've been on the Internet at the library," she said with dignity. "Looked it all up."

"You're a bright girl." Grace put her head on one side, considering. "You must have done well at school."

"You reckon." She scowled all the harder. "Nobody likes a smart-arse."

"They used to tease me at school. I was too tall, too awkward. Too buried in my books."

The girl gave another listless shrug, face going slack. "S'pose."

Grace waited but Edith didn't follow up. The light had gone out again, her animation dulling as her interest faded.

"My father died when I was fourteen," Grace said then, almost remotely, staring at a bluebottle that was flipping itself at the far window, only catching the way Edith's head came up again out of the corner of her eye. "I felt as though my world had collapsed. I had no control over anything. Do you know what it's like to feel so helpless? So utterly at sea?"

Edith started to nod, stalled, so all she gave was a stilted jerk of her head.

Grace took a breath. "I stopped eating. It seemed the only thing I could do. It gave me back control." She switched her gaze back to the girl. "For a time."

Edith's mouth opened, wavered a little, then firmed. "What happened?" It came out as a croak, as though she hadn't wanted to ask but couldn't help herself.

"I had people around me who saw how unhealthy I was making myself." Now it was Grace's turn to shrug. "Not everyone's so lucky. Left to my own devices, I believe I would have developed full-blown anorexia."

Edith's gaze swept over her, almost dismissive. "You don't know what it's like to be fat and ugly," she said in a knotted little voice. "Fat and ugly and stupid."

"You're far from any of those things," Grace said, gently. "Except, I never got as far as making myself throw up. Now, that *is* a stupid thing to do."

Edith's colour rose another notch, but she said nothing.

"And the worst thing is, it doesn't work." Grace's voice was perfectly even, detached. "All making yourself vomit does is give you bad breath and makes your teeth fall out. The acid from your stomach weakens the enamel, you see. Not very attractive prospect, is it? False teeth before you're twenty."

She glanced across, knowing she was taking a risk, but wondering if anyone had voiced the dangers. She doubted Edith's parents had even realised their daughter had a problem.

"The body goes into famine mode. It starts to process what little food it gets higher up the digestive tract, holds it in the stomach for longer. You burn lean tissue instead of fat, your sodium and potassium levels plummet, and your kidneys start to fail. Eventually, you end up on dialysis. You'd have no control there, Edith. None at all."

Edith's downcast expression never altered. She sat with her teeth closed over her trembling lower lip as a single fat tear welled in the corner of her eye and ran down her pale cheek. She dashed it away fiercely, like it was the annoying fly at the window.

Grace watched and waited. "What happened, Edith? You have to tell somebody. You won't be in any trouble."

Edith jerked up to meet her eyes again, let her breath out fast through her nose, almost a snort at this very adult lie. As her head came up, Grace saw the marks on her neck for the first time.

"Oh, Edith," she murmured, agonised. "What did he do to you?"

"He didn't mean—"

"Oy! What d'you think you're up to?"

Jim Airey shouldered through the inner door from the station, all bristle and bluster.

Grace eyed him calmly as she got to her feet, refusing to be intimidated. "Edith and I were just having a chat," she said pleasantly. "It looks like it's going to be another hot day. I thought she might like an ice cream."

"She wants one, she can get it herself," Airey said, truculent. "You've no right to go bothering her. You just leave her alone, you hear me?"

Grace heard desperation rasping through his voice and, knowing she'd never get permission from either of them to take it further, made an instant decision. She stepped in close and pushed a deliberately insolent finger into his chest. "I will if you will, James," she murmured.

Airey's face flooded with furious colour. Almost experimentally, Grace prodded again, harder this time. His arm came up, swept hers aside, grabbed at her, hand closing around her bare arm, gripping tight.

Grace pulled back instantly and swatted at his fingers where they overlapped under her forearm. The unexpectedness of the move surprised him. The realisation of what he'd come close to doing made him release her abruptly. He almost stumbled back, mortified, the anger dropping clean out of his face.

"Sorry," he muttered, voice hollow. "I'm sorry, but just you leave her be, all right?"

Grace clutched her arm, her own fingers where his had been, as though he'd hurt her. She ignored Airey, glanced over to find his daughter watching the exchange intently. "It was nice talking to you again, Edith. You know where I am if ever you need me."

56

JIM AIREY WATCHED with narrowed eyes as the tall crime scene technician left the waiting area. She was still holding her arm, he saw, as if he'd done her any damage. But if she wanted to make trouble for him... Airey spun to his daughter.

"Just what have you been saying?" he hissed, voice low. "If you've been making up your stories again, Edith, I'll—"

"You'll what?" Edith said, sullen.

Then she looked up at him and for the first time, Airey saw real defiance in his daughter's face. More than just childish rebellion; true contempt. And he knew instantly that she realised he'd seen it.

"I—"

Airey felt the ground shift beneath his feet. It was like she was a block of wood he'd been working on in his cellar, sculpting, whittling away in odd moments, forgetting for weeks on end because he'd always thought he'd have time later. There always seemed to be something more important, more interesting to be getting on with.

Only now he'd been told that his creation was finished, ready or not. And whatever knowledge or values Airey had once hoped to pass on to his only child had either taken or they hadn't. Out in the cold light of day, he was suddenly aware of how much more could have been achieved in the time he'd been given. She seemed such a poor effort for his labours.

Too late.

"You just tell the inspector what you told me," he said. It should have been an order with a hint of threat to it, but somewhere along the line it became a plea. "About the bloke you saw on Orton Scar, yeah? The day you—" He stopped, reddening. "The day that dog was killed."

The door opened behind them and a uniformed sergeant stuck his head round. "All right, Jim. Mr Pollock will see you now. But I warn you—he's in a right foul mood."

There was a long pause, then Edith got to her feet. She passed him the cold assessing stare of a stranger. "You want to be careful," she said in a whisper only he could hear. "That kind of slip is going to get us *both* into trouble…"

57

GRACE WAS STILL GRIPPING her arm when she reached her office, to find Ty Frost, the young CSI from Workington, installed at her desk. He was tapping furiously at his laptop and slurping Red Bull straight from the can. She paused in the doorway and he glanced up, instantly sheepish.

"Sorry, Grace." He pushed his frameless glasses further up his nose. "Mr Blenkinship said it would be OK to set up shop in here."

She found a reassuring smile as he scrambled out of her way. "Don't worry about it."

Frost's embarrassment faded as he noticed her odd stance. "Are you all right? What's the matter with your arm?"

"Nothing," Grace said, distracted. "I just need...ah, could you uncap that felt pen for me?"

Frowning, Ty reached for an indelible marker, holding it out nervously as though offering lump sugar to a bad-tempered horse.

"Um, if you could just put a couple of little dots on my arm... there and there. That's it. Right where I've got my finger and thumb... Thanks." She finally let go, took the pen and recapped it.

"And what was that in aid of?"

"Do you know a Special here called Jim Airey?"

"Don't think so." Frost shook his head. "Why?"

"Well, he's in reception with his daughter, who's got some

very suspicious looking marks around her neck. So, I provoked Airey into grabbing me—"

She didn't need to finish. Understanding leapt into Frost's moon face. He nodded to the pen marks he'd just made on her arm. "You should be able to use those as an exact frame of reference to calculate his hand span and see if he's the one who tried to throttle her," he finished. "Sneaky."

He closed down the file he was working on, hardly glancing at the keyboard, then opened up another program from the menu, flicking her a sideways grin. "Want to give me those measurements, then?"

Grace rummaged for a tape measure, wound it around her arm from one pen mark to the other, reading off the distance between Airey's forefinger and thumb. Frost input the information, peering at the screen.

"Ah. One other thing," Grace added as the image of the hand morphed to fit the parameters. "Airey is missing the top of his right index finger. To the first knuckle—there."

Frost pursed his lips but bent over his keys without a murmur.

"There you go." He turned the laptop round slightly to face her, tried putting his own hand over the top. His rather long digits overlapped by half a centimetre at the ends.

Grace looked at the image. "Is this actual size?"

"Uh-huh." Frost wiggled his fingers. "Small hands for a bloke, hasn't he?"

"Hm." Grace sighed. "The trouble is, I won't get the girl's agreement to examine her closely enough to prove a match, so I've probably done more harm than good."

Frost held up a finger. "No. No, not necessarily. They were in reception, did you say? Let me just…" He spun back to the desk, fingers scuttering over the laptop keys. "I just downloaded some new software from the States. Allows you to freeze video footage and work up a 3D model."

"And reception is covered by CCTV." Grace moved to the phone, dialled down to the front desk. "Thank you, Tyson," she said while the line rang out, flashing him a brilliant smile. "You're a genius."

"It's just basic photogrammetry techniques. They developed it originally for digital effects—you know, in the movies," His face was the most animated Grace had ever seen it. "Did you see *Fight Club*? No, never mind," he muttered before she could answer. "Um, of course, it might not actually *work*," he pointed out. "I've agreed to be one of the beta testers. It's still kind of experimental."

He had an untidy air that brought to mind an overgrown schoolboy, with his shirttails hanging out of his trousers and his tie knot askew. But the laptop was the latest state-of-the-art design that had easily cost more than the old banger he drove.

"They're going to nip up with a copy DVD of the security footage," Grace said a few moments later, putting down the phone. It rang almost immediately.

"CSI McColl."

"Grace? Chris Blenkinship," said the voice at the other end, making an obvious effort to inject cordiality. The volume was such that Ty Frost gave a guilty start, as though caught shirking. "I just, ah, wondered how you were getting on with those calculations for the direction of the shot. I've had this CTC lad, Mercer, chasing me. Any joy?"

"I'm working on it." Grace allowed no irritation into her voice. "Don't worry. Richard's still down at the scene. As soon as I have anything, I'll take it straight to him for the search teams."

"Oh, ah, right you are, pet. Knew we could count on you."

Grace put the phone down wondering if she was being too sensitive in bridling at his use of "we", found Frost eyeing her anxiously.

"Chris is not a bad bloke. *Most* of the time."

She gave a rueful smile, brought her own computer out of standby and clicked into the maps she'd been studying before her encounter with the Aireys. She was tired, she recognised. Perhaps too tired to be doing this, but she couldn't leave it. If she didn't see it through now, the long night's labours would be for nothing.

By reconstructing the showjumping wall and pinpointing as accurately as she could where Angela Inglis, Major Frederickson, and Max had been standing at the moment of impact, she reckoned she had just about narrowed down the only possible flight path of the bullet. The theodolite had been invaluable for calculating the angles. From the statements and sketches of the scene, she knew the round had passed within a hairsbreadth of Max.

Reaction sent a cold wash of fear down her spine. She shook her head, put it aside. According to Major Frederickson's information, the most likely type of gun had a range of more than a mile. She zoomed out, put a radius around the GPS location she'd taken and there, as close as she could call it, was the search corridor.

As the printer spat out a dozen hard copies, Grace turned to the second shot. It was more difficult to track than the first. The bullet had passed through Danny Robertshaw and apparently nothing else. Blenkinship was trying to find the spent round, but no luck so far—at that kind of velocity, how far it might have continued on was anybody's guess. Without knowing its point of origin, there was no way to tell where it might finally have gone to earth. They needed to narrow it down somehow.

Suddenly, Grace remembered the last image she'd taken. She'd spotted something in the distance, a vehicle perhaps, and snapped off just one frame before setting aside her camera and walking away from Sibson, calling to Robertshaw. *Bringing him out into the open...*

She shut her eyes, squeezed the bridge of her nose with forefinger and thumb, then reached for her camera bag. The memory card she'd been working on was tucked away in an inside pocket and she slid it into the reader permanently wired into her computer.

The card held four gigabytes and was close to capacity. The images downloaded with frustrating slowness.

"Come on, come on," she muttered, ignoring the way Ty Frost glanced round nervously.

"Going as fast as I can," said a voice from the doorway. Both CSIs turned to see a uniformed sergeant with a DVD disk in his hand.

Grace took the disk, smiling an apology.

"Something important, is it?" the sergeant asked.

"We're just checking out a new piece of recognition software," she said, which wasn't entirely untrue, but Ty Frost flushed, suddenly busied himself with his keyboard again.

The sergeant gave a disinterested grunt and departed. Grace handed the DVD to Frost, who slid it into his laptop. Grace wheeled her chair closer to hang over his shoulder.

The footage was a half-hour segment, which showed Grace

leaving as well as returning. In between, the Aireys walked in, Jim ordering his daughter into a chair and bending to have what looked like a few fierce words before he disappeared into the station proper. Edith sat alone with her face averted, hardly moving. She didn't react to Grace's return until she actually sat down alongside.

"Can't get a good look at her neck from this angle."

"She looks up—when her father reappears and I rattle his cage."

"You're right," Frost said moments later, slipping a covert glance in her direction. He let the footage run a little further, then backed it up to the best spot, froze the image, selected and enlarged it. His fingers danced over the keys, delicate as a concert pianist. Grace leaned in a little closer.

Gradually, Frost's movements slowed and his eyes slid to meet hers, panic in them. "Erm, give us a bit of room, eh?" he said, squirming. "I can't do it with you breathing down my neck."

"I'm sorry. I'm just interested. This is fascinating."

His Adam's apple bobbed and he jerked his head towards her own desk. "Your pictures have finished downloading," he said with an air of hopeful desperation.

Grace took the hint and pushed back across. She scrolled right the way down to the last shot that had come off the memory card. It was a landscape, quite ordinary and innocent-looking. Except that a few moments after it was taken, every-thing had changed forever.

She had been about to get a tripod so she could take a picture with maximum depth of field, which required a relatively long exposure to eliminate camera shake. But the light had been good and Grace knew she had steady hands. As she zoomed in she was pleased to see the definition remained reasonably crisp.

And as she did so, she glimpsed something pale blue and blocky shaped, like a van. Or…a 4x4; the type farmers favoured.

Something about the shape, the colour, teased and tormented at Grace in whispers too indistinct to be more than an annoyance.

The answer unfolded out of some corner of her mind like an inflating life raft, almost overwhelming her with its sudden arrival. There had been a pale blue vehicle, like a van, in the lay-by at the top of Orton Scar on the day Frederickson's dog was killed. But where else had she seen it?

She hunted through the files, called up the right image and opened both on the screen. Even magnified as far as the resolution would allow, both remained frustratingly obscure. The distances involved were just too great to get a clear picture before it started to break down into individual pixels.

Grace sat back in defeat. *It can't be coincidence,* she thought. *There* has *to be a connection.*

And as her mind ran back over the first incident, she remembered waiting for Nick to turn around to follow her back to the cottage. He'd disappeared up the hill in that blue Subaru of his. Would he remember a parked vehicle from a week ago?

While the images were printing off, she dialled Nick's mobile number. It went straight through to his answering service. Hiding her impatience, she left him a brief message and got to her feet, gathering the printouts.

"I need to get back to the scene with these," she said to Frost.

"Erm? Yeah, OK, right." He barely turned his head, eyes glued to the screen. He groped for the Red Bull again. "Soon as I have something, I'll let you know, OK?"

"Great." Grace got to the doorway, hesitated a moment and turned back. "Oh, and Tyson—I'd appreciate it if you kept this Airey thing just between us. Whatever we get has been gathered without the Aireys' knowledge or consent. It'll be worthless in court."

That did make him look up. "Yeah, but *we'll* know," he said. "Won't we?"

58

"PATRICK!" Opening the back door of the farmhouse to Bard-well's knock, Ian Hogg's voice betrayed both pleasure and surprise. "Come in, man. I was just having breakfast. Will you join me?"

Bardwell hesitated briefly before stepping over the threshold. He'd done a few tours alongside the UN peacekeeping forces, knew that refusing hospitality could be taken as an insult or a sign of pity—that you didn't think they could spare it. Better to take a little than nothing.

"Cuppa tea maybe?" he said, wary.

"Good." Hogg beamed. "Oh, don't worry about your boots. Take a seat."

Hogg hobbled over to the scrubbed pine table where a huge stained teapot sat under an insulated cosy. The tea he poured from it was thick and hot and the colour of old beer, turning chestnut with milk. Bardwell took the proffered mug and sank into the chair nearest the Aga so he could lean down and scratch the terrier's ears. She propped her head on the side of her basket and submitted blissfully to his attentions with her eyes squeezed shut.

"Bad business, this," Hogg offered, shaking his head. "I've never seen people so frightened to leave their homes." He paused. "Like Sarajevo all over again."

"Aye," Bardwell agreed softly. "That it is."

Hogg lowered himself into the chair opposite, hooked his

cane over the edge of the table and cradled his tea. For a moment or so, neither man spoke. Bardwell felt himself absorbed by the silence, letting it swirl around him. The farmhouse kitchen had the air of being carved from time, the generations who'd passed through making only a minimal impression, so it retained its own enduring identity.

The table itself was mostly covered with the debris of old newspapers, bills and other haphazard correspondence. At the far end, a portable TV set jostled for space amid the paperwork. It was tuned to some breakfast news channel, with the sound muted.

Bardwell kept half an eye on the screen.

"So—I never asked—how did the welding go on the Land Rover?" Hogg ventured casually. "Only, I called in at the garage, and the chap there swore the chassis was sound last time he checked it."

Bardwell shrugged at that. "Well, it's done now. Not hard to remember the knack, once you get your hand to it."

"Good, good. Nice to have you looking out for the old girl, anyway."

"No trouble." Bardwell sat up, tried to keep his voice relaxed. "I saw you've got some tins of coach-paint in the barn. Wondered if you'd mind if I gave her a few coats?"

He watched Hogg go still, cautiously consider. "Well…yes, I suppose so." Then, more firmly, "Yes. Why not? Nothing outlandish, I hope."

"There's some darkish blue, looks all right." Bardwell felt his shoulders drop a fraction. "I'll get started today, then," he said, nose in his tea mug to cover his relief. "Before this weather breaks."

Hogg looked momentarily taken aback by the speed events had overtaken him. He frowned a little but evidently couldn't find a real reason to object.

A flash of red amid greenery on the TV screen caught Bardwell's eye. His head jerked at the sight of it. The red showjumping wall, taken through a long lens so it reminded him starkly of the view through the scope. Only, when he'd last seen it, it didn't have a hole through the centre.

They should have surrounded it with screens to keep the prying press at bay, he knew. Only reason to have taken them down was that they needed to see further. *Will they find the hide?* he wondered. *Will they know it, even if they do?*

Hogg saw, misread his reaction for interest and reached for the remote to turn up the volume. Together they listened to the sober voice of the TV reporter detailing events of the day before. His piece was hazy in places, outright wrong in others, but delivered so supposition carried equal weight with what facts were known. Bardwell held his peace, face neutral, but the casually twisted lies set an anger burning in his hands.

As the reporter handed back to the studio, Hogg thumbed down the volume again. "A sniper," he said, shaking his head sorrowfully. "I thought I'd left all that behind a long time ago. And you must have, too, Patrick." That intense gaze again. Hogg got stiffly to his feet, carried his empty mug slowly across to the Belfast sink and rinsed it under the tap.

While his back was turned, the silent screen flashed up an old colour photograph, the face of a man about ten years younger than Bardwell was now. In uniform, clean shaven, with his hair trimmed well back, the man had stared straight at the camera for the picture with a mix of bravado and apprehension, yet to witness the reality of what he'd signed up for.

Hogg turned away from the sink just in time to catch the last few seconds of the face. "Is that who they think is responsible?"

Bardwell shrugged again, held his gaze like a man with nothing to fear. "Must be."

"Some army lad gone off the rails, by the look of him." Hogg moved back to the table, dragging his leg. "They train them for the life, then let them go and wonder why they can't cope with what that comes after. It always ends in tragedy of one magnitude or another." He shook his head. "We only get to hear about the big ones."

"Dunblane—he wasn't army," Bardwell pointed out. "Nor was Hungerford."

"True enough," Hogg admitted. "Not to mention that taxi driver here a few years back, over on the coast." He regained his seat, looked at Bardwell intently. "Did you ever kill anyone, Patrick?"

Bardwell looked away, took another swig of tea, wiped his beard. "Part of the job description, wasn't it?"

"Soldiers, yes—the enemy," Hogg said quietly. "I meant civilians. People who were simply in the wrong place at the wrong time." He nodded to the TV set. "Like that poor woman, and the policeman."

"Not for no reason. Not if there was a way to avoid it." Bardwell put the mug down. "Orders come and they don't tell you *why* something's to be done. Would do you more harm than good to know it, most of the time. You just got to trust somebody somewhere made the right call."

Hogg seemed about to argue, then gave a sad shake of his head. "I suppose so. In time of war we can't have every lowly private second-guessing the generals, can we? It would be chaos."

"Might not get any fighting done, though," Bardwell said with bleak humour. "That would be no bad thing, eh?" Both men smiled. Bardwell paused. "He dead then, is he? That policeman?"

"Hm? Oh, I'm not sure. Last night on the news they just said 'critical condition', which sounds pretty bad however you take it. Either way, he's lost his arm, poor devil. Just for doing his job."

"You were doing your job," Bardwell said, nodding to Hogg's cane. "Didn't get much pity for that, did you?"

"I asked for none, Patrick." Hogg's voice was gentle in its chastisement. His eyes slid to the screen again, although the picture now was a weather map. "But the man can hardly be classed as a combatant. That makes him an innocent in my book. Nobody has the right to kill innocents."

Amen to that.

Bardwell stood, suddenly restless and looked down at the former priest. "Plenty of vengeance in the Bible," he said.

He had a sudden flash of a young face, fresh and smiling, filled with vitality and the willingness to learn. Such a small coffin.

There are no innocents left.

59

Nick sat in the lobby of the North Lakes Hotel on the outskirts of Penrith, staring gloomily into the dregs of his third cup of coffee. Not that he didn't need the caffeine, he acknowledged. Even his legs ached with fatigue. He would have sold his soul for a short run, a long shower, a meal and a bed.

Instead, on his inspector's orders, he was waiting at the convenience of Superintendent Mercer, who'd checked in and disappeared off to his room, ostensibly to make phone calls too important to be overheard.

Left kicking his heels in the baronial lobby with its huge central stone fireplace, Nick thought savagely that it was a pity the CTC man had not always been so security conscious.

He leaned back in his plush armchair and resisted the lure of sleep. He could just imagine Mercer's comments if he found his designated driver snoozing on the job.

The hotel had a coffee shop as well as the usual bar and restaurant, and the constant bustle helped. Nick people-watched out of habit. At the reception desk, built into an arched alcove, a family was just checking out, surrounded by the paraphernalia of small children. He thought of Sophie and something tightened in his gut.

Into a lull, his cellphone bleeped. He pulled it out to find a voicemail from Grace. With one eye in the direction of the rooms, he dialled her number.

"Hello Nick," she said as she picked up, and he thought he could hear her smiling. He wondered why that small fact should please him.

"What can I do for you? Please tell me it's some kind of emergency that requires my immediate presence?"

She laughed softly at the pleading note. "Sorry. It's only your mind I'm after. You remember the day I called you out to Major Frederickson's dog?"

"I'm not likely to forget. Why?"

"When we left the field, where did you turn your car round to follow me back to the cottage?"

Nick heard the underlying tension, shut his eyes briefly, let the memory unfold, opened them again. "There was a lay-by at the top of the hill," he said. "Just before a cattle grid, on the left. Quite a big one, rough, full of potholes."

"Do you recall seeing any other vehicles?"

"An old Land Rover." The picture sprang straight into his mind. "It was pale blue, a bit decrepit—the paint was scabby."

"I suppose it would be too much to ask if you got the number?" Grace said then, almost breathless.

"The first or last letter was L for lima." *L for Lisa*, he'd thought at the time. "Other than that, no, sorry."

"Goodness, don't be sorry. I'm amazed you've retained that much."

Movement near the reception desk caught Nick's eye, made him glance up. Four men had just come in, wearing suits and carrying small overnight bags. They put the bags down, looked about them. The girl behind the desk appeared almost instantly, greeted them with a professional smile.

"So," Nick said into the phone, "am I allowed to ask what this is all about?"

"I found a pale blue vehicle in the extreme background of one of the images from the show field yesterday. The last one I took just before Robertshaw was shot," Grace said, nothing in her steady tone. "So far, the colour and shape matches. It could mean we were right about Frederickson's dog—taking it seriously, I mean. I can't make out any detail as yet, but I'm going to try and enhance the photo…"

As he listened to her explain the process, Nick watched the

new arrivals. Big guys, muscular under their business attire, moving with a physical awareness of their surroundings uncommon in civilians. And the way one of them stood, a little back from the others, with his weight even-spread and his hands clear, made the hair prickle at the back of Nick's neck.

"...so, thank you," Grace finished. "That's been a great help."

Nick still had his eye on the man, saw his head start turning in his direction and focused himself into the phone call instead, putting effort into showing no unease. He crossed his legs, let his foot swing negligently. "I do my humble best."

"If there's one thing I'll never associate with you, it's humility."

He grinned. "Well, if this leads to a startling breakthrough, I'd be grateful if you'd mention my part in it to Mr Pollock," Nick said. "I'm not exactly in his good books at the moment."

"I can't imagine what you've done—," she began, stopped suddenly. "Ah, this is because of yesterday—on the field. I'm sorry, Nick, if I've caused you grief. Would it do any good if I spoke to him, tried to explain?"

"No," Nick said, just as Mercer reappeared. "Best to let it lie, don't you think?"

"Well, if you're sure? Either way, I owe you the most enormous favour."

Across at the desk, Mercer was dropping off his key, smiling that crocodile smile of his. The receptionist was still dealing with the newcomers and was too distracted to recoil at the sight of it, Nick thought nastily. But as Mercer turned away, he made eye-contact with one of the four. Mercer clearly picked up the same vibe from them. Nick caught the slightest hesitation in his stride. *Interesting.*

"I've got to go," he said quickly. "I'll catch you later, OK?"

He ended the call before Mercer reached him. The CTC man had changed his suit and his slicked-back hair was damp from the shower, Nick noted. He squeezed out a bland smile while cursing roundly inside.

"Sorry about that." Mercer gave an insincere grimace. "Shall we make tracks?"

It was posed as a question, but he'd turned and headed out without giving Nick much choice but to follow.

As they passed the front desk, the men were being handed their keys amid the usual explanations of breakfast times and use of the indoor pool. They had casually positioned themselves to cover all the exits, jackets unbuttoned, hands empty. Nick kept his face placid, but for the first time since he'd walked into that warehouse ambush, several lifetimes ago, he had a sudden desire to be armed.

The men said their thanks to the receptionist politely enough, picked up their bags without drama and headed off. As Nick followed Mercer outside, he was careful not to make the mistake of looking back.

"Always did like your snazzy motors, didn't you?" Mercer said as Nick blipped the locks on the Impreza. "Thought you'd have bought yourself a nice people-carrier by now—you being a family man."

Nick ignored the jibe, pretending to be side-tracked by the sight of an outside broadcast truck pulling off the roundabout, bristling with antennae.

"The vultures are circling," he said as they climbed into the car. "We'd better hope we get this guy quick."

"Oh, we'll get him, Nick—one way or another," Mercer said with relish, reaching for his seatbelt. "Don't you worry about that."

It was the smug little smile that did it. Nick had already slotted the key into the ignition, but at that, he withdrew it again, opened his door.

"Ah, sorry," he said, with every appearance of innocent regret. "Just remembered I didn't pay for my coffee."

Mercer waved an impatient hand. "They can afford it."

"Not the point, sir. Won't be a minute." And he hopped out before Mercer could object further, jogging back across the car park to the entrance.

Mercer wasn't to know that Nick's years working undercover and surveillance had made him always prepared to move off at a moment's notice. Therefore, he'd made a point of paying for his coffees when he ordered.

Now, he walked back into reception and checked the four men had gone. The professional greeting of the girl at the desk faltered a little when he produced his warrant card.

"There's no problem," he assured her, "but I need to borrow one of your security tapes."

"Well," she said, fluttering. "I'm not sure—"

Aware of his unwelcome passenger sitting drumming his fingers in his car outside, Nick leaned on the counter and turned up the intensity of his smile.

60

"WELL, Edith, I hope you're proud of yourself." Jim Airey's voice was guttural with anger.

In the passenger seat of the old family Vauxhall, Edith barely turned her head. *Didn't ask me if I wanted to come and talk to your stupid old inspector, did you?* she thought furiously. *You just dragged me up here like a piece of meat and thought I'd play along like a good little girl. Well, not anymore, Daddy dear.*

But she said nothing out loud, just continued staring blankly out of the side window at the fields and hedges flitting past the glass.

She'd been shaking with nerves by the time her father led her into his inspector's office back at the station. After what that stuck-up redhead had hinted, she thought they'd somehow uncovered her and Patrick. Why else would her father haul her in there, all "say nothing to your mother", cloak and dagger?

It was only when she listened open-mouthed to his explanation to his boss that the rage finally overrode the fear. Even to her own ears, it sounded like a lame story. The way he told it, she'd been out shooting rabbits and seen some apparition with a long gun lying hidden in the grass overlooking Angela Inglis's house, stalking her. He was so busy steering things away from the fact it had been Edith with the AK that what was left was meagre, unconvincing.

If he'd bothered to tell me what he was about, I could have come up with something much *better,* she seethed. Not, of course, that she had any inclination. Not now.

"You made me look a right idiot back there, telling Mr Pollock you made it all up." Airey's tone was petulant now, whiny. Edith glanced across at him. She'd baulked when Patrick had suggested her father as the next target. Next time, she wouldn't argue. *Next time...*

On the opposite carriageway of the motorway, heading north, were a stream of outside broadcast vans with the logos of satellite news channels emblazoned up the sides.

Her father saw the way her head turned.

"They've been arriving all day." He flexed his sweating fingers round the steering wheel. "You're not to go anywhere near them reporters, d'you hear me, Edith? I know their sort. Won't stop until they've dug up all your dark little secrets. Can't afford that, can we?"

Edith barely heard the contempt. Her mind was seeing the rush of the press surrounding her arrival at some glittering event. She saw herself stepping out of a chauffeur-driven limousine onto a blood-red carpet, illuminated by the strobe of flashbulbs. The women would all be craning, envious, to see what designer gown she was wearing. The men would just be craning.

She'd pause, poised, graciously allowing them to take the pictures that would litter the following morning's society pages.

She'd be interviewed on all the chat shows, dazzling them with her candid charm. And the photo spreads in the glossy celebrity magazines, showing the all-white mansion where she would make her elegant home. Huge window drapes and four-poster beds, an indoor swimming pool done up like a Greek temple. She'd pored over them enough to hear every lavish word of praise, visualise each frame.

And at the centre, there she'd be. Her. Edith Airey. In a variety of easy poses, the man in her life holding her close, her arms wrapped around his neck as he stared adoringly into her eyes.

Patrick Bardwell, looking like some kind of James Bond in a black tuxedo and a startlingly white shirt. In her mind she dispensed with the beard, the shaggy hair, leaving him ruggedly handsome, younger than he seemed in his casual clothing, darker, more brooding.

The last time they'd made love, at the byre after the kill, he'd hardly been able to keep his hands off her, tumbling her into bed like something out of a late-night movie. Blushing furiously at the memory, she pressed her narrow thighs together, desperate to hold in the secret need.

And as she did so, the real truth of it landed, soft as snow. Because, surely he couldn't want her so passionately, so urgently, and not love her the same way she loved him?

61

MERCER DIDN'T ATTEMPT to engage Nick in conversation during
the run down to Orton and for that, at least, Nick was grateful.
Instead, the CTC man spent his time engrossed in the case
reports, leaving his driver alone with his thoughts.

Behind him, underneath his jacket on the rear seat, was the
security video from the hotel. It had taken a bit of fancy foot-
work to get them to hand it over, but having a long-range killer
on the loose had already caused cancelled bookings and short-
ened stays. Fear alone was making people unusually co-
operative.

He wasn't entirely sure what made him go back for the tape.
Something in the momentary look that passed between Mercer
and the men in the hotel lobby tweaked his instincts. Now he
wanted to know who they were, why they were here.

Nick resisted the temptation to make Mercer carsick, keeping
it smooth and to the speed limit. More TV crews were heading
north on the other carriageway, he noticed, just as packed-up
cars and caravans were flooding south. Tourists cutting short
their holidays.

Eventually, Mercer reached the final page with a grunt. "Well,
it seems your crime scene people are reasonably on the ball."
And Nick almost heard, *even if nobody else is.*

"They seem very thorough," he said neutrally.

"And easy on the eye, huh?" Mercer flicked him a sly glance.
"Let's face it, Nick, you weren't thinking with your brains when

you rushed out to play the white knight to that McColl girl, were you?"

Grace is a woman, not a girl. Nick busied himself with over-taking a dawdling Vauxhall saloon in the left-hand lane, making more of it than he needed to, just to negate a reply.

Mercer took his silence for guilt, continuing to pin Nick with a cool indolent stare. "So, how's the luscious Lisa and that little moppet of yours? Chlöe, wasn't it?"

"Sophie," Nick bit out. "They're fine."

"Really?" Mercer lounged in his seat. "Only, when I called round to see you the other morning, I rang the bell at your flat and there was no reply. Bit early for her to be out, I thought, with the kiddie." He left a long pause but Nick kept his eyes stead-fastly on the road. "Do I detect a hint of trouble in paradise?"

You couldn't detect your own backside with both hands and a sniffer dog, Nick raged silently, kept his face bland.

"This is our turnoff." He put the Impreza hard enough into the tight curling slip-road to throw his passenger against the belts and send him grabbing for the armrest.

Little victories...

Mercer didn't try to score any more points for the remainder of the drive up through undulating countryside to Orton village. The road was edged by dry stone walls, aged to grey and coated with lichens. It was flanked alternately by small stands of trees and sweeping fields, colours soft and hazy as the sun crested towards midday. Mercer looked vaguely bored.

They had to run the gauntlet of the press photographers at the gates to Duncan Inglis's imposing house while they were cleared to enter. The driveway was long and winding, the shrub-bery thick enough to keep prying lenses at bay.

As Nick swung onto the gravel forecourt, he saw a dark blue Jaguar saloon with the doors open. A young man in a discreet suit was lifting matching luggage out of the boot. Another man stood near the Jag, also wearing a suit, but there the similarity ended. He was larger, fleshy, more opulent and arrogant, in his politician's pinstripe and his handmade shoes. Even without researching the man, Nick would have recognised Duncan Inglis, MEP.

"Good timing," Mercer said. "Inglis only flew back from Brussels this morning." Just for a moment, his voice lost its mocking edge as he added, "He's already made the necessary identification."

And for all Inglis's haughty manner, Nick hoped the usual compassionate job had been done to reassemble the man's wife before he was obliged to view her body.

Inglis stood his ground and let them come to him, his eyes on Mercer. Close up, he had the confident air of a man who wields a great deal of power and is totally aware of the fact. He might once have been handsome but now he was beginning to redden and jowl. Nick could understand why his well-preserved wife had sought entertainment elsewhere.

He also did not look happy at this intrusion and, for a man in his profession, was taking surprisingly little trouble to hide it.

Mercer stepped forwards. "Mr Inglis." He thrust out his hand. "Matthew Mercer, Counter Terrorism Command. I'm very sorry for your loss, sir."

Inglis's gaze narrowed sharply and he regarded Mercer with a certain wariness.

"Really?" He had a deep orator's voice. "Tell me, Mr Mercer, what involvement does the CTC have in this tragedy?"

Nick caught the fractional flinch, quickly smothered. *Curiouser and curiouser...*

"We can't rule out anything at this stage, sir," Mercer said tightly.

Inglis nodded. His eyes flicked over Nick, managing to impart both contempt and lack of interest in a single brief glance.

"We'll continue this inside," Inglis said and turned on his heel.

Face white, Mercer twisted to Nick. "I'll speak with Mr Inglis alone," he snapped. "Wait in the car, Weston."

Nick hid a smile, nodded. "How long will you be, sir?"

A muscle clenched in the side of Mercer's jaw. "As long as it takes, detective constable. Do you have somewhere more important to be?"

"I need a shower," Nick said flatly. "If you're planning to be here a while, I've time to go and get one."

For a moment he thought the CTC man would refuse just out of spite, but then he made an impatient gesture. "Oh, do what you have to." He yanked open the car door to retrieve his paperwork, checked his watch. "Just make sure you're back here inside an hour." And with that, he strode away across the gravel.

Which barely gives me time to get home and back, never mind shower while I'm there. Nick thought bitterly as he watched Mercer disappear inside the house. But there was somewhere else he could think of, only minutes away, with a shower. He didn't think he'd ever forget the picture his imagination had painted the last time he'd heard it running.

He pulled out his mobile phone, hit redial.

"Hello again," Grace's voice said in his ear.

"Hi." He couldn't keep the sheepish note out of his voice. "That favour you owe me—can I collect?"

It only took a moment for her to agree to meet Nick at the cottage. As he started up the Impreza's engine and moved away quickly down the drive, he slotted his phone into the hands-free kit and dialled a London number he'd almost forgotten since he moved north.

"Hello, Bill," he said cheerfully when it was picked up. "How's life in the Met? Have they turned you into a soft southern shandy drinker yet?"

"Nick! Gawd, it's good to hear a friendly voice, mate. Where are you?"

"Oh, still up in the wilds of Cumbria. About eighty miles past a sign on the M6 that says 'Here Be Dragons'."

There was a splutter of laughter at the other end. "Yeah, I heard you applied for a transfer. I always thought you were a city boy, but I can't say I blame you, not after..." His voice trailed away, became a little more cautious. "Anyway, doesn't sound like life's dull up there from what I hear. What can I do for you, mate?"

"I was hoping for some inside info—on the quiet," Nick said. "Do I recall that you used to have ties with Special Branch?"

GRACE WAS at the scene when Nick rang. She took a shortcut through Raisbeck to get back to Orton but Nick's car was already in the driveway. He was leaning against the driver's door in his shirtsleeves, face tilted up towards the sun, eyes hidden behind dark glasses. He straightened slowly as she slotted the Navara in alongside.

"You look tired," she said as she climbed down. "You need some sleep."

He peeled off the glasses with a jaded smile. "Are you offering me your bed?"

"No." Grace put her head on one side for a moment, fingers sorting through her keys. "But it would probably do you more good than a shower." She moved past him to unlock the front door.

He just groaned, passed a hand across the back of his neck. "Don't tempt me."

Tallie, initially ecstatic at her return, slunk sulking under the dining table when she realised Nick was being allowed inside again. He'd retrieved his jacket and a small sports bag from the boot of his car.

"I'll put out some clean towels." Grace headed for the stairs. "Is there anything else you need?"

He shook his head, hefted the bag. "I always keep an emergency kit in the car. Just in case."

Upstairs, Grace hastily checked she'd left the bathroom in a decent state. She naturally leaned towards order, but her visits home since yesterday morning had been fleeting and tidiness had not been uppermost in her mind. It only took a few moments to clear away the discarded clothing, make sure the bath itself was reasonably clean.

"All yours," she said when she reached the foot of the stairs again, saw him hesitate. "What is it?"

"Borrowing your shower isn't the only favour I need to ask." He sounded uncharacteristically unsure of himself. "I need you to look at these."

Cautiously, Grace took the video cassette and the sealed plastic bag he offered.

"What's this?"

"Security tape from the lobby of the Lakes Hotel. Four men check in at about 11:30." He shrugged uncomfortably. "There's just something about them I don't like the look of. I wondered if you might be able to discreetly identify them."

"I'll try, of course." Grace looked at the tape, dubious. "Wouldn't it be easier just to sneak a look at the register?"

He pulled a face, wouldn't quite meet her eyes. "I did that, and ran the names and addresses on the way over here. They're dummy."

"Nick," she said quietly. "If you want my help, at least do me the courtesy of being completely honest. Who do *you* think they are?"

He met her gaze then, straight and unflinching. "I think they might be something to do with the CTC guy, Mercer, who's just muscled in on the investigation. They were hardliners, all of them." He stopped, shrugged in frustration. "I don't know. It has the feel of a covert op. I don't like it, and I'd feel a hell of a lot better if I knew what we were dealing with."

Grace gave a fractional smile. *Instinct,* she thought. *He puts as much store by it as I do in cold hard physical evidence.*

"Leave it with me. I'll do what I can." She held the clear bag up to the light, noted the scrawled time and date, saw the little matt of hair in the bottom corner. "And this?"

"Now there I *am* going to have to ask you to trust me. I think there's an outside chance it might match the dog hair we pulled from the workshop break-in in Staveley."

"And if it does?"

He shook his head again, passed her a weary look. "I'll deal with *that* when I have to."

She watched him trudge upstairs. Something warm and smooth bumped against her hand and she glanced down to find Tallie close alongside her leg, staring up with hurt reproach at this unchallenged invasion.

"Don't be mean," she chided the dog, who twitched out from under her fingers and took herself off, looking offended.

Grace heard the faint sound of the shower start to run upstairs. She looked at the tape. *CTC.* It didn't take a genius to work out that she could be opening a whole Pandora's box by prying into the men's identities. Not difficult to search; far harder not to be caught doing so.

You'll just have to be careful, then, won't you?

But when there was a knock at the front door only moments later, her first instinct was to hide the tape, shoving it under a couple of others next to the TV. She grinned at her own paranoia as she went out into the hallway.

Whoever she'd been expecting, the man who stood hesitantly on her doorstep wasn't it.

"Max!"

"Hello, Grace. I wasn't sure if you'd be here, what with... well, you know." He gave her a slightly sheepish smile. "Can I come in?"

Grace had a momentary image of Nick upstairs. *I am* not *going to feel guilty when I've no reason to,* she determined. "Of course." She stepped back. "How are you?"

He gave her a wry look. "All right, all things considered."

He was wearing one of his most devastating, expensive suits, she saw. For Max that counted as full armour, reassuring himself that yesterday was a temporary aberration in the successful life he'd carved for himself, rather than some kind of prophetic fore-runner of doom. The slight pallor and the dark circles under his eyes were the only giveaways of what it had cost him to step outside today as if nothing had happened.

Grace had known Max well enough, for long enough, to see beyond the exterior gloss to the trembling centre.

"I'm sorry," she said softly, her hand on his arm. "I know how scared you were."

He opened his mouth as if to deny it, couldn't form the

words. His eyes were suspiciously bright as he threw her a helpless glance and brought both hands up to touch her face, lightly,
almost with wonder.

"I could have lost you," he said faintly, eyes on her mouth.
"Oh darling, I thought I had."

"I'm still here," she said, wary of the emotion brought on by
fear and stress and shock. Max had always known how to play
her. She stepped back, careful not to be cruel. "What can I do for
you?" She formed a regretful smile. "I'm sorry, I need to be back
at the scene very shortly. Was there something in particular you
wanted?"

He took the hint, also moving back, swallowed a couple of
times, gathering himself. Grace waited without impatience until
finally, he looked up, spine very straight, very Italian. "Yes.
Grace, you know how I feel about you—how I've always felt
about you. And you know that all I want is for you to be happy.
So I want to ask you a question and I'd appreciate an absolutely
honest answer, no matter what."

63

NICK STAYED under the needles of hot water as long as he dared, oblivious.

The shower was over the bath on a fixed rail. Normally such an arrangement wasn't positioned high enough to accommodate his frame unless he crouched. But Grace was tall, and the pipe went right up to the ceiling before turning into a rose the size of a dinner plate.

Reluctantly, he closed the dial, towelled himself roughly dry and opened the bathroom door a crack to let some of the steam escape. The first thing he heard was a man's voice, slightly compressed, asking, "Do you love him?"

"Of course," Grace said, detached. "But not in the way you mean. After all, I've known him since he was little more than a child."

Nick froze. There was a long pause after that, then: "It's not that you aren't a passionate woman, Grace. I shared a bed with you for twelve years, so I should know, but there was always something so *appropriate* about that passion." Nick recognised the voice, could picture the baffled shrug that accompanied the words. Silently, he pushed the door wider. "I fooled myself into thinking what we had was perfect."

"I never faked anything with you, Max," Grace said gravely, but there was a hint of lazy amusement now. "I never had to, and if you believe otherwise then you're doing both of us a disservice."

"Oh, I don't just mean sexually, darling," Max Carri drawled. "When I first met you I took one look at that wondrous red hair and thought to myself, she's going to have a temper to match, you better watch yourself. But I never really got beneath the surface, did I?" He sounded regretful rather than bitter.

"The cliché that all redheads are fiery and impulsive is just that—a cliché."

"Is it? In all the time we were married I never saw you so"— he reached for the right phrase—"so *magnificently furious* as you were on that field. You saw that young man dying with nobody prepared to help him, and you were almost incandescent with rage. Is it any wonder that I ask if there's something between you?"

"If I have passion for anything now, it's for my job. For not making mistakes that get people killed. Besides, it *is* possible for men and women simply to be friends, without designs on each other. Do you understand the difference?"

"Honestly? No," Max admitted with a wry trace of humour. "I saw the emotion he inspired in you and it brought out all my least attractive possessive male instincts. Inconvenient, but I don't seem able to do very much about them as far as you're concerned."

"It's over, Max," she said, gently. "We're divorced. You have no rights of possession any longer."

"Listen, Grace—"

But Nick heard the thread of strain that wove into her voice. *Enough,* he thought, took a step forwards onto the landing and leaned casually over the balcony. They both caught the movement, twisted to look upwards. The towel around his hips meant he was decent enough, but from below it must have seemed like he was naked. If the consternation on Max's face was anything to go by, that was his assumption.

"Sorry to interrupt," he said pleasantly. "Do you have another towel, Grace?"

"Top shelf of the airing cupboard in the bathroom," she said without expression. "Help yourself."

"Who the hell is that?" Carri demanded, unsettled enough not to recognise Nick.

Embarrassed as much as angry, Nick thought. He smiled blandly. "Oh, I'm just a friend."

64

By the time Nick re-emerged, clean shaven, in a fresh shirt, Grace's ex-husband had departed. She was standing in front of the TV in her living room with the remote control in her hand, running through the security tape from the hotel.

Nick watched her frown of concentration as he came down the stairs. He'd acted on a protective impulse which, he acknowledged with an inner squirm, might not have been wise. Independent women like Grace did not always appreciate what they viewed as macho posturing...

As he reached the bottom step she slid him a sideways glance. "Feel better for that?"

Damn. "Probably better than I've any right to."

Grace let that go, nodded to the frozen picture on the screen. "These are the four you were meaning?"

The security camera above the reception desk was designed to cover as wide an area as possible. As she ran the tape forwards again Nick saw one of the men flick his eyes towards it and look away almost immediately.

Pros. But what kind? "That's them. Think you can get anything off this?"

She gave a fractional shrug. "They're using a very wide-angle lens—practically a fisheye—which is creating distortion in the features. Can you leave it with me?"

Nick nodded, checked his watch and winced. "I'd best get

back or Mercer will be stirring it with Pollock. Thanks, Grace. Now I owe *you* one."

"Several, probably," she agreed, leading him out.

On the driveway she watched him throw his overnight bag into the boot, close the lid.

"Why did you do it?" she asked then. "Intervene with Max, I mean?"

"Interesting that you choose the word *intervene* rather than *interfere*," Nick hedged. He glanced at her but read nothing from her face. *Max was right*, he thought. *She's a cool one.*

"I do hope"—she allowed a careful anger to show for the first time—"that you're not also being overwhelmed by any inconveniently possessive male instincts."

Nick had intended to be flippant but instead said seriously, "There was a certain tension in your voice, like he was crowding you. I just wanted to make him back off and give you a little space. That's all."

She raised an eyebrow. "I didn't realise I was so easy to read."

"Don't take it to heart." He opened the driver's door. "It's part of my job to listen to what people say in the spaces between the words."

After a moment, she nodded. "I see," she said remotely.

He sighed. "I'd like very much to be your friend, Grace." He saw the question in her eyes and smiled. "And yes, I *do* know the difference."

65

IN THE BACK SITTING ROOM OF the little house in Tebay, Edith Airey sat filled with a silent rage so fierce she thought her head might explode from the sheer intensity of it.

She was at the dining table, her parents on either side of her, picking over a desultory lunch of limp salad with cold baked beans and slices of tinned corned beef that her mother had prepared on her return from church.

Normally, her father spent every Sunday morning washing the car, weather permitting, leaving a scummy layer of suds trailing into the gutter. This morning he'd carted her up to Penrith for her abortive interview with his bad-tempered inspector instead. He'd barely spoken since they got back, apart from a gritted warning to say nothing to her mother. *Like I'm going to blab about it to her!*

The long afternoon stretched away ahead. Edith's mother would retreat to the kitchen to wash and iron, leaving her father to slump in front of the TV watching some pointless sport or another. European athletics. No glamour there.

It was the same every week, year in and year out. The banality was slowly driving Edith insane. She flicked a little look under her fringe at her mother's dull features, placidly shovelling food in and chewing like a mechanical cow. Her father was no better, his eyes on the paper folded next to his plate despite her mother's half-hearted protests about reading at the dinner table.

She wanted to jump up, to toss the old willow-pattern crockery into the air and scream at the pair of them. *Everything's different now! I'm different!* As she surreptitiously spat another lump of corned beef into her milk, it all seemed horrifyingly the same as it had ever been.

"I don't get a mention," Airey grumbled, sitting back. "They've made that new lad, Weston, out to be a right superhero." He sniffed. "Ought to be on a disciplinary charge, disobeying orders like that. And that McColl woman."

"I think she was very brave," Edith's mother said. "Going out to help poor Danny. She could have been killed."

Next time, Edith thought savagely, *she will be.*

The phone rang unexpectedly enough to make her start, sloshing milk onto the table.

"Oh, Edith," her mother said automatically. "Don't just sit there, lovey. Fetch a cloth."

Her father went out into the hall to answer the phone. Edith shoved her chair back and grabbed a dishcloth from the kitchen, heart thumping. As she hurried back to the sitting room, her eyes flitted over the door leading to the cellar steps, to what lay in her father's locked hideaway at the bottom.

Jim Airey was back before she'd finished mopping up the spill, making a show of annoyance but secretly buzzing, she could tell.

"That was Carleton Hall," he said pompously. "They want me in this afternoon."

"Oh, Jim," her mother protested. "Haven't you done enough?"

Her father's chest swelled. "I'm needed. With this sniper on the loose, it's all hands to the pumps."

They must be desperate, Edith thought, and didn't miss the dark look her father threw in her direction.

"Well, when will you be back? What about your tea?" her mother fretted. "I've got sausages defrosting."

"I'll grab something from the canteen when I get the chance," Airey dismissed. "Apparently, some Special Branch bloke's come up from London to take charge. He's shaking things up good and proper."

"Special Branch?" Edith queried, her voice slightly squeaky.

Her father nodded. "Must think there's some terrorist

connection. They're bringing in the big boys. We'll get him now, that's for certain."

Edith sat in a daze, her mind paralysed, while her father gathered his gear, her mother fluttering round him. The slamming of the front door behind him jolted her out of stasis.

"Well," her mother said with a tremulous smile, coming back through from the hallway. "Just the two of us, then, lovey."

Edith jumped up, her legs suddenly unstable. "I gotta go out."

"Oh, no. Where?"

"The Retreat," she mumbled, then invented, "Mr Hogg's got a—a new tenant arriving tomorrow. I forgot. He asked me to go in, special, like."

"Oh Edith," her mother moaned. "He can't ask you to work on a Sunday."

Patrick, Edith thought desperately. *I can't let them take him. Not when it's taken me this long to find someone to get me out of here…*

As suddenly as it had arrived, Edith's sense of panic left her. She turned, looked her mother straight in the face. "He's relying on me," she said calmly. "I can't let him down."

Her mother's brow smoothed as her face cleared. "Of course not. Well, it's nice that he trusts you with the responsibility, I suppose. Make sure *you're* back in time for your tea, though, won't you?"

Edith mumbled a noncommittal reply, scrambled into her coat and slipped out through the backyard to the scooter. She rode down to Grayrigg hunched over the handlebars, the throttle twisted open as far as it would go. It still took an agonisingly long time to reach the Retreat.

She flung herself off in the yard at the byre door. When there was no answer to her frantic knocking, she looked around, almost hysterical, saw the main doors to the barn propped open and ran up the yard, arms pumping.

Inside the barn, Patrick Bardwell was sitting on an old oil drum, stripped to the waist, very carefully laying on dark blue paint to the rear panel of the Land Rover. He glanced up sharply as she came flailing into view.

"Patrick!" she cried, and promptly burst into tears.

Bardwell set down his paintbrush across the edge of the open tin and got slowly to his feet. She thought he'd come to her then, but he moved over to the workbench and stood there, wiping his hands on a bit of rag, not taking his eyes off her.

"What's the matter?" he said at last, when her initial sobs had subsided into noisy sniffs.

"Special Branch," she managed to get out. She moved over to the oil drum, idly picked up the paintbrush, managed to get paint on her hands and put it down again, flushing, wiping her fingers on the sleeve of her shirt. "Dad says they've called in Special Branch—some bloke from London. They think you're a terrorist! Dad reckons it won't be long before—"

"You trust your dad more than me and we call this a day right now," he cut across her quietly, throwing the rag back onto the bench. Edith was fascinated at how the muscles in his chest meshed and slid under his skin. He had the look of a man race fit, carrying weight for purpose not just for show. She swallowed, mouth going bone dry.

"I–I don't," she whispered, suddenly embarrassed, looking at her toes.

He came forwards then, close but not touching. Edith risked lifting her gaze a little, was confronted by a hairless male chest only a foot or so away, a small tight nipple. She flushed scarlet at the surge of lust, let her head droop again. His fingers hooked under her chin, tipped her head up, callused thumb smoothing her jaw, mesmeric.

"If they're from London, your dad doesn't know what he's talking about," Bardwell said, matter-of-fact. "Special Branch changed their name a good few years ago to the Counter Terrorism Command, SO15. MI5's bully boys."

Edith heard something in his voice. Slowly, her head rose, past the temptation of his bare chest to fix on his face. Often it was hard to tell his expression, what with that beard, but this time there was no doubt. He was smiling.

"You knew," she choked. "You knew they were coming!"

"Knew? I was counting on it."

66

THE LIGHT WAS NEARLY GONE. Walking at a funereal pace behind the ragged line of the search team, the steadily dropping sun elongated Grace's shadow until it stretched across the grass to brush their feet.

She rechecked the coordinates again on her hand-held GPS.

"How much further, d'you reckon?" one of the sergeants asked, waving through the clouds of midges. There was doubt in his words, his face, that he was only just keeping in check. He would not continue to do so, Grace recognised, for much longer.

"Not far," she said, more confident than she felt. Richard Sibson had backed her theory or he wouldn't have let her tie up personnel, she reminded herself. Even if Chris Blenkinship pointedly chose to stay behind at the field. If he'd thought there was any chance she was right, he wouldn't have let her do this without him.

"We must be close to a mile out." The sergeant shaded his eyes as he turned back to stare in the direction they'd come. "Can't have fired from this far, surely?"

"The witnesses agreed there was a gap of several seconds between Mrs Inglis being hit and the sound of the shot. That points to distance."

The sergeant looked about to comment on the well-known veracity of witnesses, but shrugged instead.

Then one of the search team stopped and raised his hand, creating a bow in the line until the message filtered along. They halted, heads turning in a long ripple. Grace and the sergeant hurried forwards.

"Been some digging here," said the searcher who'd stopped. A young lad, not long out of training and red-faced at the attention.

Grace squatted down, careful to keep a distance.

Behind her, the sergeant said dismissively, "Animals, most likely."

"Only if they've mastered using a turf cutter." Grace pointed to a faint outline just visible in the grass. "OK, mark it." She rose, giving the young searcher a brilliant smile. "Well done. I think you might have found our hide."

"You want me to radio in to Mr Sibson?" the sergeant asked. Grace nodded, already unshouldering her camera, but a minute or so later he returned with the news that Sibson had not been available. "But Mr Blenkinship says he's on his way," he reported without inflection. "You want to wait until he gets here?"

"I don't think so," Grace said briskly, hiding her disappointment. No point in asking the ground troops to take sides.

She worked quickly. By the time Chris Blenkinship arrived, flustered, nearly an hour later, Grace had confirmed the find. Dressed in another Tyvek suit, hood pulled tight around her face, she had carefully dug round the cut edges of turf and discovered a chickenwire layer underneath, so the whole thing could be lifted as a whole to reveal the dugout hide beneath, the framework of crushed branches that had supported the roof of the structure, like a tent.

"Grace!" he said, striding forwards. "What—?"

"Stop there, Chris," she commanded. He froze, angry. "I'm still waiting for treadplates. Until then, I'd rather no-one else approached the scene."

He simmered visibly. "I've some in the van. Sergeant! Give me a hand."

Nevertheless, laying the protective plates to form a common approach path enabled Grace to sift through the location for a short while longer. She was still working, head down, when Chris's figure finally towered above her.

"You were told to wait!"

"We're already past dew-point and time is of the essence," Grace pointed out calmly. "Where's Richard?"

Blenkinship jerked his head and she saw the tall gangling figure of Sibson making his way across the grass. "So, what have we got?"

Grace sat back on her heels. He was a big man, she noted dispassionately, who nevertheless lacked the physical presence of Nick Weston. It was in her analytical nature to wonder why.

"It's a very cleverly dug hide." As Sibson drew nearer, she switched her attention. "That bank of nettles shields it from the front and, because of the slight drop of the land and the way it's constructed, it would be very difficult to spot when it was occupied." She nodded over to where some of the search team still lingered. "If a sharp-eyed young constable hadn't had his wits about him, we would have walked right over it."

"Yeah, good work," Blenkinship dismissed, impatient. "Anything left inside?"

"Well, I've only just started, but there's some hair that might have come from our sniper. I've bagged it and—"

"OK, pet," Blenkinship interrupted. "You've done enough."

Grace straightened slowly, flicked her eyes towards her boss who was standing silently alongside. "Enough?" she queried, looking to her boss for support.

"You worked all through last night, Grace," Sibson said quietly. "Tired people make mistakes, and we can't afford any on this one." He skimmed her stunned face. "Chris will take over."

"How does anything I've done so far classify as a mistake?"

Blenkinship coloured. "Well, getting your face plastered all over the tabloids isn't exactly a good career move."

"Maybe not," Grace returned. "But it was either that or watch a man bleed to death in front of me." She stepped up out of the hide, so she could meet him on a level. "I didn't realise at the time that anyone chose *not* to go to his aid because they were worried how it would look on their next performance review."

I must be tired, she thought with an inward groan, watching the anger tighten his features. He stepped in closer, would have bitten back had Sibson not put a warning arm between them.

"Go home, Grace," Sibson murmured. "You've done good work here, but don't spoil it. Let's just say emotions are running high and leave it at that, shall we?"

Grace stepped back, face blank. Blenkinship held out his hand and, for a ridiculous moment, she thought he was asking her to shake. Then she realised what he wanted and dropped the sealed evidence bag containing the few strands of hair into his outstretched palm.

He nodded shortly, dismissing her.

"We'll get this rushed through the lab," Sibson said.

But Grace had already walked away.

67

MIDNIGHT. Nick sat in a nondescript Ford Mondeo in a lay-by just off the main road from Kendal to Windermere, listening to the ache in his bones like they were whispering the story of his past. They hurt more when he was keyed up, as if to remind him of the price of overconfidence.

He shifted pointlessly, knew he wasn't going to find a comfortable position. There was a time when he had the patience of a crocodile for surveillance. Not anymore.

Finally, a set of unsteady headlights appeared down the narrow lane ahead to his left, bumping cautiously between the high stone walls. He slid down a little in his seat as they reached the junction, so his silhouette didn't break the line of the head-rest. Just another parked car.

The traffic on the main road was sporadic and the vehicle pulled out without stopping completely, a white Luton box-van. It trundled away, all legal and sedate, towards Kendal, but it had paused just long enough for Nick to make out a familiar face behind the wheel—Lisa's brother, Karl.

Nick had already run the numberplate, knew it belonged to the firm Karl worked for. The same one he'd used to collect Sophie's Wendy house. Was it only yesterday morning? Foolish of Karl to wave it under Nick's nose like that but then, he'd always possessed more low cunning than outright smarts.

Hence the fact the barn workshop at the top of the lane was not rented in Karl's name, but one of his workmates'. It had taken only minor digging on Nick's part to uncover the connection.

He gave them another ten minutes, so they'd be almost back to the firm's base on one of the trading estates in Kendal. Locking the car behind him, Nick slipped across the verge and hopped over the gate into the nearest field. The dry stone walls that bordered the lane were close to six foot, with the bank under them, and he was mindful of Grace's warning on their first meeting about the perils of trying to get over such an obstacle in a hurry.

Grace had called him earlier that evening to tell him she'd done a preliminary exam of the hair sample he'd given her.

"So far, it's a visual match to the hair I collected at the break-in. If you want me to stand up in court and say so, I'll need to send it away and have the lab confirm it. I assume you don't want to be quite so official at this stage?"

"You assume correctly. Thanks for getting to it so fast when you're up to your neck. I heard you found the hide. Well done."

"I'm being 'rested', I believe is the term." Though her voice was dry, he caught the vibrations.

"I'm sorry. Blenkinship can be a right prat."

"Mm, well, if not full time, he certainly helps out when they're busy," she agreed gravely. "Let me know how it goes, won't you? Whatever it is."

So here he was, trudging up a rough field in the dark, dressed head to foot in black from his watch-cap to his boots. Tucked inside his jacket were a slim jemmy and a lock-pick set, either of which would have earned him a trip to the cells if he was caught with them. Hell, he would have arrested himself.

There was hardly any moon. Nick carried a five-cell Maglite with his gloved hand cupped round the head shading the beam of light, and the heavy stem resting on his shoulder. That way, he could use it as a club if he needed to, with less chance of breaking the bulb.

Not that Nick expected to encounter anyone. The workshop was part of a cluster of converted farm buildings. The land was long-since swallowed up by neighbouring farms, the farmhouse itself derelict. Wouldn't be long before some developer got hold of it.

There was a rustle ahead of him in the darkness, a stamp and snort. Startled, he swung the torch up, caught the reflection of strange oval green eyes in the dark, then the scutter of feet against the rocky ground as a trio of shaggy ghosts fled away up the hill.

Just sheep.

Nick's heartrate had settled by the time he passed through the collapsed metal gate into the yard at the top of the field. All was silent. He was after the smaller of the two barns, slate rather than stone, with a solid new door to keep out the curious. It was secured with a well-oiled padlock that made Nick's job easier. Even so, he was out of practice, juggling the torch awkwardly under one arm while he finessed the tumblers.

Inside, there was no peripheral light. The Maglite's beam was a pale cone surrounded by utter blackness. Nick cast about, saw piles of what seemed like junk, scattered tools, rusting farm machinery that could have been medieval instruments of torture.

And three similar-shaped humps under dustsheets.

He pulled back the corner of the first. Under it, the quad bike was so new it still had the shiny release agent on the bulbous tyres. He pulled a printout from his pocket, checked the serial numbers, took his time about it so there'd be no mistake. All three matched his list.

When he was done, he covered them over again, exactly as they were, even looked to see what footprints he'd left in the dust on the concrete floor. He didn't want to leave anything for someone as keen-eyed as Grace to lift afterwards.

He left as quietly as he'd come, clicked the padlock shut on its hasp, retraced his steps down the field, this time without ovine interruption. The whole operation took twenty-three minutes, start to finish.

It wasn't until he'd regained the driver's seat of the Mondeo that he began to swear at Karl's arrogant stupidity and—with entirely selfish awareness—at the position he'd put Nick into.

Solving the robberies wasn't the hard part. They had physical evidence linking Karl to the crime scene of at least one, and now the goods in his workmate's lockup. Wouldn't be difficult to get the other man to roll over. In Nick's experience, there was very little honour among thieves.

Open and shut. Even a chance that DI Pollock might smile favourably on him once more.

But Lisa would be a different story. She'd see it as persecution. Getting back at her by lifting her brother, regardless of Karl's part in his own downfall. And he'd milk his own innocence alongside Lisa's anger until the only glimpse Nick was likely to catch of Sophie would be birthdays and Christmas, if he was lucky.

Bloody idiot…

With a sigh, Nick drove back towards Kendal. But as he reached the turnoff to Staveley, he took it. After all, Karl wasn't the type to have kept his activities completely under wraps. And he was unpleasant enough to have made enemies on his own doorstep.

Nick drove through the middle of Staveley and spotted what he was looking for opposite the fish-and-chip shop—a public phone box. Not many of them left. He parked further along the street and jogged back. Quickly, he dialled the number of Kendal nick, hoping it wasn't anybody he'd recognise on the desk tonight.

"Hey, listen up," he said when the phone was answered, laying on the Manchester accent. "You want them scallies what took them quads?" Knowing they'd be taping the call, he gabbled through a brief description of the barn's location, vague enough not to be suspicious but leaving no doubt, rang off when they asked for his name.

No glory, he reflected as he started up the Mondeo and headed home, *but, with any luck, no grief, either.*

68

GRACE LAY CURLED on the sofa with Tallie sprawled alongside her, head resting on her thigh. Distracted, she played with the Weimaraner's silky ears, ignoring the pair of anxious amber eyes regarding her.

She was aware of a grinding fatigue, knew she ought to go to bed, but the effort required by the short climb seemed too much. Easier to sit in the semi-darkness, taking comfort from the dog's proximity.

Grace was still smarting at Sibson's betrayal. She couldn't see it as anything else. Logic told her that Chris Blenkinship had seniority, but she still took it as a personal slight that she wasn't trusted to take charge of the scene *she* had discovered.

After Blenkinship's curt dismissal she'd gone back to Hunter Lane, desperate to still be of some use. When it became clear there was little for her to do, she'd analysed the dog hairs Nick had given her. He'd sounded grim at the news they were a match, as though it was an unwelcome confirmation.

Back in Orton, Tallie trembled with excitement in the hallway at her return, and the prospect of her nightly walk. Guiltily, Grace took her for a swift circuit of the village in the gathering darkness. Her feet were on automatic pilot, leaving her mind to roam. She faltered over an evening meal, her appetite shut down, but Tallie had no such troubles, wolfing what was put into her bowl.

Later, flipping through a pile of borrowed DVDs, she found a copy of *Fight Club*, the film Ty Frost had mentioned, put it on. It proved a good, if fleeting, distraction. So she sat in silent contemplation, telling herself that, despite Blenkinship's attitude towards her, she *was* good at her job. Better than he was. Sibson had indicated the Carlisle CSI would be next in line for promotion, and if her boss was thinking of retirement as he'd hinted, Grace suddenly saw all her recently found satisfaction and security slipping away.

She tipped her head back, closed her eyes.

I can't go yet. I haven't finished making amends…

Blenkinship might not want her at the scene, but there was plenty more to be done. Identifying the pale blue Land Rover, for a start. If she could work to enhance the photos, she might—

The phone made her jump, sent Tallie skidding off the sofa, letting out a single muted bark. Grace checked the time. One a.m. Knew instinctively that it would not be good news.

69

BARDWELL HAD ALWAYS FELT TOTALLY at home in the dark. Sometimes a velvet warmth, sometimes cruel, it embraced and concealed. Reminded him of his boyhood, camping trips and smoky fires, the feeling that he could touch and hear and smell his surroundings in a way that was somehow stunted by daylight.

In the wastes of Iraq, temperatures had plummeted with the sunset, so those who'd dropped from heat exhaustion during the day stumbled and fell away to hypothermia at night. Bardwell treated the landscape with the respect it deserved, almost reverence—an awareness of the dangers alongside the stark beauty. He survived because he harmonised rather than tried to master.

Now, in the moderate cool of an English June night, he moved across the unfamiliar terrain of Birkett Common like a ghost, picking his way by the light of a gibbous moon. He'd started out on the old Tommy Road, named after the First World War squaddies who constructed it, then broken away onto the rough ground, over the railway line, and dropped down towards the valley floor with Wild Boar Fell looming behind him.

In the quiet, Edith tumbled into his mind, the girl's near hysteria when she'd come to him earlier. She was becoming a worry all right.

Have to do something about that.

Bardwell's vision turned inside out, shooting backwards like speeded-up film, to a girl in Bosnia who'd shown him those same lustful eyes, brimful of cunning and promise while she'd fingered the muscles under his uniform and haggled about the price. She'd looked the same age, too, but had probably been younger. At the time he hadn't cared.

Besides, she was the wage-earner of the family by dint of attrition. Her father was dead in an artillery strike, she told him, matter-of-fact. Her mother had gone one day to the market and simply never returned. One older brother claimed by ethnic cleansing. Another to shrapnel from a landmine. She had just a younger brother and a baby sister, barely walking, in a half-shattered apartment building on the eastern side of the town. She locked them in every day while she went out to provide for them.

As he'd laid down with her, Bardwell had thought he'd heard weeping somewhere at the back of his soul. He'd closed his mind to it, and had laid down with her anyway.

Two days later, she was reportedly caught in the open by a Serbian sniper. It was another week before he'd heard. Ironic that it should be one of his own select band of brothers who'd taken her. He tried, from her hazy descriptions, to locate the apartment block where she'd lived and to trace the two lost little children trapped inside. His failure, not knowing if their existence was real or simply imagined—maybe some justification for the acts she felt compelled to perform with strangers—shaped his waking dreams, even now.

Bardwell crossed the drowsy River Eden, plotted a course towards the main road to give each of the sporadic dwellings the widest berth. Not that most people chained their dogs out anymore, but the habit was ingrained.

His objective was a derelict barn, standing east of the road with a curve of trees less than a hundred yards behind it and no houses close by. He'd seen it by chance, driving down the valley. It had only one obvious approach, the incline steep enough to ensure all but the fittest would be moving nice and slow by the time they reached it.

Perfect.

Now, Bardwell followed the well-worn sheep tracks to mask his passing. He circled the building once, hands on the old stones as if to gentle them before he went inside. The rafters stuck out naked from the crumbling walls like ribs picked clean by time and weather.

It was empty save for the footprints of animals who'd sought shelter, and docks almost up to his chest. In the north end was a small doorway, an aperture that provided a portal from which to look up the valley, towards Nateby and Kirkby Stephen. A little fortress.

It wasn't going to be easy, he recognised, to lure his canny prey into this designated killing ground. Harder still now they were forewarned. But Bardwell had a plan. Might work, too—if the girl could be relied upon just a little longer. And what more proof did his faceless former masters need that he was still up there, at the top of his game?

He stood in the doorway for a long time, listening to the owls in the wood behind him, the faint drift of the wind skittering through the branches. Above him, a shooting star trailed across the heavens, arced and died.

"Always a price to be paid," he told the unclouded moon. "For all of us."

PART VI

70

By the following morning's briefing, three days and two nights with precious little sleep were taking their toll on Nick. He did his best not to show it.

Things weren't helped by Mercer, who'd called vindictively early on the pretext of informing Nick his chauffeuring services were not required.

"Just wanted to catch you before your morning constitutional." Mercer's disgusting cheeriness only increased at the bleary note in Nick's voice.

At least I've made somebody's day.

Knowing his sleep was ruined anyway, Nick dragged himself out for a haphazard run and went in early. By the time he reached Hunter Lane, Mercer was already there, looking sharp and dapper.

But his attitude towards Nick had definitely altered yesterday. Trying to pin it down, Nick placed the change after the meeting with Duncan Inglis, who had treated Mercer with disdain. Maybe Mercer hadn't forgiven Nick for being witness to that minor indignity. Either that or the CTC man objected to Nick taking a shower.

Well, tough! He would have objected even more to sitting in a hot car with me all afternoon if I hadn't—air con or no.

Now, Pollock opened with a sober announcement: "For those of you who haven't heard the news, I regret to inform you that Police Constable Daniel Robertshaw died of his injuries late last night." He paused at the sharp hiss, the restless anger that paced the room. "So, I don't need to remind you that we will redouble our efforts on this one."

Pollock stepped back as Mercer stepped forwards, smoothing his jacket. "And I'm sure *I* don't need to remind you that PC Robertshaw was not the only victim yesterday," Mercer said silkily, and summarised the investigation so far in a quietly patronising tone.

"So, gentlemen—and ladies, of course," he finished, with an obsequious tilt of his head that had the female officers present craving a return to Pollock's all-purpose 'lads', "it looks very much as though we are no further forwards."

Which might be true, Nick considered, but he didn't have to rub it in.

"We haven't found anyone who might be out to get Inglis," objected DC Yardley. "Nobody with the capability of firing some thunking great sniper's rifle, at any rate."

Mercer let the smile linger for a moment while he stared him into flushed silence. "Ever heard the term 'contract killer', detective constable?"

"We haven't found anyone with a big enough grudge to warrant spending that kind of money, either," Pollock said bluntly, cutting in. "So far, there's nothing to indicate this wasn't a totally random choice."

"What about this Tawney character?" Mercer asked. "Any joy tracking him down yet?"

"No," Pollock admitted. "We've circulated his picture nationally. There've been more than two hundred sightings, everywhere from Perth to Penzance, but nothing concrete."

"Hm." Mercer allowed his disappointment to show. "At least you located the hide. Nice to see your CSIs do something other than modelling for the newspapers." He let his gaze slide over Nick. "How soon before we have any results back from forensics?"

"Everything my team found has gone to the lab with a rush on it," Pollock said. "Soon as I know anything, you'll know."

Nick had been hoping, since Mercer had dispensed with his services, that he would be reassigned closer to the heart of the investigation. As he listened to the inspector hand out tasks for the day, that expectation dwindled.

"Weston," Pollock said at last, looking round.

"Sir."

"Right, lad. How far had you got on those quad bike thefts?"

"My report's up to date, sir," Nick said smartly. "Just waiting for lab results on the last one."

"Right. Hand over what you've got to DS Crowther at Kendal," Pollock said, and Nick schooled his face into a slightly peeved expression. "Nothing personal, lad. They had a tip-off last night that's looking promising. It's on their patch, so let them handle it. I've another job in mind for you."

Nick nodded like it was all routine, the relief flooding his chest. A moment later he was glad he hadn't looked too pleased.

"Someone needs to go and talk to the bloke in charge of the military lockup where Tawney did time for assaulting Giles Frederickson. See who he was friendly with, who visited him. If he blew his nose in there, I want to know the contents of his hankie, got it?"

"But sir." Nick didn't bother hiding his dismay. "That's in—"

"Colchester," Pollock finished for him, grim. "Yes, I passed O-level geography. I know where it is. Essex. Your old stamping ground, more or less, wasn't it?"

"Not quite, sir." Nick ignored the grin Mercer made little attempt to hide. Yardley was smiling, too. First time *those* two had agreed on anything.

"It's all south of Watford to me, lad," Pollock said. He glanced at the clock on the CID office wall. "And it's a bloody long way, an' all. You'd best get a shift on if you're going to get any sense out of them today."

71

TYSON FROST SAT up from his laptop keyboard the moment Grace walked into the CSI office.

"You heard?" he asked, tentative.

"About Daniel?" Grace said, nothing in her voice. "Yes. His mother called me last night."

"Oh." He shuffled his fingers. "Look, I'm really sorry—"

"You don't have to say anything. Let's just concentrate on work, hm?"

"Oh," he repeated, fumbling with awkward relief. "Well, erm, you remember that clip of the girl's neck you asked me to have a look at?" He punched a few keys and twisted the laptop to face her. "I think I've got something for you."

On the screen was a wire-frame outline of a female figure. Frost brought up the image of a handprint alongside it, which Grace recognised as Jim Airey's by the missing finger, and juggled the two together so the hand shrank and rotated, fingers closing round the girl's throat.

Frost gave her a sideways grin and the hand tightened almost to a fist, making the figure suddenly dance and jerk. Grace smiled in spite of herself, cuffed his shoulder.

"Sorry," he said, sheepish, returning the image to a more normal aspect. "Basically, though, it's not a match. Even without the missing digit, his hand's too small for the bruising."

"So, if Airey didn't try to throttle his own daughter, who did?" she wondered aloud. She put her bag down slowly, still frowning, then turned back to Frost. "How's that 3D imaging software on facial recognition?"

"Not bad." He leaned back in his chair and swivelled slightly. "Depends what you're doing with it, I suppose. I mean, they've been trialling a system linked into all the CCTV cameras in one of the London boroughs, but as far as I know, it's never identified anybody fully auto." He shrugged. "If your target's not obliging enough to be looking full at the camera, in more or less the same lighting conditions as your comparison photo, well"— he shrugged—"there's still no real substitute for the human eyeball."

"Shame," Grace murmured. She'd captured the best images she could from the footage Nick had given her of the four men in the hotel lobby. Three of them, she felt she'd picked out quite successfully, but the fourth remained a more elusive figure. "I need to identify these men." She handed over the best printouts of the covert mugshots. "They might be connected to our case. I was hoping it would save legwork."

Frost leafed through them. "Video stills?" He pursed his lips.

"From a hotel security camera," she agreed. "They went for coverage at the expense of clarity, so it's got quite a fisheye lens on it."

"Hm, I can try using a standard biometric facial recognition application, I suppose." He frowned, flashed her a quick look. "Yeah, I might be able to do something with these. Have you got the original footage?"

Grace reached into her bag and pulled out the video cassette. His eyebrows climbed. "Wow, old school."

"Won't the distortion of the lens confuse the program?"

Frost shook his head. "As long as there's something with known parameters somewhere in-shot, I can use the photogrammetry application to un-distort it," he said, hurried. "That will give me a set of parameters to work with, then I can apply the same correction factors to the images of your guys, make a pass through FIND. That's—"

"The Facial Images National Database. I *do* read the memos." Grace couldn't help smiling at his obvious enthusiasm. "I just thought it was still in the experimental stage, and I didn't know Cumbria was taking part in the pilot scheme."

"Ah." Ty studied his fingernails. "Strictly speaking, we're not."

"Ah," Grace echoed solemnly, sitting at her own computer and firing it up. "Oh, by the way, on your recommendation, I watched *Fight Club* last night."

Ty squirmed. "You did?" he asked, reddening. 'Oh, I, erm, only mentioned because of the digital effects." His Adam's apple bounced, convulsive. "I mean, erm, I wouldn't have thought it was your kind of thing, and—"

"I thought it was a strikingly thought-provoking piece of film-making. Probably David Fincher's best work as a director since *Se7en*." She turned back to her computer screen so he wouldn't see her smile. "And a wonderful opportunity to see Brad Pitt with his shirt off…"

72

BARDWELL SPENT all morning clearing up the barn at the Retreat. He'd wedged open the main doors to allow a drift of gentle air through the old stone building. Sunlight seemed reluctant to enter, bunching up into intolerable brightness at the threshold so everything outside took on the bleached whiteness of bones in the desert.

Bardwell had found an old portable radio on one of the high shelves at the back. He'd taken it apart, blown out the dust, painstakingly run over a few dry joints on the circuit board with a soldering iron, fitted new batteries.

Resurrected, it sat on the workbench tuned to a classical station that didn't go much for chatter. The treble part of the speaker was shot, buzzing on the high-frequency like a bottled wasp, but good enough for background. Bardwell had spent too many years in amongst artillery fire to have much of an ear left for music.

He'd already sorted the end furthest from the hay, stacked a dozen ageing bags of fertiliser into sandbag order, swept and tidied. He'd found a stash of old jam jars, a throwback to the days when farmers' wives bottled their own fruit. He'd lined up the jars on the workbench in parade ground order, was filling them with odds and ends.

Just after lunch, Bardwell heard Ian Hogg's scraping foot-steps, the tick of the terrier's claws on the concrete. He looked up, saw Hogg halted in the doorway, a dark silhouette against the light.

"Hello, Patrick," came the greeting, a hint of strain in the voice. "You're quite the new broom around here." He came forwards then, features taking on definition as the shadows equalised. "The place will never be the same again."

Bardwell scooped a handful of assorted bolts into one of the jars. "Just a bit of order."

Hogg limped further in, leaned against a fifty-gallon oil drum, shifted his weight off his bad leg. "And the Landie's looking very spruce." He waved in the direction of the yard where the vehicle sat in its usual place outside the byre, new dark blue paintwork gleaming.

"Turned out all right."

Hogg didn't respond right away. Bardwell put down the copper roofing nails he was sorting, wiped his hands on the seat of his old combat trousers. He leaned against the bench, a mirror of the other man's stance, and waited.

Hogg reached down and fussed with the terrier for a moment. "You heard the news?" he asked finally, jerking his head to the radio. "That young policeman who was shot—he died, God rest him."

"Did he?" Bardwell wondered if that changed things and, if so, how.

"He was only twenty, apparently. Just a boy."

He was old enough to put on the uniform. Old enough to fight. But he said nothing, folding his arms across his chest.

"Look, Patrick, the thing is…will you talk to them?"

Bardwell's only reaction was to let his eyebrows come up sharply. "Talk to who?"

"The police," Hogg said, not meeting his eyes. "After all, you were an army sniper, weren't you?"

"Not anymore." Bardwell turned back to the bench, grabbed another handful of nails and cupped his palm to funnel them into another jar, speaking over his shoulder. "Army reckoned I wasn't up to the job and, truth to tell, by the end I reckoned it, too."

"But you understand how this man's mind works. You—"

"No," Bardwell said. Roughly, he put the jar aside, braced his hands on the bench for a moment and let his head drop, as if seeking strength. He turned back. "Came here to get away from all that—orders and questions and senseless killing."

Hogg regarded him with an unfathomable gaze. "Well, it seems to have followed you."

73

AFTER ALL HER EFFORTS, the red showjumping wall had been carefully dismantled and moved to one of the workshops at the police headquarters building, Carleton Hall. Grace spent most of the morning there with Richard Sibson, processing that and other evidence from the field.

When they walked back into the office at Hunter Lane, it was to find Ty Frost sitting uncomfortably on his hands, head bowed. Chris Blenkinship was towering over him.

Both glanced up as they entered. Frost with a panicked little flick of his eyes, flushed and miserable; Blenkinship with a narrowed anger. Clenched in his fist were the printouts of the four men from the hotel, which she'd handed to Frost earlier that morning.

Uh-oh.

"Ah, the very woman," Blenkinship said meaningfully. "Would you care to explain to me, why—in the middle of a major enquiry—you set young Frost here off on a stupid—not to mention probably illegal—search of military records? Don't you think we've got enough on our plate at the moment, without wasting time looking up dubious hotel guests?"

Without daring to glance at Sibson, she said, "You're absolutely right." And as surprise dropped his mouth open, she added calmly, "If I'd thought for a moment it *was* a waste of time, I wouldn't have asked him to do it."

A muscle twitched at the corner of his jaw. "You know your

trouble, McColl?" His voice crackled. "You don't know how to be a team player. Just because you were born with a silver spoon up your—"

"That's enough, Chris," Sibson interrupted smoothly. "Professional disagreements are one thing; personal insults are another matter entirely."

Blenkinship settled for scowling at her instead. "Well, if you want to search the military personnel database in future, *pet*, just make damn sure you follow procedure," he said, almost shouting. "You *don't* just send Cyber Boy here to hack his way in by the back door. All right?"

Sibson turned to Frost, blinking in admiration. "Is that so, Ty?" he inquired, which incensed Blenkinship all the more.

"I got no hits from the FIND database." Frost was staring at a patch of carpet six inches in front of his toes. "So I thought, what with this Tawney bloke being ex-army, it was worth a look-see if this lot were, too."

"Well, I think that shows excellent initiative." Sibson threw Blenkinship a warning glance over his glasses. "Although, naturally," he added, "you should have gone through proper channels."

There was a long pause, then Grace asked diffidently, "I don't suppose you found any matches, did you?"

"Just one, so far, then—" Frost swung his head up just long enough to meet her eye, let it slide towards Blenkinship and away again. "Just one," he repeated. He reached for his keyboard, cringing as though expecting a cuff round the back of his head. Two pictures appeared on the screen, side-by-side. One was the captured image from the security camera at the hotel; the other a formal military mugshot.

"Gary Quinn," Frost muttered. "Former SAS. Left the army six months ago. Now works for some posh private security outfit on Canary Wharf in London."

"SAS," Sibson repeated, thoughtful. He turned to Blenkinship, who was still glaring down at Frost as though flogging was too good for him. "Yes, Chris, we are indeed in the middle of a major enquiry. One that involves a sniper who more than likely has past military experience." Sibson nodded to the image. "And now a four-man team has suddenly arrived on our patch, at least one of whom is a former member of the SAS." He let that sink in. "I wouldn't classify that as a waste of time at all, would you?"

Blenkinship took a deep breath, right from his shoulders, let it out again.

"Thank you," Sibson said, as if he'd spoken. "Now then, Ty, I'll pretend I haven't seen that, and I'll go and ask Brian Pollock to put in an official request to the Provost Marshal for access to their database," he continued briskly. "Then you can 'find' it again later, hm?"

But as soon as he'd gone, Blenkinship moved in close.

"You think you're so *entitled*, don't you, McColl?" he said through his teeth. "Well, you won't always have the likes of Sibson to watch your back."

"Nor yours, Chris," Grace said quietly.

He merely glared. "As for you, Frost. I ever catch you doing anything like this again, and you're out on your ear. Understand?"

Frost, chin sunk almost to his tie, mumbled an affirmative.

For a few moments, after Blenkinship had stalked out, neither spoke. Frost flinched when Grace put a hand on his shoulder.

"How could you...?" she said, reproving. She waited a beat. "...Let him catch you?"

He stiffened, then looked up slowly, a faint smile tugging reluctantly at his mouth.

"Sorry, Grace," he said in a wretched voice. "He walked in when I was in the middle of a search, caught me on the hop. I just...blurted it out."

"Oh, Tyson." She shook her head, an answering smile on her face. "Don't you know the first rule of Fight Club...is that you *never* talk about Fight Club?"

74

IT TOOK Nick over five hours to reach Colchester MCTC, as the former POW camp was officially called. Known as the Glasshouse, it was the only remaining military prison for UK forces after one in Hong Kong was closed in the mid-seventies. He got the full spiel from the Adjutant who greeted him on arrival.

He learned more about the facility's work to retrain recalcitrant troops, but very little about Pete Tawney's period of incarceration there. Eventually, the staff passed Nick on to the padre, a big bluff man with the look of a professor more than an army officer.

"Well, detective, I'm not sure I can be of much help to you."

Nick suppressed a sigh at the now-familiar opening gambit. "To be honest, sir, that's been the line since I got here," he said with candour. "At the moment we know nothing about this guy Tawney except what's in his official record. We've no feel for the man. You've met him, at least. Anything you can tell me might help."

The padre sat with his chin propped on his linked hands for a moment, considering, then got to his feet.

"Walk with me." He led the way briskly out of his office and along a stripped-down corridor. Their footsteps echoed on the mirror-polished lino. They didn't speak again until they were outside, crossing an immaculate open area.

"The thing is, Mr Weston, Tawney was a bit of a problem for us."

"What kind of a problem? Troublesome, you mean?"

"Not at all." The padre frowned, eyes on the immaculate gravel a few feet in front of his boots. "You have to understand the philosophy behind this place," he said at last. "The name is a bit of a clue, I suppose—although we come under Her Majesty's Inspectorate of Prisons, we're actually a Military Correctional Training Centre."

Nick nodded, barely hiding his impatience, and the padre went on. "We can have over three hundred men and women here at any one time, from every branch of the services. Some of them are here for summary offences and will eventually return to their units. While they're here, in A Company, they receive ongoing training. And for those detainees, I have to say, this place does its job. Very few re-offend."

"And the others?" Nick asked.

The padre offered a tired smile. "Ah, yes," he said. "In C Company we have the violent offenders, or those awaiting transfer to civilian prisons. But over half our detainees are in D Company. They're the ones who will be discharged at the end of their time with us—usually dishonourably. For them, there is little by way of preparation for return to civilian life. I'm afraid we have few resources available to provide the skills they need to cope with the outside world. Many are simply marking time until they get out."

"And where was Tawney while he was here?"

"That's the thing. Under normal circumstances, for the nature of his offence, he would have been in A Company. His record up to that point was exemplary—a decorated and highly skilled soldier. There were many who believed he was fully justified in his actions. Only one two-hour visit a week is permitted, at the weekends, but he had no shortage of visitors. Men he'd served with, usually. I don't believe he had family. He should have had a relatively easy time of it here."

Nick had already emailed the list of Tawney's visitors back to Penrith from the Adjutant's office. "But?"

The padre sighed. "Tawney was coming up for his end of contract at the time he was sentenced and I understand he made it clear to his commanding officer that he would not be re-enlisting. After that, well"—he shrugged—"I'm not sure they knew quite what to do with him."

"Did you see much of him?"

"No more than other detainees. Many feel too intimidated to ask for help or advice through official channels, so I provide personal as well as pastoral care, but Tawney struck me as a rather self-contained individual. Did his time without complaint. Never caused any trouble. We had some rather interesting discussions."

"What did you talk about?" Nick asked. "Providing it's not privileged information, of course."

A faint smile touched the padre's lips. "Not at all. Books, mainly. The majority of detainees have a very low standard of education, can barely read and write, but Tawney was surprisingly erudite for a man who'd never been to university."

Nick, who'd also never been to university, hid a smile. "Did he give any indication why he'd decided to quit?"

"I understand there was talk of him being removed from sniper duty—temperament issues, rather than skill," the padre said slowly. "Indeed, he once told me he'd finally had enough of following orders that made no sense to him, something of that sort."

"Did he say if he had anything lined up after he got out?"

"No, now you come to mention it." The padre paused, turned towards Nick with troubled eyes. "We have an advisor comes in from Colchester Jobcentre and those facing discharge are strongly encouraged to see him, to discuss their future options." He gave Nick the rather sad smile of a man who realises he might have done more. "Tawney never showed the slightest inclination. Now I come to think of it, I always rather got the impression he had something already planned."

75

AFTERWARDS, sitting in his car, Nick rang Hunter Lane and spoke to DI Pollock. He delivered a brief précis of the interview, which was greeted with guarded praise. Nick was left with the hope that he wasn't permanently out of favour.

With the prospect of a long return drive ahead, he picked a local Indian restaurant from the well-thumbed copy of the Curry Club Guide that lived permanently in his driver's door pocket, and headed the Impreza into the middle of Colchester.

It was early for an evening meal. He was the first person in the small converted shop-front restaurant, greeted with enthusiasm and fed quickly. He'd almost finished demolishing a particularly good lamb madras with mushroom rice and keema naan, when his mobile phone started to vibrate in his pocket.

Half expecting it to be work chasing him down, Nick glanced at the screen, frowned at the unfamiliar number.

"Hello?" he said around a mouthful of naan bread and lime pickle.

"Ah, Mr Weston, I'm glad I caught you." Nick recognised the voice of the padre from Colchester MCTC. "We met—"

"Yes, of course," he said, swallowing hastily. "What can I do for you?"

"Well," the man's voice sounded hesitant, "I think it might be a case of what *I* can do for *you*, as it were." There was a short, nervous laugh, quickly snuffed. "I seem to recall you saying you thought Tawney was using a large-calibre sniper's rifle of some kind, yes?"

Nick's eyes flicked to the two waiters, but they were well out of earshot, deftly folding a stack of paper serviettes at the bar.

"That's correct," he said cautiously, heard the conflict in the other's voice and added, "Certainly, a weapon of that size was used to kill Mrs Inglis and PC Robertshaw."

There was a pause at the other end of the line, then the padre said drily, "You don't have to call to my conscience, Mr Weston. One of the chaps came to see me this afternoon, shortly after you'd left. He'd seen the news reports and wanted to come forwards, but he's anxious not to jeopardise his future."

"I'll be as discreet as I can."

"Yes, I appreciate that. Mm, yes, OK then. This chap's an RAF armourer, here with A Company on a drug-related issue—only been with us a month but making good progress, I understand."

"An armourer?" Nick said, quickening, keeping his eyes on the staff. They were still chatting at the other side of the restaurant, oblivious.

"Yes, it would seem he was doing a bit of work out of the side door, as it were, to fund his habit. He supplied some spare parts for a fifty-calibre rifle to someone he now fears could be your sniper. He wants to make a clean breast of it. Said he never thought the man intended to use the weapon on home soil."

"Can I talk to him—now?" Nick asked, checking his watch. "I can be back with you in fifteen minutes." *At least I got to eat my main course*, he thought, with passing regret for a bowl of pistachio kulfi.

"Leave it with me." The padre's voice was resigned. "I'll see what I can do."

76

GRACE WAS ALONE in the office, staring at her computer screen. On it was the hugely enhanced version of the last image she'd taken before Danny Robertshaw was shot. The one that showed the distant shape of a blue vehicle, which she'd been attempting to identify ever since.

The vehicle had been parked at an oblique angle to the camera, and she could only see the top half of it above a wall, making it harder still. From the dark patch in the centre, it looked like the rear door had been open when she'd clicked the shutter, further confusing the silhouette.

On a second screen, Grace went online and brought up a national car sales website, typed in a search for 4x4s. According to the database, there were over six thousand listed. She sighed as she began to scroll quickly down the first page, her eye running over the thumbnail images of each vehicle, looking for a shape that seemed right, familiar. Often the adverts contained multiple pictures taken from different slants. She investigated any that seemed to have the right boxy outline.

Grace was thirty pages into the website when her desk phone rang. Absently, she reached over and hit the speaker button, leaving her hands free to roam keyboard and mouse.

"Grace McColl, is it?" A man's voice, a little wary, often the case with people making first contact with the police.

"CSI McColl, yes," she corrected automatically, distracted.

Daihatsu Fourtrack? No, windows are too big at the back. "How can I help?"

She scrolled further down the page as she spoke. The older Nissan Patrol models had the right square cast, but still not quite there. It took Grace a few moments to register that her caller hadn't responded. She frowned at the silent telephone.

"Hello? Are you still there?"

"Still here," the man said without impatience. "Just wanted to say I'm sorry, that's all."

Grace froze. Very slowly, as if he could see any sudden moves, she took her hands off the keyboard and sat upright. Pushed back from the desk so she was out of sight of the window.

"To whom am I speaking? And what is it, exactly, for which you have to be sorry?"

"Won't do any good to give you my name," the man said. "And I think you know what I'm on about, right enough."

Grace let that go. Her mind darted through a hundred possibilities, eyes scanning the room as if for some means of self-defence. Her gaze touched on Richard Sibson's desk, abandoned by Ty Frost now. The memo recorder Sibson habitually used was sitting on a pile of papers. Silently, she grabbed it, held it low behind her to muffle the click as she activated the record button.

"So, why are you calling me?' she asked, using the cover of speech to set the recorder down, very gently, near the phone.

"Not to crow, if that's what you're thinking." There was a long pause. Grace tilted her head, shut her eyes, but heard nothing in the background, no convenient trains going over points, no nearby construction, no traffic.

"Why, then?"

"Fired at the uniform, not the man." He sounded casually regretful. "Won't happen again."

Grace heard no suppressed emotion in his voice. No madness, no fanaticism; a sane mind, if that were possible.

She knew she was supposed to humour him, but couldn't bring herself to deference. Not with two bodies in the hospital morgue.

"You mean you won't shoot again?" she asked, deliberately flat. "Or you won't miss?"

That got a reaction, a slight grunt. She'd surprised rather than angered him.

She heard footsteps and the office door was pushed open. Grace signalled furiously for silence, glanced up and saw Chris Blenkinship wrong-footed in the doorway, mouth open.

"Saw what you did on that field," the man's voice said, measured. "Wanted you to know you're not a target. Never were."

"How can you say that?" Grace demanded quietly, ignoring the way Blenkinship had come forwards, looming. "You fire at one of us, you fire at all of us. Wasn't it the same for you—in the military?"

"*Ah...fishing now.*" She panicked as she heard him detach, losing interest.

She added quickly, "Tell me what you want. Talk to me. Perhaps I can help you." It stuck in her throat to make the offer, to mould sincerity into her voice.

"What I want, I'll get without your help," he said. "I know you found the hide. Good work that was, but it won't make much difference in the long run."

No triumph still, no smug satisfaction. He was entirely matter-of-fact. Maybe that's what touched a nerve with Blenkinship. He leaned over her shoulder, snapped at the phone.

"Listen, you lunatic, we'll get you—!"

Grace made a grab for his arm.

"Don't need to listen to that." A quietly underlying anger gave cut to his words. "You won't find me. You certainly won't stop me. Don't put your people in my way. This is not your fight."

"What about Angela Inglis?" Grace shot Blenkinship a warning glare. "Was it her fight? What did she do to become a target?"

"When you work that out, you'll know," the man said. "Meanwhile, there's rules of engagement. Don't change 'em."

Rules? There are rules to any of this? "I have my job to do," Grace said, stubborn. "I won't be scared out of doing it."

"No, you won't at that. You be careful, now, CSI Grace McColl."

And with that he rang off, leaving them both staring at a dead telephone. The reels of the little memo recorder wound on into the silence.

77

IF IT WASN'T for the sultry night, Edith would never have known. But the temperature had climbed relentlessly during the afternoon and failed to dissipate at sunset. By the time she dragged herself off to bed, the weight and the pressure were almost unbearable.

She lay sweating in the darkness, sprawled on top of her bedclothes, hoping the promised thunderstorm would bring some relief. Her bedroom was stifling. In a vain attempt at cross ventilation, she threw the sash window up as far as it would go and propped open her bedroom door with an old shoe to let the listless air pass straight through.

And, because of that, she heard her father on the phone in the hallway.

She'd been dozing—too hot to sleep, too tired to do more than attempt it—when something furtive, gleeful, in his voice alerted her. She rolled over and lay motionless on her back, listening.

"You got a front-page exclusive and paid me a pittance, so you better make it worth my while this time." Her father's voice was low and greedy, amplified up the wooden stairwell into a ghostly echo. "Turns out the other mob would have paid double for that picture and not turned a hair. If you want what I've got now, it'll cost you."

There was a pause, while whoever was on the other end

considered, or argued, or placated. *Flattery*, Edith decided, scathing. *That's the best way to deal with my father.*

They must have come back with the right amount, though, because the next thing she heard was her father say, "Aye, OK then," in an eager rush that he tried to swallow back with a grudging, "That'll do, I suppose." But they'd know they had him hooked. And with that flimsy agreement, he couldn't wait to spill what he knew, like a kid with a secret too hot to hold onto.

"It looks like the bloke we're after is an ex-squaddie, name of Pete Tawney... Yes, of course I know you've already got that in the press handouts!" he said, irritated. "Coming to that, aren't I?"

Pete Tawney? Edith wondered. *Fools! They've got the wrong man.* But another, less welcome emotion followed on right behind. Had Patrick given her—*her*—a false identity? It made a mockery of the special bond between them. Her Patrick would never lie to her...would he?

"All right, then," her father went on, mollified by whatever oil was being poured down the line. "Like I said, this guy Tawney's ex-army, right? So, who do you think checked in to one of the local hotels at Penrith yesterday morning, fresh up from a certain army base in Hereford? Does the phrase 'Who Dares Wins' mean anything to you?"

Edith's heartrate stampeded. She got the significance without needing her father's heavy-handed hints. They'd sent trained killers after him, not policemen. So, they didn't want to capture Patrick; they wanted him dead.

"Yeah, you got it." her father's voice was unbearably smug now. "Of course, the army's claiming they've left the SAS, all gone into 'private security' but a bit too much of a coincidence they turn up here, now, isn't it? And I'm sure if one of your nosy reporters went asking questions about these four blokes..."

He must have shifted position, turned away from the stairs, because his voice dropped to a murmur and Edith reared upright, straining to make out the words in the darkness.

"Oh, and you remember that McColl woman in the last picture? Well, looks like our boy took a shine to her," Edith heard him say, and was flooded with a jealous rage. *No! He wouldn't...*

"Cocky sod called her to apologise for taking out one of our boys. Said it was a mistake... Yeah, I thought you'd find that interesting. Worth the price, eh?" He gave a fat chuckle. "That's right, same account as last time, in my daughter's name—Edith. Can't be too careful, eh? A pleasure doing business with you again."

Edith heard the receiver go down and her father let out a long noisy exhale, a physical reaction to his own treachery. The door to the back sitting room opened, suddenly increasing in noise from the inane TV show her mother used as nightly anaesthetic.

Edith wanted to go down there and launch herself at her father, screaming and kicking, incensed by his loathsome actions, shocked by the violence of her own response.

How dare he sell Patrick out and put those thirty pieces of silver in my name?

But as she swung her legs over the edge of the mattress, a cold fear gripped her. Even now, some shadowy Black Ops hit-squad were out there somewhere in the darkness, hunting Patrick down.

She'd been born way after the famous storming of the Iranian Embassy in London by the Anti-Terrorism team of the SAS, but she'd seen the TV clips replayed often enough to believe the mythology woven around the Regiment. They were invincible, invulnerable, without mercy.

No! The single word was a stark and plaintive denial inside her head. *They won't get him. Not if I can help it...*

Creeping unnoticed out of the house wasn't hard. She scrambled into her clothes without turning on the light, pulled her bedroom door shut behind her, knowing her parents wouldn't bother to look in before they went to bed.

She tiptoed down the stairs, avoiding the squeaky treads, grabbed her helmet and keys from the hall as she passed through, went out silently through the front door. Then she ran along the street and round to the alleyway at the back, slipping the chain on the scooter.

She pushed the bike to the far end before she thumbed the engine into life. It seemed very loud in the close, still night, but it wasn't late enough to be a cause for curtain twitching. As she phutted up the steep hill and out onto the main road she was filled with a fearful sense of adventure, of being absolutely alive.

She met little other traffic and reached the Retreat without incident, despite expecting balaclava-clad soldiers to abseil into her path at every turn.

There were no lights showing at the byre when she arrived, and she dithered outside, anxious. He'd seemed so unfazed by her announcement that Special Branch was on his trail. The last thing she wanted was for him to think her an idiot.

Then, just as she finally raised her hand to knock, the door fell away inwards and there he was in the opening. Edith jerked in surprise.

"You going to stand around out there all night?" he asked, not sounding at all like a man groggy from sleep. He was wearing loose black trousers with a drawstring waist, his long feet bare. She was struck again by the lack of spare flesh on his now-familiar torso, the slim slabs of muscle across his bare chest.

"I wouldn't have come if I didn't think it was important." She was aiming for casual indifference as she stepped past him into the kitchen. "Didn't want to wake you, that's all."

"Oh aye?" He flicked on the kitchen light and lit the gas under the kettle.

Edith suddenly wished she was a smoker. That she could slant a long French cigarette between her fingers and thread smouldering glances through the smoke. But she'd tried it and didn't like the taste, or the way the stink clung. Couldn't afford it, anyway.

She wandered around the kitchen, running her finger along the edge of the moulded worktop. He leaned with his back to the sink, folded his arms across his chest.

"I found out my father was the one who took that picture that was on the front of the newspaper," she said, abrupt. "He was talking to them again tonight. I heard him on the phone, doing some nasty little deal." She almost spat. "Traitor."

Bardwell shrugged. "He is what he is."

The kettle boiled. He dropped a handful of teabags into an old brown teapot and splashed water onto them. Edith watched in silence, leaning against the fridge, her head tilted so she could feel the buzz of its motor tingling through her scalp.

His attitude was so *right*, she realised. She'd been enraged by her father's behaviour whereas Patrick—the one directly affected by it—was simply impassive, unconcerned.

She tried for a similar languid pose as she asked, "Why did you call her?"

Bardwell prodded inside the teapot with a spoon, poured out. He had to come very close to get the milk from the fridge and she didn't move out of his way, just stood and stared up at him. His eyes met hers, seemed to loiter. Her heart picked up again, flushing her skin.

"My business." He stirred, handed over a mug. She made sure their fingers touched as she took it and he didn't pull back. "All part of the plan."

It was too hot to drink tea. She cupped her fingers round the crazed earthenware, gazed into the depths, ignoring the bubbles of buttermilk that scummed the surface. "So, you don't, like, fancy her or anything?"

He sipped his tea, eyes steady. "What d'you think?"

She squirmed. "I just wondered, that's all. She *is* attractive, I suppose." She couldn't prevent a sniff. "If you like that sort of thing."

"She's a fine-looking woman," he agreed solemnly. "But she's a better investigator. Best they've got, though they probably don't know it. Does no harm to throw her off her stride."

But Edith didn't like the way he let his gaze droop, like a man who was lying.

"Nothing else?"

"Now they think I'm interested, they'll try and keep her back. Their mistake." He shrugged, put down his tea. "But you didn't come out here this late just to ask that, did you?"

"Partly," Edith admitted, artlessly casual now, turning to dump her own mug onto the table. "And partly to ask you if you knew the SAS are up here to kill you?"

That got a response—*finally*. She gasped as his arms looped around her from behind, though she never heard him cross the kitchen floor. She felt his heat, his hardness, pressing against her back, one forearm under her chin. His voice was a whisper in her ear.

"What have you heard?"

"N–no more than that," she stammered, suddenly fearful, tripping over her own tongue. "Just that's they're SAS, well, ex-SAS. Four of them staying at some hotel in Penrith. That's all I know, I swear!"

He paused, as if considering, then murmured, "Not getting cold feet, are you, Edith?" His breath tickled against the pulse beating wildly at the base of her neck.

"Of–of course not!"

Just for a moment, he stilled, then his head ducked. She gasped as his teeth nipped at that little pulse. His hands shifted, roaming the front of her body, pushing her shirt open. Edith had never needed a bra, and his roughened fingers found one aching nipple without hesitation. His other hand dipped lower. She revelled in his strength, his utter confidence, as he sent the lust drenching through her.

She knew there was something else she'd wanted to ask him. *Something important.* Right now, she'd no idea what it was.

78

SHE REMEMBERED MUCH LATER, lying beside him in the darkened bedroom, letting her fingers draw swirling patterns on the damp skin of his chest.

The weather had finally broken and the rain beat steadily on the slates overhead. It was going to be a wet ride home, but Edith didn't care.

"I did hear something else tonight," she admitted. She felt his skin stiffen, couldn't be sure if her words or her touch caused it.

"Oh aye?"

"Mm. Dad said they're looking for someone called Pete Tawney. That's...not you, is it?" she stumbled. "I mean, you're Patrick Bardwell... Aren't you?"

This time, there was no mistaking the quiver. "Would it matter," he asked, careful, "if I wasn't?"

She propped herself up on one elbow, stared down at him. It was hard to make out his expression in the gloom. "Does that mean I can change my name, too—after?"

"After what?"

"Well, after we're away from here."

For an endless, utterly deafening moment, he lay silent. Then he sat up abruptly, twisted to grip her shoulders, close enough to see his face now.

"There's no future with me," he said, quiet enough for her to hear the sound of her heart, breaking into fragments. "Never was. Never will be. Never done anything to make you think things were different, have I?"

"You're just saying that because you think I'm too young, but I'm not! I'm nearly eighteen—a grown woman. Haven't I proved that? I'd go anywhere with you!"

"Where I'm going, you can't follow."

"So, what am I to you?" She began to cry then, ugly rivulets that sent her vision blurring. "Just a cheap lay? A quick—"

"Don't!" he said roughly, shaking her. "I never thought of you that way. We both knew I wasn't going to be around forever."

"But I l–love you, Patrick! I—"

"No, you don't," he said, certain as stone. "You might think you do, but you don't."

A huge hiccup welled up, turning into a wail of fresh tears. Edith wrenched free and scrambled out of bed, unable even to look at him. He sat quietly amid the rumpled sheets, watching her snatch up her clothes, fumble into them. At the doorway, she hesitated, threw him one last look of utter reproach, and fled into the downpour.

She still harboured a last slim hope that he'd come after her, call her back, tell her it was all a mistake, that she was the one for him after all.

Nothing followed her out into the night but her own humiliation and despair.

79

GRACE WAS in her tiny study at home, her back to the wall of photographs, face grave in the reflected light from the computer screen. Tallie was stretched full length behind her chair, taking up much of the remaining floor space. She was sulking at the lack of attention over recent days, and Grace suspected the obstruction was deliberate.

Absently, she reached for her wineglass on the desktop, found it empty. She nudged the dog, who reluctantly shuffled back a few inches. Grace took a moment to run her hand apologetically along the sleek coat before she rose.

There was a bottle of Cabernet Sauvignon open on the worktop in the kitchen. She knew she ought to supplement it with food, but she hadn't felt much like eating.

This counts as fruit, doesn't it?

Back in the study, she put down her refilled glass next to the two blowups of Angela Inglis—alive and dead—and studied the slightly aristocratic features, the haughty gaze.

"So, what *did* you do, Angela?" she murmured aloud.

When you work that out, the man had said to her, *you'll know.*

With a sigh, Grace went back to the hotel CCTV footage she'd been poring over. Three of the men had been identified, but the fourth kept himself angled away from the cameras just enough to evade recognition. Accident or design, she wasn't sure.

She let the section run on. Maybe they'd passed through the lobby later and there'd be a clearer shot. She sipped her wine, reached down and fondled the dog's ears. Tallie made snuffling noises of satisfaction but otherwise didn't stir.

Grace smiled down at her, glanced back at the screen. Another figure had moved into shot, turning to make momentary eye-contact with the elusive fourth man as he passed. There was something vaguely familiar about him.

She saw the new arrival stop by a seated figure in the far background, who rose to meet him. Nick, she realised. So this had to be the CTC man she'd heard so much about, Mercer. *But...*

Grace put her glass down slowly and hit the rewind, going back to the moment Mercer first appeared. As he walked into shot he turned his head...yes, *there,* just enough for her to get a good view of him in three-quarter profile.

She zoomed in, enhanced the picture to soften the harder edges of the pixels, filling in the missing information between them, until the CTC man's face nearly filled the screen, sharp and distinct.

She sat back hard enough to make the chair rock, frowning.

"What on earth—?"

Before she could finish, lights flared across the drawn window blinds as a car swung onto the gravel outside, the movement triggering the outside security light. She tensed as the engine died to silence.

The holiday cottage next door was currently empty. She'd exchanged brief hellos and comments about the weather and been noncommittal about the dreadful events in the news with her temporary neighbours, but they'd announced this morning they were leaving early. Joining the exodus of tourists who'd been jamming the M6 to a crawl all day.

It could be him.

He knew her name, where she worked, that she'd found the hide. What else did he know?

The knock on her front door startled her, even though she'd been tight with expectation. She gave a little gasp and Tallie jerked out of slumber, let out a couple of jumpy barks that Grace did nothing to silence. She minimised the current program and clicked an icon on the desktop, so the screen filled with a distorted image of her driveway.

The first thing she'd done when she came home that evening

was rig the wireless miniature webcam above her front door, an extra precaution. Not that she had expected the sniper to actually doorstep her. Not when he could deliver his particular calling card from nearly a mile away.

Instead, Nick Weston stood a pace back from the door, looking directly up into the lens she'd thought so well-hidden amid the Boston ivy. He had a long object under one arm, tagged and wrapped in plastic. In his other hand he held up what was clearly a bag of takeaway food, and he was smiling.

She opened the front door, using her knee to stop Tallie squeezing out to take on the intruder. The dog forced her head through the gap anyway, ruffled at the indignity.

He eyed the dog warily. "I assume you haven't eaten."

"You assume correctly." She nodded to the long bag under his arm. "What have you got there?"

"Vital evidence, I hope," he said. "But nothing that won't keep until we've had some food. I hope you like Thai."

"I adore Thai." She opened the door, her hand through the dog's collar. "Max and I went. Bangkok is fascinating and the cuisine was superb."

He paused a fraction, eyebrow raised, then stepped over the threshold. "Well, I didn't quite go that far for this." He indicated the takeaway. "I stopped off at the one in Kendal as I came past. It's pretty good, though; should still be warm enough."

She led him through, shooing Tallie out of their way. The dog retreated to the far side of the living room and stood to watch in disbelief.

Nick unloaded the foil containers onto the worktop, listing the contents. "Beef green curry, prawn pad thai, sticky rice, fish-cakes. Any of that sound appetising?"

"All of it," Grace said fervently, fetching down plates and another wineglass. "And red will go with the beef, so that's all right. You're OK with wine? I'm afraid I don't keep beer in."

That eyebrow again. "I have been known to guzzle the odd glass of cheap plonk."

"I apologise," she said immediately. "You were brought up in the trade, so to speak. There's no reason why you shouldn't be a connoisseur."

Perched on stools at the breakfast bar, they ate in companionable silence. Only when the first throes of hunger were satisfied did Grace indicate the long black object, like a pipe, that he'd brought in with him.

"So, are you going to enlighten me?"

"You know I was sent down to Colchester to see Tawney's jailers? Well, I ended up speaking to the padre, which would have been a waste of time had another inmate—sorry, detainee—not had an attack of conscience and come to him for absolution."

"Isn't that Catholics only?" Grace said, offering to top up his glass.

Nick shook his head. "One's enough. I have to drive home." He reached for his notebook, flicked through the pages. "Anyway, turns out this guy's an RAF armourer with a drug habit, which he's been funding by selling off bits and pieces to a dodgy dealer. He told me that, before he was caught and sent down, some bloke turned up in his local pub one day, out of nowhere. This guy knew all about his bit of private enterprise, and wanted him to swap out the barrel of"—he found the right place in his notes—"a Barrett M82A1 Light Fifty, which is a fifty-calibre anti-matériel sniper's rifle."

"Did he do it? And why did it need swapping?"

"Yeah, cash in hand, no questions asked. Apparently, they had a spare barrel in the armoury and he said providing one was still there at the next audit, nobody was any the wiser," Nick said grimly. "The one the guy had was pitted to all hell and back. Bad ammunition and poor routine maintenance, so the armourer reckoned. Too much salt in the primer corroded the inside of the barrel. He thought the gun had probably been used in Afghanistan, somewhere like that."

"And that's the original barrel?" Grace asked, moving to inspect it. The size and weight of the single component surprised her. *The complete weapon must be huge.* "How much has it been messed about since he got it?"

"He wiped it down and oiled it, unfortunately, so I doubt you'll get much by way of fingerprints, but the armourer said it was full of Vaseline."

"Hm, that makes sense." Grace caught his frown and looked up. "If you pack something in Vaseline and hide it in a refrigerated truck full of meat, say, it would be a good way to bring it into the country—confuse the sniffer dogs at Customs."

He shook his head. "Sometimes it's frightening, what you know."

"So, why did the RAF happen to have one of these going spare?" she wondered. "And how did our man know about it?"

"Not a secret, so he said. They use them for bomb disposal." He grinned. "Stand well back and plink at the suspect device with half-inch rounds until it goes bang, seems to be the recognised method."

"Oh, *very* scientific. I'll go over it with a fine-tooth comb in the morning, see if there's anything to be gleaned. I don't suppose he gave you a description of the man?"

"Big, menacing, obviously a squaddie or ex-squaddie." Nick shrugged. "It was several months ago, and the guy's a junkie, so his memory for faces isn't exactly photographic." He paused, took a swallow of wine, added carefully, "So, are you going to tell me why you rigged up that camera outside?"

"I had a strange phone call today," Grace said calmly, and recounted the conversation.

He froze. "You must have been terrified."

"Unsettled, yes," she agreed. "But it's difficult to shoot somebody along a phone line. And he didn't make direct threats against me, anyway."

"But still—"

She put her glass down very deliberately, fixed him with a cool stare.

"I already said it unsettled me." She hid behind a light tone. "Talking about it just before bedtime is not a ploy designed to give me a restful night's sleep."

"You just don't take any of this seriously, do you?" he said, edged with frustration.

Blenkinship's words had come dangerously close to the same thing. "Take what seriously?" she asked frostily. "My work?"

"No—life." He let out a long breath. "Life bites, Grace. Didn't you realise that—out there on that field?"

"I have to stay objective."

"Yes, but you behave as though nothing touches you." He skimmed her with those piercing eyes. "As though nothing can."

He was angry, she realised, the same way Max would have been. *Dangerous.*

"I'll be careful," she promised.

He held her gaze. If she ever had the opportunity to photograph him, she would go with black-and-white for everything except those eyes, she decided suddenly. The hard planes of his face would carry the shot in tone and structure, but retouching the colour back into those eyes would make it stunning.

For a moment she thought he'd argue, but then his shoulders came down a fraction and he gave a wry shrug. "OK," was all he said, but the comfortable mood was broken. He stood, gathered his keys.

Grace straightened. "I've been looking at the CCTV from the hotel again," she said, aware of the awkward tension smoking between them. "I spotted your chap Mercer."

"He's definitely not 'my chap' Mercer."

"I wasn't implying ownership. But, there's something interesting about him. Do you want to see?"

He nodded reluctantly, and Grace led him to the study. Tallie trotted after them, but there wasn't room for three. She hovered from foot to foot in the hallway, letting out the occasional snubbed whimper.

"Here." Grace sat and he leaned over her shoulder, one hand braced on the desktop, close enough that she could smell the faint overtones of his aftershave. She woke the sleeping program, and Mercer's face popped up, almost life-size.

"Hey," Nick protested, "that's not nice when I've just eaten."

She allowed the faint twitch of a smile. "Look at him." She pointed. "The shape of his ear, the line of his eyebrows, his nose, his chin. See anything familiar?"

"I should do," Nick said flatly. "I spent long enough working with him."

Grace reached for the 'before' photograph of Angela Inglis, held it up alongside the screen so the two faces were cheek-to-cheek.

"And now?"

It only took a moment. She heard the slight intake of breath, glanced sideways and saw the way his eyes had narrowed. *Oh yes, he's got it.*

"My God," he breathed. "They could be—"

"Related? Yes, I do believe they are…"

80

THE MEMORIAL SERVICE for Angela Inglis was held at All Saints' Church in Orton village, strictly limited to close friends and family at Duncan Inglis's request.

The press pushed it as far as they dared, milling around in the two lanes that led up to the church, smoking and talking and giving the occasional burst of inappropriate raucous laughter, expensive cameras slung from shoulder straps like status symbols.

The narrow approaches were clogged with private-plated Mercedes, BMWs, a couple of Bentleys. The grieving widower arrived by stately coach-built Rolls Royce, chauffeur-driven and painted a noncommittal shade of battleship grey.

Nick had worn his darkest suit by way of camouflage, but was already regretting the choice for its heat-absorption qualities alone. The overnight rain had done little to relieve the humidity. The over-saturated air seemed to condense inside his lungs.

He stood in the graveyard, mindful of where he put his feet. The church was a low building dating back to the thirteenth century. At one end it had a huge bell tower with heavily buttressed corners. The tower looked to Nick like a later addition, painted household magnolia. He saw Mercer the moment the CTC man came through the gates.

Mercer made a beeline for him, pointedly checking his watch. "I got your somewhat cryptic message," he said as soon as he was close enough not to shout, voice clipped. "I can give you five minutes."

Nick turned, began to stroll along the line of ancient canted headstones, forcing Mercer into step alongside.

"So," Nick said, conversational, "does DI Pollock know the real reason why you're up here?"

"Real reason?"

"Does he know that Angela Inglis's maiden name was Angela Mercer?" It hadn't taken much finding, once Grace had shown him what to look for. "That she was your sister?"

Eventually, Mercer said quietly, "No. Do you intend to enlighten him?"

Nick side-stepped that one, knowing Mercer would be quick to exploit any sign of weakness. "There *is* no political connection, is there?" he said instead. "You're on this purely as a personal thing."

"Wouldn't you be, in my place?"

Nick shrugged. Mercer was tense for the inevitable next question. Only trouble was, Nick wasn't sure what that should be. *What else are you hiding?* he wondered.

"What gave it away?" Mercer asked then. "Duncan?"

"Partly," Nick hedged, mind still backtracking furiously. He'd already decided to keep the flak away from Grace, if he could. After the picture in the newspaper, Mercer seemed to have the tall CSI singled out. "He disliked you on sight and he doesn't seem astute enough to make that kind of a snap character assessment."

Mercer gave a cynical little smile. "Yeah, well, we never were one big happy family. It'll come out, of course." He jerked his eyes in the direction of the press, who were studying them the way a pride of lions watches for the lame zebra. "I've done what I can, but I can't expect to keep it under wraps indefinitely with that lot hanging around. I was hoping to get more of a handle on the whole thing first."

"Or that your boys would take care of it for you."

Mercer raised an eyebrow in obvious surprise. "My boys?"

"At the hotel," Nick said, his voice casual. "Former SAS, now working for a London private security outfit who just so happen to hold a number of government contracts. Didn't know you were contracting out your dirty work these days. I wonder if they still operate a shoot-to-kill policy."

Mercer paused. "You were Firearms, Nick," he said at last, evasive. "You of all people should know you always shoot to kill." He shot a cuff, glanced down at his watch. "Time's up." But he didn't immediately move away, nodding instead to another batch of new arrivals, walking with suitably sombre stride along the pathway to the front door of the church. One of them was a tall thin man that Nick had no trouble recognising, very upright and correct in khaki number two dress uniform.

"If anyone's got the ear of the SAS, past or present," Mercer murmured, "perhaps you should be talking to the good major."

Nick was about to question that when his phone buzzed. Mercer took the opportunity to flee while Nick was still reaching for his inside pocket, disappearing briskly into the church.

With a muttered curse, Nick clicked open the phone. It was Grace.

"Bad timing?" she asked pleasantly.

"No, sorry. I think I'm allergic to Mr Mercer. What can I do for you?"

"I'm at the North Lakes Hotel."

At the morning briefing, Pollock had assigned DC Yardley to follow up on the four men, a task which should not have routinely called for the presence of crime scene technicians, unless...

"What's happened?"

"Relax—nothing. They're gone. Checked out yesterday to go off 'rambling', if you please. Their rooms have been turned over and cleaned—more thoroughly than normal housekeeping would warrant, unfortunately."

"So, what did you find?"

"Nothing, which I take as a personal affront to my skills, as I'm sure you can imagine," she said with cool amusement. "No hairs, no prints, no fibres. It's as professional a wipe-down job as I've ever seen."

"Which is a lot of trouble for a group of lads on a hiking trip." Nick watched more people in sober hats and dark suits arrive and hurry into the church as if determined not to be left with the cheap seats.

"They didn't put down a car registration number on their

check-in form, but I went over the CCTV covering the car park, anyway," Grace continued. "It shows them walking in from the main road, so we don't even have a line on their vehicle."

Nick muttered a quiet oath under his breath, then glanced in silent apology at the surrounding gravestones.

"If they *are* here to track him down," Grace's voice murmured in his ear, "then we need to find him before they do."

"Well, they'll certainly deal with him, you have to give them that," he pointed out, not sure if he was entirely ambivalent. "Justice of a sort."

"Death's too easy," she said. "I want him in prison for the rest of his life, and I want to know I helped put him there."

81

GILES FREDERICKSON LEFT the church sad, thoughtful, and thoroughly unsettled.

Weston had collared him with indecent alacrity as soon as the service was over, asking what he knew about a hit squad made up of former SAS men.

As if I'd let someone else do my wet work.

He'd been short with the man, denying all knowledge, which was the truth. But the more he thought about it afterwards, the more questions arose in his own mind.

The man they were chasing was almost undoubtedly ex-military. Not many others who would have the necessary skills. The army, as he was well aware, liked to handle its own mistakes in-house where it could—and quietly. But there were no rules that said ex-military cleared up the mess left by other ex-military personnel.

On the other hand, certain private companies *were* used, on an ad hoc basis, for strictly off-the-books operations. When Her Majesty's government required ultimate deniability.

Seems like everything's been privatised these days.

But if there was some kind of covert op in progress, it was disturbing that he hadn't been kept in the loop. This was his territory now. Surely he could have provided local knowledge, if nothing else?

He was still frowning over the ramifications, smarting at the implications, when he suddenly became aware that Duncan Inglis had closed at his elbow with deliberate purpose.

"Giles," he said in the deep stentorian voice of a parliamentarian. "You'll come back to the house, of course." It was issued as a command to which Frederickson murmured assent.

"Good," Inglis said. "Ride with me." He strode on, a man without time to waste. The rear door of the Rolls Royce was being respectfully held open by the grey-suited chauffeur. Inglis climbed in without acknowledging the courtesy and Frederickson tagged along behind him. They were followed by a slender young man, who folded himself neatly into the jump seat opposite, oozing deferential discretion. Frederickson vaguely recalled he was Inglis's private secretary.

The gathered press shouted a few desultory questions, but were being kept well back and their heart wasn't in it. The younger, keener ones raced for their cars, no doubt hoping to beat the graceful bulk of the Rolls Royce back to the Inglis residence. For what purpose other than to justify their own mean existence, Frederickson had no idea.

The rear of the car was voluminous. It smelt of cavalry leather and furniture polish and, ever so faintly, of dead flowers. The private secretary rapped on the glass partition and they pulled away almost silently. Inglis waited until they were on the move before he spoke again.

"They don't wear a uniform these days. Drivers, I mean. Poor show, don't you think?"

Frederickson was not entirely sure to whom the question was addressed. When the private secretary raised a politely enquiring eyebrow in his direction, he cleared his throat.

"A man looks better in uniform," he agreed solemnly. He paused, careful. "I wanted to offer my condolences, of course."

"Thank you," Inglis said in neutral tones. "Angela and I were married for nearly twenty years and one does tend to become accustomed to another's…habits." Inglis's tone was devoid of emotion. He might have been talking about a favourite hat.

Frederickson shifted a little in his plush seat, discomfited. The officer and the gentleman in him felt the sudden urge to confess.

"Duncan, I—"

Inglis held up his hand. "Oh, my dear chap, please don't feel the need to confide anything," he said, almost kindly, piercing him with a heavy-lidded gaze. "I am well aware that you were my wife's lover. Not her first, I might add, but at least you have the distinction of being her last."

Frederickson tried not to flounder. The private secretary gazed at him blandly.

"You didn't object to her...indiscretions?" Frederickson asked, with as much composure as he could muster.

"I think you'll agree that the last thing anyone could say of Angela was that she was indiscreet." He stared out of the window, oblivious to the passing scenery. "We reached an agreement very early on in our marriage," Inglis went on, with what seemed like candour. "She had her little diversions, and I had mine."

He turned back towards Frederickson. As he did so, his eyes flickered across the pretty-boy face of the private secretary. And in that one brief, furtive glance, Frederickson knew that Duncan Inglis's interests lay in another direction altogether.

"If you're concerned about my own discretion in this matter," he said, masking his distaste, "I am hardly likely to invite a scandal."

"So I gather," Inglis said, a smile on his fleshy lips that Frederickson took to mean he'd been thoroughly vetted for his role. Bitterly, he wondered at Angela's complicity. Had she coolly waited until her husband's people had checked him out before she took him into her bed? *At least there was nothing calculated about her responses there,* he thought with truculent pride.

"I see," he said stiffly as the big car glided through the turn into the driveway, with no discernible change in ride quality as it transitioned between tarmac and gravel. "So, if I may ask, what's the purpose of this...audience?"

"I understand that Angela made a rather *rash* gift to you last Christmas." Inglis sounded almost bored. The private secretary studied his fingernails. "A pair of antique cufflinks."

"Yes," Frederickson admitted, stifling colour. It had been an impulsive gesture that had subsequently caused her some embarrassment. As soon as he'd realised her dilemma, Frederickson had, naturally, offered to return them. She stoutly refused, claiming she'd found an alternative solution. The girl, Edith, he remembered with a twinge of guilt, had ended up the scapegoat.

"Mm, they were my father's." Inglis leaned forwards a little as the car swung round slowly to present him at the front entrance. "They have a value of a somewhat sentimental nature."

"I'll see they're returned."

"Thank you," Inglis said in a remote voice. As soon as the car halted, the private secretary hopped out to hold the door for his employer. Inglis climbed down after him, straightening his jacket.

"They'll get him, Duncan," Frederickson said abruptly from the depths of the Rolls Royce. He thought of the team Weston had mentioned and knew he wasn't necessarily talking about the police. "Whoever did this to Angela. They *will* get him."

Inglis ducked his head to meet the other's eyes. "Yes." His voice was impassive, but something base flashed behind his eyes, something savage. It passed almost too fast to register and was gone. He nodded. "Yes," he repeated, "I know they will."

As Inglis strode away, Frederickson belatedly recalled Angela mentioning to him, some months before, that her husband sat on various hush-hush committees concerned with matters of national security, and the resources he undoubtedly had at his disposal.

And he realised that Inglis wasn't referring to the police, either.

82

THOUGH HE WOULD HAVE RATHER BITTEN out his own tongue than admit it, Matthew Mercer left the memorial service in a state of some anxiety. He sat broodingly silent in the passenger seat of the patrol car he'd commandeered for the return trip up to Penrith. Like his brother-in-law, Duncan Inglis, he barely acknowledged the actions of his driver.

Privately, Mercer had always known his state of comparative anonymity wouldn't last forever, that they'd suss him out eventually. He'd just hoped it would take longer.

Nick always was the bright one, he thought with resignation. *He'll soon find out the rest, and then the game really* will *be up.*

The paper trail of official authorisation Mercer had concocted for this visit was reasonably solid, but wouldn't stand determined scrutiny. If DI Pollock had done more than go through the motions of protesting his involvement, Mercer would have been out on his ear before lunchtime the first day. When he realised that error, the inspector would likely scream blue murder.

It was pure luck that Nick was still an outsider up here. Mercer freely admitted that his own actions had probably fuelled the alienation and disfavour, otherwise he would have been sent packing already. But Nick was too used to working undercover, with too much autonomy. He'd acted on the information himself instead of passing it dutifully further up the line.

Still, it wouldn't be long, Mercer realised, as the car deposited

him outside the Hunter Lane station. He hadn't hidden his
surprise well and Nick would dig hard now. He had another day,
two at the most.

Best make them count, then.

He'd just reached the office they'd grudgingly assigned him,
when a uniformed female sergeant appeared.

"You're back are you, sir?"

No, I'm a hologram. Mercer smiled. "Of course. What can I do
for you?"

"We've got a caller on the tip-line," the sergeant said. "They
reckon they've got important information about this sniper and
they want to speak to you."

"Me specifically, or the chief investigative officer?" Mercer
queried, still smiling. "I'm sure you can deal with him, can't
you?" *Think of it as an initiative test.*

The sergeant fixed him with a no-nonsense stare.

"It's a *she*, not a *he*," she said. "And she's asking for the
Special Branch bloke at the top. Won't talk to anyone else."

"Ah well, there you go." Mercer slid behind the desk, his
attention already on the latest forensic reports put there in his
absence. "Just some glory-seeker, no doubt."

"Well, if you're sure?" The sergeant paused long enough for
Mercer to look up, the smile cooling. "Only, she said to be sure to
mention the name Barrett, if that means anything to you, sir?"

"Barrett?" Mercer echoed sharply, feeling the hair rise at the
back of his neck. "You're sure that's what she said?"

"Yes sir," the sergeant said, gleeful at this reaction.

"And she's still on the line?" Mercer demanded, got an
answering nod. "Well, put her through, woman!"

"Yes, *sir*!" the sergeant said heavily, turning away. Mercer
barely heard the muttered, "And that's *Sergeant* Woman, to you,"
that accompanied her departure.

He waited, chafing, for the call to be redirected, still standing
behind the desk, hand poised over the phone. He forced himself
to let it ring out twice before he picked up.

"Who's that?" demanded a voice at the other end of the line.
Mercer's heart twisted a little in his chest. She sounded young, a
kid on a prank. *But how did she know about the gun?*

"My name is Mercer." He smiled into the empty office so it
filtered into his voice, friendly, unthreatening.

"You that Special Branch bloke, are you?" the girl said, suspicious. "The one they sent up from London to catch him?"

And how does she know that? "That's right," the CTC man said easily, not correcting the name, aware his hand had tightened painfully around the plastic receiver. "Can you tell me who *you* are?"

"Might do—later, maybe, when you know I'm telling you the truth. Reward, is there?"

One had been discussed but not set. Duncan Inglis might not have cared much for his late wife one way or another, but he was wealthy enough to pay a substantial sum, and fully exploit the political capital to be gained from it.

"Naturally," he said warmly. "A big one. You give us something that leads to arrest and conviction, and the money's as good as yours."

She made what sounded like a disbelieving snort but it wasn't a good line, noisy in the background with traffic and voices. Mercer hoped the lab rats would be able to determine plenty from the recording he knew was undoubtedly being made.

"He's using the name Patrick Bardwell," she said.

Mercer slid the desk pad closer. "Where is he?"

"What, now?"

"Yes, now." He bit back a snap of anger. "Do you know?"

"Course I do! Old barn about halfway between Nateby and Outhgill, along the Mallerstang valley road. Up on the left-hand side, can't miss it. He's been messing about out there the last couple of nights. I don't reckon he's done yet, not by a long chalk."

Mercer scrawled the gist. "You, um, mentioned Barrett?" he asked, striving desperately for casual. "Who's that?"

"It's not a *who*," she said, matching him. "It's a *what*. A Light Fifty. You know what one of them is?"

"Oh yes," Mercer said softly. "I think it's safe to say I've come across one before."

"Well, then." There was a long pause. "You going to catch him, like he said?"

"I'm going to do it personally," Mercer promised. "But what's your connection to him? Why are you doing this?"

A long silence followed his question. If it wasn't for the background swell, Mercer might even have assumed she'd hung up. Eventually, her voice low and bitter and filled with a wail of lost longings, she said, "I thought he loved me."

And with that, she was gone.

83

GILES FREDERICKSON WALKED into his office at Warcop Training Ground and found Corporal Parrish on the phone.

As he entered, still in his dress uniform, she said, "Just a moment," and clamped the receiver to her shoulder. "Penrith police," she told him. And when he hesitated, added, "They say it's urgent, sir."

"Very well." Frederickson was still weary from the memorial service and his encounter with Duncan Inglis. He strode through to his office, tipping his peaked cap upside down onto the filing cabinet, peeling off his gloves. The phone on his desk rang.

"Yes?" he snapped into it.

"Major Frederickson?" A woman's voice, young, brisk. "Penrith CID, sir. Mr Mercer's asked me to contact you."

"Mercer?"

"He's in charge of the investigation, sir, and he's requested your urgent expert assistance with this sniper case."

Despite himself, Frederickson's interest quickened. "What kind of assistance?"

"We've just had a tip-off that's led to the discovery of what we believe may be another hide, sir," she said. "It's in a derelict barn on the Mallerstang road between Nateby and Garsdale Head—place called Outhgill. D'you know it?"

"Of course." Only weeks before, Frederickson had run the Mallerstang Yomp, a twenty-three-mile feat of endurance that took in three peaks of the valley and involved climbing a thousand metres. *Plenty of old barns out there.*

"Right, sir. Mr Mercer thought your expertise might be invaluable, if you wouldn't mind?"

"Of course," Frederickson repeated, clipped to mask his eagerness. "I'll be there directly."

He put down the phone and checked his watch. *Just time to change,* he decided. *Best to dress for action.*

It was only as he was speeding down towards the main gate five minutes later, in a Defender and combat DPM, that he wondered if he should have asked for more details—like the name of the female officer who'd called.

Probably not. From the background noise level, it sounded like pandemonium going on down there.

AT THE BUSY bus station terminal in Kendal, Edith Airey ran from the public phone box she'd been using, head down, scarlet, shaking.

She'd imagined herself back in the role of fearless Edith the Spy. In reality, she'd been sweating and terrified, expecting the squad cars to come screeching up at any moment, trapping her inside the booth, that she'd be dragged away in shackles.

Would they do that to him, if they caught him? Or would they try to claim self-defence and shoot him dead?

She bolted across the road, weaving through traffic waiting at the lights, and fled along Sandes Avenue, a panicked ungainly run, arms pumping, her bag swinging awkwardly against her hip. By the time she reached the bridge over the river, she was gasping. She could hardly see for the tears that wracked her body and wrecked her vision.

Oh, Patrick, cried a silent voice, twisting inside her head. *Oh, Patrick...*

NICK ARRIVED BACK at Hunter Lane just in time to see Mercer disappearing at high speed in the front passenger seat of a Volvo estate patrol that was also an Armed Response Vehicle. As he watched the ARV reach the end of the street with unobtrusive haste, Nick knew he'd missed something vital while he'd been away. He hurried across towards the station entrance.

Just as he stepped up onto the kerb he picked up a small blur of colour in his peripheral vision, closing fast, accompanied by a shriek of, "Daddy!"

His head snapped round as the small figure clamped onto his legs and stuck there like industrial Velcro.

"Sophie? Sweetheart!"

She let go then, stood back a pace and held her arms wide in mute demand, eyes huge. He hoisted her up immediately, held on tight, burying his face in her hair, inhaling baby shampoo and the blueberry Ribena that was her latest favourite. The smell of his child instantly triggered every memory of her Nick had ever had. He shut his eyes, breathed deep, and let them all wash over him.

When he opened them again, it was to find Lisa standing awkwardly in front of him with her fingers tucked into the back pockets of her white linen Capri pants. She was watching the two of them together and there was something wistful in her gaze.

"Lisa," he said, wary after their last parting, shifting Sophie so she was balanced on his hip facing her mother. "Is anything wrong?"

Lisa gave a little lift of her shoulder that didn't quite make it into a shrug.

"You're all right, are you?" he tried again. He glanced at Sophie. She was a bit flushed but that could simply be the heat, the excitement of seeing her daddy. He stroked the little girl's hair away from her face, ran his knuckle gently down her soft cheek.

"Yeah." Lisa's eyes were fixed on Sophie. "*We're* OK."

Ah... Nick kept his face carefully blank. "I hear a 'but'?"

"It's Karl," she said miserably. "Your lot have arrested him."

Nick had to work hard not to break into a triumphant grin. When he didn't immediately speak, Lisa threw him a quick, wounded glance. "Did you know about this?"

Nick shook his head slowly. "No," he said truthfully. After he'd handed off his file on the quad bike case to Kendal, he purposely hadn't kept up to speed on it. "I'm sorry." He rocked Sophie automatically and she gazed at him, fingers in her mouth. "We've been kind of busy."

Lisa nodded, doleful. "Yeah, I know. I've been watching the news. It's horrible, and I'm really sorry to ask, but..." She shrugged helplessly. "He's my brother. Mum's worried sick. What can I do?"

Cut him loose before he sinks the lot of you, he thought bitterly.

Instead, he said, "I understand."

"Do you think you might be able to find out anything?" she asked in a rush, as though knowing she was pushing her luck. "Karl swears he's done nothing wrong. That it's just some mate he works with, dropping him in it."

"Nice mates he's got." Nick's tone was dry.

Lisa's colour rose, and she took a breath to blast at him, but then the fire went out of her. Her gaze flicked to Sophie again, fell away.

"Yeah, well," she muttered. "He's been really good, helping out with Sophie since—," she paused, swallowing. "Well, since we split up."

Since you left, you mean?

"Leave it with me. I can't promise, with all this going on, but I'll look into it when I can."

"Thanks, Nick." She checked her watch, frowned. "We need to get back to the car." She gave an embarrassed little smile. "Otherwise I'll be asking you to get me off a parking ticket as well." The joke was strained, but Nick smiled with her anyway.

She held out her arms to Sophie. Nick's heart twisted at the way his daughter instantly wriggled to go to her mother. He gave her a final kiss, a tight squeeze, and set her down.

Lisa started to turn away, stopped. "I know he's a bit wild, but he's still my big brother," she said, uneasy. "I don't want to see him in trouble for something he's not done."

Nick stood and watched them, mother and daughter, until they reached the end of the street. Sophie looked back twice. He waved each time, and she waved too, happy now.

"Yeah," he murmured when they were well out of earshot. "But what about seeing him in trouble for something he *has* done?"

He was still wrestling with his dilemma when he reached the CID office, hung his jacket over the back of his chair. Yardley was the only other occupant.

"Where's Mercer gone haring off to?" he asked, not expecting much of a reply.

To his surprise, Yardley rocked his chair back, grinning at him, almost friendly. "Some anonymous call to the tip-line about a possible sighting down in Mallerstang. Don't know what they said, but he went chasing off like his tail was on fire, eh."

"We live in hope." Nick sat down. "Where's Mallerstang, anyway?"

Yardley rolled his eyes. "Mallerstang Common," he said, like that helped. "East side of the M6, between here and Tebay." He swivelled back to his desk, paused. "Oh, someone called Bill rang—said you used to work together and wanted a word, eh. Your mobile was off."

"Must have been at the funeral." Nick reached for his phone. *Wow, a message actually passed on.* "Thanks," he added as the number connected.

It was quickly answered. "Nick, mate! Can you talk?"

"Uh-huh," Nick said easily. "I'm listening."

"Oh, like that, is it?" Bill said. "I called in a few favours about this Mercer bloke." He hesitated, his voice dropping into seriousness. "Bearing in mind what's been going on up there, you're not going to like it much."

"Tell me."

"Couple of years ago, Mercer was in charge of vetting asylum seekers from countries that were, shall we say, *sensitive*, sniffing out potential terrorists. He cleared a lad who went straight into some radical extremist group. It caused a right stink. Mercer took heat for it, and by the looks of it he was pretty anxious not to make the same mistake twice."

"So he went too far the other way?"

"Got it in one, mate." Nick could picture his former colleague sitting back in his chair with his feet up on the desk. "Anyhow, he finds this other kiddie, in from Afghanistan, and he's convinced he's looking at the same again. The kid's only sixteen, but he can field strip an AK-47 blindfolded. He's from some troublespot province in the arse-end of nowhere, got relatives in the Taliban, the whole shebang."

"So, what happened?" Nick asked. "Deported?"

"Would have been better all round if he was. Think Guantanamo Bay," Bill said grimly. "Mercer got it into his head he needed a full confession to restore his credibility, so he locked the kid up in a detention centre and went at him, practically day and night."

With a creeping sense of unease, Nick knew where this was going.

"Anyway, after days of interrogation, the kid tore up his bedsheets and hanged himself," Bill went on, sad disgust in his voice. "Mercer, of course, took it as a sign of guilt. Case proved."

"But?"

"You always did spot the 'ifs' and 'buts', didn't you, mate?" Bill gave a humourless laugh. "Turns out the kid had been working as a local guide for our boys out there. Ended up as a spotter. Practically earned himself a medal, by all accounts. The sniper—one Sergeant Conor O'Keefe, would you believe. Irish father, Scottish mother—was the one who persuaded him to come to the UK, promised him a better life. So, O'Keefe brings him over, expecting he's going to pass straight through the green channel—priority case. He goes back to finish his last tour and next thing he knows, the kid's dead. There were some nasty reprisals out there, apparently. Messy all round."

"How did O'Keefe take it?"

"Ah, now we're talking. He went ballistic, as you'd expect. Swore he'd get Mercer 'a bit at a time'. Not sure what to make of that, eh? The old death of a thousand cuts, maybe? Women and children first?"

"No," Nick said tightly, pushing his chair back. "More like death at a thousand yards. And he's already started with the women."

86

MERCER COULDN'T DECIDE whether to be annoyed or gratified to find another vehicle already parked by the side of the road when he arrived. As he climbed out of the Volvo, he saw a tall figure standing on the verge near the sagging wire fence, arms folded, staring up towards the barn at the top of the field.

"Afternoon," Mercer called, and the figure turned. "Thank you for being so prompt."

"You're welcome," Grace McColl said coolly.

Mercer hadn't met the red-haired CSI before, and realised now that the fuzzy newspaper pictures had not done her justice. The way her manner lightened towards the two uniforms accompanying him did not escape notice, and he smiled his most ingratiating smile.

Then, behind her, the passenger door of the crime scene van opened and a gangling man got out. "You know my boss, Richard Sibson?" Grace said.

"Of course." Mercer's smile hardly slipped as the two men shook hands.

"When do the rest of the team get here?" Sibson asked.

"We're it, for the moment," Mercer said with forced cheerfulness. "Think of us as the advance party."

"Really?" Sibson scanned the surrounding territory. "Bearing in mind we have a sniper on the loose with a weapon capable of causing considerable destruction at more than a mile," he said, slightly scathing, "are you seriously suggesting we walk up that hill, in full view of the far side of the valley, before it's been swept? I'd bring in an ammunition dog at the very least."

"There's a time issue," Mercer said baldly. "If we go in mob-handed, we might scare him off." But he heard his own desperation, sensed their withdrawal. "I don't know about you, but I want to catch this guy."

"Because Angela Inglis was your sister?" Grace asked.

Mercer tried not to squirm. He'd been a comprehensive school boy and while his university years had given him a certain polish, women clearly born advantaged always made him feel inferior.

One of the uniformed officers came forwards, one hand on his radio. "DI Pollock's ordering us to pull back until the area's secured."

Mercer looked pointedly at his watch. "Unless there's been a bloodless coup in the last half hour," he snapped, "I believe I am still in charge of this investigation." The uniform shuffled his boots.

"If this is turning into a mine's-bigger-than-yours contest, you can count me out," Grace said calmly. "I simply don't have the equipment for it."

She started to turn away. Mercer put his hand on her arm, knew at once it was a mistake by the way she stiffened. He let it drop, along with his voice.

"Look, I really need you in on this," he said. "You've both seen what he can do." He flicked his eyes to Sibson, standing impassive beside her. "Yes, Angela was my sister, but that young copper was one of *your* boys. You, more than anyone, should want to catch him before he kills again."

"You don't have to try to appeal to our emotions as well as our professional pride," Sibson said with asperity. "We want him as much as you do, trust me."

"So—?"

"I'm in." Grace glanced at the silent uniform, adding with bleak humour, "But, should the worst happen, find someone to look after my dog, would you?"

87

Nick sent the Impreza hurtling through the roundabout in an agile four-wheel drift, balanced between throttle and steering, ignoring the blown horns that marked his rapid progress. As he accelerated down the slip-road onto the motorway, a glance in the rear-view mirror told him both patrols following had dropped back a good fifty metres.

Alongside him in the passenger seat, DI Pollock loosened his death-grip on the armrest.

"I wondered why you bothered with a car like this, lad. Now I think I understand."

Nick's answering smile was terse. They'd wasted valuable time trying to find out where Mercer had gone in such a hurry. The sergeant who'd passed on the tip-line call was the same one who'd sent Nick down to Orton the day he'd first met Grace, and she was no less obstructive now.

It wasn't until DI Pollock got involved that any real sense of urgency took hold. The call recording was retrieved and replayed. When Nick added what he'd just learned from his Met contact about Conor O'Keefe, things stepped up another gear altogether.

Pollock seemed to shrug off his usual bluff exterior, focus in tightly on what was needed, concise and in command. When the news came in that Mercer had requested CSI presence at the scene, and now neither Grace nor Sibson could be raised, Pollock stabbed a finger in Nick's direction.

"You're driving, lad. So shift your arse."

Now, as Nick weaved through traffic with the speedo needle quivering at one-thirty, the inspector leaned over to stab the re-dial button on the hands-free kit again. "Phone reception always was terrible right along Mallerstang."

"The number you have dialled is not available," the irritating automated voice informed them. *"Please try later."*

"I'll give 'em 'please try later'!" Pollock growled.

Nick gritted his teeth and pressed his right foot down a little harder. Something in his gut told him that if they weren't fast enough, or lucky enough, there might not *be* a later.

88

MERCER STEPPED THROUGH THE GATEWAY, mindful of his leather-soled shoes amid the dusty ruts. Grace, he noticed, was wearing some kind of high-tech hiking boots below lightweight cargo pants. She looked more like a climbing instructor than a crime scene specialist.

Sibson, by comparison, was in moleskins, a check shirt with the sleeves rolled back, and a knitted tie. He carried a compact video camera. Grace had an expensive-looking Canon slung over her shoulder, the flashgun wired to a battery pack on her belt. They both had several pairs of nitrile gloves protruding from pockets, but apparently no other equipment.

"Is that all you need?" Mercer asked, dubious.

"Let's see what we have first, shall we?" Sibson said equably. "You said yourself that we're merely the advance party rather than the main event."

Mercer glanced back, nervous, to where the ARV sat by the verge. The two uniforms were still waiting for authorisation from Control to unlock their weapons from the gun safe in the vehicle, and would not be swayed to deviate from procedure. Not that they could have provided much defence against a Barrett, Mercer acknowledged, but he would have felt better with them alongside him.

The two CSIs struck out across the grass. The land soon began to slope upwards and Mercer saved his breath for the climb, staying close to Grace's shoulder as if offering protection.

She moved easily on those long legs, he noted sourly, trying not to gasp as the incline bit.

Halfway up, they stopped. Grace snapped a couple of shots of the barn up ahead. The main building was a straightforward rectangle, roofed with the graduated stone flags that were typical of the area. It looked in good order. The smaller single-storey extension at the northern end was more ramshackle. Part of the corner was missing, the roof repaired with corrugated tin that had been partly blown away by the winter gales.

"It's a strange place for a hide." Sibson turned to stare uneasily across the valley, video camera in his hands. "What's he laying up to shoot from here?"

"Who knows?" Mercer, deeply uncomfortable to be a static target in such open ground, edged a little closer to Grace.

Without looking at him directly, she said in a conversational tone, "You might like to remember that he shot your sister at more than eighteen hundred metres and didn't touch a hair of the man on her arm at the time." She glanced at him then, a slightly supercilious look, he felt, that mocked his lack of courage.

"Meaning?" he snapped.

Grace raised an eyebrow. "Just an observation. Shall we go on?"

For Mercer, the barn's sanctuary couldn't come soon enough. Although wide open to the west, it was sheltered to the rear by the thick plantation of conifers which stood in a high semicircle on the barn's eastern side, a hundred and fifty metres back.

The two CSIs circumnavigated the building, pushing aside their own fears to make a professional record of what looked to Mercer like agricultural detritus against the back wall of the barn, accumulated over years. A rusting machine that he couldn't begin to guess the purpose of, a stack of broken pallets leaning near the open doorway, a couple of old oil drums standing close up against a piece of sheet steel and some rusting sections of corrugated iron, probably carried up here in some rush of unfulfilled enthusiasm to patch the roof of the smaller section.

"What can I smell?" Grace murmured, frowning. "Diesel?"

Sibson paused, sniffing. Mercer waved at the piece of machinery. "Probably that thing leaking," he suggested. "These farmers claim they're guardians of the countryside, then pour more pesticide into the rivers than all the chemical plants put together."

Grace smiled thinly, making no reply.

Frustrated by their slow pace, Mercer had nevertheless worked with a lot of crime scene people in his time. He had to admit they were thorough, treating this as a crime scene until it proved otherwise. When—or *if*—this came to trial, it would be a high-profile case. They couldn't afford mistakes.

Finally, putting their feet down with careful precision, they moved towards the barn's narrow doorway.

And just as they were about to enter, a figure in dark green camouflage stepped round the far corner of the stonework and said calmly, "I wouldn't do that, if I were you."

Mercer stumbled back, barely containing a yelp of fright.

"What the *hell* are you doing here?"

Major Giles Frederickson frowned in disapproval. "I received your message," he said. "I understand you've discovered another hide—wanted my opinion."

"I'm not sure quite *what* we've discovered as yet," Sibson said. "But we'd certainly value your opinion."

"Wait a minute," Mercer said. "What message? When?"

The major checked his watch. "Approximately twenty-five minutes ago. Some woman from Penrith CID rang me at camp."

Mercer hesitated. *He* certainly hadn't asked for the major's assistance, but without any other official back-up, he wasn't about to turn him away.

"Why didn't you want us to go inside?" Grace asked.

"Booby-traps," Frederickson said succinctly. "Standard operating procedure in hostile territory. May I?"

Mercer took a hasty step back. "Be my guest."

Frederickson approached the entrance cautiously, dropping to put his head close to the grass, looking for disturbed ground or tripwires. After a few minutes, he rose, straightening his tunic.

"You may want to move a little further back," he suggested with a grim smile. "Just in case."

Led by Mercer, Sibson and Grace walked thirty metres or so uphill towards the plantation. When they stopped, looked back, the major had disappeared inside the barn.

They stood in silence, listening to the quiet rustle of the trees, the distant bleating of sheep, the occasional noise of traffic. Mercer glanced into the forest behind them, edgy. The branches were so thickly layered the light could not penetrate, leaving the ground a rusty brown carpet of dead needles where nothing grew. Not that he could see much of it. After maybe ten metres the darkness became absolute. He shivered, turned away again.

The curving ends of the plantation reached down on either side of where they stood. The barn was directly in front, offering no direct line of sight across the valley.

So, if O'Keefe—or Bardwell, or whatever the hell he's calling himself now—is out there, at least he can't get a clear shot.

They waited another minute. Sibson began to hum distract-edly under his breath. Grace reviewed the shots she'd taken, eyes fixed on the small screen on the back of the camera as though to shut out her surroundings.

Then Frederickson appeared in the doorway, beckoning. They hurried to join him.

"No sign of explosives." He stepped aside. "See for yourself."

The CSIs both paused to pull on gloves and the four of them went in. The interior of the barn was dim but not dark. Light spilled in from several open apertures that might once have contained windows, and a second open doorway in the northern corner.

Next to this, neatly rolled, was an army surplus sleeping bag on a thin sheet of camping foam, mess tins, utensils, an opened twenty-four-hour ration pack with half the contents gone, bottles of water. All the signs of clandestine habitation. Grace fired up the flashgun, took numerous pictures both overall and close-up detail.

"So, *someone's* camping out here, but is it him?" Mercer said tightly.

"I would have thought so." Sibson was crouched near the sleeping bag. "Look at this."

They approached, leaned over him. Sibson had carefully peeled open a roll of oiled cloth. In the centre were two of the biggest bullets Mercer had ever seen. Almost the length of his hand, they were polished brass and copper and lead, with strangely flattened tips. The thought of something like that tearing through his sister made the rage punch at the inside of Mercer's skull.

"VLD rounds," Frederickson said, clipped.

"What?"

"Very Low Drag. I would say this is our boy."

Sibson stood. "Right, we've disturbed the scene more than enough," he said briskly. "By the book from here on in."

"Shall I go down to the van and fetch our kit?" Grace asked, earning a reproving stare from Sibson over the top of his glasses.

"I'm hardly too decrepit to manage that gentle hill without keeling over, McColl."

"And there was I just trying to be a polite and efficient junior," she said demurely. "You go, by all means."

He snorted. "Oh, just get on with it! And don't forget we'll need plenty—"

"—of evidence bags," she finished for him, smiling. "Yes, oh wise one." And she went out.

"If you wouldn't mind, gentlemen?" Sibson nodded to the exit.

"Not very gallant of you," Frederickson murmured to Mercer as he followed him out, "bringing the woman along as cover."

Mercer shrugged. "Like you, major, I'll take whatever cover is to hand," he said bluntly, checking Sibson wasn't close enough to hear. "It's me he's after, not her, but he clearly likes our CSI McColl or he wouldn't have called her. I'm not going to waste that." He nodded to the barn that loomed over them. "And as long as we stay this side of something with three-foot-thick walls of good old Lakeland stone, we should be pretty safe, don't you think?"

"What makes you think he's after you?"

Mercer shoved his hands into his pockets. "I was perhaps over-zealous—just doing my job. But somebody died who probably needn't have done."

The major pursed his lips. "There seems to be a lot of that going around."

Mercer moved to the corner of the barn, looked down the hill. Grace had stopped to take another couple of pictures and was about thirty metres away. He could see the Firearms boys milling around at the roadside. More uniforms had just arrived, and that flashy blue Subaru Nick Weston drove.

End of the line for me, he thought. No way they'd they let him stay with the investigation now. He turned back to Frederickson.

"Does the name Patrick Bardwell mean anything to you?"

The major looked shaken. "Yes," he said. "But I hope you're not suggesting he's the one behind all this, because I can assure you quite categorically that he is not."

"Very sure of your facts aren't you, major?"

"If we're talking about the Patrick Bardwell I knew, he's dead."

89

"COME ON, COME ON!" Nick muttered under his breath. Through a spotting scope filched from Firearms, he watched Grace begin her walk down the hill, cursing roundly when she stopped after only a short distance. Did she have no concept of the possible threat?

"What the hell's she playing at?" Pollock growled.

"At a guess? Trying to give us all heart attacks."

"Hang on, who's that?" Pollock pointed. "Man in army uniform."

Nick swung the glass up, adjusted the focus onto the figure who'd just appeared and was striding quickly after Grace. "It looks like Major Frederickson, sir."

"What the heck is he doing here?" Pollock shook his head. "I don't like this. I told them to stay back." He turned, scowling, to a couple of the Firearms team who were hovering nearby. "Get them back down here, all of them. Do it now!"

The two men had just started to jog away from the gateway when there was a massive crump from the far side of the barn, so the fabric of the earth appeared to momentarily heave and buckle underneath their feet. He saw both Grace and Frederickson go to ground.

The grass around the barn flattened as if in a strong wind. Then a tongue of dirty orange flame shot high into the air, sending roofing flags half the size of a man cartwheeling lazily.

And at last came a tremendous booming thunderclap as the noise of the explosion finally reached them.

90

MERCER WAS DOWN. Conscious, bleeding, still alive, but badly down.

He couldn't hear anything for the roaring in his ears, the burning in his lungs. He shook his head, trying to clear it, but all that did was provoke a spasm of pain that wrenched his entire upper body. As it rolled over him, he realised he couldn't feel his legs.

He lay panting, aware of an overwhelming coldness that reached into his gut and was spreading slowly upwards. In a panic, he clutched at his stomach. His hands came away greasy.

He twisted his head, saw Richard Sibson lying a few metres away. He could see half the CSI's face. His eye was open, staring, already beginning to glaze.

Mercer tried to scream, but could only manage a gurgle more animal than human, cornered, feral. He fought to rise, fingers scrabbling uselessly at the soft earth. Something jarred at his right hand, causing another spike of pain. Clumsily, he raised into view and found a nail speared through his palm like a crucifixion, blackened and hot to the touch.

Shrapnel. He gripped it in his other hand, pulled it loose with a snarl and threw it away, noticed small fires burning at the edges of his vision, patches of scorched earth.

He realised he could smell charred flesh like the last outbreak of Foot and Mouth when they'd burned whole farms of cattle in the open fields.

And suddenly he was assailed by memories of old family barbecues; he and Angela as children, teenagers; attending her wedding many years ago, and her memorial service only this morning. They hadn't yet released the body. He had a terrible sensation that he would not survive to see her buried.

A pair of booted feet came into view. He lifted his head in hope but saw a tall apparition in full camouflage, a strange other-earthly figure, draped in strips of rusty brown cloth and bits of dead conifer. A perfect match to the barren ground beneath the trees...

We were looking the wrong way, he realised dully. *We were looking for a long-range killer. Ignored what was right under our noses.*

He watched the boots move alongside Sibson, deliberate, without haste. They stopped, and the man leaned into view, placed two fingers briefly against the empty pulse point.

Mercer saw him rise, the boots twist in his direction. He knew what came next. The blood was in his mouth now, too thick to swallow. He wanted to be brave, but all he felt was a desperate fear.

I'm not ready!

"They were none of them ready," said a deep voice from somewhere above, and he realised he'd voiced the craven thought. *Famous last words.* He squinted up through tears to the distance face, bearded and remote.

The last thought that went through Mercer's head was one of total bewilderment. He opened his mouth, his voice a rusty remnant.

"Who in God's name...are you...?"

91

EDITH SAT KICKING her heels against the wall near the petrol station at Morrison's supermarket on the outskirts of Kendal.

It was not her first choice for a mysterious rendezvous point. A railway station would have topped the list but only if they still had steam trains. She'd be wearing a snappy suit with a pencil skirt and box shoulders, and a fox fur stole and one of those little hats with a veil that just covered her smoky eyes. Patrick would suddenly stride out of the billowing clouds, in a long overcoat and a rakish trilby. He'd run the last few yards to sweep her off her feet, whirl her around, as the last express to Paris pulled in behind them.

But this was not one of those old black-and-white films her mother indulged in when her father was off playing copper on drizzly Sunday afternoons. Where everyone smoked elegantly and were too terribly well-spoken, and the women never went anywhere without gloves.

This was dreary real life, with all its dirt and vulgarity. Its shabby disappointments made all the more graphic for being rendered in full Technicolor.

She checked her watch again, but no time seemed to have passed since she'd last looked. If it wasn't for the slow arc of the second hand, she could almost believe the stupid thing had packed in. It was only some market stall knockoff, the wafer-thin gilt already rubbing off the bezel. She'd promised herself the real thing—after. When she and Patrick had left all this far behind them.

Only he hadn't come.

She'd been fretting for the past hour, even before he was late. She'd done everything he asked, followed his instructions to the letter like she was defusing a bomb. Dialled the numbers he'd given her, acted her little heart out. No slips, no errors.

That copper from London, who was supposed to be the Big I Am, he'd lapped up every word of it. And the stupid army bloke never suspected for a moment that he wasn't dealing with a real policewoman.

But despite how brilliantly she'd played her part, Patrick hadn't come for her.

The only possible reason was that they must have taken him. Somehow, somewhere, his grand design had unraveled, come undone. She harboured a fierce hope that, knowing capture would mean their ultimate separation, he'd fought them to his last breath.

The weather was finally turning, clouds gathering overhead to block out the sun. It fitted Edith's mood perfectly. *If I can't be with Patrick,* she thought tragically, *the sun will never shine again.*

She'd gone from one extreme of emotion to another, roller-coastering, after that night she'd run from the byre. It was only the next day, when she'd knocked wretchedly on his door to clean for him, that he'd swept her into his arms, held her close and told her how much he needed her. And then he'd shown her. The loo at the byre didn't get scrubbed that day. Edith had grinned under the visor of her helmet all the way home, struggling to mask her delight in front of her parents.

Because at last—*at last*—everything was starting to go right for her.

Of course, looking back, Patrick hadn't actually explained much. He'd carefully gone over *what* he wanted her to do, but she realised she was hazier on the *why* of it. Maybe she should have asked more questions, so she'd have known what to expect from their new life together.

But what does any of it matter now, if they've taken him?

She drummed her heels against the stonework behind her legs, a random pattern that picked up rhythm and speed to match the dreadful bellow inside her head.

Further along Appleby Road, towards the middle of town, she heard the frantic wail of sirens. Two squad cars hurtled towards her, their strobing headlights searing her eyes, roof lights ablaze. She froze like a rabbit, waiting for them to screech alongside, the slam of doors, booted feet, shouted commands to lie on the ground while they cuffed her.

Both cars rocketed past without a pause, headed on towards Grayrigg. The thudding of Edith's heartrate faded slowly with the distant wail, yelping in and out of sync. Foreboding lay like a stone in the depths of her belly.

Edith waited another two hours, by which time a steady rain had begun to fall. She caught the bus up to Tebay. The route went past the entrance to the Retreat, which she half-expected to see barricaded with policemen, but there was no sign that things weren't just as they'd ever been.

Edith sat in the furthest back corner of the bus, clutched her running-away bag to her chest like a baby, and wept silently for the rest of the journey.

92

TWO MILES FROM OUTHGILL, further up the valley towards Nateby, Jim Airey stepped into the road and waved an imperious hand. The approaching Land Rover slowed to a stop and some hairy old farmer stuck his head out of the sliding window, blinking against the rain.

"What the 'eck's goin' on, son?"

"There's been a serious incident locally, sir," Airey said, pompous, trying not to recoil as he got closer. The man smelt like he'd been rolling in sheep dip. "I'm going to have to ask you for some ID."

"ID?" the farmer spluttered through his beard. "We in a police state now are we? Don't you think I got better things to do than carry me drivin' licence around all over the place just on the off-chance the likes of you take it into your head to pull me over?"

Airey sighed. Just about everyone he'd stopped so far had made the same point and he was getting sick of arguing about it.

He gestured to the back of the Land Rover. "What have you got in here, then?"

Grumbling, the farmer climbed awkwardly down from the driver's seat with the stilted gait of a man whose knees gave out on him decades ago. He yanked open the back door.

Three startled-looking sheep jostled inside, accompanied by the overwhelming stink of lanolin. One of the sheep began to urinate with nerves, a yellow stream that splashed onto the bare metal floor. Airey stepped back hastily.

"Seen enough, son?" the farmer asked. "Or d'you want to ask them for ID an' all?"

"Oh, get off with you," Airey said, flushing.

The farmer merely grunted by way of reply and stumped unevenly back to his cab.

Farmers! Airey shook his head. Who else would put a load of dirty, incontinent animals into the back of their car? That Land Rover might be old, but it looked in surprisingly good nick, the dark blue paintwork gleaming almost freshly as it sped away.

93

ANOTHER MILE FURTHER ON, Patrick Bardwell pulled over into a gateway selected at random. He hopped nimbly down from the cab and opened the back door. The trio of Herdwick ewes he'd taken hostage scrambled out without further invitation, fleeing into the open field.

Underneath the Land Rover, wrapped in the remains of Bardwell's ghillie suit, clipped neatly into its custom bracket, the Barrett lay hidden and secure.

PART VII

"THE BOMB DISPOSAL team have done a preliminary exam of the area," Grace said. "They reckon from the general blast pattern and the dispersal of the debris, that the explosion most probably originated in the two fifty-gallon oil drums placed against the east wall of the barn."

Brian Pollock peered at the tall redhead from under bushy eyebrows. She was dangerously calm, he thought, her usual smooth gait now coltish and stiff, and it wasn't just the drizzle that was making her shiver. *Shock—she shouldn't be here.*

"They didn't waste any time."

"Well, I was able to provide them with detailed images of the scene just before..." Grace gave him a ghosted smile. "I nearly left my camera in the barn."

"Do we know what the explosive itself was?" Pollock asked quickly, not liking the sudden brightness in her eyes. "We *are* near an army camp, after all—not to mention local quarries."

"ANFO is the mostly likely candidate, they tell me—ammonium nitrate and fuel oil. When we first arrived up here I thought I could smell diesel, but it didn't alert me because diesel is so difficult to ignite. And the major checked out the area for any obvious signs of a booby-trap." She paused in memory and regret. "It would seem he filled the drums with ammonium nitrate—probably in the form of fertiliser—and then poured in a mix of diesel and petrol."

Pollock's eyes narrowed. "Two fifty-gallon drums' worth? Bit more than he could siphon out of his car, then."

Grace nodded. "He must have got it from somewhere, and there's always CCTV on petrol station forecourts. It's somewhere to start looking, anyway."

"What about the detonator? Any word yet on how he set it off?"

She took a deep breath, steadied. "They're being cagey at this stage, but judging from the impact point on the steel sheet directly behind the drums, it looks like our man simply waited until his targets were in place, and then ignited the device with some kind of incendiary round. They reckon he could have dropped a couple of live rounds into the drums, too, just to make sure."

Pollock's lips tightened into a thin line. "When will they know for certain?" He tried to ignore the pale reproach in her face.

"As soon as possible. I appreciate the urgency, but we've only had a few hours," she pointed out wearily. "And now the weather's turned on us we have our work cut out simply trying to preserve the scene."

Since the explosion, a makeshift shantytown of EZ-Up tents had sprouted across the area between the barn and the woods.

Pollock had dragged in all his people, put Chris Blenkinship in charge. No choice, really. The lad was pushy, but he'd done the time, and with Sibson gone…

Blenkinship had the site split down into sectors, had them all combing the grass for the myriad of scattered fragments. Grace was back on drone work. Dressed now in her Tyvek suit, booted and gloved, she was carrying two handfuls of loaded evidence bags down to the van when Pollock intercepted her—partly for a progress report; partly an excuse to see how she was holding up.

Better than expected, he realised. "It's caused a right mess, that's for sure." He paused, shook his head. "Set us up good and proper, didn't he?"

"Mm," Grace said remotely. "He must have known we'd try and stay away from the open area, keep to the uphill side of the barn where we felt safer, less exposed."

"Aye, and he was right."

Her expression chilled. "When Major Frederickson was

carrying out his inspection, he advised us to move back. We must have been so close to him then..."

"You couldn't have known," Pollock said, almost gently.

Grace swallowed. "Um, the barn itself acted as a deflector to concentrate the force of the explosion into the area immediately adjacent to it, much like a giant shaped charge."

"Like a Claymore," Pollock glanced at her. "That's a—"

"—an M18A1 anti-personnel mine," she said, neutral. "Yes, the bomb disposal people made much the same comparison. And, as with a Claymore, our sniper had packed his own makeshift version with shrapnel. Clearly, he didn't have ball bearings, so he used whatever loose junk happened to be at hand." She lifted the bags, which contained a variety of blackened and distorted nuts, bolts and nails. "We've been picking these up all afternoon."

"Nasty," Pollock commented. "I've seen the initial report on the injuries sustained by both victims." He hesitated, picked his way with care. "Richard must have been right next to one of those drums when it went up. He wouldn't have known anything about it."

Grace gave a nod and gleaned what he hoped was comfort from the news. He'd heard the rumour about her and Sibson, taken note even if he hadn't entirely believed it. After all, they were both free agents. None of his business as long as it didn't bleed over into work. But, even if their relationship *was* purely professional, she was a cool one.

They'd all been kept well back for a time after the explosion. By the time Firearms had OK'd them to go forwards, Blenkinship had arrived, so at least she'd been spared the job of gathering pieces of Sibson personally.

The dog teams had been out all afternoon, picking up a profusion of different trails that ultimately led nowhere. Even the helicopter, drafted over from the north-east with thermal imaging equipment, had drawn a total blank.

Like chasing down a damn ghost.

He sighed, rubbed his forehead. The death toll was up to four. Since Weston's discovery about Conor O'Keefe and his feud with Mercer, things had become more complicated, not less. The press was going berserk behind the roadblocks set up to keep prying eyes and lenses at bay.

He turned, gave her a considering stare. "You all right, lass? You should—"

"No," she said abruptly, forestalling his suggestion to take herself home. "I need to be here."

"No-one's going to think any less of you, Grace, if you call it a day."

"*I'll* think less of me," Grace cut in, brittle as glass. "Two people are dead and I'm not one of them. How can I clock off now?"

95

STANDING BY THE GATEWAY, Nick saw the way Grace's shoulders slumped as she turned away from the inspector and headed in his direction. *What the hell is she still doing here?* he wondered savagely, and in the next breath realised he would do exactly the same. *Working through it.*

"You all right?" he asked as she neared. Her stride faltered, and for a moment he almost expected her to bite back at him. But then her face closed down again into that seamless mask.

"I suppose you could say I've been better."

He straightened, dragged the gate open and followed her to the van, where she dumped the fresh collection of evidence. It hit the metal floor with an ominous dull clank.

"He waited, didn't he? Until I was clear." She turned, sank onto the open side-step of the vehicle, sitting with her forearms clamped between her knees, hunched, eyes on the ground. "He could have set off that bomb the moment we got up there. So, why did he wait?"

Nick crouched in front of her, tilted his head until he was sure of her gaze. "If it *is* Conor O'Keefe who's responsible for this, not Pete Tawney, maybe *he* does have a problem killing women."

"What about Angela Inglis?" Grace pointed out. "He didn't have any problem killing her."

Nick gave a sigh. "Women he considers innocent," he amended. "Women who are not his primary objective."

"You think he has one? Perhaps we're looking for logic in a madman."

"No, there's an agenda here. We just don't quite know what it is yet."

Grace nodded slowly and sat for a moment longer. "I'm sorry." She stiffened her spine as she rose. "I didn't mean to go all maudlin on you."

"If that's your idea of maudlin, you've led a very sheltered life."

Her smile lost heart before it was fully formed. "What are you doing back here?"

"Just come to update Pollock on O'Keefe." Nick reached into his jacket for his notebook. "He's no longer at the last address we had for him in Liverpool—surprise, surprise," he said gloomily. "I spoke to his ex-landlady, though, lives in the flat above. She was the usefully nosy type, told me O'Keefe apparently went 'up north to some religious place' about a month back. Found out last Christmas that he had something terminal, so she reckoned, and either sold everything he owned or gave it away, even his dog."

"He gave his dog away?" Grace queried.

"That's what she said. It's not a bad cover story, if this is what he had in mind." He gave a twisted smile. "She was halfway through telling me about the very nice TV set he'd given her when she obviously realised that if the cops were asking questions about him, it might be stolen, so she started back-pedalling madly."

But Grace didn't return his smile. "He gave his dog away," she repeated, meeting his gaze with troubled eyes. "So, wherever he went, he knew he wasn't coming back."

96

Giles Frederickson had a raging headache and a desperate thirst.

He'd been far closer to the detonation than Grace McColl, still remembered the tremendous compression through his chest as it buffeted his internal organs and sent him diving.

He'd got away with a bump on the head, possibly a wrenched knee from landing awkwardly. All in all, nothing much. A few seconds earlier, he realised grimly, and it would have been another story.

Like it was for those two poor devils.

The medics argued he should go to hospital, of course, but Frederickson had survived enough skirmishes to know when injuries were serious. On a battlefield triage scale, he didn't even count as walking wounded. Nothing that couldn't be cured by a stiff brandy and a soak in the bath. He intended to indulge in both as soon as he got home.

Leaving the scene, he drove the Defender north through the pretty market town of Kirkby Stephen, accelerated out past the cemetery and turned off towards Warcop village.

The road was tight and twisty, but the most direct route. A convenient shortcut that avoided the regular traffic jams of the main A66. Frederickson drove automatically, his thoughts churning.

The bomb disposal chaps told him little, of course, but he

knew by their questions what they were thinking. Those oil drums must have been packed with shrapnel as well as explosive.

He'd seen such damage often enough in Iraq. And on home soil, come to that—two nail-bombs in London parks in the early 'eighties.

But this was more than simple mindless carnage. As soon as Mercer mentioned the name Patrick Bardwell, all Frederickson's very well-developed survival instincts warned him to get out fast.

The Bardwell he'd known had died in Afghanistan, his entire squad killed when the vehicle they were travelling in had come under sniper attack. Those mountain roads were narrow and treacherous, and no-one ever knew if the driver had jerked disastrously as the anti-matériel round hit, or if the steering gear itself was shot away. Either way, the result was the same. A long deadly plunge and yet more body bags loaded into the belly of a Hercules.

They should never have been there, he thought fiercely. *I followed my orders, saw that Tawney followed his…*

But Frederickson remembered Mercer's certainty that *he* was the target. If the sniper in the trees above the barn *wasn't* Pete Tawney, then perhaps he had been waiting for Frederickson and the woman to clear the scene. But if he was minimising civilian casualties, why take out the CSI chap, Sibson as well? And it didn't explain using the name Patrick Bardwell.

No coincidence, Frederickson was sure of that.

He massaged his grazed temple under the band of his beret, hoped the painkillers the medics had given him would kick in soon.

In his breast pocket, the major's iPhone began to buzz. He slipped the Bluetooth earpiece in place.

"Frederickson."

"You were lucky today, major." A man's voice, quiet, not gloating.

It took a startled moment before Frederickson's brain put it together and he was suddenly glad the Defender's steering was forgiving enough to absorb his reflexive twitch.

He ducked, scanning the rapidly passing terrain. Trees, low

fields, a couple of barn conversions. Unfavourable territory for a sniper. Too enclosed and twisting, without enough commanding high ground. Nevertheless, his right foot lifted momentarily.

"Mr Bardwell, I presume," he said, recovering. "Sounding very much alive for a dead man."

"Wondered if you'd remember."

Do I stop or go on? Frederickson had walked away from one ambush by the skin of his teeth. Was he being herded towards another, or just being taunted?

He pressed his foot down again, hard. The Defender lurched forwards and picked up speed, diffs whining.

"I know you, don't I?" Frederickson strove for casual. *Not Pete Tawney, but that voice...*

"To the likes of you, I'm just another piece of equipment. Long as it functions, you look after it. Soon as it doesn't, it's on the scrapheap, regardless. Plenty out there just like me."

Frederickson heard the bitterness behind the even words. He pushed the Defender through another bend, cutting it fine, the protruding hedgerow thrashing against the bodywork. *Unsettle him. Distract him.*

"So, you were decommissioned," he said, drawling slightly. "Is *that* what this is all about?"

Bardwell grunted. "Ironic, isn't it, major? You reckon a man's mentally unfit to fight, but you of all people know we can't do what we're trained for, tour after tour, and stay entirely sane."

"When history looks at what you've done here, everything you were before won't matter," Frederickson crossed a hump-back bridge over the Eden, fast enough for the suspension to unweight at the crown. "You'll be immortalised as a monster."

"Who's to blame for that? You train us to forget we're human, then condemn us when we do. And when *you* decide we're done, you expect us to turn back into civvies again overnight. Flick of a switch. Can't be done."

Don't I know it. "If you're hoping to punish the army for their indifference, they won't even notice."

"Somebody like me, loose on home ground with a weapon like this?" Bardwell jeered. "Trust me, they've already noticed."

A reference to the team of ex-SAS mercenaries Weston mentioned? The turnoff for Musgrave village appeared ahead and Frederickson hesitated. Should he take it—deviate from any expected route? Surely Bardwell, whoever he was, hadn't had time to set up another hide. *That voice was tantalisingly familiar.*

"So you're out to prove a point?" he said. "Using civilians—non-combatants?"

"They were connected, one way or another," Bardwell said, and Frederickson clamped his jaw, reminded himself that this man had murdered Angela in cold blood for the actions of her brother. "The army gave me the only family I've ever known, then tried to take it away again. Combat forges bonds that can't be broken. Stronger than blood."

"You talk like I've never been there," Frederickson snapped, finally goaded into temper. And his brain finally flashed him an image of his office wall, of the line of photographs, and of one in particular, taken in the mountains. Of a big guy, standing at the major's shoulder amid the rocks, cradling his beloved Barrett, surrounded by his grinning fellows. *Gotcha!*

Distracted, Frederickson braked late for a ninety-degree blind corner onto the bridge over the dismantled railway line, almost locking a wheel. "What the devil did you think you signed up for, man?" he demanded. "A chestful of medals and glory?"

Another grunt. "We all of us, at one time or another, fall some way short of glory, major. You should know that."

And the line clicked off, abrupt.

As Frederickson turned onto the bridge, the soldier in him realised his mistake. The bridge was narrow, straight, about thirty metres long. Dead ahead, the land rose maybe fifteen metres up towards the tree line at the top of the hill. Perfect uninterrupted visibility into a controlled and measured kill zone.

He stamped on the throttle, but he'd misjudged the gears. From a near standing start, the Defender's non-turbo diesel responded with utter lethargy. Frederickson's gaze skimmed across the top of the field, just catching a glimpse of chimney pots through the trees. He almost gasped his relief.

Madness to risk a shot so close to habitation…

The .50 calibre round punched through the radiator grille like it was paper, ripping straight into the cast iron engine block. The motor seized instantly, with an explosive detonation.

Power gone, the Defender coasted gently towards the exit of the bridge, scuffing against the stonework.

Out! Get out!

Frederickson just had time to reach for the door.

97

"GRACE! THERE YOU ARE!"

Grace looked up from her laptop, which was balanced across the front seat of the crime scene van, plugged into the auxiliary socket, to see Chris Blenkinship bearing down on her along the grass verge. There was something baleful about the tilt of his head.

"I'm just downloading another memory card," she said as he neared.

Blenkinship might have coveted command, she thought, but he was rapidly discovering how deceptively easy Richard Sibson had made it look. At the very thought of her mentor, Grace felt her throat close up.

"Grace, pet, I'm going to have to ask you to leave the scene."

The download was in its last five seconds. Grace waited for it to finish, then turned and eyed him calmly.

"Might I ask why?"

Blenkinship puffed out a breath. "I've just had word from the lab. You remember those hair samples you collected from the first hide we found?"

Grace did not miss his usage of "you" and "we". Manoeuvring, taking credit and shifting blame. Her mind skated back but could find no loopholes.

"I remember."

He sighed again, more heavily this time. "They've just run another DNA sample you collected, totally unconnected, and got a match." He shook his head. "You cocked up somewhere along the line, cross-contaminated the evidence."

Grace closed down the program, ignoring the hollow clench in her belly, turned to face him. "We both know that didn't happen. I'm good at my job, Chris. That would be a basic, careless mistake."

He flushed. "Well, maybe you're just not as good as you think you are," he snapped. "You might have jeopardised the validity of this whole case. I always thought Sibson set too much store—" Even he stopped just short of saying it. "Just go home, Grace." And he turned away.

"Compromised the samples how, exactly?"

He halted, irritated now. "I don't have time to argue about this."

"If you're suspending me—officially or unofficially," she added when he opened his mouth to protest, "then I have the right to know why, surely?" She masked her distress with a cool indifference she knew annoyed him. It was preferable to letting him see her rattled. He'd take the slightest hint of self-doubt as sure-fire guilt, and that was the last thing she could afford.

Blenkinship rolled his shoulders as though spoiling for a fight, said in a flat voice, "The hair sample came back a match to the routine DNA swab you took from the Airey girl over that thing with the dog. If you can manage to contaminate two totally different samples, taken more than a week apart—"

"—I'd be a genius," Grace cut in. "Oh, come on, Chris! It would be hard enough to do on purpose, never mind accidentally. Even if I was as sloppy as you believe." She frowned. "You are, of course, ignoring the other explanation."

"What?" Blenkinship gave a snort of laughter, waved a hand up towards the remains of the barn, still smouldering. "That an anorexic teenage lass might be the one responsible for all this?"

But Grace had a sudden flashback to her conversation with Edith at Hunter Lane. The girl's knowledge of the Ukrainian female sniper, her alienation, her rage. And the fingermarks around her neck did not correspond to the size of her father's hands, that much they knew. So, who had tried to strangle her? And why?

"Responsible, no," she murmured. "But she might be involved."

Blenkinship made a swat of annoyance. "You're clutching at straws, pet," he said, exasperated now. "Your wild theories might have been given free rein in the past, but I'm not Sibson."

"No." Grace lifted her chin, giving way to the anger simmering just beneath the surface. "You most certainly are not."

Blenkinship flushed dark red, features closing down into a scowl. He opened his mouth, just as Ty Frost appeared at a run along the verge behind him.

"Boss! There's been another shooting!"

Just for a second, Blenkinship's face was haunted, then he said coldly, "Go home, Grace. If I have to make it official, I will. Like it or not, I'm running this scene, and if I can't trust you to do the job right, then you're no use to me here."

98

Bardwell drove into the yard at the Retreat and shut off the Land Rover's engine. He sat for a moment with his arms resting on the hard rim of the steering wheel, head bowed, one thought circling inside his mind.

It's done.

He'd allowed himself to break his own rules by killing Frederickson. He'd paced the bridge and calculated he had four to five seconds of viable exposure. There'd been no need to disable the vehicle first. At only three hundred and twenty metres, the range was child's play for the Barrett.

But he'd wanted the bastard to *know.*

The relative proximity of the farmhouse had been a worry, but between the regular blasting from nearby quarries and artillery fire on the ranges at Warcop, he reckoned the locals would be hardened to the sound of gunfire. No doubt by the time the farmer had his boots on Bardwell was already across the field to the Land Rover and away.

He sat up. The logical, clinical part of his brain was telling him coldly to get moving. Escape and evade.

He let out a long whistling breath. Half of him hadn't expected to ever get this far. He'd thought he'd feel elation but in reality, there was nothing.

What have I done? he wondered. The answer came quickly. *My duty.*

His mind spun back through a thousand flickering images, like a riffled book of photographs, to a very different kill. He'd begged for clearance, finger curled inside the guard, almost trembling with the effort required *not* to shoot. Alongside him, he'd barely heard the increasingly frantic whispering of his spotter's signals traffic with the nearest command post.

A group of soldiers were raping civilians, women and girls. It was a small town, little more than a village, just outside Srebrenica, after the partial evacuation during the Serb bombardment. The women were supposed to be safely out of harm's way. They were not.

The soldiers seemed to take no pleasure in their own depravity, acting with a tense purpose, as though under orders. A colonel had been overseeing the degradation, a big man with his greatcoat slung around his shoulders. Bardwell's hide was less than five hundred metres downwind, close enough that he could smell the cigarette smoke, sex, blood, and fear.

Command wanted him to stand by, observe, not to compromise his position for no tactical advantage. When they'd cut the first of the little girls struggling from the herd, he'd stopped listening.

He'd shot the fat colonel deliberately high, in the throat, so his head popped off like that of a suicide bomber. The ragged troops should have massacred both him and his spotter afterwards, but they scattered in shameful disarray.

As Bardwell fell back, he'd known only a raging satisfaction, to be in the right place at the right time, with the ultimate power at his disposal.

That must have been when his superiors decided that he could no longer be relied upon. How had Frederickson put it? When they'd decided to *decommission* him.

He sat up, unclenching his stiff fingers, and let himself into the byre. As soon as he closed the kitchen door behind him, he felt some small difference in the viscosity of the air, as though he could feel the vibrations of another heartbeat.

His eyes flicked to the door again. *No time.*

He stepped sideways, quietly opened the drawer next to the sink and slid out a carving knife with an eight-inch blade. As he moved silently towards the living room, he shifted his grip so the blade slanted upwards, lying alongside his forearm where it was hidden by his sleeve. Easy to use; hard to take away, even by an expert.

He slipped through the doorway. The curtains were drawn, but in the dim light, he saw a man sitting empty-handed in the wingback chair. A man who'd become very familiar.

"You won't be needing that, Patrick," Ian Hogg said gently.

Bardwell regarded him for a moment, then lifted his arm and let the knife clatter, handle first, into the coal bucket.

"Didn't know it was you." He didn't reach for the light switch.

"I don't even know who you are," Hogg said, great sadness in his tone.

Bardwell moved further into the room. Hogg didn't make any attempt to rise, but his fingers tightened on the arms of the chair.

"You know me," Bardwell said quietly, looking down at him.

Hogg shook his head. "It was on the news this afternoon. They want you for all this killing."

Bardwell's lips thinned. *Aye, there was a time when they did.*

"Shouldn't believe everything you hear on the news."

"I didn't want to believe it." Hogg gave a watery smile. "But I called a lieutenant-colonel I used to serve with, who's now based at Credenhill. He was very interested to hear where you were because he reckoned he went to your funeral last winter. So, who *are* you, Patrick?"

Credenhill, Bardwell thought bleakly. He remembered Edith's garbled report of the men who'd apparently been sent to track him down. She's seemed to think they were SAS, up from Hereford. She'd probably got her facts wrong, but he couldn't be sure. And the army would not want the embarrassment of a trial. If they didn't know already where he was, Hogg's innocent enquiry might have set the hounds on his trail. *I've less time than I thought.*

"You ring the cops, then?"

"Not yet," Hogg said evenly. "You came to me for sanctuary. I couldn't betray that trust without giving you a chance to explain."

Bardwell sighed, overwhelmed with regret. "I've watched

people herded into churches and burned alive, padre." He leaned over the chair, watched the man who'd so nearly become a friend try not to shrink back. "There is no sanctuary."

99

EDITH JERKED upright as she heard her father slam the front door. She'd been in her room, sobbing, since she arrived home and channel-hopped through all the news reports she could find. They all had the same sketchy information.

There'd been an incident, an explosion. Two men were dead, believed to be police officers. And then had come the breaking news of a third man shot and killed in a roadside ambush, his Land Rover found adrift. Military connections were hinted. The name Patrick Bardwell had been released. Anyone with information should come forwards. No further details at this time.

Edith filled in plenty of her own.

Now, she scrambled off her bed and galloped downstairs. Her father was in the back sitting room, peeling off his stab vest. Underneath it, his shirt was stuck to his body with sweat and rain. He glanced up briefly as she froze in the doorway, clutching at the jamb.

"Your mother not back from her shift yet?" He dumped the vest onto the table with a gusty sigh. "Make yourself useful and put the kettle on then, will you? I'm parched."

"What happened?" Edith burst out. "Is he dead?"

"What are you on about, Edith?" He turned to stare at her. "Is who dead?"

Edith came forwards, face white. *How can I begin to explain what there was between Patrick and me?*

"What. *Happened*?" she ground out.

Her father continued to regard her in irritation. He shook his head but was clearly gleeful to have an audience for his part in the unfolding drama.

"We had a tip-off this morning. Some tart, giving us the fake name he's been using. Matey-boy obviously got his leg over, then dumped her. She said he'd holed up in an old barn just south of Kirkby Stephen. Who'd have thought he'd be right on our doorstep, eh?"

Airey wandered into the kitchen looking for food. Edith followed, watched as he pulled a lump of cheese from the fridge and took a bite out of it, talking with his mouth full.

"Anyway, the Special Branch bloke, Mercer, he went rushing down there with a couple of CSIs and that army bloke, Frederickson. The one who owned the dog...well, you know who." He eyed her as he pushed more food into his mouth. "When they got there—boom! Whole place had been booby-trapped, according to the bomb squad. It was a set-up from the get-go."

"A set-up?" Edith mumbled dully. "So it's not Patrick who's dead?"

"Patrick?" Airey said, distracted, opening the bread bin and pulling out a couple of slices of curling white loaf. "Who's Patrick? No, a couple of our own got it. Made a right mess of them, from what I hear. Just missed Frederickson, but popped him on his way back to Warcop, cool as you like." He found a knife and glooped lurid yellow piccalilli onto the bread, dotting it with lumps of cheese, squashing the other slice on top with the flat of his hand.

With a grunt of satisfaction, he scooped up his feast, headed for the sitting room again. "I'm going to get changed. Edith, did you hear what I said? Don't just stand there, girl, put the kettle on. I'm dying for a cuppa. We've been run ragged this afternoon. I've had nothing since lunch."

He went out. Edith vaguely heard his feet heavy on the stairs, but still she didn't move.

If Patrick isn't dead, then why didn't he come for me?

The truth descended slowly onto Edith, standing there in the dingy kitchen, watching a blob of piccalilli make its painstaking slide down the outside of the jar her father had left lidless on the worktop.

The temperature seemed to plummet. Edith felt it in the

shimmy of sensation that ran up her shins, across her stomach and ended at the back of her neck, crawling through her scalp.

He lied to me.

She twisted, staggered, grabbed hold of the sink and shut her eyes, but there was no escaping it. No other spin to put on what he'd done.

He used me.

He'd taken the devotion, the love that Edith had showered onto him, taken it all with selfish arrogance and left her with nothing. The depth of his betrayal ripped at her soul. She'd given him everything, *everything*.

He won't get away with this.

Edith pushed herself away from the sink, caught a glimpse of her reflection in the liver-spotted mirror her mother kept hanging by the corner of the cooker. Her sunken eyes burned, ferocious, as the anger swelled inside her until she thought she'd split wide open and it would all come bursting out like a giant solar flare.

Nobody does this to me.

She spun away from the sink, stumbled down the cellar steps. The padlock her father kept on his illicit gun store was secure enough, but the wooden door it was attached to was old and soft.

Edith grabbed a long flat-bladed screwdriver from the shelf by the stairs. She jammed the blade between the hasp and the door, heaved. Even with her skinny frame behind it, leverage was on her side. The screws pulled out and the door swung wide. Before, she had needed the key so her father wouldn't know she'd been there. Now she didn't care.

Edith stepped into the narrow space, lifted down the AK-47 from its rack, grabbed a handful of reloads, began feeding them into the magazine with cold determination. Her hands shook as she forced each round into place.

He'll be sorry.

She was almost done when she heard her father's voice in the kitchen above, exasperated to find the kettle empty and the gas unlit. She didn't answer.

Her father stumped down the steps, stooping to look as soon as he was low enough. His face congested at the sight of the broken door, and the assault rifle in Edith's hands.

"Edith! You little—!" He bounded the last few treads. "What the hell d'you think you're up to?"

Edith pushed the last round home, snapped the long curved magazine into the receiver and flicked the selector lever all the way down to the Cyrillic ОД for single shot. Her hands moved without a fumble now. *Like this was how it should be. Fate.*

Then, with an enormous sense of power flooding through her, she worked the charging handle to chamber the first round and swung the muzzle of the AK towards her father. He froze in mid-step, anger quickly changing to consternation, then to fear.

The fear brought him right back round to anger, she saw. Anger that his own pathetic, useless, fat, ugly little daughter dared to threaten him. In his own house, with his own gun. With a roar, he lunged for her.

Edith pulled the trigger.

100

NICK WAS on the motorway when he dialled Grace's cellphone number, not expecting her to answer, but she picked up after half a dozen rings, sounding distracted.

"Sorry, Grace," he said. "I thought I'd have to leave you a voicemail—that you'd be at the scene."

"No. I'm at home." And there was something fragile in her voice that he hadn't heard before. It sent the hairs rising at the back of his neck.

"What is it?"

"Blenkinship thinks I contaminated DNA samples from one of the earlier scenes. He doesn't believe Edith Airey could possibly have been at the hide, so I'm...off the case." He heard her take a shaky breath. "I'm off all cases."

Nick swore under his breath. "That's—" He broke off, saw his junction coming up, checked his mirror and slid the Impreza over into the left-hand lane. "Look, from what I've just found out, she could well have been. I'm at Tebay. I'll be with you in a couple of minutes, OK?" He hit the End Call button without waiting for a reply.

By the time he reached Grace's cottage, she was outside on the gravel with her hands in her pockets and Tallie at her feet.

Max Carri was standing beside her. He ran faintly amused, superior eyes over the Impreza as he leaned negligently on the front wing of his expensive Mercedes. Nick noted the additional AMG badges sourly.

She still divorced him, though, didn't she?

He climbed out, waited silently while they said their good-byes. Max backed out of the driveway and put his foot down. The Mercedes disappeared with impressive speed, which Nick tried to tell himself was a sign of Max's insecurity.

"What was he doing here?"

"I called him," Grace said. "After what happened to Richard...I–I needed someone." He'd never heard her sound so unsure of herself. He put his hands on her upper arms and stared straight into her eyes, ignoring the warning growl from the dog.

"Are you all right?"

"No," she admitted, stepping back out of his grasp, rubbing her arms as though cold. "I've never been suspended for incompetence before." She threw him a brief smile. "The ground suddenly feels rather unstable underfoot."

"It shouldn't do. I've watched you work, Grace. We both know you didn't make a mistake."

She took a grateful breath. "What did you mean on the phone, about Edith?"

"Pollock's had me chasing down the fuel angle for the bomb," he said. "Seemed a better bet than the fertiliser. This is farming country, after all. Must be hundreds of places with old bags of the stuff stored. Anyway, I've just been interviewing a guy from one of the motorway services who's admitted to selling off two drums of diesel/petrol mix. Amazing how many people fill up their car with the wrong fuel and have to get it syphoned out again."

Tallie butted against Grace's leg and she leaned down to stroke the dog's head. "And didn't ask what they wanted it for."

"Says he did, actually. To run a Chieftain tank on." At her raised eyebrow he added, "One of these old military vehicle enthusiasts' groups, so the bloke he sold it to claimed. They scrounge what they can."

"Oh." He watched her absorb that information. "Did he give you a description?"

"A vague one—big, bearded." He grimaced wryly. "But he knew our man was driving a dark blue 1956 long-wheelbase Land Rover Series Two. Bit of a car nut."

"And where does Edith fit in?"

"He mentioned it specially, said he wasn't suspicious because the guy had his daughter with him."

"It could be a coincidence." Grace seemed listless. "Lots of people have daughters, after all."

"True, but we've been in touch with every military vehicle enthusiasts' group. They all deny anyone has been in this area collecting fuel to run a tank on. And then there's the Land Rover."

Grace's face grew thoughtful. "I know they're pretty common, but they do seem to keep cropping up, don't they? What colour did he say it was?"

"Dark blue." Nick saw her disappointment, added quickly, "but he also said it wasn't a standard colour and it looked fresh. Like I said, he was a car nut. There's no reason why our man couldn't have repainted it, although you would have thought he'd go for a more drastic colour change."

"No, he wouldn't," Grace said, frowning. "Merely going from light to dark blue means he wouldn't need to alter the designated colour on the vehicle documents. And if anyone did a PNC check, it wouldn't raise any flags."

"Damn," Nick said, offering a smile. "Why didn't *I* think of that?"

Grace smiled back, the first real animation since he'd arrived. "That's what you have *me* for."

"We need Edith Airey picked up." He pulled out his phone, dialled Hunter Lane. "I doubt she was on the trigger herself, but I'd bet she knows who was."

"And quickly. If our mystery man was behind the marks on Edith's neck, he may have already tried to kill her once. And the tip-off this morning came from a young woman. If he realises she's turned against him…" She broke off as his expression hardened through the short call. "What?"

"Someone shot Jim Airey at his home," Nick said. He jerked his head to the Impreza. "Grab your gear."

Grace didn't argue. She shooed the dog inside, emerging a moment later with her camera bag and basic crime scene kit. By the time she was in the passenger seat, clipping her seatbelt, Nick was already pulling out into the lane.

"Did he come for her, do you think?" Grace asked as they

accelerated away. "And Airey tried to protect his daughter, got in the way?"

"Either that or she plugged the old man herself. She's familiar with firearms, don't forget, and you've met Jim Airey." He took his eyes off the road to flash her a brief dark glance. "Wouldn't *you* want to shoot him?"

101

An ambulance and an ARV patrol were already parked outside the Aireys' house when Nick rounded the last corner.

He braked to a fast halt alongside, just as two paramedics manoeuvred a stretcher down the front step onto a pavement crowded with ogling neighbours, necks craning to see who was on board. Grace scanned their faces, saw the same horrified fascination that marked crime scene spectators everywhere.

Strapped onto the stretcher, Jim Airey's eyes were closed, his skin a waxy beige. He lay quite still, making no complaint at the bumps on the way into the back of the ambulance.

Grace heard Nick's breath suck inwards on a soft hiss. She glanced across, saw the bleak expression on his face and knew he was regretting the crack he'd made about shooting Airey, now he was faced with the reality.

"Don't." She put a light hand on his arm. "I've worked with the police long enough to know how the humour-under-stress thing works."

A muscle pulsed in the side of his jaw but he didn't reply while she collected her gear, just showed his warrant card to one of the paramedics.

"What happened?"

"Single gunshot wound to the leg," the paramedic said shortly. "Large calibre, I'd say. He's lucky it didn't hit an artery or he'd have bled out." He finished securing the stretcher in place and climbed out, closing one door, nodded towards the house. "Wife called it in. Says she got home from work and found him almost unconscious the cellar."

A large woman in a stained tabard had stumbled out onto the pavement, weeping into a handkerchief, unaware of the blood coating her hands. Nick caught her arm.

"Mrs Airey, I'm very sorry about your husband. Did he say who did this?"

She looked at him, face ravaged. "He said it was our Edith." Her voice was a bewildered wail, causing a ripple through the avid crowd. "I tried to be a good mother." She gave a great heaving sob. "What have we done?"

The paramedic glared at Nick, grasped Mrs Airey's arm and whisked her up into the ambulance, slammed the final door behind her.

"They've got beds at Lancaster Infirmary, so we're taking him there," he threw at Nick. "Question him later."

As the ambulance set off, lights blazing, Grace followed Nick into the house. It seemed a long time since she'd carried out the FDR test on Edith here. *If only we'd known then…*

Hearing their footsteps, a uniformed Firearms officer appeared at the back sitting room doorway, greeted them warily.

"Is the place secure?" Nick asked.

The officer nodded. "Our shooter's long gone. Looks like poor old Jim got it in the cellar." He jerked his head. "He's got a proper little arsenal down there. I knew he was into his guns, but I would never have guessed at that lot."

"His wife reckoned it was the daughter," Nick said. "Any sign of her?"

"Nothing," the officer said. "Car's still outside, but there's a scooter registered in the mother's name and that's gone. I've put out a call for it." He gave a brief smile. "Those things only do about thirty miles an hour, so she can't have got far."

Nick moved forwards. "Let's have a look at this armoury, then."

"I'll go and check out Edith's room," Grace said.

Nick looked back at her with a questioning gaze.

"Are you sure?"

"We won't find where she's gone by looking in the cellar."

She went straight up the staircase. It didn't take much guess-work to pinpoint Edith's room. These houses were all laid out the same; two up, two down, with the kitchen and bathroom bumped out on an extension at the rear. Edith's was the tiny back bedroom.

Still smarting from Blenkinship's dismissal, she put down her kit and pulled on gloves and bootees before she ventured inside.

The room was gloomy in the afternoon light. When Grace flicked on the single overhead bulb it only made the space look more shabby.

The wallpaper was childish, girlie, peeling posters of film stars and celebrities stuck to the walls around the window, where she could lie in bed and gaze at them and dream.

If it wasn't for those posters, she'd struggle to age the occupant of this room. It was as though Edith was tied to infancy, trying to make the leap to adulthood without passing through a natural adolescence.

Grace felt the stark contrast to her own bedroom at home, long since vacated. She'd never had the desire, even as a child, to adorn the place with twee wallpaper or soft furnishings that owed more to merchandising than to function. She'd been encouraged to express her individuality in other ways, secure, safe, loved.

At least, until her father died.

Grace hadn't even known that he was ill. Looking back, she saw how much they'd hidden, believing it best to let her assume things would go on forever as they were. She regretted their decision. Knowing would have been painful, yes, but it would have given her time to prepare…

She shook her head to clear the dust of memories, looked about her.

"Come on, Edith," she murmured. "Talk to me. What's driving you?"

She searched the room thoroughly, found the stack of well-thumbed magazines, concentrating on fashion and the lifestyles of the rich and famous, the pages creased from constant rereading.

She found the loose floorboards under the window, the large plastic Tupperware box hidden underneath, containing what remained of Edith's illicit food stash. It broke her heart to find that, but she put it aside, sat back on her heels. It told her nothing she didn't already know.

"How's it going?" Nick asked from the doorway.

She glanced up, found him leaning against the jamb.

"Nothing useful," she said wearily. "She must be the first teenage girl in history not to keep a diary. How about you?"

Nick ran a hand round the back of his neck. "It's a mess down there. She must have hit him with something pretty big. Bullet went straight through Airey's thigh and buried itself in the stairs. I'll leave it to your expertise to recover the round."

"Do we have any idea what the gun was?"

"Well, Airey's got a little hidey-hole all racked out, even got his own gear for reloading the brass. Found a boxful of these."

He reached into his pocket and picked out something small and cylindrical, flicked it across to her. Grace caught it, looked down to see a long slim bullet casing. She turned it over in her hands. Stamped into the bottom was 7.62x39.

"Seven-point-six-two was the old NATO calibre," she said, frowning, "but thirty-nine is—"

"—Russian," Nick said grimly. "There's nothing down there that takes that size of round, but looking at the other stuff Airey collected, I'd guess she's on the loose with an AK-47."

"My God," Grace said quietly. "The damage she could do with one of those."

"Are you sure there's nothing in here that might tell us where she's gone?"

Grace's eye rested on the single bed in the corner of the room. She'd already checked under the mattress, but now she leaned down flat on her hands and peered beneath the frame, catching sight of something bunched up near the headboard. She snapped a picture before reaching under to snag it clear. What seemed at first like a bundle of rags, unfolded into a shirt, obviously Edith's.

Nick grunted, losing interest. "If she was a teenage boy, that wouldn't be all you found under the bed."

But Grace looked around her. "She's tidy," she said slowly. "She doesn't leave her clothes all over the place. So why did she hide this away…?"

She straightened the shirt out carefully in the middle of the floor, examined it, but no spots of blood marred the ugly stripe. She turned it over, then picked up each sleeve in turn. And there, on the left one, she found a dark mark, a dried-in smear.

"What's that?"

"I don't know." Grace rose, went to the window and pulled the thin curtain aside, peering at the shirt in natural light.

"Is it blood?"

"No," Grace murmured. "It's dried hard, like...paint." She turned. "Dark blue paint." Her eyes flew to his as certainty grabbed her. "Oh, I am such a fool," she said fiercely. "I know where he is. And I know where she's gone."

102

EDITH RODE over the cattle grid into the farmyard without slackening her vice-grip on the throttle, so the scooter's engine squealed as the rear wheel spun up over the slick steel rails.

She lurched to a halt outside the byre and threw herself through the door into the kitchen without knocking. The AK, one round gone, was slung on its webbing strap over her shoulder.

"Patrick!" she yelled. Her ears still rang from firing the rifle in the confines of the cellar. She shook her head again. The persistent clamour clung like guilt.

There was no reply to her shout, but she heard movement in the living room, rushed to the doorway, chest heaving as though she'd run a marathon.

The sight of Ian Hogg, sitting on the sofa, gaping at her arrival, barely registered. Her eyes were locked on Patrick Bardwell, in the wingback chair in the corner with the Barrett on the low table in front of him. She let out a cry of protest when she saw what he was about.

He looked up then, eyed her calmly, hands still working almost of their own accord.

"What are you *doing?*" she demanded.

"What's it look like?"

He'd already removed the Unertl sight from its mount on top of the receiver and the muzzle-brake from the end of the barrel, unbolted the folding bipod legs, withdrawn the two screws that held the shock-absorbent Sorbothene pad to the end of the butt.

"Stop it," Edith whispered. He ignored her. She jerked forwards, roared, "STOP IT!"

"Edith, my dear girl..." Hogg protested, eyes wide at the sight of her unexpected vehemence, of the gun over her shoulder. If she'd been paying more attention, she would have seen the utter desolation in his eyes.

But Bardwell did stop what he was doing, his expression close to pity. "What did you think was going to happen next, Edith?" he asked quietly. "Where did you think this was going to end?"

"Not here." The tears scalded the back of her throat. Furious with herself, she swallowed them down. "Not yet."

"It's done." Those cold eyes flicking over her face. "Nothing left to do."

"Nothing left for *you*, you mean?" she tossed back. "What about me? What about my dreams?"

"Dreams?" Hogg repeated, and she heard an edge of incredulity. "Good Lord, Edith, who dreams of killing?" He struggled to his feet and she stepped back instinctively.

"This has been about loyalty and respect," Bardwell said, subdued. "You think it's been about fulfilling some kind of sick ambition?"

"We'll never know, will we?" Her voice was a low growl. "Whatever we've done, it was always your choice. Never gave me a chance, did you?"

"Chance to do what? You made your choices, Edith, right enough."

"When you'd let me!" she flung back at him. "And even then, you didn't take me with you, did you? You *knew* I wanted to be there. You *knew*—" Her voice choked. "I *loved* you." She blanked Hogg's groan, hoping to push Bardwell into his own declaration. His silence was a bitter blow.

Hogg dragged in a breath. "Listen, child—"

"I am not a child!" Edith yelled. "I'm a woman. A grown woman!" She swung back to her lover, crying openly now, rivulets streaming down her cheeks. "You left me—sitting there like an idiot, waiting for you—and you weren't *ever* coming, were you, Patrick?"

"This was never about you." Through the haze of tears, she read nothing in his face. She might as well have been looking at a block of stone. "Go home. Forget all about me and go back to your life."

With a snarl, Edith unshouldered the AK, gripping it tightly in her hands, saw his head come up.

"What life?" she said bitterly. "I don't have a life, not now. I gave it to you."

Very calmly, he put down the screwdriver, spread out his hands. "Then do what you must."

"For pity's sake..." Hogg lurched between them, made a clumsy grab for the gun. The barrel arced wildly, Edith's hands tightening in reflex.

This time, she was ready for the noise, the flare and the recoil, but not for the way Patrick reacted as if to a massive punch in the gut.

His mild surprise was the first emotion he'd shown since her arrival. He gave a soft grunt as he doubled over, slumping sideways across the arm of the chair.

Oh, my God. Patrick...

Edith yanked the gun free of Hogg's suddenly nerveless grip. He knelt over Patrick, hands shaking.

"Don't you touch him!" she screamed. Blinded by rage, she jammed the muzzle against Hogg's temple and pulled the trigger. The effect was devastating and instant. Blood spattered the far wall in a fine mist. Hogg dropped like a side of meat in the shop where her father worked, cannoning off the table to lie twitching on the worn carpet. Loose rounds from the stripped magazine scattered around him.

Edith threw down the AK and rushed to Patrick, tried to cradle him in her arms, whimpering apologies, endearments, her voice broken and her mind shrieking.

His chest had started to flutter as he shallow-breathed around the pain. He pushed her away with one hand, the other pressed hard against his belly to stem the flow.

The blood was dark and greasy, oozing from the wound just above his belt on the right-hand side with the inevitability of a mudslide. Already, half his shirt and hip, the cushion and the arm of the chair were saturated with it. Edith stared at the growing pool with horrified fascination. She hadn't stayed long enough to watch her father bleed.

"Patrick, I—"

"Shh." His smile was sad and soft, his face sheened with sweat. "You need to go."

He reached up, tucked a strand of hair behind her ear. She didn't think anyone had looked at her with such wonder, touched her with such infinite gentleness. He started to gasp, his hand falling back. She folded into another raucous round of sobbing.

"I can't leave you!" she hiccuped. "I won't!"

"They're coming, Edith." He spoke in short bursts now, harder to make out. "Hogg tipped 'em off—SAS, but message'll get through. They'll finish this. Won't be long now. Go... Don't let 'em...take you."

His eyelids started to droop, then fluttered closed entirely.

Edith gripped his hand and wailed out loud, shaking him, but he didn't stir. She sat back, still crying, sniffing, looked across at the part-dismantled Barrett on the table.

The SAS... They'll finish this...

She scrambled to her feet, grabbed the sight and reattached it to the top mount. Her fingers fumbled with the bolts for the bipod legs, inserted the screws for the butt pad more surely, reattached the muzzle-brake. She grabbed the heavy magazine and snapped it into place with something like a flourish.

After all, she'd lain alongside Patrick and worked the distances, hadn't she? All he'd done was operate the trigger, and she'd proved she could do that.

Edith picked up the Barrett, arms straining under the weight of it. She took one last long look at Patrick, slouched in the chair with eyes closed.

"The SAS or whoever they are won't finish this, Patrick," she vowed, determination burning bright and savage inside her. "*I* will."

103

Patrick Bardwell drifted, somewhere between this world and the next.

The pain drove him from his body, to the outer reaches of his mind, where a hazy mix of slurred images tripped and danced and tumbled until he could no longer tell reality from imaginings. Ghosted recollections, freed of the constraints of conscious thought to range abroad.

Some time after Edith had gone, he'd attempted to rise, driven by the instinct of an animal to survive. He'd staggered a monumental distance that was only a few feet, and fallen, slippery hands clutching at the kitchen door frame as he went down.

Now he lay there, neither in one room nor the other, convinced in his more lucid moments that he was upright and everything else was somehow spinning ninety degrees out of kilter.

Sliding behind his eyes now he was assailed by the brutal majesty of the desert. He could feel the sand whipping at his skin as the sun died red and golden behind the rocky outcrops to the west. The vision shimmered into the high country of the Afghans, the bare limestone Dinaric Alps that dominated the border between Croatia and Bosnia, the lush rainforests of South America.

The places he'd travelled, the people he'd been sent to kill. The days spent lying up, waiting, watching, feeling himself absorbed into each landscape, part of the earth, unborn.

"What was it all for?"

He jerked, assailed by the overwhelming stink of goats, swivelled his eyes upwards and found the Iraqi boy standing over him, bleeding from his severed throat.

"Did you make a difference?" the boy asked. "Did you change anything?"

The girl was next, proud, sensual beyond her years, her face distorted by the sniper's bullet that broken away half her skull. At her feet, two young children, a boy and a girl, hands outstretched, skeletal, starving.

"You didn't look hard enough." The girl turned them away from him sadly. "You didn't try."

I tried.

"Tried what?"

His lips moved, but he had no voice. There were three figures before him now, strangers in camouflage, flying no colours. They tiptoed into view across the kitchen lino, their booted tread so soft he felt no echo beneath his cheekbone.

Whose memory is this?

The soldier in him noted automatically that they carried H&K MP5s. Good covert weapons—the SD with the fat suppressed barrel, so the sound of the mech working was louder than the shot. Interesting to know, even in the depths of this hallucinogenic fantasy, his tactics were sound.

Then one of the shadows knelt, rolled him roughly onto his back. Something tore deep inside. Swamped by reality, Bardwell bucked and screamed, a long howl of agony that ripped up from his belly to emerge as no more than a desperate gasp within the quiet room.

Somebody swore—at or because of him, Bardwell wasn't sure. As the pain receded, he heard more voices, low murmuring. Caught the words *morphine, and hurry.*

He felt their bootsteps now there was no need for stealth, moving quickly through the byre. The first shadow patted him down, tore open his shirt and probed the wound, carelessly efficient but impersonal as a surgeon or a butcher.

Another figure closed in, sought bared skin. Bardwell felt the scratch of a needle.

The opiate dulled the fire in his gut like a dose of ice, left him frozen, shivering. Then the second man said, "Hold him," and drove a needle the size of a fencepost straight into his chest.

The adrenaline dose roared through bloodstream like potcheen on an empty stomach. He rode the surge upwards, snarling, his dulled senses exploding back on line, overcrowding him with vivid detail, colour, smell, noise.

"Look at me," the first man was saying above the background clamour inside Bardwell's head, grasping his chin with steel fingers, forcing eye contact. "Where is it? Where's the gun?"

"Not here," Bardwell managed, little more than a croak. He thought of Edith. They'd kill her if they caught her—no option. It was always the young ones who haunted him and, for all her protestations, at seventeen she was still a child. He closed his eyes. "Broken up," he lied. "Buried. Won't find it."

Another figure appeared from the living room. Jerked his head. "Slaughterhouse in there," he said, tense. "Looks like two of them slugged it out with an AK."

The first man, the team leader, swore, let go of him and moved back. The one who'd injected Bardwell packed field dressings against the sodden entry hole in his stomach and the exploded exit just behind his hip, ripping off lengths of duct tape to hold them in place. His hands slowed.

"I know you," he said, turned to the team leader. "I know him."

"Yeah." The team leader looked down, grim. "So do I."

"What now?" the medic asked, hushed. "Do we still—?"

"What d'you think? Call Gary," the team leader said. "Tell him to bring the vehicle up. Local fuzz can't be far behind. Tell him we need a rapid exfil."

The medic got to his feet, went outside. The team leader continued to stare down at Bardwell.

"How the hell did you come to this?" he said softly, sounding bitter, angry. "I know your work. You were a bloody hero."

"Made a promise," Bardwell said, rasping now, barbed wire in his throat. "Nothing else left...they took it all."

After a moment the man nodded, as if that were enough.

The third man finished his search, stepped over Bardwell into the kitchen, handed something to the team leader. Bardwell heard a metallic jingle, saw him turn two objects over in his gloved fingers and hold them up with a small smile. A pair of the rounds he'd stripped from the Barrett's magazine. The girl was unaccustomed to the weight of the mag, full or empty. Had she realised?

"Not much use without these." The team leader stared a moment longer. "Guess you might have buried it, after all."

The medic came back in, MP5 slung over his shoulder. "Gary's on his way," he said. "ETA three minutes."

"All right, let's get him outside." He leaned down, face close. "Sorry, soldier, but someone wants a little chat before we slot you," he said, unrepentant. "Nothing personal."

Bardwell managed the faintest glimmer of a smile. "Orders," he murmured.

"You got that right," the team leader said. He paused. "When the time comes I'll make it quick, all right?"

Bardwell didn't so much nod as give a slow blink of acceptance.

Even after the morphine, moving him set light to the wound, racked him. They drag-carried him out through the kitchen, propped him shuddering by the old galvanised trough, just as a dark red Discovery thundered over the cattle grid at the bottom end of the yard.

The initial hit of the adrenaline was wearing off now, leaving his head muzzy, his limbs unbearably heavy as the opiate depressed his blood pressure still further.

So, they were going to disappear him. He'd had no doubts about that. No real feelings either. Not much he could do about it, anyway. There were four of them, armed, serious. Wouldn't have been sent on this job if they weren't pros, committed. The odds wouldn't have been good even if he'd been in one piece. But wounded, without a weapon...

And then, as he lay with the metal trough imprinting its edge along the side of his temple, Bardwell remembered his insurance piece. With painful slowness, his fingers crept up under the trailing foliage and made contact with the string he'd so carefully hidden.

His eyes flicked upwards. The man nearest, the one who'd carried out the search, was standing with his MP5 at the ready but his back was slightly towards Bardwell, looking for outside threat. The other two were opening the doors of the Discovery.

He pulled, hard as he could manage, but feeble. The soft

earth of the flowerbed fought him briefly, then the oiled bag silently broke the surface and flopped into his hands. He traced the outline of the revolver and hesitated.

Not here, not now. Police on their way, probably. Can't drive like this. They'd track me easy from here.

He glanced up at the covert extraction team who'd been sent to dispose of him. A simple execution would raise too many questions. He was an embarrassment that had to disappear like he'd never existed. Ironic, in its way, considering all the trouble he'd taken to disappear before he came here.

Better to let them do their job. First part of it, anyway.

He felt the leaden cold of the bullet wound through his gut, knew he was getting weaker by the moment. By the time they got him where they were going, some deserted stretch of moorland most likely, there was a chance he'd be finished anyway. The drugs they'd pumped into him were a quick fix, but probably fatal in the end. Maybe that's what they were hoping.

Clumsily, he shoved the oiled bag into the leg pocket of his old combats and let his eyelids droop again, vision blackening down.

We'll see…

104

"I saw him." Grace clung to the door-pull as Nick sent the Impreza careening into a tight series of bends. She flicked her eyes across, took in the clenched concentration in his face. "I met him and I never knew."

"At the Retreat?"

"Yes. That day we had lunch in Staveley. I called in on my way back, looking for Edith. A man came out of the old byre, told me to try the farmhouse, but she wasn't there."

"Would you know him again?" Nick asked as the car went light over a vicious crest. She braced her knee against the camera bag wedged into the footwell as they landed hard, sped on.

"Probably, although I didn't get close. There was a pale blue Land Rover parked outside. I looked right at it—" She broke off abruptly as he skimmed the apex of a right-hander and almost exchanged paint with a dark red 4x4 coming the other way, drifting wide from its own excess speed.

"Sorry," he said between his teeth as they rocketed out the other side, miraculously unscathed. "If it's any comfort, I got top marks on all my defensive driving courses."

"Mm," Grace said. "Perhaps I should point out that I went quiet so as not to distract you, rather than because I was struck dumb with fright." She flashed him a quick smile, added diffidently, "My mother drove rally cars for Sunbeam in the 'sixties. I was eight before I realised the handbrake was intended just for parking."

He gave a short bark of laughter but, she noted, nobly resisted the temptation to drift the car into the mouth of the Retreat driveway when they reached it shortly afterwards.

"There it is," Grace said as they reached the yard, pointing. "And you're right—it's been repainted."

She remembered the first time she'd asked him about the Land Rover in the lay-by at the top of the hill above Orton. The last letter of the plate was L for Lima, as he'd suggested, but it was an old number without the later prefix or suffix indicating the year of registration. As a vanity plate, it was worth more than the vehicle it was attached to.

"The door's open." Nick slowed to a crawl. "Do we go in, or wait for the bomb squad?"

"My head says we wait, of course. But my heart...?" She shrugged. "If the man who killed Richard is here, I want to catch him—before he kills anyone else."

Nick pulled up close to the farmhouse, far enough away from the byre to avoid obliterating trace evidence. *Doesn't want his nice car blown up, either,* Grace thought.

They climbed out. Nick scanned the yard with narrowed eyes. As they cautiously approached the open doorway, Grace slid her hands into a pair of nitrile gloves. Nick paused by the water trough just outside the door, squatted by the dark stains on the concrete.

"What do you make of this?" he asked quietly.

Grace put the bag down, knelt, bent low and sniffed. "Blood. Not yet fully congealed." She looked at him. "It could be Edith's."

"Or anyone who got in her way," Nick said darkly. He took a pained breath. "We have to go in, don't we?"

Grace felt the tightness in her own chest echoed in his voice. *He's scared,* she realised, and was somehow comforted by his vulnerability. *That makes two of us.*

He put a hand on her arm when she would have led the way. "I don't always believe in women and children first," he said with a tight little smile, moving past her.

She managed a cool smile of her own. "I prefer to think of it as CSI before CID." But she let him take the lead.

There was more blood in the kitchen, much more. It lay pooled on the floor by the doorway into the living room, scraped and smeared down the woodwork of the frame, like someone had been holding on with their last breath.

Grace studied the pattern with as much objectivity as she could manage, attempting to push aside the knowledge that the scene was unsecured, the dangers unknown. At last, she stepped carefully over the bloodstain and moved into the living room.

The body of a man lay awkwardly between the sofa and the coffee table, the area around him saturated with blood. One side of his head was missing, the skin of his face ingrained with burned powder. His lips were parted as if in surprise.

Grace had never met Ian Hogg, so failed to recognise his corpse. She put gentle fingers to the dead man's cheek, gave it a little wobble.

"I don't claim to be an expert, but I don't think you'll bring him round that way," Nick said from the doorway. "Even I can tell he's been shot."

Grace accepted the grim humour as a release of tension. "Rigor mortis usually starts in the small muscles of the face," she said over her shoulder. "And he's still warm." She got to her feet. "We need to call this in."

"Wait a moment," he murmured. "Let's just check there are no other nasty surprises in store first, shall we?"

Without waiting for a reply, he moved through the other rooms. His nerves seemed to have settled, she noted, as though his sudden fear before they'd entered the byre was an aberration.

What happened to you, Nick?

Alone, she looked carefully at the blood-soaked wingback chair, the spattered walls and sodden carpet by the kitchen door. Who was the dead man? Had Edith come in, brandishing a weapon, only to be met with a more deadly force? If so, did the empty cottage signify the mysterious Bardwell had gone to dispose of her body? And had not gone far, or he would have taken the Land Rover...

Grace was enveloped by a sudden chill that sent goosebumps springing up in its wake. She was glad of Nick's return.

"All clear. Is that the man you saw?"

"No—he had a full beard," she said after a moment, studying the victim, her imagination infusing him with the animation of life, thought, emotion. "If he'd shaved in the last few weeks, he would have an uneven tan." She straightened. "And he was bigger all round—taller, heavier. This isn't him."

"Great," she heard Nick mutter. "So the body count just went up again."

"And may do so again. There are two distinct bullet holes in the wall. Here and here." She pointed to one, surrounded by a spray of blood and bone, and a second behind the chair. "From the amount of blood I'd guess at a second gunshot victim. I couldn't say what calibre at this stage, but large enough to go through-and-through—furniture as well as flesh. We may have to take half that wall out to recover the rounds."

"It was an AK," Nick said.

"Just because we *think* that's what Edith took, we can't make assumptions."

"OK, what about this?" He nodded to an assault rifle lying half-tucked underneath the valance of the sofa.

It was a sad sign of the times, Grace thought, that she had no difficulty recognising the distinctive curved magazine of the AK-47. This was not the first time she had come across one at a crime scene. He reached towards it.

"Don't," she said quickly. "Not until I've photographed it at least. I'll get my gear from outside."

105

EDITH AIREY'S eye fixed on the open doorway to the byre, the image overlaid by the mil lines in the reticle of the Unertl scope.

She'd managed to carry the Barrett only six hundred metres from the farmyard, up the sloping field that rose behind it, before she'd heard the raucous approach of an engine, driven hard, and she'd sought the shelter of a small stand of trees.

The copse stood about halfway up the hill, which she realised would give her ideal cover to set up the gun, the way she'd watched Patrick do it. Now, lying behind it, copying his position, she felt empowered and all-conquering.

From here she had an unobstructed view of the front of the byre in the narrow gap between the farmhouse on one side, and the wall of the barn on the other. She'd hoped to get further away, to use something of the Barrett's awesome power and range, but for her first time out this would do.

I'll get better with practice, she thought, her belly warmed by the thought.

The gun was much heavier than she'd expected. Patrick always made it look so easy. She'd taken his ghillie suit, too, like a trophy, lugged that up the hill with her, staggering under her awkward burden. By the time she'd reached the safety of the trees, she was light-headed with both exertion and elation.

She'd chosen a roundabout route to her present location, following the hedge line that ran down to her left, so her view of the yard had been blocked when the four men had arrived in the dark red Discovery. By the time she'd scrambled into position, they were just climbing back into the vehicle, scribing a rapid circle and driving away.

Patrick!

Edith felt the bitter pang of a missed opportunity, angry that they'd come before she was ready. But it wasn't long, only a matter of minutes, before she heard the other car accelerating up the farm track, caught a glimpse of it pulling into the yard. Moments later, the two people she'd most wanted to see through the scope of a sniper's rifle, walked into shot.

She spread the ghillie suit out beneath her, wriggled into position behind the gun. As she concentrated on regulating her breathing, she was suddenly overwhelmed with doubt. Not for what she was about to do, but her own readiness.

Flustered, she realised she hadn't adjusted the sight for this distance. She hadn't worked out the direction or speed of the wind, the difference in elevation. Her own little .22 was incapable of this kind of range and she was unsure of the amount of bullet drop to take into account with something as powerful as the Barrett. So close to her target, would it make a difference?

And while she dithered, she watched the couple linger tauntingly by the doorway, bending to examine something near the old water trough, then disappear inside.

Damn!

For a moment she slumped, defeated, letting tears of self-pity start to form, but she dashed them away and set her jaw, mulish.

Lyudmila Pavlichenko hadn't given up so easily. From what Edith remembered reading of the Ukrainian-born sniper, she was already a sharpshooter when she volunteered to fight after the Nazi invasion back in 1941. Ancient history.

Had she been as frightened as this when she made her first two kills near Belyayevka? If so, she overcame her fear quickly. Less than a year after Pavlichenko had marched into the Red Army recruiting office, she received a commendation for killing two hundred and fifty-seven enemy soldiers in the battles for Odessa and Sevastopol.

After the war, she'd toured America, been greeted by cheering crowds, met the President at the White House, been heaped with praise and medals for valour. As Edith lay behind the Barrett, she felt certain triumph awaiting her.

She fidgeted again, trying to adopt the same effortless sprawl Patrick used. But the gun was so much bigger than her Gaucher, not just in calibre but in every way. With the butt nestled against her shoulder, she could barely reach the pistol grip. Her hand was stretched by the distance to the trigger. But she curved her index finger inside the guard and felt the tunnel-vision of panic begin to recede. She took a breath, let it out shakily.

Calmer now, Edith reached to wind down the elevation on the sight, but her hand stilled, reluctant to alter Patrick's perfect settings. Just as she hadn't wanted the detective to mess with the scope on her own gun. *I can work out the hold-off.* The last time she and Patrick had used the gun was at a thousand metres, wasn't it? From the back of the Land Rover near Raisbeck. She was a little more than half that distance now.

I can do this.

She closed her eyes, finally feeling her pulse begin to steady. But she needed to be prepared to take the shot, mentally as well as physically.

Him first, she decided, already able to visualise the pink mist and the falling, recalling the way bits of Angela Inglis had actually cartwheeled through the air. One moment human, and the next...

Besides, if last time was anything to go by, the woman—that bitch McColl—would go to him once he was down. She would present herself, brazen, foolish, and Edith would be able to take aim at her leisure.

With only waiting to occupy her mind, Edith's memories surfaced. The way Ian Hogg had simply ceased to exist in human terms, the moment she'd pulled the trigger. The shock on her father's face as the bullet from the AK had taken his leg out from underneath him, spun him back. He'd ended on his rump, clutching stupidly at his leaching thigh and looking like he might cry.

He can't be my real father, she thought with fierce contempt. *My mother must have had some fling with a mysterious stranger.* But the image *that* conjured was too ridiculous for words. The thought of her fat little anxious mother indulging in a passionate affair. *Adopted, then.* That was better! Delivered to their doorstep as a new-born, in the dead of night, never to be told her true heritage.

Blood will out.

Suddenly, there was movement in the doorway below and they came out. He moved quickly across the yard and was out of sight before she could collect her scattered thoughts. But the McColl woman was a different story. She retrieved her bag, lifted out a camera and began snapping away at the side of the water trough.

Edith wiped her sweating palm down the side of her leg, slipped her finger back inside the guard, but hesitated, not liking to abandon her original plan. She swept across the yard, but the blond detective had disappeared completely. *In combat, snipers have to adapt to circumstances,* she told herself. *How else can I hope to equal Pavlichenko's record?*

Through the scope, she followed as the redhead cast slowly across the concrete, eyes down, following some kind of trail invisible from this distance. Finally, she stopped, more or less where the Discovery had stood, bent low to inspect something on the ground more closely. *How does she know?* Edith wondered. Could she really see their tracks?

Edith settled her aim. She centred her finger on the trigger, took in a deep lungful of air.

Here's to fame and glory…

106

"THE BLOOD DRIPS from the front door simply stop here," Grace called over. "There are tyre marks. It looks like he, or she, got into a vehicle."

Over by the Impreza, Nick was on the phone updating Pollock on their find. He glanced across as Grace spoke, saw the intent frown as she lifted the camera again, at the precise moment the ground at her feet erupted.

She landed brutally hard, enveloped in a cloud of shards and dust as her head cracked back onto the concrete. The monstrous sound of the shot transported Nick instantly to the show field, to the vulnerability of flesh.

The phone went tumbling. "GRACE!" he yelled, already sprinting.

He scooped her limp body into his arms and almost threw her into the byre doorway, rolling inside after her. The force of his momentum sent them both skidding across the lino. They crashed into the far cupboards, Nick taking the brunt of it, trying to shield her. He was still gasping from the shock, the sudden overwhelming bolt of fear.

She's not moving!

There was blood everywhere. He ripped her T-shirt up out of her waistband to find the wound before it registered that if she'd been hit there wouldn't be much left of her.

"You've a one-track mind, Mr Weston," she managed, voice muzzy. Her eyes flicked open, so close he could make out the individual colours of her iris. Her point of focus seemed to be somewhere over his left shoulder and several miles beyond the cottage walls. *Concussion*, he realised.

"My God, Grace…" he said, weak with it. "I thought he'd got you. I thought—"

"—wrong," she said, still hazy. "He missed." She put a hand up towards her head, a gesture that ran out of energy before she could complete it. She winced, let the hand flop. "Mostly."

"Not by much," Nick said on an unsteady breath. Gently, he smudged a trickle of blood from her eyebrow with his thumb.

She began to shake then, a faint quiver. Nick put his arms round her. 'You're OK, it's all OK,' he murmured, hiding a tremor of his own. "I've got you."

"I know you have," she said distinctly, and closed her eyes again.

Nick waited a beat. "Grace?" No response. "Grace!"

Carefully, he eased out from under her sprawled limbs, checked her over. Apart from numerous small cuts from the splintered chips of concrete, there were no obvious signs of a wound. But when he stripped off his jacket to support her head, his fingers found the alarming lump on the back of her skull, the broken skin, the blood. In slow-motion recall, he saw her fall again, her head striking the concrete with sickening force as she went down.

Could be fractured, he registered with a hollowness at the base of his stomach. *She needs a doctor—an ambulance.*

He looked round for a phone, then realised there wasn't a land-line. His radio and mobile were in the car.

He swore under his breath, eyed the gap out into the sunlit yard, the distance to the Subaru. He just had to hope that, even over a mobile phone line, Pollock had recognised the sound of the massive gunshot for what it was, that the Firearms team were already on their way.

Meanwhile, he had to just sit tight and wait.

Meanwhile, said an invidious voice in his head, *she might die.*

Keeping well under the level of the kitchen window, Nick crabbed into the living room, trying to avoid the blood. He reached for the AK still by the low table in the centre of the room.

"Sorry, Grace," he murmured as he picked it up, snapped the

magazine out to verify a full clip. He slapped it home again with the palm of his hand so it re-seated firmly.

It was a long time since he'd last held an assault rifle in his hands.

Grace hadn't stirred, her breathing shallow. For a moment, he hesitated over leaving her. If her skull *had* been fractured in the fall, she might stop breathing. He could breathe for her, if he had to, until the paramedics got here. But not if he'd gone charging off trying to get himself killed...

Telling himself that the most sensible thing was to stay put—the relief such a decision would bring—did not make him feel any less of a failure. And it did not make his terror at the prospect of going out there any less real.

You coward. You utter bloody coward...

Tilting his head sideways, he peered over the top of the worktop, out through the window. The shot had come from the direction of the farmhouse, but he saw no open windows on either storey. The barn door was firmly shut and devoid of gaps.

That left the field behind the farm, open except for the single clump of trees halfway up. Nick didn't see any stray reflections from the scope, but instinct told him that's where he'd find the sniper.

With a last regretful glance at Grace, he backed up as far as the confines of the room would allow, clutching the AK across his chest. His hands were shaking. He took a couple of deep breaths, and launched. By the time he passed through the doorway, he'd already hit his stride.

He ran for the car, gabbled a message into his radio and ignored the squawked order to keep his head down until back-up arrived again. All the time he was trying to work out why nobody had taken a pot-shot at him.

He knew the rules of fire and manoeuvre as well as anyone. Was the sniper repositioning himself so the next shot would come from a totally different direction, as it had at the show field? Nick tried to close his mind to it.

Just before they'd gone into the byre, he'd experienced a sudden burst of fear that had both shamed and surprised him, as memories of walking into that undercover ambush took hold.

Is that why you're doing this? he asked himself, mocking, cynical. *Trying to prove you're still the man?*

Nick gripped the stock of the AK tighter and bolted for the corner of the farmhouse. Still no high-pitched whistle, no concussive follow-up boom of the shot. Carefully, he took a peek around the edge of the stonework, assimilated the landscape in an instant. Back to the wall, he took another couple of breaths, then he was out and running again, for the wall into the neighbouring field this time, vaulting the gate, rolling out through the fall on the other side. He pounded up the field with just the hedge between him and the stand of trees, fiercely glad of the stamina from his daily runs.

At any moment he expected the bark of the Barrett to come rampaging through the branches. That alone sent the sweat dripping into his eyes. He blinked furiously. *Why is it worse when you're expecting it?*

Just past the copse was an adjoining gateway, standing open. Nick threw himself through it, went flat to the ground on the other side, the AK out in front of him.

Still no shot.

After a moment, he raised his head, cautious, but nothing stirred except a slight breeze fingering the grass. It was wet from the earlier rain, soaking his shirt.

Nick's nerves stretched, his breathing ragged and his heart beating a brutal tattoo behind his breastbone. He clambered to his feet, went across the distance dividing him from the trees like a hare from hounds.

He was on the uphill side, the incline adding momentum. He reached the trees and jerked back to walking pace, the rifle up and ready, butt pulled tight into his shoulder, finger inside the guard. For a moment he wished for body armour, dismissed the thought.

No use against a Barrett, anyway.

Then above the pounding in his ears, he heard the quiet sound of stifled sobbing. He crept towards it, mouth dry.

At the front of the copse, facing down towards the cluster of farm buildings, he found Edith Airey, sitting weeping amid her ragged camouflage, with the mammoth gun over on its side in front of her. The AK in his hands was a toy by comparison.

The reason for the lack of secondary shots was immediately apparent from the hunch of her body, the way she cradled her arm.

Her shoulder was broken.

She heard his approach and looked up blindly. Nick wondered if it was his imagination—was it just the tears that gave her eyes a shining glitter?

"Well? Did I do it?" she demanded. "Is she dead?"

PART VIII

107

"WHY DID YOU KILL HER, EDITH?"

"Because I hated her, of course." Edith gave a tinkling laugh, as though the question was quite absurd. "She accused me. How was I supposed to react?"

"And you killed her for that," DI Pollock said flatly.

He'd used the same neutral tone throughout. Subdued, Edith thought, to be in the presence of such greatness.

"Yes." She lounged nonchalantly in the hard-backed plastic chair.

She scratched absently at her shoulder under the sling. The hospital had inserted a plate to reattach her shattered collarbone. It itched constantly.

Now, sitting restless in yet another interminable interview, she still wasn't sure exactly what went wrong. Only that the recoil of the Barrett was like nothing she'd experienced before, a sledgehammer blow that blocked her mind to everything except the pain.

At first, in shock, she'd been devastated that all her plans had come to nothing. But now she realised this could still turn into a huge opportunity. After all, she'd been there, hadn't she?

For most of it, anyway.

"So, Mrs Inglis accused you of stealing a pair of antique cuff-links, and you obtained a large calibre sniper's rifle and shot her dead for it?" Pollock said, and Edith thought she detected a hint of wonder.

She nodded.

"Please speak." The other detective, Weston, gestured towards the recorder that sat at one end of the table. "For the record."

He was the blond one, Gestapo good-looking in a mean and dangerous way. The one who'd come bursting out of the woods behind her with the AK in his hands and death in those cold blue eyes. She thought he'd shoot her right there. But if he had, she would have missed all this.

Edith made a show of leaning closer to the microphone. "Yes," she said clearly and distinctly, "that's why *I* shot Angela Inglis. And her dog."

"Really, Miss Airey," protested the drippy solicitor the Legal Aid people had assigned her, hands fluttering, "I strongly suggest you volunteer as little information as possible."

Edith looked at her with astonishment and contempt. "Why on earth would I want to do that?"

"Where did you get the rifle, Edith?" Pollock said, almost gently, the sweat beading at his temples and across his broad forehead. It was hot in the interview suite at Hunter Lane, almost stuffy, but Edith had never felt so cool.

They'd never caught Lyudmila Pavlichenko, however hard they'd tried. Hadn't her tally of kills included thirty-six enemy snipers? But she was injured, too, in the course of her work. A mortar blast. A major by then, they'd withdrawn her from active duty. The Russian hierarchy had considered her too great a propaganda asset to risk again in the field.

"My father's been a collector for years," she said demurely. "You'd have to ask him."

"We have. *He* claims he's never seen it before, that it's nothing to do with him."

"Well," Edith smirked, "he *would* say that, wouldn't he?"

Pollock sat back heavily in his chair and waved Weston forwards for his bout, as though they were tag-team wrestling.

"You haven't asked us about your father." Weston propped his elbows on the scarred tabletop. "Don't you care how badly you hurt him?"

"I only hit him in the leg," she scoffed, as if it was calculated, intentional. She lifted her chin. "If I'd wanted him dead, he'd be dead." *A fine piece of bravado—worthy of Pavlichenko herself.*

Weston let his eyes drop for a moment as if acknowledging her skill, then he flicked them up, piercing her. "Did he ever hurt you?" he asked then, hesitated. "Touch you in any way?"

It took Edith a moment to get his meaning, and then she flushed a deep, unbecoming red. Did he really think there'd been anything like *that* going on?

"Don't be disgusting."

"How far out where you?" he asked, changing tack. "When you made that first shot?"

"Eighteen hundred and thirty metres, give or take," Edith said promptly. "But you uncovered my hide, so surely you know that?" She found the courage to stare into those vivid eyes. "The execution was flawless, wasn't it?"

"And the second? Another hide?"

"Of course not." She frowned at his refusal to be drawn. "That was more a spur-of-the-moment thing. Fire and manoeuvre, you know? I was in the back of the Land Rover with the bipod resting on the top of a dry stone wall. It may even have left marks." She glanced from one face to another. "I could show you, if you like?" she offered, disdainful, flicking her gaze into the corners of the room. "Could do with a ride out from this dump."

Weston sat back again, let his inspector take over.

"And your choice of target?" Pollock asked, allowing a hint of heat to slide through. "Did you hate Police Constable Daniel Robertshaw, also?"

"After the lies he spread about me?" Edith flushed anew at the memory. "Yes!" She shrugged as well as she could with only one working shoulder.

"And why try and kill CSI McColl?"

Edith gave another careless half-shrug. She wasn't about to recount the conversation they'd had that day at Hunter Lane, where the tall redhead had speared her with a frighteningly accurate picture of her life, her secrets. *How dare she try and claim something of this pain for her own?*

No-one had ever been through precisely this before, and no-one ever would again. Edith's position was unique, and she clung to it. She set her jaw.

"Why not? She came into my home, took away my rifle—one

of my rifles," she added quickly. "I couldn't let that go unpunished."

"And Ian Hogg?" Pollock persisted. "What had he done?"

"He tried to get in my way," Edith said, flooded with a reflex burst of rage as she remembered him wrestling with her for the gun, the discharge, Patrick falling... "Hogg was a traitor." She curled her lip. "He deserved what he got."

Pollock exchanged a glance with Weston that she couldn't decipher.

"Who's Patrick Bardwell?" the inspector asked, head tilted slightly to watch her reaction. She tried to show nothing.

"He was just some loser, staying at the Retreat," she said, as casual as she could. "I used to clean for him."

"How well did you know him?"

"Not well. He wasn't the chatty type."

"We have a recording of a female voice telling us Patrick Bardwell was behind these shootings," Pollock said, stony. "It now seems that call was made solely to lure our officers into an ambush." He paused, went on quietly, "When our experts finish running voice comparison tests, they're going to find you made that call, aren't they, Edith?"

A slow smile spread across Edith's face, then she began to laugh. "Of course. You should have just asked before you went to all that trouble, and I'd've told you." She looked from one to the other. "He tried to strangle me, if you must know. Here." She pulled the collar of her shirt down, tragic, showed them the last pale smudges around her throat.

"Why would he do that?"

"Because he was a loony. Post-traumatic stress or something. Why else would he be at the Retreat?"

"So, why did you tell Mr Mercer he was the sniper?"

"Because I wanted rid of him," she said. "And I wanted to fool you into thinking it wasn't me with the gun. Worked, too, didn't it?"

"Two men died," Pollock pointed out, hushed and solemn.

Edith scrambled to recall what her father had said about the explosion at the barn, but she'd been so paralysed with worry about Patrick she hadn't paid attention. It had only sunk in that he'd tricked, used, and abandoned her. *So, he was a traitor, too, in the end.*

She shrugged again, tried to look mysterious.

"We found a lot of blood at the byre," Pollock said now. "What happened to Bardwell?"

She opted for partial truth over invention. "Oh, some SAS hit squad came and took him away—in a dark red Land Rover Discovery."

She shifted in her chair, trying to appease the ache in her shoulder. The plate under her skin was lumpy and awkward, and it was itching unbearably again. Her solicitor was on the ball for that, at least.

"We need to stop there for a break," she said primly. "My client has only just undergone surgery. She needs to rest."

"I'm done for the moment." Pollock threw a sideways look at Weston. "Anything else you want to ask at this point, Nick?"

"Just one final question." Weston eyed her again, a butterfly pinned under glass. "Why, Edith? What made you want to do anything like this?"

Edith stared at him. *Surely he can't be serious?*

"To be somebody, of course." She realised that three expressionless faces had turned in her direction. She almost laughed at their lack of comprehension. *After this, Edith Airey will be a household name.* "Oh, come *on*! How else was I going to be famous?"

108

As NICK CLOSED the interview room door behind them, DI Pollock let out a long breath, as though he could no longer hold it in. The big man sagged back against the opposite wall of the corridor, wiped a hand across his eyes.

"*Famous*...hell's teeth. I've dealt with some psychos in my time, but this?" He shook his head.

"Terrifying, isn't she?" Nick agreed. "I can't work out which is worse. The fact that she *wants* to be held responsible, or the fact there's a faint possibility she believes it herself."

"Do *you* believe any of it?"

Nick made a 'maybe, maybe not' gesture. "She's clever. There's enough truth mixed in with the fantasy to make you stop and wonder. There might be little to see now, but Grace *did* notice the marks on Edith's neck. And we passed a dark red Discovery on the road not two miles from the Retreat that could have been those ex-SAS guys, like she says," he added. "They were going like stink. We nearly wiped each other out, which would have made things interesting."

Pollock gave a grunt. "Their firm is still giving us the runaround on exactly what those lads were supposed to be doing up here. If it was them spirited him away, we may never get to the bottom of it. Still, looks like Edith certainly fired the shot from the AK that killed Ian Hogg. We'll clear that one, if nothing else." He eyed Nick without expression. "Should have let you have that warrant for Airey after all, eh?"

Nick wisely didn't comment. "Regardless of whether you believe Edith was behind the Barrett or not, she knows details that could only mean she was there. So it must have been her DNA that was found in the hide," Nick felt compelled to point out. "Whatever doubts Blenkinship had about it."

"Aye, lad, point taken. It's not like Grace to make that kind of cock-up," Pollock agreed. "Have you been to see her?"

Nick checked his watch. "I'm on my way from here."

"Good," Pollock said. "Give her my best, won't you? Tell her we need her back at work. And tell her well done."

"I will. Thank you, sir."

The door to the interview room opened and the solicitor came out, shut it behind her, clutching her briefcase.

"We'll be asking for full psychiatric reports, of course," she said, her voice dry.

"Thought you would." Pollock nodded glumly. "Last time I saw anything that fruit and nut, it came in a Cadbury's wrapper."

The solicitor left, trying not to smile.

Pollock looked about to speak again when a uniform appeared at a doorway further along the corridor.

"Hey, Weston!" he called. "You're wanted in reception."

"Thanks. Any idea why?"

The man shrugged. "Don't know, but she's blonde and pretty, apparently, so you might want to take a look."

Nick turned back, found Pollock watching him. "Get on, then," he said, gruff. "Oh, and Nick—?"

Nick paused inquiringly.

"Well done yourself, lad," Pollock said, scowling in case Nick should make the mistake of believing he'd gone soft. "I mean, don't let me catch you doing anything that bloody silly again, mind, but...well done, all the same."

Nick kept his face grave. "Thank you, sir."

But he was still grinning when he reached the reception area to find Lisa waiting for him, alone. She certainly fitted the description his messenger had given, he considered, wearing a flimsy little summer dress and high-heeled strappy sandals.

"Lisa! Is everything OK? Is Sophie—?"

"She's fine," Lisa said, awkward. "I–I'm here about Karl."

"Oh?" Nick ran a hand round the back of his neck. "Look, I'm sorry I haven't been back to you, but what with—"

"No, no, I understand," she said quickly. "It's been all over the news." She paused. "Dad said they were talking about giving you some kind of medal."

"Yeah, well." He shrugged uncomfortably. "Talk's cheap, isn't it?"

She shifted a little, and the sunlight from the window caught the wheat-gold of her hair. She'd taken time with it today, he noticed, put on full make-up. Was this another charm offensive on her brother's behalf?

"They're letting Karl go." She smiled, hesitant, with no sign of the recent edge. "Insufficient evidence, so they reckoned."

"Oh," Nick said again. "That's…good, isn't it?"

"I told you he'd done nothing." But Nick heard relief rather than conviction in her voice. "Apparently, it was one of the blokes he works with," she went on, oblivious to his silence, anxious to repeat the story as if to reinforce it in her own mind. "They both occasionally borrow the same van. Nothing to do with Karl at all."

Nick forced a smile, hiding the bitter taste in his mouth. "Ah, good." *So, the jammy little sod's got away with it, again.* He heard himself say, "I'm glad it worked out."

"I know you had something to do with it, Nick."

He froze. "With what?"

Keep calm, he warned himself. *Deny everything. I phoned in the tip anonymously. Nobody knows. If she ever finds out, I'll never see Sophie again without a fight.*

She sighed at his deliberate obtuseness, but her tone was more indulgent. "With Karl getting off, of course," she said lightly. "I know you put in a good word for him with that DS Crowther. I just wanted you to know I'm, well, grateful for you getting them to take his story seriously."

Nick realised it would not be in his best interests to deny it. *If I'd said anything to Crowther, it would have been to keep digging until he found proof,* he thought. *Karl was guilty as sin, so there had to be some.*

He was suddenly aware that Lisa was watching him closely. "I, er—"

"It's OK." She mistook embarrassment for modesty. "You don't have to say anything."

She stepped in, reached up to place a gentle kiss, nominally on his cheek, but landed it, sneaky, on the corner of his mouth. Nick could smell the perfume he'd bought for her last birthday, softened by contact with her skin into a scent that was uniquely hers. He let his eyes close for a moment. She stepped back, smiling.

"So," she said haltingly, "I, erm, wondered if you were doing anything this weekend?"

"I'm not sure as yet," Nick said. "But I'll pop round and see Sophie, if I'm off."

"Well, I thought we could maybe go out somewhere, the three of us, have a picnic or something?"

Nick stared, remembering Grace's words after Lisa had made a scene in Staveley when they'd had lunch. That things weren't quite as over as he'd thought.

"Can I get back to you?" He wondered at his own lack of elation. "We're still flat out on this case. Lots of loose ends to tie up."

"Yeah, of course," she said hastily, collecting her handbag from a chair. "I'm sure Sophie would love to spend time with you, though, if you can manage it." She reached for the handle to the outer door before adding softly, "And so would I."

Nick stood and watched her go, knew she was aware of it by the swing of her hips. And suddenly he had a vision of another woman's movement, very different from Lisa's. Long-limbed and self-contained, displaying less outright femininity. More subtle and somehow infinitely more attractive.

And where once he would have stated without doubt that he preferred bubbly petite blondes, now his tastes had shifted towards redheads. Tall, slightly superior redheads with a cool meticulous eye and a dry sense of humour. But where did that leave Sophie in all this?

"Damn," he said.

The door into the main building opened behind him. He turned to see Pollock eyeing his consternation with undisguised curiosity.

"Glad I've caught you, lad," he said, holding out a slip of paper. "We've had a possible sighting…"

109

GRACE STARED out through the French windows into the rain. The sudden change in the weather fitted her mood. Within minutes, the normally vibrant landscape had transformed into a shapeless monochrome blur in the mist.

Rationally, she knew her current malaise was a combination of delayed shock and grief, and the after-effects of the head injury. For the first few days after she was discharged from hospital, she'd mostly slept, allowing her physical self, at least, to recover. They'd signed her off for a fortnight with the possibility to extend. Her psychological self might have healed faster, she recognised, had she jumped straight back into the fray.

Now, she was beset by doubts.

Max hadn't helped, although with best intentions. Behind her on the coffee table were the glossy brochures for the ornate Grand Hotel in Florence, part of his plan to gradually wear down her resistance. His inconvenient male instincts *protective* this time.

"What's the point of moping around here?" he'd coaxed. "Come to Florence with me, darling. Plenty of time to think about all this when you get back. And if this Blenkinship really doesn't appreciate you, why not simply tell him to go to hell?"

The same day Blenkinship was made acting head CSI, she'd heard her suspension was rescinded, but he had not been in touch. Not even to enquire after her health. Grace, who'd been properly brought up to send thank-you notes at every occasion, couldn't help feeling slighted.

The beating rain on the skylights above the living area masked the sound of a vehicle approaching, so her first warning was the doorbell and Tallie's customary half-hearted bark.

She found Nick on her doorstep, hunched into the upturned collar of his suit jacket, had no choice but to invite him in.

"It was sunny in Penrith," was his opening gambit. He jerked his head towards the ivy as he shook off the excess water. "No more webcam?"

"No need."

"We haven't caught him yet, Grace."

"Maybe not," she agreed, leading him through, "but you have the gun."

He saw the brochures and the pair of empty coffee cups immediately, she noted, but didn't comment.

"We traced the Barrett's serial number through the manufacturer," he said instead, watching her closely. "You were quite right. It most likely came in from Afghanistan."

She shrugged, moved through to the kitchen to make fresh coffee.

He asked quietly, "When are you coming back?"

She filled the kettle, glad of something to do with her hands. "Well, the headaches have stopped and the lump's nearly gone, so I suppose...as soon as they pass me fit to drive." That calm cool stare unnerved her. "Poor Tallie has never been for so many long walks. She's exhausted."

"You're having second thoughts about the job, aren't you?"

Grace stopped fussing with the cafetière. "Honestly?" She sent him a level stare. "Yes, I am."

"Why?"

Another shrug, almost an irritated twitch. "Didn't you have doubts—after your last undercover assignment went so badly wrong?"

"You've been checking up on me." Something quick and bright flashed behind his eyes. "Oh, I probably would have made myself get back on the horse, but there was Sophie to consider." He gave a rueful smile. "At the time, I was glad of the excuse."

"Well, there you go." She lifted down clean cups.

"I didn't say I'd never regretted that decision, but I would have been a liability." He leaned his hip against the worktop, arms folded.

"And if *I* can't be relied upon to do my job in the field," she agreed, ignoring the ache in her chest, "then I'm no help to anyone, either."

"So, that's it, is it? The going gets tough, and you throw in the towel?" And when she turned, surprised by such lethal calm, he added, "You've never had to *want* for anything, have you?"

Masking her hurt, she said, "That's not fair and not true!"

"People like you have had it so easy all your lives and you just can't cope when things get difficult. Is that what happened to your marriage, Grace? You ran away?"

"And of course you're such an expert on relationships." She stopped, lifted her chin, her voice brittle as ice. "I don't have to justify my decisions to you."

"No, you don't, but you have to justify them to yourself. You know what I think?"

"No, but I'm sure you're about to tell me."

"I think you had it too easy with Sibson. You were his discovery, his pet project, and he cut you a lot of slack." Those merciless eyes raked her, derisive. "Now Blenkinship's taken over, you're going to have to fight to prove yourself. And I don't think you've ever had to do that before, have you, Grace?"

"I've worked hard to get where I am." But the shake in her voice lent uncertainty to the words.

His lips twisted. "You worked hard, sure—surrounded by people who supported you, believed in you. And now, for the first time, your abilities are being questioned." His voice grew harsher. "And you can't handle it."

The kettle boiled, clicked off. In silence, Grace turned away, measured in coffee, poured the water, hands moving automatically.

With her back to him, she said, "Max is wonderful in many ways—generous, unselfish—but he's so single-minded, so clear in his vision, that living with him left no room for me. I spent twelve years living in his shadow; an appendage rather than a separate person in my own right. Richard understood that. Without him..." She trailed off helplessly, looked over her shoulder and wished Nick wasn't so hard to read.

He shifted. "He wasn't the only one who could see how good you are at your job, Grace. Don't let an arse like Blenkinship make you throw it all away."

She blinked. "You're being deliberately mean to goad me, aren't you?"

"Yes," he said, almost cheerful. "I imagine Max has been round, patting your hand, saying 'there, there' and doing you no favours whatsoever." He grinned, suddenly boyish. "You needed a good kick up the backside."

"Thank you, I think," she said gravely. "Is that why you came round—just to rattle my cage?"

"No, I thought you might like a ride out." Something in his voice nudged her interest like a half-remembered scent.

She raised an eyebrow, asked coolly, "Where did you have in mind?"

"I hear Wythenshawe's nice this time of year."

"Wythenshawe?" she repeated. "Manchester, isn't it? What's in Wythenshawe that's so important for me to see?"

"We've had a report of a man admitted last night with a badly infected gunshot wound. Like to take a guess at his name?"

Grace stared. "You don't mean—?"

"Pete Tawney. The very same. I'm on my way down to interview him and I'd like you to come along."

"But any trace evidence will be long gone by now," Grace pointed out. "You may believe hygiene standards are low within the NHS, but it's been more than a week and—"

"You saw him," Nick interrupted quietly. "That day you went looking for Edith at the Retreat. You saw his face. One of the few people who did and lived to tell the tale."

Grace paused. She'd done some sketches. There was something about the man's eyes she would not forget. However much she might try…

"Come on, Grace," he murmured. "Let's go lay some ghosts, hm?"

110

TRAFFIC on the motorway was light. Less than two-and-a-half hours after leaving Orton, Nick turned in to the Wythenshawe Hospital on the south-western side of Manchester. He was surprised how quickly the time passed.

As she'd slid those long legs into the Impreza's passenger seat, Grace had said, "I hope you don't mind, but I brought my iPod. I noticed your stereo had an input for one."

He'd stifled a groan. "No opera," he warned. "It all sounds like fat women strangling cats to me." But he was heartened by her flicker of amusement.

"I've been to Glyndebourne several times with Max, of course."

"Of course," he muttered, pulling away.

"But, to be honest, I always preferred Glastonbury. Now, Goldfrapp or the Foo Fighters?"

By some tacit agreement, they'd avoided discussing the case during the drive, talked instead of music and movies, food, travel. She was good company, a good listener, with a sharp wit he found deeply satisfying.

More's the pity…

Now, directed through the hospital's maze of corridors and wards, they found Pete Tawney in a private room. Nick showed his ID to the uniformed constable guarding the door and jerked his head to indicate the man inside.

"So, what's his story?"

"Says he's only just got back in the UK, doesn't know a thing about it," the constable said. "Not exactly Mr Informative."

"Mind if we take a run at him?"

The constable shrugged, eyes drifting over Grace. "Help yourselves."

Inside the room, a man lay almost naked on the bed, rumpled sheets thrust roughly aside. An IV drip was plugged into the back of his right hand, and an electric fan stood close by, running at full chat like an aeroplane propeller winding up for takeoff. Even so, he was sweating badly.

When he saw Nick, Pete Tawney swore, short and heartfelt, letting his head drop back against the pillows.

"Not more coppers," he muttered, ignoring the proffered warrant card.

"Who were you expecting?" Nick asked mildly.

As they approached the bed, he saw that Tawney's right leg was horribly inflamed, a dark mottled discolouration spreading outwards from a vicious wound to his upper thigh. Even the normal dense cocktail of hospital aromas failed to disguise the sour, fetid odour that emanated from it.

Tawney laughed without humour at his instinctive recoil.

"Yeah. Whatever you've come about, mate, don't forget anything, 'cause chances are I won't be around long enough for you to come back."

"You have wet gangrene," Grace said, entirely dispassionate. "That's uncommon in an exposed area like the leg unless you've been in a very humid climate."

"Oh, very good," Tawney jeered. "Give the lady a coconut."

Grace raised her eyebrow, but didn't respond. Nick treated him to a hard stare until he dropped his defiant gaze.

Tawney had the look of a man once bulked up with muscle, now skimmed back to a feral minimum. He had a number one buzz-cut even a Marine would have thought severe, scalp deeply tanned through the stubble. And although his face was clean-shaven, the signs of a recent beard were clear in his two-tone tan.

"Africa would be my guess," Grace said. "If you'd been in South America you would have gone for treatment in the States, maybe Mexico, rather than risk a transatlantic flight in your condition."

Nick glanced at Tawney's face, saw the accuracy of Grace's statement in the scowl that bunched around his mouth.

"So what?" Tawney said. "Had some work out there. Congo, Nigeria, Chad. Good money."

"What kind of work?" Nick asked.

"Missionary—what do you think?" Tawney said and laughed again, a harsh rip of sound. "I can bring down the hand of God at fifteen hundred yards."

"How long have you been away?"

Tawney wiped a hand across his clammy face. "Dunno, lost track of time. Mate of mine offered me the job just before I got out. Nothing to keep me here, so I went."

"There's no record of you leaving the country."

Tawney bared his teeth. "Another mate runs a Sunseeker out of Southampton. Amazing how quick you can be in France, no questions asked, in a nice little speedboat that does sixty knots."

"Interesting mates you have," Nick murmured. "So, how did you get yourself shot in the leg?"

"Call it an occupational hazard," Tawney said. "You going to tell me what this is all about?" He glanced between them, almost hopeful. "What am I supposed to have done?"

"Nothing." Grace caught Nick's eye. "It wasn't you."

"Oh, come off it!" Tawney protested. "Who's dead that you had me in the frame for? I haven't exactly been keeping up with the news."

Nick considered for a moment. "Major Giles Frederickson," he said baldly.

Tawney went utterly still, then he gave a soft chuckle. "Well, well," he said, almost in wonder. "Sorry, mate. If you'd been talking about a couple of crackpot African dictators, I might've been able to help with your enquiries, but as you can see," he waved a hand, "I've been out of town."

"What's the going rate for a mercenary these days?" Nick asked, voice mild. "And what, exactly, have you been spending your wages on?"

"Wine, women and song, mate." The colour was leaving him as he tired, skin turning waxy. "You want to try and prove otherwise, good luck to you."

"Frederickson cost you your career. Didn't you hate him for that?"

Tawney shrugged, but wouldn't meet Nick's eyes. "Had my fill of the army long before that." His voice was starting to slur. "Least in the private sector you're not squabbling over who goes out on patrol with the radio that works, or drawing lots for body armour."

111

"SHE COULDN'T POSSIBLY HAVE FIRED the Barrett before she took her pot-shot at you, of course," Nick said. "Otherwise she would have known the recoil from that kind of cannon was going to kick like a demented mule."

"It was a monstrous weapon," Grace agreed. "In every sense of the word."

"You only had to look at the length of the stock and the size of the grip to know it had been customised for someone twice the girl's size. You have to mould yourself around a gun like that or it really clobbers you. Hardly surprising it smashed her collar-bone to pieces the first time she tried it. She must have been off her head even attempting to put a round through it."

"Which might be something of a Catch 22," Grace pointed out. "Didn't you say Edith's solicitor is calling for psychiatric reports?"

"Mm, I think you're right." He gestured with chopsticks. "How's your sashimi?"

"It's excellent," she said warmly. "I'd no idea this place was here."

They were seated at a quiet corner table in a little Japanese restaurant in Lancaster, with plates of sushi, sashimi and tempura spread between them. Nick had tentatively suggested dinner on the way back up country and Grace, thinking of her empty fridge, readily agreed.

"I've always loved Japanese food," he said. "When I first

moved to London, I sublet from an ex-barman I knew. He left the pub trade to train as a sushi chef. He taught me to cook." Nick deftly dipped a piece of yellowtail on a finger of rice into his soy sauce and wasabi mix, and took a bite, swallowed. His gaze turned cynical. "I suppose you're going to tell me you've spent time out there."

"Japan's one place I've never visited," Grace said sedately, "although I'd love to, of course. All the little shrines and temples, and those sublime Zen gardens."

"I went a few years ago," he admitted. Almost diffident, she thought, to be able to claim one experience over on her. "Tokyo, Osaka, down to Nagasaki. Took the bullet train past Mount Fuji. All the usual tourist stuff." He shrugged. "It was a blast."

Grace sipped her green tea, poured them both a refill from the bamboo-handled pot on the table, and felt compelled to ask, "Did Lisa enjoy it?"

Nick grimaced. "She went to Tenerife with her mates from the salon where she was working, and I went to Japan with mine —including the sushi chef. Big advantage, as it turned out. He could nose out good food in the most unprepossessing places." He nudged a plate across the table. "Try the eel. It's delicious."

"It sounded much more appetising when you called it *unagi*."

There was something rather intimate about sharing dishes, she considered, a togetherness she hadn't felt since Max. Except that with her ex, of course, the conversation would not have turned to motive, or murder.

"I still can't get my head round the poor kid's notion this would be her ticket to fame and fortune," Nick shook his head. "Who's so desperate to be famous they'll try and take the blame for slaughtering people in cold blood?"

"What was that old song? Something about being wary of young girls who craved nothing more than to cry at the wedding and dance on the grave."

"Who sang that?"

"Dory Previn, I believe. Strangely appropriate in this case," Grace said. "But we live in a shallow, image-driven world. For some people, it seems being remembered for anything, however horrific, is better than not being remembered at all."

"Yes, but Edith obviously hasn't cottoned-on to the fact that, because she's not yet eighteen, we can't release her name to the media," Nick pointed out. "Chances are, nobody will ever know the part she played—whatever that turns out to be."

"'The mass of men lead lives of quiet desperation'," Grace said softly.

"You're very poetic this evening. Henry Thoreau, wasn't it, who said that? 'And go to the grave with the song still in them'." Nick reached across to load his chopsticks with *gari* sliced pickled ginger and grinned at her raised eyebrow. "I'm not a total peasant, you know."

Grace ignored the jibe, focused on his previous comment instead. "From what you've told me, the saddest thing seems to be that, if this man at the Retreat *was* the one who tried to throttle her—and we know *somebody* had a go—she didn't come to us then."

"What good would that have done?"

"Well, if it wasn't Edith firing that rifle, it must have been the mysterious Mr Bardwell," Grace said slowly. "If only she'd spoken out when he tried to kill her, no doubt we would have brought him in, done a little digging. We might have found out about the gun. We might have stopped him." She looked up, saw the startled realisation in his eyes. "Then she really *would* have done something to make her famous, after all."

A WEEK LATER, Nick tapped on the open CSI office door. Grace glanced up distractedly from scanning through on-screen pictures of a burglary in Appleby.

"Good to see you back, Grace."

"After that last pep talk, how could I not return?"

He nodded, trying not to let her words ridiculously please him. "Where's Blenkinship?"

"On a leadership skills course." There was just a brush of strain beneath her brisk tone. "I have no illusions he will return a changed man. Can I help?"

"It was you I was after." He paused. "I don't suppose you'd fancy another little trip out, would you?"

She pushed back from her desk, asked in that same cool tone, "And where did you have in mind *this* time?"

"Well, I hear…Scotland's nice this time of year." He grinned suddenly. "I finally tracked down Conor O'Keefe and Pollock's given me the go-ahead. Grab your coat."

THEY WERE ON THE MOTORWAY, heading north, when Grace said, "We got all the lab results back from the byre, by the way."

"No joy?" He pulled out to overtake a line of slow-moving trucks near the crest of Beattock Summit.

"Oh, we got perfect matches on everything—prints, blood, DNA. The works." But her voice was subdued.

"Ah. Why do I get the feeling this is not a good thing?"

"Because they came back a match to one Staff Sergeant Patrick Bardwell."

"But..." Nick frowned. "I thought that was just an alias?"

"It is—unless you believe in ghosts. According to the army, Bardwell died in the friendly fire incident in which Pete Tawney and Major Frederickson were involved. There were witnesses, before you ask," she added. "Whoever he was, this man posing as Bardwell, he went to considerable lengths to ensure the trail would go cold."

"Must have had a lot of help as well," Nick said at last. "You can't swap out military medical records without someone on the inside. Never mind where he got the gun, how he paid for it all. You know the Firearms lads took the Barrett up to Warcop range to test-fire it?" His voice turned wry. "Needed all of them to do it, apparently."

Grace glanced across at him. "You didn't fancy a turn?"

He shuddered. "I've seen more than enough of what it can do, thanks."

"Well, boys will be boys," she said calmly.

His smile came and went quickly. "They found out why she missed. Another of the reasons, anyway."

She twisted slightly in her seat. "Why?"

"The sights were set to three hundred metres—that last shot at Frederickson," he said. "Edith must have been at least six or seven hundred from the farmyard, so she badly miscalculated the amount of hold-off."

Grace shook her head sadly, murmured, "Poor girl."

"Poor girl?" Nick echoed sharply. "Grace, if she hadn't cocked up the range, she would have killed you! That round buried itself into the concrete a little too close for comfort, if you ask me."

"Nevertheless, I view her as an object of pity rather than hatred. You know she's gone on hunger strike, don't you?"

"Yeah, I heard. They're letting the shrinks see what they can make of her."

"And what do *you* make of her, now you've spent so much time interviewing the girl?"

"She's one crazy mixed-up kid," Nick said. "And although there's no way she did half of what she's claiming, she was definitely there—for some of it, at least." He shrugged wearily. "Mind you, her story changes so much I don't think even *she* knows the real truth of it."

114

IT TOOK a little over four hours from Penrith to reach the coast just below Oban. To a large and sturdy grey stone house, part castle, on Minard Point overlooking the Firth of Lorn. If it hadn't been for Grace's palmtop GPS, Nick would have doubted the directions he'd been given. The last mile-and-a-half took them along a rutted track filled with muddy puddles, despite relentless late-June sunshine that had put half the country on a hosepipe ban.

Nick winced as the suspension grounded over yet another pothole.

"Perhaps we should have—," Grace began.

"If we'd come in your hulking great truck," Nick said from between his teeth, "we'd still be on the motorway."

"I wouldn't dream of making any kind of tortoise and hare comparison," she said blandly. She nodded to the house, looming large on the horizon. "Do you really think Conor O'Keefe is Bardwell?"

"Who knows?" He steered around a crater that would have happily accommodated a large dog. "But when O'Keefe left Liverpool, he cleared out his bank accounts, converted everything he owned to cash—quite a bit of it." He glanced over. "Getting hold of the Barrett and smuggling it into the country took some funding."

They pulled up on granite chippings outside the weathered front entrance. *Even the gravel up here is hard-bitten*, Nick thought.

The wind came up strong over the headland. Hazy in the distance, hunkered down, was the outline of an island Nick vaguely thought might be Mull. The glittering sea between the island and the mainland was scattered with gulls.

"How did you find this place?" Grace asked as they climbed the lichen-covered steps.

"O'Keefe's still claiming his army pension." Nick nodded to the imposing façade. "It goes to a Post Office box number, then is forwarded on here."

He rang the bell. Shortly after, the door was opened by a severe-looking woman in an old-fashioned white nurse's uniform. Her elaborate cap was long at the back, like a veil.

"Yes?" She managed to inject a wary chill into the single word, without quite stooping to outright hostility.

Nick reached for his ID. "DC Weston, Cumbria CID, ma'am," he said politely. "This is Ms McColl, CSI. We understand there's a gentleman called Conor O'Keefe here?"

"It's 'Sister', if you don't mind." The nurse gave a sniff that reminded Nick of the sergeant at Penrith. She took her time examining their credentials, returned them and stepped aside. "He's expecting you."

"Expecting us?"

She threw them a glance arctic in its disapproval. "Or somebody like you," she said, turning on her heel. "This way, please."

He caught Grace's quiet amusement and pulled a face at her behind the nurse's ramrod retreating back.

"You're a hospice," Grace said. "Cancer?"

"Mostly."

"I'll speak to my husband about the work you do here," Grace said in an uninvolved voice. The nurse turned, eyes speculative, and Grace added with a slight smile, "He's a noted supporter of worthy causes."

"Naturally, we rely entirely on voluntary donations," the nurse admitted in a fractionally more conciliatory voice. "We offer spiritual as well as palliative care."

"Admirable."

"*Ex*-husband, you mean," Nick whispered as the nurse led the way up a wide staircase, a chair-lift fitted up one side. "And shame on you, manipulating her like that."

"How?" Grace seemed surprised. "Max would be more than happy to write them a cheque if I asked him to."

Nick could only shake his head. They walked along a mirror-polished corridor. Everything was painted white, as though to prepare the occupants for their vision of the afterlife.

The nurse stopped by an open doorway, gestured them inside. "Five minutes only, if you please." She performed a rusty movement of her mouth that might have been a smile. "He tires easily."

If Nick had thought Pete Tawney looked in a bad way, nothing prepared him for the sight of Conor O'Keefe. White and wasted, the former sniper sat swathed in blankets by the window, a shrunken little figure who stared longingly at the open water beyond the salt-splattered glass.

Without shifting his gaze, O'Keefe said, "If you're here tae tell me he's dead, save your breath." His Glaswegian accent lay thick across a soft voice.

"Tell you who's dead, Mr O'Keefe?" Nick asked.

"Mercer." He treated them both to a strangely disinterested survey. By the side of his chair, on a tall stand, was a syringe-driver filled with morphine, the IV line snaking between a fold of the cream blankets wrapped around his body. His thin lips widened a little. "The Sisters may believe in simple clean living up here, but we still get all the satellite news channels."

"If you already know Mr Mercer's dead, why did you agree to see us?" Grace asked.

"Because refusing would only make you more of a nuisance and then you'd be back again." He looked at her without emotion. "Ah'm dying," he said bluntly. "Have been for months. Started in ma pancreas and now it's in ma bones, so they tell me. Not one ah would have chosen, but who gets to choose?" His pale gaze flicked across to Nick. "All ah want is tae be left alone tae go in ma own way, in ma own time."

"All debts paid?" Nick asked carefully. "All...scores settled?"

"Ah've put ma affairs in order, if that's what you mean," O'Keefe replied, without heat. "Why? You think ah might have snuck out under the wire one night and done him ma'self?"

Nick leaned against the opposite side of the window frame, looked down at him. "As well as a sniper, I understand you were something of an IED expert."

O'Keefe's mouth cracked into a bitter smile "So's anyone with an Internet connection or an old copy of *The Anarchist Cookbook*," he dismissed. "Don't ask me tae shed a tear for Mercer. He was a right royal bastard, no mistake."

"You won't hear any arguments from me," Nick muttered. He still remembered the sound of his own bones breaking.

Misunderstanding, O'Keefe gave a slight nod. "If you've done your digging, you'll know about the boy. Fifteen that kid was when he hanged his'self. Full of hope and laughter, so *excited* tae be coming here…"

He broke off, his eyes drifting away as if pulled by the lure of the sea. There was a fierce brightness to them that Nick gave him time to subdue.

"Ah identified the body." O'Keefe's voice was almost a whisper. "They said he'd tried tae cut his wrists not a week before, and they never even put a watch on him. *Fifteen*." He shook his head. "Ah had tae tell his mother, his grandparents, that ah'd promised tae take care of him, and ah'd let them down. And you know the worst of it?"

Nick gave a fractional shake of his head.

"They did'nae even look surprised. Like they had'nae really expected me tae look after the boy." He looked straight at Nick, straight and level. "Is it any wonder ah wished ill on Mr Mercer? Hell, man, if ah were capable of it, ah'd be doing a tango on the man's grave."

"You liquidated your assets," Nick said. "There's no reason you couldn't have paid someone else to do the job."

"Oh, ah could, could ah?" O'Keefe gave a wheezy laugh. "What? Go tae hire-a-hitman.com, eh? Easy as that, is it?"

"For someone with your old contacts, old comrades? Yes, it probably is."

"Gave every penny of it tae the Sisters here," O'Keefe said. "Reckon by the time ah've passed over, they'll have earned it. Ask 'em, if you don't believe me."

"We'll have a forensic accountant go over the books."

O'Keefe shook his head. "You've never served, have you?"

"Why do you ask?"

"Because if you had, you'd know you're wasting your time trying tae chase down blood money." O'Keefe's hands gestured, restless, under the blankets. "Ah've spent ma whole adult life among men who were prepared tae kill or die for each other, and if you don't understand that, you'll not catch him." He gave a wistful smile. "Some things have a price all right, but they cannae be bought."

"You sound as if you rather admire what he's done," Grace said quietly. "You may have hated Matthew Mercer, but innocent people have also died for this, including a twenty-year-old policeman, and my boss."

"Personal, is it?" O'Keefe regarded her for a long moment. "They train us tae do your dirty work, you civilians, and you can't just switch us on and off at will. Sometimes there's collateral damage, things happen, and we all of us fall a ways short of glory." He paused. "But ah'm sorry—for your loss."

The nurse who'd admitted them appeared in the doorway. "I must insist that you leave Mr O'Keefe now," she said, ominous. "He needs to rest."

"Ach, ah do nothing but rest," O'Keefe complained, but his tone was gentle. She almost smiled at him, her face growing more severe as she escorted Nick and Grace the way they'd come, as if wanting to make sure they were off the premises.

On the stairs, Nick said, "Mr O'Keefe tells us he's made a sizeable donation."

"He's been most generous," she said primly. "Not that the care we provide has any such strings attached, naturally, but we were...grateful."

Grace asked, "How long does he have?"

The nurse pursed her lips. "A few weeks," she said finally. "Perhaps a month. Not much more. He was late to seek a diagnosis, as they often are."

By the front door, she plucked a colour leaflet from a display, handed it across. Grace opened her bag to put it inside, pulled out a photocopy of the sketch she'd made of the man from the Retreat.

"Has this man been to visit Mr O'Keefe while he's been here?"

The nurse took the drawing with only the faintest hesitation, gave it due consideration and frowned before returning it. "This looks like Mr O'Keefe's brother. He came with him when he was first admitted, but has not been back since. I suppose this might be him. It's hard to tell." She folded back into herself. "I really couldn't say for sure."

She shook Nick's hand with a brief, firm grip, using both her own to cover it, repeated the action on Grace with a little more fervour, he noticed.

"We'll be in touch." Nick gave her a card. "You'll let us know if...?"

"You mean *when*," the nurse said placidly. "Of course."

They took the steps, heard the heavy wooden door close solidly behind them. Nick paused by the Impreza but Grace walked on to the edge of the gravel, arms wrapped round her body as if cold.

He moved alongside her, hands in his pockets, and they stood side by side in silence for a few moments. The sun was starting to sink, streaking the sky with the palest blues and pinks, washing the landscape mellow gold.

The wind was blowing her hair back gently from her face and she looked unbearably sad, he thought.

"He knows, of course," Grace said. "Even if he didn't fund it, he knows."

"If he does, he's planning on taking that knowledge with him to the grave."

"And dancing on it, as he said." She turned, eyed him. "Do you think we'll ever understand?"

Nick shrugged. "I doubt it." He paused. "O'Keefe doesn't have a brother, by the way."

"No, you're wrong," Grace said, in that remote voice she'd used the first time they'd met. "He has hundreds, and one of them was prepared to kill for him."

EPILOGUE

EDITH STEPPED out of her cell onto the top floor landing and felt the atmosphere inside the prison change. It was as if a ripple passed through the stone and steel of the building.

She moved to the railing, a slender and defiant figure in the standard-issue orange jumpsuit. The collar was open just far enough to show one end of the fading scar from her plated collarbone, and her rolled-back sleeves revealed a series of scabbing parallel cuts along her forearms. Vivid slashes, almost tribal, against pale skin.

Ignoring the eyes watching through industrial mesh beneath her, she leaned on the railing. As she stared down through the catch-nets to the main floor below, all she could see were upturned faces.

Every one of them was looking.

Looking at her.

She kept her face blank, concentrated on projecting nothing through her eyes as she studied them. The smell of this place hit hardest. The smell of pent-up aggression, frustration, desperation, greased with sweat and shaken down with fear.

She tried to imagine how Patrick would have handled this, but in the months since her capture, his features had grown gradually hazier until she could hardly even bring them to mind.

She didn't know if he was alive or dead—there'd been no news one way or the other. A part of her mourned his disappearance the way all doomed love affairs were mourned. Oh, he'd never truly loved her—she saw that now—but it made her feelings for him all the more bittersweet.

Because despite the depth of her love for him, in their last moments together she'd held the balance of his life in her hands, and had still pulled the trigger. That kind of ruthlessness, she'd discovered, was real currency in here. It earned admiration, respect, maybe even just a tinge of awe.

Word had gone out that she was one crazy, cold-blooded bitch.

Around her, she could hear the murmurings, the whispered rumours, embellished and handed on as solid fact. And she realised that they might have taken away her freedom, but they had replaced it with something so much more powerful.

In here she was finally free of the suffocating spectre of fat little ugly, useless Edith Airey. Edith the loser. Edith the dreamer. Edith the 'things-like-that-don't-happen-to-the-likes-of-us'. Edith, whose mother had snivelled through every day of her trial, and whose father had been too ashamed of his own cowardice even to look her in the eye as her sentence was handed down.

Over to her right, there was some shuffling. Those nearest on the landing parted and flattened themselves to the edges, keeping their gaze averted like frightened sheep. Edith eyed them with contempt, although she accepted there was a time when she would have done the same.

Flexing her hands a little she stepped away from the railing and turned to meet the reception committee who swaggered from amidst the crowd.

There were three of them, which was unexpected. Oh, she'd known she'd get a visit from the current Top Bitch but for it to happen so soon after her arrival was…instructive.

The woman was flanked by two minders, strapping women who looked more male than female. *Studs*—Edith already recognised the type. They stood a pace back on either side like some kind of honour guard, towering over their leader and carrying twice the muscle but nowhere near the menace.

The trio stopped close enough to state their authority without the insult of crowding her, the distance finely judged.

The woman in the centre treated her to a frank appraisal. Edith returned the favour. The woman had short-cropped hair around a face that had clearly smiled little and laughed less. She was old—maybe in her forties. Her orange jumpsuit fit better than the others, like it had been tailored.

"Heard about you," the woman said at last. "Say you killed a copper." She gave a jerk of her chin. "That so?"

"No," Edith said, allowing her voice to mimic Grace McColl's remote drawl. She waited a beat before adding carelessly, "Actually, I killed three."

OK, so one of them was just a civilian crime-scene technician, but he still worked for the cops, didn't he?

Another ripple spread outwards through the women on the landing, was passed down and along. There were a few gasps then, and—almost at the far end—a distinct snigger.

Edith sucked down an unobtrusive breath, willed her face not to heat, her heart not to race.

"I killed a soldier too—some cocky major. And a politician's wife who once tried to frame me. And the bastard who turned me in, an' all," she said, loudly enough to carry into the far corners. "Stood trial for it. Went down for it." The snigger died away and did not return. Edith checked the nearest faces, saw that for once nobody rushed to rubbish her word.

The woman was watching her minutely again. Her gaze pierced a moment longer. She had dark grey eyes like wet slate. Her expression never altered.

"That the lot, was it?"

"Shot my own father as well, if that's what you mean." Edith shrugged. "Only, the dopey bastard was too stupid to lie down and die."

This time the laughter was nervous, sliding away when she failed to join in.

That earned her a slight nod in acknowledgement. She saw the woman's eyes skim over her lacerated forearms.

"So...you going to cause trouble for us?"

Edith didn't miss the way the question was phrased—was *she* going to cause trouble for *them*, not the other way around. Her shoulders unlocked just a fraction but she covered it by folding her arms, letting her head cock to one side as if considering.

"Not if none of you don't cause trouble for me."

"We'll see they don't, eh?" The woman glanced over her shoulder and seemed to sense rather than see the meaningful nods from the studs.

"Good enough." Edith allowed an artful hint of doubt in her voice. It was slight enough to be easily missed, but she knew the woman missed nothing. Nor did she rise to the challenge.

Instead, she said, "Come see me when you've settled in. Give you the lowdown on this place." She jerked her head in the direction she'd come. "Next door but one. We get the penthouse suites up here."

"Sure," Edith said. "I will."

The woman hesitated a moment then thrust out a hand. "I'm Nadine. You?"

Edith didn't need to think about her answer as she took the proffered handshake.

"They call me Pavlichenko."

———

"...*Pavlichenko*."

"What's that, Edith? Not back to that again, are we?"

The nurse rapped on the reinforced glass pane in the door to the girl's secure room. No response. She took out her keys and twisted one in the lock.

The girl didn't seem to register another person entering. Her eyes were open but utterly unfocused as she slouched on the bed, lips mouthing the same words over and over like a mantra. Her forearms were laced with blotchy scratches as she scraped her nails rhythmically across her own skin.

"Come on, Edith," the nurse coaxed, looking at the untouched tray of congealed food. "If you don't eat, you know they'll put you back on the meds."

She reached out and stilled the restless fingers.

"Pavlichenko..." Edith mumbled.

The nurse sighed. Some of the patients committed to this facility could be helped, while others arrived total space cadets and were likely to remain so. She shook her head and left the room, locking the door behind her. She took one last look through the glass. Edith hadn't altered her position. A pathetic little figure who'd resumed clawing at her arms and muttering that damn silly name again.

"...*They call me Pavlichenko.*"

"On *your* home planet, maybe," the nurse muttered under her breath. "But I very much doubt they ever will on mine..."

———

AFTERWORD

Liked it?

If you've enjoyed this book, there is no greater compliment you can give an author than to leave a review on the retailer site where you made your purchase, or on social media. Doesn't have to be long or in great detail, but it means a huge amount if you'd leave a few words to say what you liked about it, and encourage others to give my books a try. Thank you so much for taking the time.

I'm only human...

We all make mistakes from time to time. This book has gone through numerous editing, copyediting, and proofreading stages before making it out into the world. Still, occasionally errors do creep past us. If by any chance you do spot a blooper, please let me, the author, know about it. That way I can get the error corrected as soon as possible. And I'll even send you a free digital edition of one of my short stories as a thank you for your eagle-eyed observational skills! Email me on Zoe@ZoeSharp.com.

ACKNOWLEDGEMENTS

Brian Price, Crime Science Advisor
Caroline Moir
David Farrer
Derek Harrison
Dina Wilner
Fred Rea
Gill Lockett
CSI Helen Pepper
CSI Ian Pepper
Jane Hudson, NuDesign
Jill Harrison
Joanna Joseph
John Lawton
CSI John Routledge, Cumbria Constabulary
Jon Rush, Cumbria Constabulary
Judith Baxter
Jules Farrer
Keith Caladine
Maggie Topkis
Matt Johnson
Mike Jecks
Patti Ruocco
Robert Roper
Sarah Williams
Shell Wilbye

DIE EASY # 10: A deadly hostage situation in New Orleans forces Charlie Fox to improvise as never before. And this time she can't rely on Sean Meyer to watch her back.

ABSENCE OF LIGHT # 11: In the aftermath of an earthquake, Charlie Fox is working alongside a team who dig out the living and ID the dead, and hoping they won't find out why she's *really* there.

FOX HUNTER # 12: Charlie Fox can never forget the men who put a brutal end to her army career, but she swore a long time ago she would never go looking for them. Now she doesn't have a choice.

TRIAL UNDER FIRE # 0: The untold story. Before Charlie Fox was a bodyguard, she was a soldier...

standalone crime thrillers

THE BLOOD WHISPERER Six years ago CSI Kelly Jacks woke next to a butchered body with the knife in her hands and no memory of what happened. She trusted the evidence would prove her innocent. It didn't. Is history now repeating itself?

AN ITALIAN JOB (with John Lawton) Former soldiers Gina and Jack are about to discover that love is far deadlier the second time around.

Made in the USA
San Bernardino, CA
01 September 2018